"Casey Jones is a gal, there's no other word for her.
Not only that, she's a gal with attitude, an attitude she
earned the hard way . . . Casey's funny and shrewd,
not least about herself . . . She's a heroine with a
difference, and someone you'd like to know better."
The Mystery Review on *Legwork*

"The book, the first in a series,
is a wonderfully entertaining read."
Publishers Weekly on *Legwork*

"The atmosphere is thick with greasy foods and pervasive
corruption, but Casey makes this a delightfully funny read,
perfect for a rainy afternoon or long train ride."
Publishers Weekly on *Out of Time*

"It is always refreshing to discover a main character that
immediately captures the reader and that absorbs one into
the story. This is the case with Katy Munger's spicy leading
lady, Casey Jones . . . Her strong personal presence, pride
in outrageous outfits, and quick wit add much . . . and
make her quite the 'off-the-wall' kind of detective."
The Mystery Review on *Out of Time*

"Casey Jones is not your typical heroine . . .
Hopefully we'll soon see more of Casey Jones!"
The Pilot, Southern Pines, NC

Other Casey Jones Mysteries by
Katy Munger
from Avon Twilight

LEGWORK
OUT OF TIME

MONEY to BURN

A CASEY JONES MYSTERY

Katy Munger

AVON
TWILIGHT

AVON BOOKS, INC.
1350 Avenue of the Americas
New York, New York 10019

Copyright © 1999 by Katy Munger
Inside cover author photo by Greg Feller
Published by arrangement with the author
Library of Congress Catalog Card Number: 98-91009
ISBN: 0-380-80063-2
www.avonbooks.com/twilight

First Avon Twilight Printing: July 1999

AVON TWILIGHT TRADEMARK REG. U.S. PAT. OFF. AND IN OTHER COUNTRIES, MARCA REGISTRADA, HECHO EN U.S.A.

Printed in the U.S.A.

WCD   10 9 8 7 6 5 4 3 2 1

For Cabana Boy,
who taught me that life is a daring adventure

ONE

"I never smoke after sex, though I have been known to purr." I offered this tidbit only because the skinny guy in glasses was asking.

I've had clients in all flavors, but Thomas Nash was a new one. At around six foot four, he weighed about as much as my left thigh and had unruly light brown hair that waved at the temples. His face had a perpetual sleepiness to it. Drooping eyelids and wide, narrow lips made him sexy in an intellectual sort of way.

He reminded me a little of Leslie Howard in *Intermezzo*. I wanted to pull off his glasses and plant a big one on that expressive mouth, just to see if smoke would billow out of his ears and steam blow from his nostrils. Unfortunately, I am more early Courtney Love than Ingrid Bergman. I suspect he would have fainted from fear had I attempted the maneuver.

"Are you listening to me, Miss Jones?" he asked politely.

Miss Jones? Yikes. He must mean me. I'm Casey Jones, private detective sans the official license (though I keep that little fact to myself), tethered by fate and cruel necessity to a 360-pound blimp named Bobby D., who does have a license and who fancies himself my boss—though never my superior.

"Could you repeat the question?" I asked, still imagining what he looked like naked and wondering why I cared. The man was wimpy but he had . . . *something*. It wasn't

1

athletic grace, however. So far he had tripped over a leg of Bobby's chair, run into the back of my office door, knocked over his coffee, kicked my trash can and dropped his pen three times. The guy would be positively lethal on a dance floor.

"I asked if you smoked at any time at all," he repeated. "It's very important that I know."

"No," I assured him. "I absolutely do not smoke. Not even after six gins in a row. In fact, I have been known to swat cigarettes from the mouths of fourteen-year-old strangers on the street while lecturing them on the evils of tobacco."

"Good," he said, sighing. He settled back in the chair. "It's incredibly important you be on my side one hundred percent."

I wanted to assure him that it was my job to be on the side of my clients, but I was currently going through the charade of "deciding whether I would take him on." The truth was that I was flat broke and, if he had the money, I had the time.

"Why don't you tell me what the problem is?" I encouraged him, though I was really wondering whether he wore boxers or briefs.

"I've been receiving death threats, midnight phone calls, that sort of thing," he said. He glanced out to the hallway as if some unknown assailant was lurking there with a club. "I think someone is out to destroy me."

"Is that all?" I joked.

"Isn't that enough?" he countered indignantly.

Uh oh. No sense of humor. His sexiness quotient just took a big dive.

"Can you be more specific?" I asked, resisting the urge to look at my watch. Never mind that I deserved to be lying on a lounge chair by a hotel pool with a bevy of college boys oiling my suntanned body. It was nose to the grindstone time. By now, I was willing to pull teeth if I was getting paid by the hour. And I'd be willing to pull a lot more than teeth if my dire financial straits kept up.

"I'm a tobacco researcher," he explained. "Have you ever heard of the Clean Smoke?"

"Sure," I admitted. "With a two-billion-dollar ad campaign, who hasn't?"

"I invented that for Teer & Talbot. It's not all that flavorful, but it is relatively tar and nicotine free."

I stared at him. This was no time for niceties. "You must be loaded," I said.

He shook his head. "My employer at the time owns the patent. I received a nice bonus, that's all."

"Hope you bent over all the way for that one," I observed.

"I know," he agreed. "I have a lawsuit pending asking for a share of the royalties. In the meantime, I jumped ship and formed my own company. I own half of King Buffalo Tobacco now. I'm working on the Safe Smoke, a chemical-free curing process that's as efficient as modern day methods."

"Great concept," I interrupted. "People can light up a Safe Smoke after having safe sex."

He blinked at me without smiling and continued. "I want to change the world of tobacco. Instead of tearing down the industry, I hope to transform it by removing the dangers and saving the farmers. King Buffalo is my vehicle."

Thomas Nash was off to a good start. King Buffalo Tobacco was one of several independent firms that had sprung up in the past decade to provide yuppies with a way to get lung cancer naturally. The firm produced charmingly crude cigarettes that appeared hand-rolled and had given more than one street cop a heart attack when lit up in their vicinity. They tasted like crap, but they allowed rich white kids to pretend they were as cool as the crowned buffalo on the label.

"I hear your company is doing okay," I said.

He nodded. "Being privately owned, we can focus on the big picture instead of quarterly profits. I make enough to fund my research. I'm not interested in short-term sales, it's the long term I have in mind."

"Got any partners?" I asked, wondering if they were as equally unenthusiastic about current profits. Money was always a motive.

"One. His name is Frank Cosgrove. He's a marketing

whiz, used to work at Liggett & Myers and at T&T with me. MBA and the whole bit. We make a good team. He supports my long-term view."

Sure he did. Show me a marketing whiz with a long-term view and I'll show you a candidate for the unemployment line.

"What did you mean when you said someone was trying to destroy you?" I asked. "Tell me more about the harassment."

His foot jerked nervously. "Someone is trying to kill me," he explained. "Or, at the very least, frighten me away. The power brake cable on my car was cut and the tires have been slashed twice. I've received threatening letters in the mail, telephone calls that end in hang-ups, even a dead rabbit in my mailbox."

Yuk. "A dead rabbit?" I asked.

"With duct tape wrapped around its mouth."

Hmmm . . . Glenn Close was currently starring on Broadway, so I could eliminate her as a suspect. One down and 274 million Americans to go.

"Why do you think someone would want to harm you?" I asked.

"To keep me quiet," he explained. "Have you heard about the Hargett suit?"

"Sure. Who hasn't?" Horace Hargett was an old geezer who had a small farm tucked into the mountains off the Blue Ridge Parkway. About ten years ago, he had come down with lung cancer. His son, Horace Jr., had followed his footsteps into the cancer ward two years later. Both blamed Blue Tips, a brand of cigarette manufactured by Teer & Talbot Tobacco. Blue Tips used to be an old farmer's brand but, in the early sixties, had been successfully repositioned by T&T to appeal to a younger audience. It was one of the nation's leading brands today.

The Hargett family had been able to accept the old man coming down with lung cancer, it seemed, but when the son was diagnosed with it at age thirty-five, they had a lot more trouble accepting his fate. Word had it that an eager county health official—tired of footing the bill for treating public lung cancer patients—had talked the Hargetts into instigating a class action civil suit against Teer & Talbot. The suit charged T&T with intentionally marketing Blue Tips to underage smokers while knowingly concealing the presence of addiction-causing substances in their products. Turns out young Horace had picked up a pack at the age of ten and seldom been without Blue Tips since, though he had tried to quit many times. Now the family wanted someone to pay for the consequences.

It was a familiar story—lawsuits like this were proceeding all over the nation. But not in North Carolina, where thousands of tobacco farmers live, work, and, most important of all, vote. For North Carolina, the lawsuit was a first.

"In fact," I told Thomas Nash, "I've been following it pretty closely. Never thought it would happen here in North Carolina, but the time's they are a-changing. What's it got to do with you?"

"I've been asked to appear as a witness for the plaintiffs," my client explained. "Specifically in the matter of marketing cigarettes to underage smokers. I'm sorry, but I can't tell you anymore than that. Except to say that I could probably successfully destroy Teer & Talbot if I told the whole truth."

"I thought you wanted to save the industry, not destroy it," I said.

"I do."

"If you ask me, it's a little odd to find a tobacco scientist opposed to smoking." My own feelings about smoking were unequivocal: licking an ash tray was more efficient. But I'd grown up in the Florida panhandle where people knew damn well that smoking caused cancer but puffed away like fiends regardless. It was a way of telling the world to go screw.

"I'm not opposed to adults smoking," Nash explained. "They know the risks. But until we come up with a safer blend, no company has any business selling to young people who haven't got the sense to know what they're getting into. I quit T&T over that very issue. I feel rather strongly about it." He brushed a lock of thick hair absently off his forehead. Unfortunately, he forgot to put his felt tip pen down first and ended up drawing a zigzag of black ink across his skin. It was a wonder he didn't poke an eye out. He must have had a season pass to the emergency room as a child.

"Okay," I said. "Fair enough. So you think someone from T&T is threatening you in order to keep you from testifying in the Hargett case?"

"That's my best guess," he said. "They're sending me a message of some sort to keep silent. Otherwise, who would bother to duct tape a rabbit?"

Someone who can't find a gerbil? I kept the theory to myself. "What do you want me to do about the harassment?" I asked.

"I'd like you to find out who it is," he said. "I talked to a lawyer and we almost brought suit against T&T, but then I realized I didn't really have any proof. There was another complication, a personal matter I would prefer not to go into. But once I dropped my plans to sue T&T, the harassment got even worse. So now I don't know what to think. I thought you could follow me around and keep an eye on things, just in case it gets even uglier. Maybe even spot whoever it is that's been doing this to me."

"Who told you about me?" I asked him, stalling. I wasn't accustomed to having such an upfront, clean-cut guy for a client and, to be honest, I didn't trust him because of it. I am actually more comfortable working for slimeballs— they're so seldom subtle and I like to know who I'm dealing with.

"Francine," he told me.

"Who?"

"The girl down at Elmo's. The waitress with the gold ring in her tongue."

Oh, yeah. The tiny brunette with the very large continental shelf who had the good sense to keep my coffee cup filled to the brim whenever I staggered into Elmo's Diner seeking a morning hangover cure. We'd talked a few times. She knew I was a private investigator and how to get in touch with me. I'd helped her reclaim a stereo system and television set once when a boyfriend had moved out abruptly with half of her possessions in tow.

"You know Francine?" I asked. Maybe Thomas Nash

wasn't such a klutz in bed after all. Francine was just over twenty and maybe half of this guy's age.

He looked offended. "I understand what you're insinu- ating, and I have a very respectable girlfriend, I assure you. Francine is simply an acquaintance. I don't even want her to know I've hired you. I told her I had a missing relative I was trying to locate."

"I consider missing relatives a blessing," I said. "Better find a new cover story."

This time he didn't even blink. The guy must have been a barrel of laughs at parties. But I didn't need a client with a sense of humor, I needed one with money—which was one thing he definitely had.

"Okay, Mr. Nash," I decided. "I can help you out from nine in the morning until around midnight or so. I need a few hours off to eat and sleep, or not sleep if I get lucky." He didn't smile. "If you want, I can pull someone else in to cover the night shift," I offered.

He shook his head. "No, I'm not concerned about that. So far, all the incidents have occurred during the daytime or early in the evening. That's another reason why I think we're dealing with a corporate amateur rather than a pro- fessional."

A professional what? I wondered. All the really good professional harassers were out in Hollywood stalking stars.

After agreeing to begin work that afternoon, I asked for a nice chunk of money upfront and got it. Bobby D. would be pleased to know we'd covered the rent for the month and here it was only fifteen days into it.

After I shook Mr. Thomas Nash's hand, he charged into the broom closet instead of out the exit door, then careened through the outer office and bounced off Bobby's desk be- fore disappearing down the street with a distracted gait. I watched him bang his head on a street sign before turning the corner. Absent-minded professor, indeed. It was a won- der he was still alive.

Shaking my head, I pulled a chair up to Bobby's desk to discuss the situation. Seeing that he was not currently eating, I figured it was safe.

Bobby was fiddling with a black device that looked like

a miniature flying saucer with buttons and dials glued all over it. To say that the sight of it annoyed me was an understatement. One reason we were in a budgetary pickle was Bobby D.'s current mania for spy gadgets. A new shop promising "state-of-the-art security devices" had recently opened up in North Raleigh. Bobby had quickly become their best customer. I had explained to him again and again that when your primary assignments involve following cheating spouses so stupid they take their mistresses to the same cheap motels over and over—not even bothering to draw the curtains all the way—it's really not necessary to possess infrared laser-beam underwater high-altitude sonar, sound and sight devices that can penetrate any substance known to man, including Lois Lane's underwear. He wasn't listening. He'd spent ten thousand dollars, and counting, to date.

"This is an unbelievable little gizmo," he said, trying to convince me. "It's a phone that allows for conferencing, plus secret taping of calls. When I pull up this antenna and push these two buttons, it can record voices through up to fifteen feet of concrete and from as far away as fifty yards."

"Best of all, it looks like a Frisbee covered in dog doo," I added. "So you can stash it in the bushes under windows and no one ever tries to pick it up."

Unperturbed by my sarcasm, he put down the recording device and opened his side desk drawer. I got a glimpse of an electronic extravaganza crammed into the small space. He selected a small black box and placed it on the desk.

"This is a beeper," he explained. "You can reach me twenty-four hours a day."

"First of all, Bobby," I said. "You're so fat that when your beeper goes off, people are going to think you're backing up. Secondly, I don't want to be in touch with anyone twenty-four hours a day, including myself."

He ignored my jibes and continued searching in his desk drawer, this time selecting a small red-and-white metal square that he placed on his desk. It was supposed to look like a pack of cigarettes, but featured a brand name and design so phony that it was obviously a surveillance device—or a toy.

"Know what this is?" he asked proudly.

"A pack of candy cigarettes?" I guessed.

"Fooled you, didn't it?" he said, pleased. "This is a combination video and still camera that automatically takes pictures at any interval you specify while adjusting for lighting conditions. Yet it looks just like a pack of cigarettes." If he wasn't repeating the salesman's spiel word-for-word, he was pretty close.

"Ingenious," I said. "It opens up the entire world of illegal videotaping. You could put it on your bedside table, tape sexual encounters and your girlfriends would never know until they asked you for a cigarette afterwards."

He stared at me, finally grasping that my enthusiasm did not match his. "What's the problem, Casey?" he asked.

"The problem is we don't have any money," I explained. "If I hadn't just demanded a big advance from my latest client, we would not be paying the rent this month."

"I could ask some of my stable of lovelies for financial assistance," he volunteered.

"God, no." It was bad enough sharing a business with a 360-pound goofball. I drew the line at sharing my fate with a 360-pound gigolo.

"Really, they wouldn't mind," he assured me.

"No, Bobby. I'm not going to borrow money from your girlfriends. We have to earn it." I glared at him, a little pissed that he had recently made me a partner and then promptly stopped taking on new cases. Half of zero is still zero, no matter how glorious you make it sound. "We're in business to earn money, remember? Besides, your harem suffers enough without being hit up for loans."

That was my opinion only, understand. His harem did not appear to be suffering at all and, in fact, by all indications, was thriving. I'd learned an important lesson from watching Bobby D. in action: there are hundreds of romance-starved middle-aged women in this town and only a handful of middle-aged men who don't pick their noses in public, date one another or secretly covet their mother's underwear.

Though he was a fashion moron and a faithful wearer of bad toupees, Bobby loved his ladies with a public passion unmatched since Don Juan hung up his tights. He showered them with flowers and filthy telephone calls in the middle of the afternoon when they were the most bored at their jobs. He remembered their birthdays, while conveniently forgetting their actual ages. He considered Valentine's Day a national holiday more sacred than Easter. And he wined and dined his women year-round until they spilled over their XL Victoria's Secret panties. He thought them all beautiful regardless of weight, and frequently told them so. In return, they adored him, cleaned his apartment, cooked him dinners, and agreed to be seen in public with a man who dressed like Englebert Humperdink and made Humpty Dumpty seem svelte.

Or, at least, that was the Bobby I had come to know and love. Unfortunately, the man before me seemed but a pale imitation of his original self. Ever since he had suffered a heart attack four months before, Bobby had been much more subdued than normal and far less eager to shake down desperate wives and husbands for a fee. Recently, he had been downright withdrawn and the truth was that I missed the old Bobby. I had never realized how much I clung to his exasperating sleaziness until it was gone.

"Bobby," I told him. "I know the heart attack scared you. But you have to take back your life. You've got to get back to work."

He was quiet, chewing thoughtfully on a jumbo Tootsie Roll while he thought the situation over. "I suppose you're right," he finally said. "My mind hasn't been on work. Thoughts of mortality and all that."

"Maybe you're getting tired of peeping into the corners of people's dirty lives?" I suggested. "Just like you got tired of watching the 'Jerry Springer Show'?"

"Of course not." He looked affronted. "It's just time to get back to work, that's all. I need to get back into the swim of things. Bust the crust." He grinned lewdly. "Need any help?"

"Sorry, buddy. You're not busting any crust of mine. But I'll let you know if you can help with this latest case." I examined the camera disguised as a cigarette pack. "Tell me again what this does."

He adjusted a dial. "Turn this knob to the thirty and you set the camera to take a photo every thirty seconds, for up to a hundred exposures with the special film cartridge. You can program it to take photos faster or slower than that, if you need to. Switch the film canister and, voila, you can videotape instead, even at night. Think of how easy this makes surveillance. Just put this sucker on a windowsill, press a button and go have doughnuts and coffee while this does all the work."

"If I wanted to spend my time drinking coffee and eating doughnuts," I reminded him, "I would have joined the police force."

His chuckle was as greasy as ever. "Try it," he insisted, sliding the device toward me. "Let me know if it's reliable and when I get back into the swing of things, I may give it a go myself."

"Sure," I promised, not all that enthusiastically. "I'll let you know."

I'd agreed to start tailing Thomas Nash that afternoon. Although he lived in Durham as I did, he was in nearby Raleigh on business for most of the day. It was a simple matter to keep pace with him, thanks to my new car, a 1961 Porsche 356 B—the so-called bathtub Porsche. It wasn't as trustworthy as my former car, a 1965 Plymouth Valiant, but it had gone down in flames and was now gathering rust in a junkyard in Garner. I'd picked up the '61 Porsche for a song from an old farmer who kept it stored in his barn after its owner, his son, died in Vietnam. The farmer drove it for a couple of years until he discovered the Porsche was created by a German who had worked for the Nazis. As a World War II vet, the old farmer wouldn't be caught dead driving a German car and he'd sold it to me for peanuts. After twenty years of sitting in a dusty old barn, the car had its problems. It spent more time up on the block than parked on one, but it was getting there.

While I watched Thomas Nash do all the things an up-and-coming CEO and brilliant scientist does, I pulled a box of Snackwell's creme cookies from the backseat and ate about fifty of them, all the while congratulating myself on

the fat calories I was saving. Just for the hell of it, I placed
Bobby D.'s latest toy on the dashboard and recorded the
entire afternoon.

Not much happened. First, Thomas Nash had his shoes
shined outside the legislative building while I waited in my
car, searching every nearby grassy knoll without luck. I
couldn't even find a lone gunman. Then he hopped into a
very nice tan Mercedes SL convertible parked at the curb
and zipped over to the local Staples. I followed him through
the aisles, but he was not harassed by a single salesclerk.

After packing his car to the gills with bags and boxes—
he had to lower the convertible's top to fit in a file cabinet
he'd bought—he took I-40 back toward Durham, the tops
of his many bags flapping in the wind. Despite his tendency
to speed, I was never more than a few cars behind him at
any time.

Once we hit downtown Durham, Nash made two stops.
First he pulled into Brightleaf Square and entered one of
its buildings, leaving me outside in the parking lot trying
to figure out if I should tail him or guard his car, since he'd
left the top down and all of his recent purchases were sticking out of the backseat as an invitation to every thief in
town. Yes, Durham has its share of snatch-and-grab artists,
most of them on extended leave from New York City, i.e.,
hiding out with Grandma down South.

I took a chance and stayed with the car. Nash didn't take
long. He returned about ten minutes later and told me he
had one more stop, and not to bother coming inside with
him. Hey, he was paying the bill. I was happy to sit on my
butt, if that's what he wanted. He left his car parked where
it was and walked two blocks down Main while I stood on
the sidewalk, watching him trip over cracks and trample
flower beds. He disappeared into a tall, green-glass building
that was maybe fifteen stories high and qualified as a sky-
scraper in these parts. I didn't know much about the building, only that the neighbors had fought tooth and nail for
the city council to block its construction. They had lost the
fight—and a good portion of their daily sunshine.

Nash took a long time in the green building and looked
lost in his own private Idaho when he finally returned to

his car. I snapped a photo of him walking into a street lamp and shutting his tie in his car door, then followed him down the street toward a residential area in downtown Durham.

To my surprise, Nash's laboratory and home turned out to be a converted historic house only a few blocks from my own apartment. It was located just off Main Street, across the street from several bigger tobacco companies that routinely perfumed the streets with rich smells. I always wondered why the cigarette factories smelled so good, when their products tasted so nasty.

I parked at the curb and helped Nash lug his office supplies inside. Like I said, for $100 an hour, I'd even do windows.

"Thanks," he told me absently, dumping his packages in a corner of his office. His mind was already elsewhere as he eyed the blinking answering machine light, decided to ignore it, then surveyed the empty reception room. "My partner's out of town on business and we haven't hired a new receptionist yet. The old one quit on us."

"I thought King Buffalo was already up and running," I said.

"It is, but we're farming out the production right now to a bigger company. We're hoping to build our own factory and operations soon."

Of course. Nothing was ever what it seemed. Even the little companies were simply satellites of the big ones. When you get right down to it, there are really only two companies in the world: McDonald's and the Gap. And Bill Gates probably secretly owns both of them.

"Want to see the laboratory?" he asked, a spark of enthusiasm lighting his eyes for the first time that day.

"Sure." Why not? He was cute for a mad scientist and I wanted to see him strut his stuff. We descended steep stairs into the basement. I saw where his current profits had gone at once: a completely modern research facility had been installed in the basement of the house. Smooth white dryboard fronted the brick foundation walls and spotless counters stretched the entire width of the building. A pristine white carpet covered the floor and muffled all sound. There was a large metal desk in one corner heaped high with stacks of papers and a big-screen computer system. I counted three other computers, including one that was busy calculating numbers on its bright blue screen as if it had been working hard all day while its owner was in Raleigh having lunch.

Every counter held a series of work stations, each consisting of a different combination of beakers, plastic tubing, jars of clear and colored liquids and, sometimes, a small black box with adjustable dials.

One corner of the room was piled high with half a dozen bales of cured tobacco, the pungent smell of the leaf mingling with the odor of fresh paint.

"Wow," I said as I made my way across the carpeted floor. "Where's Frankenstein?"

"Not bad, huh?" He led me to one of the research stations. "I can't go into detail, but I'm experimenting with various extraction methods and altering the genetic code of the leaf itself. The trick is to eliminate tar and nicotine without losing flavor. You can enhance flavor by adding a substance like ammonia, but I'm working on an all natural mix of herbs and other plants, some of them common and others from as far away as the Amazon Basin. What you see are different combinations of various extracts." He waved a hand around the room. "The real secret is in the tobacco itself. I've had farmers all across North Carolina growing special hybrids for the past three years. No chemicals and no fertilizers allowed. Just my genetically altered seedlings, very specific growing techniques and selected organic compounds added at certain times. If I can get the right base of tobacco this season, I'll be able to complete my research within the next two years and we could be out with the product within three or four years."

While I watched, he took a dropper and extracted a sample from a beaker that was a third of the way full, thanks to a steady drip from a tube poised above its mouth. He squeezed the sample into a waiting petrie dish and the mingled ingredients turned a faint purple. He frowned, then slid the dish beneath a large microscope. I waited in silence while he examined the results and made notes on the nearest computer. After about five minutes, it became apparent that he had forgotten I was there.

I coughed and he looked up, startled. "Oh," he said. "Hi there," as if I had just happened to wander in. "Why don't you look around the house or something? I just want to finish this up."

Further talk would be futile. He was a man consumed by his work. I left him to his conclusions and made my way back upstairs. The house had been carefully renovated and the fireplace was spectacular. A bronze plaque embedded in the wall beside it had "May 30, 1872" etched across it.

The first floor included a living room dominated by an enormous oak conference table and a gleaming wood floor. Two other rooms had been converted into spacious offices—each with a curved window alcove that looked onto gardens outside. A long modern kitchen took up the rear of the house.

Upstairs was clearly home for Thomas Nash. One room was lined with shelves filled with books of all sizes, colors and, from the looks of the titles, topics. Nash had a fondness for wilderness books, it seemed, in addition to more scientific titles.

I continued down the hall and discovered a bedroom with a large antique bed heaped with identical pairs of chinos and blue jeans, while endless golf shirts hung from every bedpost and door knob. Was it possible he never bothered to clean his clothes and simply purchased more when he needed them? It was a great technique. Too bad I couldn't afford it.

I grew restless and wandered back downstairs in search of mysterious harassers. For the next few hours, I snooped through his mail, read old *New Yorkers*—a habit I'd picked up in prison—and ignored the blinking message light on the answering machine. No one threw a rock through the window or left a dead rabbit on the doorstep.

Finally, bored, I abandoned all self-control and headed for the kitchen. Grabbing a handful of chocolate chip cookies and a glass of milk, I returned to the office, determined to listen to the answering machine while I ingested as many calories as possible in the shortest amount of time. Nash wasn't interested in his phone messages, but I was. Maybe his harrasser had left a call-back number.

The first message had been left by someone with a cultivated, high southern voice who felt no need to leave her name. "I'm leaving Savannah now," she said in a faint drawl. "I'll be back very late and if I just can't wait, I might have to stop by and say hello." She giggled and hung up.

Okay. Now I knew he was straight. I wondered what his honey thought of his preoccupation with work.

The next caller didn't bother to leave his name, either. He was too agitated. "You're making a mistake," a deep voice informed my client. "If you drop the case now, you're sending a signal that you can be pushed around. It's not going to stop unless you confront them. It will only get worse. Call me to discuss it."

Had to be his lawyer, I thought, or possibly his partner.

The next call scared the hell out of me. The sound of heavy breathing filled the room, followed by a low rumbling laugh and a whispered threat altered by an electronic device: "Talk and I'll rip your head off. Then I'll leave it under your pillow for your family to find." *Click.*

Any doubts I had about Nash's need for protection vanished. The voice held no sign of self-consciousness and the words, which easily could have sounded silly, were absolutely terrifying. I decided to take the job a lot more seriously.

Around midnight, I tiptoed down the steps to the basement. Nash was bent low over a beaker of clear liquid that bubbled atop a small gas flame. Computers blinked and whirled around him and the air was rich with odors: tobacco, cinnamon maybe, or possibly cloves, and other less definable smells.

"Guess I'll be going now," I called out. "There's a message on your machine that's pretty grim. I think maybe we should take it to the cops. Don't rewind it."

He peered at me as if we had never met before. "What?" he asked, distracted.

"I'm going now," I repeated, knowing anything more

complicated would never penetrate his preoccupied brain. "Don't rewind your answering machine. I'll meet you at Elmo's at nine tomorrow, okay?"

"What?" He stared at me for a few more seconds, before finally realizing who I was. "Yes, yes, of course. Elmo's Diner at nine." He bent back down over his bubbling brew. "Nine o'clock sharp."

Sure. I made a mental note to stop by in the morning and drag him from his laboratory. No wonder he was so skinny. He probably had to be reminded to eat.

I left the building, congratulating myself on my good fortune: Nash lived only a block away from Another Thyme restaurant. After wandering around the house by myself all night, I could do with some company and Another Thyme had one of the nicest bars in Durham. Mahogany and brass gleamed in the candlelight, giving everyone a healthy glow instead of an alcoholic pallor. The staff was friendly and there were tables if you wanted to eat.

What I wanted to do was drink.

I ordered a Tanqueray and tonic from an efficient bartender who wore her hair cut short and slicked back. She had to be a northern transplant. No southern belle would be caught dead in such a style, unless it was underneath her Dolly Parton wig.

"Pretty quiet," I observed, looking around the near empty room.

"Yeah," she agreed. "Been this way for over a week. Ever since word got out about the campus rapist. The kids are sticking pretty close to home."

I nodded, annoyed that once again a solitary scumbag was wreaking havoc in my sleepy southern town. Recently, a rash of rapes had plagued the Duke campus and the cops were stymied. Apparently, the setup for the crime took place at a bar crowded with summer students. Someone was slipping one of the new date rape drugs into the drinks of female students, then spiriting them out of the bars without anyone noticing. The women were waking up in the morning, dumped in some corner of Duke Gardens, with no memories of the night before, headaches that could fell a horse, and clear signs of forced sex. It was real bad publicity for the school that alumni liked to call the Ivy League of the South.

So far, the cops had made little headway. They were reluctant to cause widespread panic, but their hesitation had emboldened the rapist. I knew from a friend in the department that he had struck six times in the last eight weeks and was likely to succeed again soon. What I wouldn't pay to get my hands on him.

I sat there, imagining how I'd torture the creep with a pair of pliers and a campfire, while I nursed a few drinks in solitary comfort and watched the bartender break down the bar for the night. An hour later, not a single other customer had wandered in for a drink and I wondered if the entire Thomas Nash assignment would be as quiet as this night had been.

I should have known better, really I should have. It's always calmest before the shit storm.

I staggered home around two o'clock in the morning, admiring the stillness of downtown Durham on a hot July night. Two hours later, my tangled alcohol dreams were interrupted by the persistent scream of sirens outside my window. I struggled awake. The acrid smell of burning wood and scorched rubber had lured me from sleep. I opened the window, inviting a cacophony of odors and sounds into my apartment. The fire was definitely nearby. From the sudden blaring of the many fire trucks and police cars racing toward the blaze, it was also a big one.

I threw a bathrobe over my blue night shirt, rescued my pink bunny slippers from beneath the couch and raced from the building toward the chaos.

Following the flashing lights of the fire trucks to Main Street, I saw a commotion near the railroad tracks that cut through the Liggett & Myers warehouse. Black smoke clogged the air and obscured the block from my view, while heavy fire hoses zigzagged across the sidewalk in front of me, blocking the way.

I didn't need it spelled out for me, anyway.

I had let a client down. Big time.

TWO

Thick black smoke billowed in angry columns that spread like ink across the sky. The air was hot and rancid, the fire mingling with the Carolina humidity to choke the oxygen from the air. Though the house was wood, the blaze smelled of melting rubber, discharged ions and a funky mixture of plastic and chemicals. I retreated to a spot upwind and pitied the firefighters as they dashed from the trucks to disappear into the haze hovering around the burning structure.

The street was in chaos. A half dozen fire trucks had pulled up on the sidewalks with police cars close behind. Their colored lights revolved silently, transforming the smoky haze into a multicolored fog. The fire marshal's car blocked the opening to the street and a couple of unmarked ATF vehicles flanked it. All sirens had been turned off and an eerie silence hung over the scene, spoiled only by the crackling and pops from the fire, the occasional squawk of a walkie-talkie or a shouted command.

Behind the officials, unnoticed yet by the cops, stood a row of neighbors who had been roused by the commotion and had crept from their beds to witness the disaster. At first, the blaze illuminated their figures so that they looked like actors standing before footlights. Then the wind shifted and smoke drifted across the assembled crowd, making them look as if they were waiting their turn to enter the heavy black gates of hell.

To these strangers, the fire was entertainment. But I had

known Thomas Nash, however briefly, and I had to find out if he had escaped in time. If not, it would be my fault. I had promised to protect him.

I canvassed the yard, searching for someone I knew. Chances were good I had an ex-boyfriend running around the scene somewhere. But chances were slim I could identify him. Most of the firefighters wore heavy fire-retardant rubber suits, which didn't help since I was most likely to recognize an ex-boyfriend buck naked.

I walked along the fringes of the crowd, searching until I spotted a man leaning against a truck further down the block. He was gasping for breath and had pulled his mask down around his thick neck, revealing his face. Bingo. An ex-boyfriend. True, my fling with Doodle Simmons hadn't lasted long. After his mama found out he was dating a white girl, I was out the door quicker than a cat in heat. But we'd remained friendly. Hell, if I held a grudge against every man in Durham who was an ex, I'd be reduced to dating newly arrived Duke freshmen.

Doodle was built like a professional wrestler. His head emerged like a giant monolith from his massive neck. The revolving lights on the truck swept past him at intervals, illuminating his silhouette so that he looked like a living version of an Easter Island sculpture.

"You okay, Doodle?" I asked, sitting beside him on the running board of the truck. The side of his rubber suit was still warm from the fire.

"Casey?" He looked down at me and noticed my bathrobe. "This isn't your house, is it? Because it's a goner."

"No." The blaze had broken out of the upper windows and flames were licking up the second story of the house, casting fingerlike shadows across the grass. "Has anyone spoken to the owner yet?"

Doodle shrugged. "No one's inside. I think they're trying to locate the owner by phone right now."

I thought of the steep steps descending to the basement. "I don't think they'll find him alive, Doodle," I said. "How do you know that no one's inside?"

"Freddie and Charlie canvassed the second floor when we first got here. Rita and Tommy checked out the ground.

They didn't find anyone, but the fire's burning pretty hot right now and the hoses aren't helping much. From the looks of it, I'd say the fire's been helped along. But we can't go back inside until the blaze has been checked." He wheezed for breath, sipped water from a sports bottle then squirted the liquid over his face.

"What about the basement?" I asked. "Did anyone check? There's a full laboratory down there."

He looked at me curiously. "You know the house?"

I nodded.

"You know the owner?"

"His name is Thomas Nash. He lives on the second floor and has a lab in the basement. I saw him at midnight." I hesitated. "He was a client of mine."

Doodle's eyes shifted to the fire. "What kind of a client?" he asked. He knew my line of business.

I let out a long sigh. "I was doing some bodyguard work for him."

Doodle stared at the fire. "No one came out, Casey," he said flatly. "And we weren't able to get into the basement. Maynard Pope's the cause and origination man on this one. He's gonna want to talk to you."

I hardly heard what Doodle said. The fire had reached the attic and whatever stored items were there ignited, sending the blaze to new heights. The fire seemed too strong, too towering to be real. It was like a special effect in a movie, and I felt myself being lulled into the passive state of a detached observer. I knew Thomas Nash was probably dead, but it wasn't really registering. All I could do was stare at the flames.

"Casey?" Doodle repeated louder.

I shook my head, tearing myself away from the sight of the blaze. "Sorry. Jesus, how can you watch this all the time?"

"I know. It can hypnotize you. Listen, you better stick around, so Maynard can talk to you. I'm no expert, but I'd say this fire was set. If you know the building layout and the reason why, you might be able to help. Can you stand it?"

I thought of Thomas Nash bent absently over his instruments, oblivious to the world around him as he pursued answers in a microscopic world of his own.

"Yeah, I can stand it," I said.

While I waited for the fire to be brought under control, I trudged home and changed into more suitable attire: a black tank top, matching leggings and my red high tops. Flame on. I took four aspirin and chugged a quart of water. Any trace of alcohol fogging my brain had disappeared from shock. I felt like a complete asshole for not taking my client's death threats more seriously. Thomas Nash had hired me to help him and now chances were good that he was dead.

Still numb, I stopped by Dunkin' Donuts on my way back to the scene. Listen, I was desperate. Durham is a disadvantaged town—it has no Krispy Kreme. When I ordered thirty coffees to go, the night manager knew I was heading to the fire. He gave me the coffee for free, and threw in five dozen doughnuts to boot. Durham is still a small town in many ways.

"God bless them," he told me. "It looks like a bad one."

Worse than he knew, I thought.

I staggered back to the scene bearing an armload of sustenance and was greeted like a returning hero. It didn't make me feel any more like one.

I sat on the running board of someone's pickup truck and watched in glum silence as Durham's bravest battled to bring the blaze under control. The sun was rising over the nearby Duke campus by the time the flames were finally extinguished and the remains cool enough to investigate.

Like all fire scenes, it begged the question: "Is that all there is?" The front wall of the house had been completely destroyed. It gaped open to the gawking crowd, like a giant dollhouse. The interior was reduced to a series of support walls and mounds of black ashes, dotted by melted lumps of possessions and strange charred shapes that had once been furniture. The doorway leading to the basement had disappeared, a dark hole taking its place. The bathroom fixtures on the first and second floors had survived the blaze and the sooty porcelain had been rinsed to a bright white by the high-pressure hoses. It stood out obscenely against the surrounding destruction.

Embers steamed in the morning air as firemen lightly hosed down banks of ashes to preserve any evidence that might be left. A breeze was blowing in from the north and, slowly, the choking odor of the fire lifted until the ruins smelled almost pleasant, like a campfire late at night.

Where the hell was Thomas Nash?

"Casey?" Doodle looked exhausted in the morning light, his face streaked with grime. He had shed the suffocating rubber suit and his T-shirt was soaked through with sweat. His eyes were criss-crossed with fine threads of blood. "This is Maynard Pope. He needs to ask you some questions."

Maynard Pope was a wiry little man with a white buzz cut and gray stubble dotting his pointed chin. I knew him by reputation. He'd been busting arsonists and insurance scam artists for over thirty years. His colleagues called him Mad Dog because he was so tenacious. His detractors called him nothing at all. It was safer that way.

"I ain't got but a minute," he said flatly. He had a peculiar voice that sounded like a cross between Donald Duck and Elmer Fudd. "Doodle says you think there's a body in there."

I winced. Thomas Nash had become a body.

I explained how I had left my client at midnight and that he had been in the basement. I described the layout of the house as the arson investigator listened carefully. When I was done, he pulled a notepad from his pocket and asked me to sketch the rooms.

"I'm gonna need your help," he said in his odd nasal voice. "Doodle says you're standup and I'm taking him at his word. From what I can tell so far, the flash point is on the first floor, midway into the structure. That indicates that the point of origin may have been just below, which brings us to the basement. The fire spread upward from there. We've already checked the remaining walls and what's left of the wiring. There's no signs of arcing and no internal wall fires. I doubt it was electrical. But I got a problem with the fire spread patterns and the scorch lines. They lead off in a lot of different directions.''

"Multiple origin points?'' Doodle suggested.

"Looks that way,'' the little man agreed. "Tell me again what the upper rooms were.'' He handed me the pad and pen again.

I went over the layout of the upper floors, sketching them out as best I could.

"Did anything unusual happen earlier in the evening?'' he asked. "Any visitors or indications that this Nash guy was upset?''

I shook my head. "There was a threatening phone call,'' I explained. "He'd been receiving them regularly. That's why he hired me. But he seemed unfazed when I told him he'd gotten another one.''

A short fireman appropriately shaped like a hydrant scurried up to Maynard Pope and interrupted us. "Gene's finished sounding the floors. We can get into the basement now, but the stairs are gone. We're laddering down.''

Maynard nodded, then turned back to me. "I want you to stand by in case we find a body. You might be able to identify what's left of it.''

With those ominous words, he hurried off. I watched as a ladder was lowered through the scorched opening to the basement and a line of firefighters descended, some with masks still hanging around their necks. Above them, water ran in dirty rivulets across the soggy ground floor and dripped from what was left of the second-story flooring, the sound of trickling water incongruous with the sight of the charred structure.

The men took forever down below, out of my sight, and were joined after half an hour by even more people. One was a photographer and the bounce of his flash strobed from the dark basement opening at intervals.

I had been abandoned to wait out my fears alone. Lost in my thoughts, I gradually became aware of a panting in the vicinity of my right shin. I looked down to find a shepherd collie mix sitting obediently at attention beside me, its female owner at its side. The owner wore a windbreaker emblazoned with the Durham Fire Department logo. A heavy belt encircled her waist and a large pouch hung from it. The dog was staring at the remains of the house, its tail thumping in excitement. Its fur was black but long white tufts of hair sprouted from behind each of the dog's ears to curl toward its nose, and all four of its paws where white.

"Well, hello there," I said to the dog. It looked up at me without interest, then returned its gaze to the fire.

"Annie's only interested in fires," the owner explained apologetically. "She's an accelerant dog."

"No kidding?" I stepped back to give the dog a better look. I had heard about Annie, but never expected to meet her face-to-face. Or snout-to-snout, as it were.

"I hear her evidence is good enough to be admitted into court," I said.

"That's right." The owner smiled and ruffled the back of Annie's neck. "This gal's got two hundred twenty-five million nerve endings in her nose alone. You and I have five million at best."

"Just as well, with the kind of boyfriends I have," I said.

The owner smiled. "Annie's more accurate than all current laboratory tests. Maybe you ought to have her check out your boyfriends for you."

"What does she do exactly?" I asked.

"She's trained to sniff out five different kinds of accelerants used to start fires, from petroleum to acetone and alcohol-based products. If she finds something, she bows over the spot and waits until I arrive. I mark the spot and give her something to eat." She patted the pouch hanging around her waist. "If someone has helped a fire along, believe me, Annie will find out."

"I'm impressed," I admitted.

"What's the story here?" she asked. "Chief says it's a suspicious fire." She was obviously assuming that I was there in an official capacity. That's what happens when you're a woman wearing black—and an attitude. I didn't bother to correct her.

I told her what I knew and threw in my two cents worth about where the fire originated. "I think it was probably started in the basement. They've been down there a long time."

"That means they found a body," she explained. "Annie and I will be going down next."

The watching crowd began to murmur as several men ascended up the ladder from the basement hole, poking their heads into the morning light like ground hogs about to see their shadows. They were followed up by another man gripping the front legs of a flat gurney. As the rest of the carrying board emerged into sight, I realized that the gurney held the remains of a body beneath a white plastic sheet. Its dark outline pressed against the opaque plastic with a pathetic smallness.

They had found Thomas Nash.

A few minutes later, the men had maneuvered the gurney up the ladder and were carrying it toward a waiting van. Maynard Pope walked behind it, making notations on a clipboard in his hand.

He saw me staring and waved me over. "Sure you can do this?" he asked. "The body was found slumped over an upturned metal desk and pooled water preserved a small part of the face. If you could just take a look at the height and build—and what's left of the face—it would be worth our while to send for dental records. Think you can take it?"

"Of course I can," I mumbled, dreading the moment. The gurney had been half-lifted into the back of the truck and the men carrying it were waiting for the go-ahead. Maynard stepped up and peeled the plastic sheet back, starting at the top of the head as he slowly unveiled the body.

Charred remains that had once been a face stared up at me, the flesh on the left side burned away so that the skull and teeth gleamed in a death grimace. Part of the other half of the face remained, where the body had been lying on its side in water. The flesh was covered with a black crust, but I recognized enough of the remaining features to know it was Thomas Nash. The figure was so very different from the man I had sat across from in my office that it didn't seem possible that I was looking at something that had once been human. His arms were roasted into thin black sticks that crossed his chest as if he had been warding off a blow. The rest of his body was a mixture of black ash, charred tissue and bone, and melted lumps where his feet and shoes had been.

I snapped. Overwhelming anger filled my body. I turned away from the grotesque figure on the gurney, wanting to destroy. The first thing I saw was a towering stack of garbage left on the curb by someone a few days before. I kicked the pile savagely with my right leg, hitting a metal trash can solidly enough to send it flying into the street. The stack of trash collapsed, sending cardboard boxes and plastic bags tumbling to the ground. I waded into the mess and began kicking each object methodically, only dimly aware that everyone else had backed off. I felt the weight of each container roll onto the top of my foot as I plowed through the pile of garbage, bent on destruction. I began to count each kick, moving faster and lifting harder, sending each bag soaring into the air so that it fell with a splat in the street, the plastic bursting as discarded cans and bottles skittered down the asphalt. I could hear myself cursing as if I stood at a distance from my own body, helpless to stop the attack.

Maynard Pope waited quietly until I had reduced the pile of trash to debris. When I was done, I was breathing heavily and gasping for air. My lungs felt like all the smoke of the night before had gathered in a big choking ball and lodged in my throat. I had to get the taste of the fire out of my mouth. I bent over and coughed so violently that I finally threw up, losing the contents of my stomach on the edge of the grass and not giving a shit who saw it.

When I was done heaving, I remained bent over, eyes closed, and rested myself with my hands propped on my knees. Something wet and cold touched my arm. I opened one eye tentatively. A narrow dark nose was in my line of vision, pointing obediently at the pool of vomit at my feet.

I looked up to find Annie the accelerant dog bowed at attention, her front paws daintily crossed and her hind-quarters thrust into the air as she pointed her nose at the pile at my feet. One of her two hundred and twenty-five million nose nerve endings had detected one of my three gin-and-tonics of the night before.

Maynard Pope coughed and I met his eyes across the

redraped and thoroughly toasted carcass of Thomas Nash.
"That's him," I told him glumly. "I'm sure it's him."

For the rest of the morning, Annie and her owner moved
through the fire scene, repeating the same ballet over and
over: Annie would sniff a section of surface area, find a
suspicious spot and freeze in a bowing position. Her owner
would mark the spot with a small red flag and reward Annie
with a treat from the pouch. As they moved on to another
area of floor, a forensic fire specialist would come in behind
them, carefully swabbing the area with a pad of gauze or
carving out a section of the area where Annie had scored
a hit. Each sample was placed in a small metal container
that resembled a quart-size paint can, then the top was la-
beled according to a grid code. The process repeated itself
again and again as Annie sniffed out suspicious substances
beneath the ashes. The dog was finding plenty of hits. In
fact, she was bobbing up and down more than a bunch of
Dallas socialites kissing Fergie's ass.

After a while, Annie was hoisted into the basement using
a canvas sling that caused her legs to splay out to the sides.
She endured this treatment cheerfully, the consummate professional, her ears perked high and her tail wagging as she
disappeared from my sight.

I knew she'd be a long time in the basement. As I waited
for the dog to finish, I leaned against a telephone pole and
drank a cold Pepsi that Doodle had found for me after my
public puking performance. The can was icy and I held it
against the back of my neck as I gulped in fresh air. It was
only ten o'clock and already the July day was hotter than
two foxes fucking in a forest fire.

"Know that woman?" Maynard Pope appeared at my
elbow again. I jumped at the sound of his stridently nasal
voice.

"Jesus. You always sneak up on people like that?" I
glared at him, irritated.

"Sorry. It's my job. Didn't mean to scare you." He was
old for an active fireman, more than sixty, I'd say, and he
rolled the words around in his mouth like Popeye before
he spoke. "Know that woman over there?" he repeated.

I followed his gaze. A slender woman of medium height, with straight brown hair, was standing alone at the edge of the front lawn, sobbing into a white handkerchief. Her white cotton dress billowed in the breeze, giving her the air of an apparition posed against the backdrop of black, charred ruins.

"No, but I'll find out who she is," I volunteered, thinking of the voice on Nash's answering machine the night before. I had a pretty good idea of what she was, even if I didn't know her name.

She faked me out. With surprising quickness, the woman turned her back on the fire and hurried back to the street, hopping into the passenger side of a late-model Sentra that was parked at the curve just beyond the parameters of the taped crime scene area. The car sped off before I reached it.

"Quick, ain't she?" That damn Maynard Pope was like a ghost. I flinched. Maybe what I really needed was a good long nap.

"So who was that?" he demanded. He'd stuck a toothpick in his mouth and it bobbed up and down while he spoke.

"The victim had a girlfriend," I explained. "I think it was her."

"What else do you know about this Thomas Nash?" the arson investigator asked. "Who was harassing him?"

"I don't know," I said. "You go first. What have you found out so far about the fire?"

He stared at me, content to hold his ground. I held mine right back.

"Can't tell you," he finally said.

I shrugged. "Coincidence. My information is confidential, too."

His small eyes flickered, but I stared back, determined to wait him out. I couldn't afford not to. He held the magic keys to the fire. No way I was giving information away for free.

"I'll trade you," I finally volunteered, once it became obvious that we were now in a pissing match rather than a mere staring contest. "You tell me one piece of information and I'll tell you something I know about the victim in return."

His mouth twitched. "Not very trusting, are you?" he said.

I shook my head. "Nope."

It was like pulling teeth from a tiger, but in the end I found out what I needed to know. Judging by where he was found and his position, Thomas Nash had likely been knocked unconscious before the fire even started. Maynard was willing to bet that Nash had died of smoke inhalation following the blow. Accelerant had been found at various spots throughout the basement and first floor. Maybe even on the upper floors, too. They had to wait until the floors were shored up before they could confirm it.

"In other words," I said. "This was no accident."

"Definitely not an accident," the little man agreed. "More like murder." He gave me a thin smile. "Stick around. The cops are on their way."

Funny thing, me and Durham cops. I got the hell out of there.

THREE

"Good thing I deposited his check right away." This was all the ever-sensitive Bobby D. had to say when I informed him later that afternoon that Thomas Nash was not only dead but Extra-Krispy in the bargain. Bobby had the decency to look guilty at his remark, though it didn't stop him from assaulting a large garbage pizza. His face was smeared with a sheen of oil and tomato sauce, making him look like a hyena caught in the bowels of a kill.

"Bobby, do the women you date ever go out to eat with you more than once?"

"Sure, babe." He licked his fingers with the dedication of a cat. "The women of today realize that a man with a hearty appetite has a keen appreciation for other pleasures of the flesh, know what I mean?" He wiggled his eyebrows at me and *har-harred*, causing a rope of half-eaten cheese to fly out of his mouth and across his desk. A lesser man would have apologized and whisked it from sight. Bobby plucked it from the telephone and dangled it in the air as he chewed at one end with undisguised gusto.

I stared. He chewed. I stared some more.

"What?" he finally said, defensively.

"This whole thing sucks," I told him. "Tom Nash was a good guy and you should have seen what that fire did to him. He looked like a giant spare rib. I'm not touching meat for at least ten years."

"They got any idea who did it?" Bobby asked.

I shook my head. "I was thinking about looking into it

31

on my own. He does have quite a few hours left on his retainer fee."

Bobby probed the corners of his lips with a fat red tongue for stray tomato sauce. "Casey," he said with a gentle belch, "what we need are live clients, not dead ones. Let the cops handle it. They won't let you get near it, anyway."

"If the cops won't let me near it, that's all the more reason why I ought to look into it on my own," I told him. "I owe it to the poor guy."

Bobby rolled his eyes. He is only sentimental about women, and not even women if they happen to be clients, too. "Face it, babe, the guy gave you the hots and you're sorry you never had a chance to tango. That's what this is about."

"It is not," I said indignantly. "It's about honor. I said I would protect him."

"It's about hormones. He was your type. Tall. Brown hair. Kept bumping into things."

"That's my type?" He made it sound like I enjoyed dating Great Danes.

"No, but he was breathing. And that is your type."

I punched him on the arm. My fist sank harmlessly into a sea of flesh. "I'll be in my office if any new clients come in," I told him.

"Don't worry, I'll send them your way. Hey, did I show you my new gizmo?" He started to open his desk drawer and I stopped him.

"Bobby, we agreed. No more new gizmos. I don't want to see it." But it reminded me. "How do I get the film in that cigarette pack camera developed?"

"Leave it with me, babe," he said. "I need something to do to occupy the afternoon. I'll drive out to the spy shop and drop it off."

Yeah, while he waited out those long lonely hours between his afternoon snack and his dinner. I handed the cartridge over for processing. I was curious to review just how Thomas Nash had spent his last afternoon. Maybe I'd spot something I'd missed the first time around that would point toward his killer.

Unfortunately, my good intentions died within half an

hour. Exhausted by my night vigil at the fire, I fell asleep at my desk with my cheek resting on a roll of scotch tape. I woke in the early evening, alone in the office, with a dent in my face centered by what looked like a boil the size of Cleveland. I wasn't about to visit any of my regular haunts with the outline of a giant snail on my face. So I drove home to Durham and resumed my fitful sleep in bed.

All night long I dreamed of fire and smoke, awaking at intervals, choking for breath and certain that I was trapped by flames. By morning—which was a long time coming—I knew that I had to somehow find the money to ignore my other cases, so I could find out who had killed Thomas Nash. If not, I'd be trapped in my own private hell forever.

If your intentions are pure, the universe will further them. I know because two weeks later, after a depressing but financially necessary fourteen days of boring divorce cases and missing persons work, a stunning woman in her early thirties walked into our office in downtown Raleigh. Her eyes were shaded by expensive sunglasses and she had soft brown hair that fell in waves down her back. She wore a yellow sundress with thin straps that criss-crossed her shoulders. If she'd looked any better in that dress, she'd have been wearing it down a runway.

When she walked in, I was standing at the coffee machine, pounding it with the heel of my hand to make it drip faster than the maddeningly slow pace it had recently adopted. Coffee was more important than a new client, so I decided to let Bobby handle the newcomer.

Unfortunately, Bobby was preoccupied staring at the black Ferrari that the woman had parked at the curb.

I cleared my throat loudly and Bobby got the message. He roused himself from the depths of auto lust and rose from his long-suffering chair to give the woman a courtly bow. "Allow me to introduce myself," he said grandly. "I am the proprietor of this establishment."

She slid the sunglasses down her nose and peered at him. "I want to talk to her in private," she said, pointing a finger at me.

I shrugged innocently, though I recognized her face once

I got a better look at it. "Right this way," I said, waving her in the direction of my office cubby. She looked like a nice woman, so I spared her the offer of any coffee.

The visitor sat in my extra chair and slid her glasses up on her head. Her hair bunched in silky waves around the frames, a maneuver that I swear requires hours of practice in front of a mirror to perfect. She looked around the dingy room and her confidence faltered for the first time.

"This is a pretty small office," she said.

"Bobby needs a lot more room than I do," I told her, "as I'm sure you noticed."

She answered me with an uncertain smile and I saw that she had recently survived a serious crying jag. Her eyes were red and devoid of makeup, though the rest of her was perfectly groomed.

"I saw you at the fire a couple weeks ago," I said. "You were wearing a white dress and crying into a handkerchief."

"Yes," she said in a voice that suddenly broke. She burst out sobbing and fumbled for tissues in her ostrich-skin handbag. I produced a box from my lower drawer and slid it across the desk toward her. We detectives are prepared.

She sobbed out a completely incomprehensible sentence, her voice muffled by tissue and tears. Where are subtitles when you need them? I caught the word "Maynard" and took a stab at her meaning.

"Did Maynard Pope send you to me?" I asked.

She nodded and gulped for air, then threw her shoulders back with resolve. I waited while her sobs subsided. Eventually, she blew her nose with a honk that would have caused an entire flock of Canada geese to fall from the sky. Then she daintily dropped the offending soiled Kleenex in my trash can.

"Sorry about that," she said. "Thomas Nash was my fiancé."

"I'm sorry for your loss," I told her. "I heard your voice on his answering machine. You were the woman flying in early from Savannah."

She nodded. "If I had only gone to his house from the

airport, this probably wouldn't have—" Her voice threatened to break again so I headed her off at the pass. Any more salt water and I'd start feeling like Kate Winslet in *Titanic*.

"Your fiancé was murdered," I told her. "If you'd gone to his house, you would be dead, too. And if the killer had failed the night of the fire, he most certainly would have succeeded eventually. Unless you set the fire, his death is not your fault." I should have recorded the speech and played it back for myself.

"Why did Maynard send you to me?" I asked when she threatened to tear up again. Maybe I should find her a sponge instead of a tissue.

She wiped each eye with a fresh Kleenex and let her head slump back, trying to relax the muscles in her neck. "This is rough. I don't know where to start."

"Start at the beginning," I suggested. I could tell she was wealthy, and rich people who have inherited their bucks are different from us mere mortals in at least one important respect—time is not money, it's theirs to spend as they like.

"I need a drink," she said unexpectedly. "I've been trying not to give in to the urge, but I need a drink if I'm going to get into it."

"No problem." I slid open one of my lower drawers and produced the bottle of bourbon that I keep hidden behind my box of tampons—one of the few items in my desk that Bobby D. refuses to touch. "Will this do?" I asked, displaying the label. "I keep it for emergencies." Which was true. Just the smell of bourbon can make me gag, but sometimes it was useful with hysterical clients. I had wavered between the more traditional private-eye inspired bottle of scotch, but given that my clients were almost universally southern, bourbon won out in the end. At least it was a decent brand. "Wild Turkey okay?"

"I'd drink sterno right now," she answered. She winced as she realized the irony of her remark, and I poured her a paper cup full of the hard stuff before she started blubbering on me again. She drained it in one gulp, gave a long shudder, then composed herself to begin.

"I called Mr. Pope a number of times after the fire," she said in a soft voice tinged by a cultivated drawl. "I found out his name from some, well, let's just say some 'connections.' I guess I got on his nerves with all my questions, but when he figured out who I was, he didn't want to make me mad. So he suggested I call you for help."

I raised an eyebrow. "So, who are you," I asked, "that arson investigators like Maynard Pope tremble at the very sound of your voice?"

She smiled, revealing perfect white teeth. "Lydia Talbot. My father is Randolph Talbot."

"Oh," I said, immediately tabulating the implications of that simple remark. Randolph Talbot was the chairman of Teer & Talbot Tobacco, my dead client's former employer. Randolph Talbot was also head of Durham's wealthiest family. In fact, the Talbots were probably close to being the top dogs in both Carolinas, with more bucks than Marlin Perkins had on his walls and more social influence than the president of the local junior league.

Even the most out-of-it townies knew their story. Rumor had it that a Talbot from Virginia had rolled into North Carolina after the Civil War searching for a way to improve his family's fallen fortunes. He'd founded T&T Tobacco in Durham with the backing of a friend named Eustace Teer. Within two generations, the Teer seed died out thanks to debauchery and rumored syphilis, but the Talbot family tree took firm root and, eventually, took over the company. One hundred and thirty years later, T&T had made Randolph Talbot and his relatives wealthy beyond expectation. The mere mention of their name could make bankers salivate and caterers faint with joy. If Thomas Nash really had been engaged to the young woman sitting before me, she may well have been the reason why he was so blissfully unconcerned about current profits. He'd be set for life once he married her.

Of course, now he never would, would he?

"When I first saw you at the fire," Lydia Talbot was confessing to me tearfully, "I knew you weren't with the cops or fire department. And I could tell you were upset.

So I thought maybe you and Thomas . . ." Her voice trailed off.

"You thought I was having an affair with him?" I asked incredulously. "That doesn't say much about the level of trust between the two of you."

Her shoulders slumped. "You don't understand," she said. "We were engaged and he kept saying he was happy, but he always seemed so . . . distracted. Distant. He was even passive about our wedding plans. He went along with everything I suggested. I guess I thought maybe it was because he had been seeing someone else and that you were her."

"I assure you I only met your fiancé the day before the fire," I told her. "And I can also tell you that he was more preoccupied with his work than any other man I've ever met. I'd be willing to bet my original Kid Creole and the Coconuts debut album that his preoccupation was not due to another woman. Is that why you've come to see me? To make sure we weren't having an affair?"

She shook her head. "No, it's worse and even more ridiculous than that."

Worse than what? I wondered. What was so frigging ridiculous about the idea of me boffing Thomas Nash? Yeah, sure, I had less than a millionth of her bank account and I was a good ten years older and thirty pounds heavier, but there were plenty of men who found my, ahem, big bold beauty appealing.

"Mr. Pope said it was arson," she said. "And that it was probably set to harm Thomas or cover up the evidence of some other crime. But he said he couldn't be more specific. He thought maybe you could help me and he gave me your card."

I wasn't sure whether Maynard Pope was sloughing a hysterical female off on me or whether he was trying to do me a favor. I'd let her fee decide.

"What exactly is it you want me to do?" I said slowly.

"Could you find out who set the fire and whether or not they intended to murder him?" she asked.

"That's what the cops are for," I told her. "What do you really want?"

She blew her nose again, daintily this time, stalling for time.

"I might be happy to help you," I said, then thought of her bank account. "Hell, I might even be ecstatic. But you have to be straight with me so I know what I'm getting into."

She paused, then blurted it all out before her nerve failed. "I thought maybe you could find out for sure if he was having an affair before he died and also tell me if my father had him killed."

"What?" I sat, stunned. "You think your father had him killed?"

"I don't know," she said, and this time the tears hit like Niagara Falls. I didn't even try to stop her. I heard a shuffling in the halls and knew that Bobby D. was eavesdropping outside. He doesn't normally boost his big butt up unless he has to go to the bathroom, but the Ferrari had aroused his interest. He may even have recognized Lydia Talbot from her photographs in the newspapers.

While she cried, I occupied myself calculating what I would charge her for taking on the case. Thomas Nash's retainer had gone toward rent and food, but a new month was looming and neither Bobby nor I were into starvation. I didn't want to gouge her, but I was having visions of working out of the bathroom at the Greyhound Bus station and, believe me, the scenario wasn't pretty to contemplate. By the time she quieted down, I had decided on a fair—but fat—fee and was busy thanking whatever gods hovered above for sending me an excuse to avenge Thomas Nash's death while still fattening our bank account.

"About your father," I prompted, when her fresh tears had subsided to a ladylike trickle.

"He was furious that Tom and I were engaged," she explained in a tiny voice. "Especially since Thomas had quit T&T and gone out on his own. I first met Tom when he worked at T&T, but we didn't go out until after he founded his own company. We met again at a benefit for Duke Hospital. He was very attractive in a different sort of way, if you know what I mean."

I nodded. I knew.

"Anyway, we had dinner the next night and one thing led to another. I had to do a lot of the leading, if you want to know the truth. Sometimes I wondered if he'd ever even had a girlfriend before. I didn't tell Daddy about him, but somehow he found out. He always does. And he was furious. He said Tom was just using me to get information on T&T. That was silly. I don't have anything to do with the company, so what could I tell him? Then Daddy said he only wanted my money, but Tom was earning plenty with King Buffalo. Daddy just didn't understand."

I had a feeling Daddy understood plenty.

"Were you aware that your fiancé was going to testify against T&T in the Hargett case?" I asked, "And that he had a lawsuit pending against T&T, asking for a greater share of the Clean Smoke royalties?"

She nodded. "Daddy made a big deal about that, too." She sighed as if her father had been most tiresome. "He forbid me to see Thomas anymore."

"And when you wouldn't obey him, he went ballistic?" I suggested.

She nodded. "It was after Daddy heard that Tom might be testifying against T&T in the Hargett case that things really got rough."

"How did he know about that?" I asked, curious as to how Randolph Talbot had found out so quickly. "Did you tell him?"

She shook her head. "No, Tom didn't even tell me when he decided to testify for the Hargetts. He never talked to me about work. Daddy found out some other way. He knows everything. I thought I might have to move off the family compound, it got so bad. That was just a month ago, and now I'm afraid that Daddy may have had something to do with . . ." Her lower lip started to tremble.

"You realize that this man you loved so much could have cost your family an incredible bundle of money?" I said. "In the millions and millions. It's no wonder your father was upset. Why did you let yourself get into such a mess?"

She twisted a ratty Kleenex between her fingers and

stared at the floor as she spoke. "You'll think I'm snobby if I tell you."

"Would you rather I thought you were snobby or stupid?" I asked.

"Neither." She stared at the floor near my feet and explained. "My whole life, men have come after me," she said. "From the time I was eleven years old and even before that. Some of them asked me out because their fathers put them up to it, especially when they were too young to figure it out for themselves. Others did it on their own, but for the exact same reason."

"For the money?" I surmised.

She nodded.

"You give yourself too little credit," I said. "You're a beautiful woman."

"Isn't that the same thing?" she said. "It's still not loving me. Not one of the men I ever dated, not one of them until Thomas, ever saw beyond the Talbot name or my face to who I really was inside. I could tell. I'm no idiot. They all wanted to visit the house, meet Daddy, make a good impression, land a great job, get their hands on my share of the money. I was instant fame, instant fortune, instant career success or, at best, instant decoration for their arm. I hated every one of them. I still do. They're phony and I'd kill myself before I'd spend the rest of my life with any of them."

"And Tom wasn't like that?" I prompted, envying her passion but thinking that she was a little naive for her age.

"When I met Thomas at that benefit, I don't think he connected me with those Talbots. He didn't even remember meeting me once before. And when he did find out who my father was, he didn't care. Don't you see? He was maybe the one man in the world in danger of being destroyed rather than being helped by the Talbot name. And he loved me anyway."

I shrugged. "That's a little unfair. He may have passed your test, but he was the only one in a position to take it."

"He saw me for a person," she insisted. "He didn't even care what I weighed or what I wore. No one else was like that."

"You're expecting an awful lot from men in general," I said. "They are, after all, only men."

"I know," she answered in a small voice. "But they ought to at least try to pretend those other things matter."

True. That alone would be enough to get most of them laid on a regular basis. "So you think your father had Tom killed for any number of reasons?" I asked.

She pursed her lips. "I don't know. That's what I want you to find out."

"I hate to sound like a broken record," I said. "But if your father's involved, that's what the cops are for."

She shook her head. "If my father is involved, the Durham cops will get nowhere. He would have thought of that long ago and made sure to prevent it."

"And you think I might be able to figure it out when the cops can't?"

She nodded. "Because *you* don't have to follow the law."

Ah. So that was it. She was smarter than I gave her credit for. I upped my asking price to account for the moral gray factor.

"Let me get this straight," I said. "You want to find out if Tom was having an affair before he died, to make sure that what you had between the two of you was real? And, you want me to find out if your father had him killed?"

She nodded, eyes wide.

"What do you want me to do with the information if I obtain it?" I asked. "Obviously, if I find out your father did kill him, I have to go to the police."

"I know. I just want you to tell me first, before the news goes public. I've thought about this a lot, all day and all night. If Daddy did have something to do with it, he has to pay. I love my father, but . . . ." She stopped to consider her choice of words. "I don't know that he really loves me back. He isn't capable of it. He just sort of marches through this world he has created and expects everyone to do exactly as he says. He never smiles, he never laughs, he just evaluates people to see what he can get out of them and sometimes drinks a little too much."

"Drinks a little too much?" I repeated. In the South,

depending on who you're talking to, "drinks a little too much" can mean anything from takes a single glass of champagne on New Year's Eve to pisses his pants on a regular basis.

"It really is only now and then," she explained. "He's not an alcoholic or anything. He just wants to forget."

"Forget what?" I persisted.

"Forget my mother dying and ... maybe, forget that *woman* he married after she was gone."

Great. An evil stepmother. I upped my price even more. If I had to deal with Cruella de Ville, I wanted to get paid for it.

"Got any brothers or sisters?" I asked, since I like to know who or what is going to fall from the family tree when I give it a good shake.

"Two brothers. Jake is in college and Haydon is twelve."

"Half brothers or full brothers?"

"Full." She paused. "Why?"

"I'll need to look into all that stuff," I warned her. "And before I agree to take the case, I want you to think very hard about whether or not you really want to know what I might find out."

"I do want to know," she said immediately. "I need to know. I have to get on with my life and I don't think I can unless I know the truth."

"Okay," I agreed reluctantly. "If it's the truth you're after, then I can help. But it may end up costing you a lot."

"I don't care," she said. "Money is nothing to me."

I wasn't referring to money, but while we were on the subject: how come only people who have tons of money ever say it means nothing to them?

"Do you know why Tom hired me in the first place?" I asked.

She nodded. "I was the one who told him that maybe he ought to hire a private investigator to see who was behind it."

"You thought your father was behind the harassment, too?" I guessed.

She nodded again. "I need to find out if I'm right."

If she was willing to take on the purse strings in her family, who was I to argue? "Okay," I decided. "Let's get started." I pulled out my notepad. "Tell me everything you know about how and when Thomas was harassed in the weeks leading up to his death."

"Oh," she said in a voice grown suddenly small. "I don't know anything about the specifics."

"*Nothing?*" I said.

"Not really. Thomas didn't want me to know. He said it would scare me. He said he'd take care of it and not to worry."

Had that been his real motivation, I wondered? Or had Nash known Lydia's father was behind it? It might account for why he dropped the harassment suit. Maybe he'd wanted to minimize the pain caused to her family.

"You could talk to his lawyer," she suggested. "I think he knew everything that happened."

"I thought he had decided not to press charges," I said. "What was he doing with a lawyer?"

"He did decide to drop the suit against my father. But before that, he went as far as having a lawyer draw up the papers."

"Did you tell him to drop the harassment suit against your father?" I asked bluntly.

She shook her head. "I would never tell Thomas what to do. Plus, I won't be intimidated by my father. Thomas never even told me he was dropping the suit until it was a done deal."

Nash had certainly been protective of his fiancée. I thought I understood why. Lydia Talbot had an earnest innocence about her, as if she had been protected from the ugly side of life, as well she might have been. Only a true cynic would want to be the one to burst her bubble. As cynical as I was, I didn't want to be the one.

"So you think the lawyer will know the details about the harassment?" I said.

"I'm sure the court papers contain specific incidents. Maybe you could find some clues there."

"Worth a shot," I agreed. "What's the lawyer's name?"

"Harry Ingram," she said. "Or maybe it was Henry. I'm

not quite sure. I've probably run into him at social events; I know his name is on the letterhead of a lot of the causes I support. But I can't put a face to the name. I think his office is in Brightleaf Square, so you should be able to find him.''

I wrote the lawyer's name down and asked her a few more questions about her relationship with Nash. She had never met his parents or any of his siblings. I found that a bit odd, but chalked it up to two very busy schedules. Either that or Nash had some skeletons he hoped to keep firmly shut in his family closet.

When I was done, I walked Lydia Talbot out of the office just in case Bobby D. decided to take advantage of her grief, though I didn't think a multi-million-dollar heiress would ever be that desperate for male companionship. I promised to keep in touch, accepted the retainer check when it was discreetly offered and watched her zoom away in the Ferrari. She drove down McDowell Street well over the limit, smoothly zipping in and out of traffic.

I watched her squeal around a corner as I thought about my first impression of her. There was something about her that was fragile and innocent, yet also spoiled and danger- ously beguiling, like a rare orchid that smelled so impos- sibly sweet, it made you think of decay instead of beauty.

Five minutes after Lydia Talbot left, I was on the phone to Maynard Pope. He would tell me nothing.

"Come on," I pleaded. "Just a scrap to go on."

"I sent you a big bucks client," he droned in his nasal voice. "That's enough favors for this month."

"Come on, Maynard. I can owe you one."

"What could you possibly do for me?" he asked.

That was a good question. Even I had my standards. Then I remembered something Lydia had said.

"If you ever get in a tough spot in an investigation, call me," I offered.

"What for? That's my job. To investigate."

"Yeah, but you have to follow the law," I pointed out.

"I don't. Not unless I get caught, of course."

He was silent, considering whether or not the offered

favor was worth it. In the end, he relented and threw me the scrap I wanted. "Fire was set by an amateur," he said flatly. "But that's all I'm gonna tell you."

"How do you know?" I asked.

"Only a fool would have dribbled gasoline around the house like this guy did. It's a wonder he didn't set his dick on fire. He was lucky. Very lucky. A pro would have known better."

"You sure?" I asked.

"I'd stake my reputation on it."

That was good enough for me.

Using womanly wiles on Maynard Pope would have been like trying to teach a yard-dog table manners. My ex-boyfriend, Doodle Simmons, was another story. After I hung up with Maynard, I called Doodle and demanded the inside info on the Nash fire.

"Come on, Casey," he said. "I can't do that. It's under investigation."

"Doodle," I said firmly, "When you wanted to take me to bars fifty miles out of town so no one in your family would know you were dating a white girl, I did not make a peep. And I accepted your sexual boundaries, shall we say, though I would never have tolerated such an attitude in a paler imitation of a man. I even tried to cook for you."

"Yes," he countered, "and it's a good thing I'm a fire-man and had an extinguisher handy."

"Regardless, I gave it my best shot." I played my trump card. "Most of all, when I had to hide in your closet that time your mother came over with chicken and dumplings, I did so willingly even though you had the balls to sit down and discuss whether or not the new uniforms of her church's gospel choir had been worth the money."

"But I had to give you half the casserole after she left, just to keep you happy."

"Well, of course," I pointed out. "I was burning more calories than you, remember?"

He sighed.

"The point is, Doodle," I explained firmly. "I did for you what I have done for few men. I kept a low profile and sacrificed my self-respect on the altar of your mama's racist leanings. So now you owe me."

"God almighty, Casey," he complained. "Do you have to act like I beat you or something?"

"Give it up," I said slowly.

He sighed. "I'll call you back in half an hour."

He was as good as his word, which was one of the reasons why I had gone out with him in the first place. "Okay, Casey," he said when he called back. "There's a little I can tell you, but remember—it didn't come from me."

"I can't even remember your name," I assured him as I opened up my official Thomas Nash file. I am, at heart, organized and methodical about my work, even if my personal life qualifies for intervention by the Federal Emergency Management Agency.

"Nash was shot in the back and head several times, then doused with gasoline before the fire was set."

"Ouch," I said. "What a way to go." I remembered the turned-over metal desk. There must have been a struggle. One that Nash had turned his back on—a fatal mistake.

"At least he never felt the fire," Doodle said. "It's conceivable the gunshot would have been concealed by the fire, but the killer hadn't counted on Nash falling over a metal desk when he was shot. Water from our hoses pooled in the well of the desk, preserving more of his skull than you'd expect."

Hey, I'd seen that skull. And I hadn't expected anything from it but nightmares. Damn, but that Maynard Pope was good at his job.

"Probably less of him was destroyed than the killer figured," Doodle added. "The other thing I can tell you is that the fire was set to destroy the house as well as Nash. Accelerant was found all over what was left of the counters in the basement, plus upstairs in the areas where both offices were located and in his library and bedroom. They took a chance spreading it around like that."

I thought of what Maynard Pope had said about it being an amateur. "So they were desperate. And maybe they were trying to destroy his records," I said. "I wonder why?"

"So does Maynard Pope. But he doesn't have anywhere to start."

"Or maybe he has too many places to start?" I suggested.

"Maybe," Doodle conceded.

"Did the answering machine survive?" I asked.

"No way. Anything plastic melted during the first flash. And the computers wouldn't even make good paperweights at this point. Why are you asking?"

"Nothing," I said. "Just wondering. Anything else?"

"Nope. Maynard's working hand-in-hand with some detectives named Cole and Roberts on this one. Need their phone numbers?"

"No, it won't do me any good." I'd heard of them and neither one was going to cut me any slack. "Thanks for your help, Doodle. It's for a good cause."

"I knew it had to be," Doodle answered. "For all your brass, Casey, there's a heart of gold beneath those thirty-eight D's. Old Doodle can always tell."

"Too bad your mother can't," I said ruefully.

"I love ya anyway, Casey," Doodle said unexpectedly before he hung up.

I spent the rest of the afternoon logging onto NandoNet to perform my new case ritual. I hacked my way into the *N&O* newspaper archives for articles on Thomas Nash, his company and anything having to do with the Talbots. Nash had kept a low profile. Most of the articles about King Buffalo featured his partner, Franklin Cosgrove. I made a note to talk to him pronto and kept reading.

Lydia's evil stepmother led an active social life. Wherever there was a ribbon to be cut or a champagne bottle to be cracked over a prow, there she was. To catch the drippings, from the looks of things. In such a decorous crowd as North Carolina's social elite, it's not hard to spot the dress strap that's fallen unnoticed to the elbow, the out-of-control glint in an eye, the slightly frazzled hair or the frequently inappropriate facial expression. By all indications, Lydia's father had taken a drunk for his second wife and her name was Susan Johnson Talbot.

Lydia kept a lower profile. I found her at a charity event, but she was shown in blue jeans taking a group of mentally retarded adults to the zoo rather than in a diamond tiara sipping champagne. Good for her. The conversation was probably more intelligent and certainly more honest.

For one of the most powerful men in the state, Lydia's father was also surprisingly low key. He was short and photographed wearing a tuxedo over his barrel-chested body. He had a full head of brown hair that curled like vintage Captain Kirk, circa the infamous 1980s toupee, and he had thick, somewhat brutish features that never seemed to change expression. The man could have been a wax dummy for all the animation he displayed. What would it take to get a twitch from those pressed lips or a spark in his narrowed eyes?

When I was done, night had fallen. I was starving—and broke. I drove home, but all I had in my refrigerator that didn't come crawling out at me was peanut butter and olives. And all I had in my bank account was a promise that funds would be available by the next business day. I settled for peanut butter toast and hoped that by burning the bread I might disguise the taste of incipient mold.

It was tough being penniless. I doubted Bobby D. was dining on such meager fare, thanks to his many girlfriends. The thought made me feel very alone, which was odd since I generally prefer the company of myself over anyone else's. But I didn't want a drink, and not even the thought of visiting my friend Jack—who worked on the other side of the bar at a restaurant called MacLaine's—could get me excited. Instead, I sat on the windowsill in my bedroom, watching the Duke students filter past on their way downtown. I kept zeroing in on the couples, studying them for a clue as to why they seemed so happy.

It was Lydia Talbot I was really thinking of, I finally realized. She had seemed so genuinely in love with Thomas Nash. And now he was gone. But at least she had felt that kind of love in her life and knew it was possible.

It was sick, but in a way I envied her sorrow. At least she was brave enough to face it, instead of running away and never looking back.

FOUR

The next morning, I chalked up my bout of self-pity to low blood sugar and decided that a two-thousand-calorie southern breakfast would set me to rights. Fortunately, the ATM was in the mood to spew out twenties. I drove over to Honey's on I-85 and elbowed aside a couple of territorial truck drivers to make room at the counter. I ordered country ham and eggs plus a side of sausage gravy—a southern phenomenon that relocated Yankee doctors consider liquid suicide. It's the color and consistency of glue, and flavored with crumbled bits of pork sausage. As if this weren't enough cholesterol, the gravy is ladled over biscuits before being served, which explains why everyone at the counter overflowed their bar stools. When I was done packing it in, I felt like someone had poured cement down my gullet— the true test of a good southern meal.

I was suffused with goodwill toward the world and, during the half hour drive to Raleigh, used my rare burst of enthusiasm for mankind to eliminate suspects in the Thomas Nash murder.

No one made the cut.

When I arrived at the office, Bobby D. was parked at his desk eating chicken biscuits from Hardee's like they were potato chips. He was examining the photos I had taken of Nash during my one day of surveillance—and getting greasy fingerprints on the evidence.

"Remember these, babe?" he asked. "I stopped by the

spy shop for some high speed film and there they were. I'd completely forgotten about them.''

''Do you mind?'' I asked, plucking the pack of black-and-whites from his offending fingertips. I'd forgotten, too. Now Lydia Talbot had given me a reason to remember. ''Get your own case, partner,'' I added, annoyed that, thanks to Bobby, a glob of mayonnaise now obscured Nash's head in the first photo.

His face lit up. ''Already got one. I kept telling Cheryl down at the legislative building to dump that no-good husband of hers. She thinks he's gay and fooling around down at the Pony Express. Now it looks like she's going to do it, if I can find enough evidence to make the divorce settlement worthwhile.''

Good old Bobby. He was like the glass salesman who walks through town at night lobbing rocks at his clients' windows.

''If her husband was *gay*,'' I corrected him, ''Cheryl would know it. I think the two of you mean bisexual, which seems to be the media's favorite word for gay these days. But since neither one of us is a babe in the woods, let's get it straight. No pun intended.''

''Whatever,'' he conceded. ''Can you follow the guy for me tonight? See if he hits any swish bars?'' Bobby would never qualify for membership in the Rainbow Coalition.

''No can do,'' I told him. ''I've got to work on the Nash case.''

He looked disappointed. ''Guess I'll have to do it myself.''

''Cheer up,'' I told him. ''The Pony Express is every bit as sleazy as those topless bars you love. The only difference is that the women are fake—and a lot better looking.''

''Cool,'' he said, reaching for his jumbo Pepsi. ''Just hope I don't get harassed by the clientele. I got enough trouble keeping women off me.''

I didn't have the heart to tell him that the buffed-out gay men of Raleigh, North Carolina were unlikely to give his porcine butt a second glance. I left him to his homosexual fantasies and went back to my office to examine the photos.

I had to admit that the stupid cigarette pack device was

a pretty good camera. The prints were crisp and sharp, through no fault of my own, I might add. We're talking auto-focus and auto-exposure. I examined the photos carefully, but didn't find much new to go on. Until I reached the last one of the day: Nash's final stop had been the green-glass office building on Main. I examined the print more closely and noticed huge brass letters decorating the front archway: "T&T."

I was staring at the house that Randolph Talbot had built, the headquarters for T&T Tobacco. What had Nash been doing visiting his former employer? Especially considering his multiple lawsuits against them.

Not much to go on. I'd have to take the Durham bull by the horn, so to speak, if I hoped to shake loose a lead. After wishing Bobby well for his walk on the wild side, I headed back to Durham and the offices of T&T Tobacco.

The lobby of T&T looked like it had been designed by someone who'd spent too much time in Miami. A wall of water took up the entire southern exposure, with tropical plants and white slat benches arranged in front of it. A newsstand was nestled into an alcove across from the waterfall, near the bank of elevators. I stopped for a pack of bubble gum and recognized a familiar face.

"Well, well, well," I said, staring at an old black man who had more wrinkles than a geriatric shar-pei. He was sitting on a stool behind a rack of magazines, his eyes shaded with Ray Charles specials.

He dipped his head first to one side, then the other as if searching for the source of my voice.

"Knock it off, Dudley," I warned him. "You've seen too many Stevie Wonder concerts. Besides, I can tell you're staring at my tits."

He checked to see if anyone was watching, then snickered when he saw we were alone. "Would you rather I use the Braille method to check them out?" he asked, extending two eager hands.

I slapped them away. "You couldn't tell the difference between Braille and buckshot," I pointed out. "You're no blinder than I am, you old fraud. I can't believe you're still getting away with it."

It was true. Dudley was a sixty-eight-year-old con artist from Philadelphia who moved south about ten years ago in search of greener pastures. He used to panhandle down near Brightleaf Square, pretending to be a blind harmonica player. He was such a lousy musician that, for a while, he made a good living accepting donations in return for silence. But he got rousted after making a smart-ass remark about the girth of a leading citizen's wife. So he stole a wheelchair from the Duke Cancer Center and switched to impersonating a disabled war veteran at Durham Bull games. He would score the excellent seats set aside for the handicapped, turn around and sell them for three times their face value, then demand that his companions supply him with all the beer he could hold during the games. Leaping up to wrestle a foul ball away from a screaming seven-year-old kid had lost him that gig. Now he was back to being blind and I knew why.

"How many times do you give the wrong change and people let you get away with it?" I asked, knowing southerners would be loathe to pick a fight with a blind man who'd made what they thought was an honest mistake.

"All the time," he cackled with satisfaction. "Got a twenty? I'll show you."

I shook my head. "I'll take your word for it."

"Don't go turning me in, Miss Casey," he pleaded. "I got me a tasty younger girlfriend who depends on my income." He kissed his fingertips.

"Enjoy it while you can. In a couple more years, you're going to be depending on your Depends." I took out a photo of Thomas Nash and showed it to Dudley. "Recognize this guy? Look carefully and think hard before you speak. My PMS is acting up and I'm in no mood to screw around."

Dudley glanced at the photo over his sunglasses. "Sure. He was a big cheese around here for awhile. Used to work on the tenth floor." He jerked a thumb toward the bank of elevators. "Kinda the absent-minded professor sort. Would let a dozen empty elevators go up without him before he noticed he was still standing in the lobby. I used to sit here and count them. The guy was maybe a hot dog or two short of a picnic, know what I mean?''

"He was here a couple of Mondays ago," I told him. "Did you see him?"

Dudley nodded. "He bought a pack of Rolaids and let me keep the change from a five." He stopped to reconsider. "Course, I think it was more like he never noticed what he handed me or what I handed him back."

"Where did he go on Monday?" I asked.

"You think I'm a goddamn doorman or something?" he asked indignantly, holding out his hand for a bribe.

I ignored it. "I think you better tell me or you're gonna find yourself without this cushy little franchise of yours. Or your extra state disability payments."

That last little remark hit home. He nodded toward the elevators. "He went to the tenth floor, same as always."

"Thanks, Dudley." I turned to go and nearly plowed down a plump matron swathed in pink and purple chiffon, no doubt on her way in for the latest copy of *Southern Living*. "Better count your change carefully," I muttered to her. "You'd think the guy was blind or something."

She was tut-tutting her disapproval of my rudeness as I left. She'd learn soon enough.

The tenth floor of T&T Tobacco turned out to be the Marketing Department, which was a bit of a surprise. I had Thomas Nash pegged as a laboratory rat.

The reception area was pure *Architectural Digest* and reeked of contemporary good taste. I don't know why they didn't just go ahead and paper the walls with hundred-dollar bills for the same effect. The receptionist was way too young for the job and far too pink for the shaggy blue-black mop that topped her head. Traces of heavy eyeliner told me she was one of the Triangle's music groupies plugging away at her day job. Poor thing. Ten to one, she was supporting a drummer.

I didn't bother with formal introductions. My goal was to intimidate, not ingratiate.

"How long have you worked here?" I demanded.

She eyed my iridescent purple sharkskin dress. Jealously, no doubt. "About a year. Why?" she stammered.

"You knew this man?" I flashed her a photo of Nash.

"Sure," she said quickly, her face shutting down with a mixture of suspicion and fear. "He worked for Mr. Teasdale in New Product Development. Why are you looking for him? He's dead."

"I know," I barked at her. "Where's Mr. Teasdale?"

Her eyes slid involuntarily toward a set of wide mahogany doors firmly shut behind her. "He's in a meeting right now. He's not to be disturbed."

"Disturb him," I said sternly, sliding my card across her desk.

She was too young to know that it was her job to argue with assholes like me. She plucked my card from the desk with talons that had been painted black, then scurried into the conference room. Her round bubble butt was packed in a black leather mini-skirt and red fishnet stockings. If she'd been the receptionist at a crypt, the outfit might have been appropriate. The fact that T&T tolerated such attire was proof that the local job market was insane. Thanks to a booming economy, if you could breathe, you could work. Which also explained why they had vegetarians trying to argue you out of buying meat down at Wellspring's butcher counter.

Elvira Jr. was back in a flash, her pink face gone even paler. "He's tied up," she said in a flustered voice. "For the whole day. He says he'll call you."

"No need for that," I informed her. I sidestepped her desk and marched straight toward the double doors of the conference room.

No, I'm not incredibly rude. Well, maybe I am. But that wasn't my motivation in this instance. After years of investigating assorted white collar crimes, I'm wise to the ways of corporate America—specifically the wiles of good old boys who jealously guard their office fiefdoms with petty power plays. Like making visitors wait, sometimes for days. The only reason why women have trouble breaking the glass ceiling is that they're too busy trying to wipe the bullshit off it.

My tolerance for bullshit is especially low. I decided to blast Mr. Teasdale's hopes for a pissing match right out of the water in Round One.

The double doors burst open with a dramatic bang as I marched into the conference room. I was pinned in the sudden gaze of a half-dozen corporate minions. Three of them were men with long brown hair pulled back into ponytails. The women were blondish and fond of blunt cuts. Everyone was dressed in a tailored dark suit with funky advertising-like touches like boxy shoulders. What fearless risk-takers, I thought. I was willing to bet that even their underwear all looked alike.

The group was huddled around a narrow conference table that ran the length of the entire room. It stretched before me like an alley waiting for a bowling ball, its polished surface cluttered with cardboard-mounted sketches, computer-generated comps and other paraphernalia of creative corporate minds.

I took advantage of the shocked silence that greeted my arrival to snoop. The assembled go-getters were working on a new advertising campaign. Various mascots were obviously being proposed, ranging from the photo of a studly young fellow who looked like a Cuban James Dean to a cartoon of a well-dressed panther lighting up a cigarette. Good grief. Ever since the success of Joe Camel, the entire tobacco advertising industry has been searching for an equally successful mascot, especially since cartoons tend not to demand residuals and raises. They all acted like it was some mysterious process to pinpoint exactly the right image and liked to blab about focus groups and cross-affinity. But Joe Camel's phenomenal success was pretty obvious to me. Stick a giant phallic symbol in a velvet smoking jacket and surround it by adoring girls, and of course underage teenage boys will stampede to buy your cigarettes. A mere panther would never be able to compete.

"You need something with a little more zip," I told them, sliding the panther cartoon down the table toward its creators. James Dean Jr. followed. "What you need is something distinctive." I pretended to think. "Wait, I know." My face lit up with enthusiasm. "How about a giant dancing cigarette, only round the top a little bit and color it sort of pink and . . ." I stopped when I realized that some of the professionally wacky trend-setters gathered before me were taking me seriously, assuming that I was a member of the creative team they'd yet to meet. It was too cruel to continue, so I stopped.

Just in time, it seemed, since a tiny little guy at the far end of the table was turning several spectacular shades of blue. He'd lost all of the hair on the top of his head and had compensated by growing it long in back. It flowed to his shoulders in gray waves, making him look like a cross between Ben Franklin and a Smurf. His mouth was opening and closing like he'd just been gaffed.

"You okay?" I asked with feigned sincerity. Sometimes you had to confuse them to conquer them.

"Who the fuck are you?" he sputtered, waving his arms around as he searched for the properly corporate response.

"I believe I sent my card in a few moments ago." I paused. "With the young vampire-in-training."

Enraged, the short fellow—who I pegged as Donald Teasdale, Marketing Whiz—pointed a chubby finger at the door. "Get out!" he ordered me. "This is a confidential meeting. I'm calling Security."

"This isn't confidential. This is crap." I pushed the rest of the comps down the table at him. "Do yourself a favor. Send these people back to the drawing board, give me fifteen minutes of your time and then I'll be out of your life forever."

Unless, of course, I thought to myself, you're the one who torched Nash.

I suspected him because he was shorter than a lawn jockey, which is a shallow theory but not entirely without merit. It was been my experience that short corporate guys are, hands-down, the meanest of all the suit species. They can't help it. Years of being put down for their height has warped them.

Teasdale stared at me in enraged silence, his blue-and-silver tie askew. His lackeys were gazing obediently out the large picture window with studied nonchalance. I waited him out and, gradually, his normal color returned. He found his voice—and his wits.

"Give me half an hour," he told the others. "And she's right. These are crap. Come up with something better." He flung the carefully executed ideas back toward his minions dismissively, taking out his frustration on those who depended on him for a paycheck. They gathered their rejected dreams and filed from the room, shooting me curious glances.

"I still ought to call Security," he threatened primly once we were alone.

"Oh, cram it," I said good-naturedly, pulling out the chair right next to him and flopping down in it. I'd crowd him just to let him know that I was bigger and that I knew it.

"Have we met before?" he asked suddenly.

"No." I shook my head innocently. "Don't believe we've had the pleasure." I grinned at him and winked.

"What is it you want?" he asked in a tone more poisonous than polite.

"I have a few questions about Thomas Nash."

He was silent but his eyes flickered.

"I'm investigating his death," I explained.

"I gathered." His voice was high for a man, and had gone even higher. This was not a subject he enjoyed.

"You knew him?" I asked pleasantly.

"Of course I knew him," he spit back. "He worked for me. What is it you want to know? I'm a very busy man."

I knew that. Every man in a suit is busy. If they weren't so busy, they'd have taken the time to take the damn things off.

"Nash came to see you the last Monday he was alive," I said. "Why?"

"How did you know that?" he countered, shifting his body away from me like I had cooties crawling up my legs.

"You just told me," I said with a smile. "I only knew he came to the tenth floor. But I figured it was someone high up." I could have made a crack about his height, but didn't. No sense being petty. I'd joke behind his back instead.

He fumed for a moment in silence.

"Just tell me," I said finally. "And I'll be out of your life forever."

"Who are you working for?" he asked, flicking an imaginary piece of lint off his jacket as he stalled for time.

"Sorry, but I can't tell you that."

"Then I won't cooperate."

"I can tell you that the same name that figures prominently on my retainer check also figures prominently in T&T's success."

That did the trick. Teasdale was so in awe of Randolph Talbot that he walked around with his lips puckered, just waiting for Talbot to bend over. It never occurred to him that another Talbot might be my client.

"Why didn't you say so in the first place?" he said. "I told Randolph we needed to clear our name. What do you want to know?"

"Why Nash came to see you."

Teasdale puffed up with satisfaction. "He wanted to settle."

"Settle what?"

"The lawsuit he filed, hoping to get a bigger share of the Clean Smoke royalties."

"Why would he want to settle?" I asked.

Teasdale shrugged. "Maybe he knew he was outgunned and out of line," he suggested. "He created that process while in the employ of T&T. It was ours to keep. He should have been grateful for the bonus he received."

I understood then that the little weasel sitting in front of me had been the one to parcel out that meager bonus, probably keeping most of it for himself. "What reason did he give for wanting to settle?" I asked.

Teasdale shrugged again. "He said all the legal mumbo jumbo was taking up too much of his time and energy, that he had better things to do. That he wanted it settled so he could get on with his work."

"What did you tell him?" I asked.

"Precisely this, and you may quote me: 'Tough titty said the kitty, but the milk's still good.' " Teasdale smiled thinly.

"That was mature," I remarked. Like I said, it's all a

big sandbox so far as guys are concerned. They're either flinging it, digging it or pissing in it.

He didn't care what I thought. "I told him to talk to our legal department if he didn't like my answer. He'd get the same response. No way we were settling. We don't owe him a dime. He walked out on us with three years left on his contract. He's lucky we never came after him on the basis of the no-compete clause."

"He'd signed a no-compete clause?" I asked, surprised.

Teasdale's smile faded. "Not exactly. But it was in his contract."

"Then he signed it," I said.

"Well," he hedged, tapping his fingernails on the table surface.

"He never signed the contract at all, did he?" I guessed. "It got plowed under all that other crap on his desk and forgotten." Nash had been absent-minded, not stupid. He'd used the system to his advantage.

My correct guess pissed Teasdale off. "Look, Nash is dead," he said. "What does it matter why he came to see us or why he wanted to settle?" He eyed me curiously, his gaze lingering on my black high-tops. "So why did Talbot hire you?" he asked. Then, just to make sure I understood how very important he was, he repeated, "I told him it might be a good idea to clear our name."

"Clear T&T's name?" I asked. "Do people think T&T killed him?"

Teasdale looked appropriately shocked. "I meant clear our name of having harassed him."

"You knew about the harassment?" I asked.

"Of course I did." He stared at me, wondering why, if I had been hired by Randolph Talbot, I didn't know the inside scoop. "Everyone knew Nash was being harassed and that he thought it was us. He called me, you know, when it first started. Accused me of it in his typically round-about way."

"What did you tell him?" I asked.

"I told him there was no way T&T was behind it. That's petty stuff. Believe me, Randolph Talbot and T&T Tobacco are above that kind of crap." He adjusted his necktie again.

"Besides, it's too risky. You get caught pulling penny ante stunts like that and a jury could sock you with millions in damages. It wouldn't be worth the risk. I told him to look somewhere else."

In other words, he'd have gone that route but was afraid he would get caught. Honest to God, sometimes I think dollar signs have replaced our consciences in this country. God help us when inflation hits.

"If it wasn't T&T, who do you think was harassing Nash?" I asked.

He shrugged. "Same person that killed him?"

"Could you be a little bit more helpful than that?"

He shrugged again. "If I were you, I'd talk to Cosgrove."

"Cosgrove?"

"Yeah. Franklin Cosgrove. His partner. The guy's a smug bastard. I wouldn't put it past him." Teasdale glanced impatiently at his watch. "They were arguing over the division of royalties from the new curing process Nash had come up with. Probably invented it on our dime, but I can't prove it."

"How do you know all this?" I asked.

"Listen, everyone knows everything when it comes to this business. Except for you, apparently."

Apparently. But I'd squeezed the little squirt for all the juice I could get. And I needed to get the hell out of there before he figured out I hadn't been hired by Randolph Talbot. Time to throw him off Lydia's trail.

"Thanks for your help," I told him, heading for the door without bothering to shake his sweaty little hand. "Nash's family will really appreciate it."

"Nash's family?" He jumped up from his chair and scurried after me. "You said Randolph Talbot had hired you."

"No I didn't. You did."

He glared at me, the angry flush returning,

"Hey," I consoled him, patting him on the back. "Every Napoleon has his Waterloo. I guess I'm yours."

*   *   *

Tracking down Nash's partner was a cinch. The phone may have gone up in smoke, but the line had been rerouted to King Buffalo's new offices. I called from a pay phone in the T&T lobby and hit pay dirt on the second ring.

"King Buffalo Tobacco," an ultra-polite feminine voice answered.

I asked to speak to Franklin Cosgrove and, after assuring the woman that I was not a member of the press and, in fact, believed in shooting the media on sight, was put through to the big man himself. I guess with a third of their employees burnt to a crisp, King Buffalo didn't have the manpower to sustain a bureaucracy. After hearing who I was and what I was after, Cosgrove agreed to see me at once. He even gave me directions to their new temporary offices on Main Street in downtown Durham.

I got caught in the insane traffic loop that strangles downtown and passed the damn building twice, but finally managed to park my ancient Porsche without mishap. I tracked down Franklin Cosgrove in a small office on the fourth floor. The secretary was AWOL, but the main office door was open. I considered it an invitation to march right in.

My, my. Franklin Cosgrove was enough to make me change my evil mind about red-haired men. Don't get me wrong, I'm sure the world is full of fabulous carrot-tops. I just don't want any of them in my bed, with the possible exception of Eric Stoltz. I was willing to consider another exception for Nash's business partner. He was in his late thirties, tall and trim, but definitely not skinny. A third baseman's body if ever I saw one. He had a thin mouth and nose, beautiful high cheekbones and his eyes were goldish tan. His hair was dark copper and there was plenty of it. He was wearing a white cotton shirt that had been ironed to pass inspection by a general and it was tucked into tight black jeans. A tingle passed between us when we shook hands.

He knew I was attracted to him and he worked it. "Nice dress," he said, taking my hand and leading me to a chair that was just a little too close to his. "I knew Tom had hired a private investigator. I didn't realize detectives looked like you. I'd have insisted on being tailed by you if I'd known.''

Uh-oh. A silver tongue to go with all that red hair. I made a mental note to keep my mind on my work. I've gotten myself in trouble enough times in the past to know that when all of my blood starts running south, my brain is left high and dry.

''You're pretty cute yourself,'' I admitted, but I inched the chair away as I spoke. It's not that I lack self-esteem. God knows I could do with a little more self-restraint and a little less self-confidence. It's just that warning bells go off when a potential suspect gets too chummy too quickly. Especially one who doesn't seem all that broken up about the loss of his crucially talented partner.

''Too bad about Tom Nash,'' I offered.

''Tell me about it.'' He ran a hand through his hair and sighed, as if I had no idea of the depths of despair and self-sacrifice Nash's death had caused him. ''It was terrible timing.''

''Mighty damn inconsiderate of him to get murdered,'' I wanted to say, but kept my mouth shut. No sense provoking an asshole into acting like one before the spirit moves him.

Cosgrove smiled, revealing expensive teeth. ''I bet you thought Tom was hot stuff. Women loved him. Even more than they love me. I don't know what his secret was.''

''Modesty,'' I told him. ''He was completely unaware of his appeal. Humility is such an underrated virtue.'' He didn't get the hint, so I got down to business. ''Thanks for seeing me,'' I said. ''I just have a couple of questions.''

''Who's paying your bill now that Tom's dead?'' he asked suddenly.

''No one,'' I lied. ''He has a lot left on the retainer he gave me. I feel like I owe it to him. Besides, like you said, I liked the guy.''

''Oh.'' He stared at his desktop. ''I thought maybe Lydia had hired you.''

''Lydia?'' I asked innocently. Scary how well I can lie.

''Tom was engaged to Lydia Talbot,'' he explained. ''The lucky bastard.''

Yeah, real lucky. Not everyone gets to die as the fiancé of a millionairess.

"They must have kept it pretty quiet," I said, not adding that Lydia had said it was pretty much a state secret. I was surprised that Cosgrove even knew.

"They did keep it quiet," he said. "On account of her old man. But I knew both of them pretty well, so I figured it out and asked Tom about her one day. He admitted they'd been seeing each other, then said they were engaged. I was surprised. Lydia is not exactly the marrying type."

The way he said her name got me to thinking. Specifically, it got me to thinking that maybe Franklin Cosgrove had liked Lydia Talbot even more than he'd liked Thomas Nash.

"You know Lydia Talbot?" I asked.

"Sure." His eyes slid away from mine. "We sort of grew up together. Our parents belonged to the same clubs. I know her family. She's younger than me, of course. We never dated or anything, if that's what you're after."

It wasn't what I was after, because I had already figured out that he was one of the handsome fortune seekers Lydia had complained about. I was ashamed of myself for ever having thought Franklin Cosgrove was cute. He was undeniably attractive, but he was definitely one of those guys who's always wondering what's in it for him. He probably palmed the five-dollar bills out of the collection plate at church on Sundays.

"You're young to be heading up a company," I said. "Must be nice to have it made before you're forty."

His laugh sounded practiced. "I wish. We were doing okay, but Tom's death is a major setback. I'm selling out and moving on. I've got an investment banker working on it now. There's no growth left without Tom and his new ideas."

"Going back to the corporate grind?" I asked.

He shrugged. "I have a standing offer from T&T to come back on board in marketing any time I want. For a lot of money. Easy money. It's tempting when you consider my option is either starting over with a new company or putting back together the pieces of this one."

"Yes," I said. "But then you'd be working for Donald Teasdale."

"So you've met him." His smile was fleeting. "Actually, I wouldn't be working for Donald Teasdale. He would be working for me."

That was interesting. "No love lost between the two of you?"

"It's tough to lose what you've never found."

"They could use some help in marketing at T&T," I admitted. "I was just over there. Their advertising ideas were terrible. Not a single phallic symbol in the bunch. I hear you're the marketing whiz behind King Buffalo."

"That's me."

"I also hear that you were locked in a disagreement with Nash about how to divide the royalties for the new curing process."

He tilted back in his chair. "Hold on," he said. "Stop right there." He laughed uneasily and straightened his collar while I watched in careful silence. When I didn't respond, he explained in a rush, which of course made him sound guilty though it didn't prove that he actually was. "We were in negotiations for dividing the royalties and close to agreement," he said. "He was always going to get the majority share in any royalties, as well as he should. The agreement was almost completed. Now none of us are getting anything because he was too paranoid to keep backup research files or notes. Everything went up in smoke. It's gone. I lost a lot of money when he died, in case you're fishing for a motive."

I *was* fishing—and Cosgrove looked like a pretty good worm. "What if I told you that Donald Teasdale heard that the two of you were really going at it about the royalties?"

"I'd tell you that it was all wishful thinking on Teasdale's part. Donald is still pissed we left and set up shop together, and even more pissed that Talbot would take me back in a heartbeat. As his boss."

I hated to admit it, but I believed Cosgrove. If it's a choice between believing a short scumbag or a tall, handsome one—frankly, I take the low road and choose the high way.

"Who do you think might have had a motive for killing Nash?" I asked.

"Isn't it obvious?" Cosgrove said. "Whoever was harassing him. Someone who wants King Buffalo to fail."

"But who do you think that was?" I asked. I was starting to get annoyed at this by-now standard response. "And why weren't they harassing you?"

"That's easy," he answered. "They couldn't find me. I'm on the road ninety percent of the time, meeting with suppliers and distributors. Hammering out ad campaigns. Kissing ass in Washington. That sort of thing. To tell you the truth, I never even witnessed any of the incidents. I just heard about them. The night Tom died, I was in Atlanta on my way to Mobile. I didn't even know about it until the next afternoon when I tried to call in. But if I had to guess, I'd say that it was some competitor."

"What about a possible personal motive?" I asked. "Just in case."

He thought about it for a moment. "Maybe a woman that Tom had inadvertently pissed off?" he suggested. "I mean, come on, duct-taped rabbits? That sounds like a female to me."

"Why's that?" I asked. "Men blow living things apart, but women duct tape them?"

He looked uncomfortable, having gotten it through his handsome skull that I was offended. "I just meant that there seemed to be a lot of personal anger in the incidents. At least the way Tom described them. Like a lovers' quarrel gone bad."

Why did I have a feeling he was an expert on lovers' quarrels?

"You sound almost like you aren't sure they really happened," I said, reading the skepticism in his voice.

"Oh, they happened all right," Cosgrove assured me. "Some of the phone calls were so scary, I lost two good secretaries over them. And a third after the fire. She refused to start work. I had to hire someone else."

"Which reminds me," I said. "Weren't all the harassing calls from a man?"

"Yes," he admitted. "But they could have been made

by a woman with one of those distorter things. Anyone can change their voice these days.''

I hated to admit it, but he was right. I'd have to ask Bobby D. about those gizmos and see if they were readily available in the Triangle.

''Got any spurned woman candidates in mind?'' I asked.

''Well . . .'' his voice trailed off as he looked out a window. ''Is that your Porsche?'' he asked suddenly, staring down at my lousy parking job. ''I thought I saw you getting out of it earlier.''

''Yup,'' I said. ''That's mine.''

''Wanna sell it? I'd give you a good price.''

''No way.''

He sighed. ''Seems a shame to waste a classic car like that on a woman.''

''True,'' I agreed. ''But I really need it. So I can run over men with style.''

He blinked at me without comment, then stared back out the window again. Several blocks west, the Durham Bulls stadium was bustling with an afternoon home game. I'd have killed for a seat along the first base line and a cold beer.

''Well?'' I prompted him. ''Was Tom having problems with anyone? Male or female, if you don't mind. I can't say I share your hormone-based theory.''

He thought about it, casting his scheming mind over a entire Rolodex, no doubt, before coming up with someone he could tar with his brush of suspicion. What a worm. Ever notice how you can't help but hate a tattletale, even when you're glad to be hearing what they're tattling?

''Tom had a big problem with a farmer out near Lake Gaston,'' Cosgrove finally offered. ''The guy was using unapproved chemicals on his crop, or something like that. Tom got pissed. He'd contracted with some farmers to follow his guidelines exactly, but said this guy could compromise his pilot program. So Tom fired the guy from the project. I think it was some old geezer who lost a lot of money because of it. He might have been mad enough to kill.'' He stood up and started for a file cabinet, then stopped. "Shit. I forgot. The files are all gone. What was his name?"

He picked up the phone and dialed an outside number. "Roberta?" he said in a voice so fakely cheerful that I knew at once that Roberta hated his guts and had told him so. "It's me and I'm not calling to talk you back into working here. I found an excellent replacement."

Whoa. There was a hell of a lot of subtext in that one word "replacement." If he'd slapped Roberta across the face, it might have been kinder. I knew then that Cosgrove was one of those guys who thinks that screwing his secretary is a well-deserved job perk for a successful man, ranking right up there with a company car and a private bathroom.

"I need to know who that farmer was that Tom had a problem with. Cops want to know," Cosgrove was saying, proving he'd just as soon lie as blink. "I think he was from over by Lake Gaston. Remember? It happened last spring. Just after our Bahamas trip, if that helps you remember." His laugh made me want to turn my head away, but it worked on the woman on the other end. Cosgrove was silent for a moment, listening, then thanked her, made some meaningless promise to call back soon and hung up.

"The name is Hale," he told me. "Sanford Hale. Like I said, he lives in some small town near Lake Gaston. I'd talk to him if I were you." He held up a finger to forestall any more questions and picked up the phone. Punching an intercom number, he went into his oily act again. Only this time he managed to convince his current secretary to pick up his dry cleaning after work and find a nice gift for his mother in time for her weekend birthday. "Take an extra fifteen minutes for lunch tomorrow," he magnanimously offered. "Get her something personal."

Watching him in action for twenty minutes had convinced me that Franklin Cosgrove was a sleazeball. Still, that might turn out to be in my favor. Under the theory that it takes one to know one, he might be the perfect guy to help identify suspects. If he was telling the truth about being out of town the night Nash died, he was off the hook. Unless he'd hired someone, of course, but his explanation of the money that Nash's death was costing him rang true. Besides, Maynard Pope said it had been an amateur and I believed him.

"Did you have key man insurance?" I asked him casually, having seen *Double Indemnity* only the week before.

"Of course." He stared at me, affronted. "Why?"

"How much?" I countered.

"Two million." He looked uncomfortable.

I thought about it. That was two million more reasons than anyone else I could think of had to kill Nash.

"That's nothing," he protested against my silence. "Every penny of it will have to be used to whip the company into good enough shape to sell it. And we owe a lot of people money, believe me, we were in the building-up phase. No bank is going to lend to us now that Tom is dead. I'm not seeing any of that two million. I need it for cash flow. I'll be lucky to walk away from here with the shirt on my back."

Soon he'd be on his knees, sobbing about a vow of poverty. His hypocrisy was choking the oxygen out of the air so I decided to pull the plug on his performance. "Who irons that shirt for you?" I asked suddenly. "They're good."

"A friend does," he said, but his eyes flickered to the open door. Creep. He was paying her a crummy salary and making her work around the clock, all for the privilege of serving him.

"What about Randolph Talbot?" I asked. "Think he might have had something to do with your partner's death?"

"God, no!" he exploded, looking nervously around the room as if listening devices were planted everywhere. "And I'd advise you not to go around saying that, if I were you."

I found his reaction odd. Why the sudden fear?

"Talbot is that powerful?" I asked.

"Too powerful to care about Tom," Cosgrove insisted. "Even if he was going to marry his daughter. Besides, Randolph Talbot liked Tom. Always did. He was happy they were getting married."

"What?" I asked, confused. Lydia told me her father had been furious.

"Sure. Tom talked to him on the phone about it just a week before he died. I heard them. He was assuring the old guy that his intentions were honorable, that kind of crap. He wanted to go over and talk to the old man in person. It made me sick to see him groveling like that over a woman, but it kind of amused me at the same time. Tom Nash, oblivious to the female species, gaga over some girl."

Yeah. But that "some girl" was *some* girl, I wanted to say. I found Cosgrove's seeming detachment just a little too studied and I was also confused by his contention that Nash and Randolph Talbot had been on speaking terms. If they were, Lydia sure as hell had never known. I'd need to find out more.

I didn't think I'd get anything else useful out of Cosgrove. I could practically hear the wheels turning in his mind as he sat behind that desk. Everything from here on out was likely to be too self-serving to be useful. I thanked him for his time and stood to go.

"How about dinner?" he asked. "They make a great Cosmopolitan at Papa's."

"No thanks," I told him. "I'm trying to quit." I was sticking to my guns about red hair, I decided. Especially when it covered a devious mind like his.

He didn't look too disappointed. He was a serial charmer and had asked out of habit, not desire. Screw him. Or, more to the point, don't.

I took a look at Cosgrove's new secretary on the way out. She was plain and plump, with pale stringy hair and a wrinkled blouse that gaped open at the bustline. Guess she'd been too busy ironing his shirts to give her own a glance. She gave me a quick look, toting up whether or not I was competition, then avoided my eyes. I felt bad about it. Her boss had started using her in less than two weeks and I knew she had a lot of heartache ahead of her if she was naive enough to think that Franklin Cosgrove gave a shit about her.

*　　*　　*

It was early evening and the secretary's pathetic melancholy proved contagious. Feeling sorry for myself was getting to be a habit. Not even the thought of Bobby D. standing in front of his closet, trying to decide what to wear to a gay bar, could pull me out of my slump. I didn't want to go home to an empty apartment, but I didn't feel like having a drink, either. Maybe I needed to get a dog. I'd had one once—for twenty-four hours. Until he had pissed on my rug while stoned out of his gourd. If I wanted to put up with behavior like that, I'd get a steady boyfriend. So I'd found the old mutt a new home. Now I missed the company, wet spot and all.

I opted for a drink as the lesser of all available evils and headed to MacLaine's to see Jack. MacLaine's is located on 15-501, about halfway between Chapel Hill and Durham. It was happy hour when I got there, but it didn't make me any happier. The place was jammed with off-duty nurses and cops, along with the usual office and university employees. I took a spot at the bar near the kitchen door and Jack brought over a Tanqueray and tonic without asking.

"Hey, babe," he said. "Hard day at the office? You look kind of blue." He gave me one of his famous smiles in an attempt to cheer me up, but it lacked its usual dazzling magic.

"Hard day at everyone else's offices," I told him. "I spent the entire day with a bunch of creeps."

"You spend your nights with creeps all the time," he pointed out, teasing me. At least, I hoped he was.

"Yeah, but it's easier to spot them in the daylight."

"You need to have a love affair, Casey," he told me, glancing toward the far end of the bar. "With someone nice, not me. There's a nice guy down at the other end. Owns a construction company. Not a bullshitter. Big. Smart. Your type."

"I have a type?" I asked. Maybe if enough people told me that, I'd finally be able to figure out what it was.

"Sure." He smiled broadly. "Me. But I get this sense I'm wearing thin."

Poor Jack. He was a good-natured, faithless and basically insecure cad who was human flypaper to babes. He loved them and left them with the speed of a Canadian sprinter. Most of them minded, but I didn't. I always knew he was a snake when I picked him up. But he periodically suffered a slight sense of the guilts at his failure to maintain even a token semblance of monogamy when it came to our relationship. Probably his Catholic upbringing.

"You're not wearing thin," I assured him. "Life is wearing thin. Maybe I need a vacation."

"What you need is a love affair," he repeated. "Trust me on this one, Casey."

He hurried off to refuel a couple of out-of-control nurses, leaving me to my drink. If I didn't snap out of it soon, I'd end up permanently parked at the bar, begging the piano man to play me a tune.

"Buy you a drink?" a deep voice asked.

I turned to find a burly man dressed in a nicely pressed golf shirt and khakis at my elbow. Jack's friend from the other end of the bar.

He had red hair.

"Sure," I said. "Why not?"

It had been years since I'd taken home a stranger. I made up my mind to get to know him fast.

FIVE

I woke up alone the next day, my newfound red-headed friend having had the good taste to slip from my apartment before dawn. He didn't leave a note. Either he'd figured out I wasn't the mushy type, or I had snored.

I decided to skip my morning weight-lifting session since I had burned a zillion calories the night before and was currently flexible enough to take on those ten-year-olds who keep winning Olympic gold medals. Instead, I sat at the kitchen table and looked out over my backyard as I slurped down my morning coffee. The air conditioning was cranked up to the max and the window fogged with the suffocating humidity of a Carolina July day.

Speaking of suffocation, maybe Jack was right. Maybe I did need a love affair. But you couldn't just order one up like a pizza from Domino's. Me and last night's redhead was a case in point. I had managed to scratch an itch, but that was about it. Odd how two people either click or they don't.

I didn't want to dwell on my romantic drought, so I took the cold shower I probably should have taken the night before and thought about the Nash case.

I needed to warn Lydia that I'd have to speak to her father. I could hide her involvement in hiring me, but I couldn't ignore the inconsistencies I'd heard about Randolph Talbot and his relationship with Thomas Nash.

I phoned Lydia at home, aware that, though she only

lived a few miles from my apartment, our lives were a million miles apart.

I was living in a three-room apartment perilously close to the wrong side of the tracks. Meanwhile, the Talbots lived on an enormous ten-acre compound smack in the middle of Durham's oldest and most expensive neighborhood. A forbidding wrought-iron gate surrounded the entire lot, keeping the riffraff at bay. The acceptable practice was to grasp a metal bar in each hand and gaze longingly through the gate at the twin mansions built atop a central hill. They were matching pink stucco, sort of miniature San Simeons, and were lit with tiny white Christmas tree lights all year long to inspire awe in the simple folk. A carriage house that was about ten times bigger than my own apartment guarded the single entrance gate. There were various smaller cottages scattered around the estate, most of them well-hidden by the huge old oaks that dotted the rolling green lawn or the weeping willows that lined the large creek meandering across the Talbot grounds.

I wasn't sure if Lydia lived in one of the big houses or in one of the smaller cottages. Wherever she was, she had live-in help. A man with a faint accent and a formal manner answered the phone. I gave only my name; he recognized it and put me through without comment. I was vaguely relieved that she did not live alone. Until I found out who had killed Nash and why, there was a chance she could be in danger.

"Did you find out something already?" she immediately asked, oozing the effortless morning energy of a person who lives a cleaner life than my own.

"Not really," I said to stave off more questions. "I just want to check a few things with you. I understand you know Franklin Cosgrove." I wanted her take on King Buffalo's remaining partner.

There was silence.

"Lydia?"

Her tone was cool. "Yes, I know him. In fact, I've known him since I was about ten years old."

"I gather you don't like him."

"I don't."

"Can you tell me why?"

"Is he involved in Tom's death?" she asked.

"I have no indication he is," I answered carefully. "I just want to get your take on him. He told me some interesting things and I don't know whether to believe him or not."

She was silent as she chose her words. "I think he's truthful," she finally said. "And certainly he's a talented marketer. A lot of Tom's success in King Buffalo was due to Frank. He came up with a great marketing strategy, selling expensive handrolled-looking cigarettes to yuppies. But I don't think Frank is a very nice person when you get down to it."

"Why's that?" I asked, thinking of his sad-sack secretary and her dreams of a future with him.

"He uses people and has no clue that he's doing it. He thinks of himself first, second and last. I doubt it even occurs to him to consider other people's feelings and emotions." She paused. "His mother worshipped him. It didn't do Franklin a lot of good, either. He's only thirty-eight and he's already been married and divorced twice. He likes to marry up and he's always shopping around for a new rich wife."

"How far up does he have to go?" I asked. "He seems to be on speaking terms with the good life."

"He has a fair amount of money, but he spends it fast. Everyone in our circle knows that when Frank's father died, he left behind a trust fund for his wife and instructions to distribute the rest of his estate among all his children— which included three daughters—even though it cost him a lot of money in taxes. I guess he figured that if it were left up to his wife, Frank would get it all. So the family money has been diluted and there's no way Frank can get more than his share. He has to work. Unless he marries rich, of course."

Good God, she knew everything but his bank account number. I had no doubt she knew his balance. Talk about money recognizing money. These people treated each other like balance sheets. "But he has married rich twice?" I asked.

"Yes," she admitted. "Both times to women I know.
But he made the same mistake twice. He married pampered
southern belles whose fathers were still alive and looking
out for their little girls. When he proved to be a lousy husband, the divorce proceedings were like surgical strikes.
Frank walked away with nothing in each case. My guess is
that now he's holding out for an orphaned harelipped heiress whose trustee is asleep at his desk."

Her opinion made me glad that Franklin Cosgrove had
not been the only person holding out the day before. "Cosgrove makes it sound like there was once something between the two of you," I told her. "It's in his tone of
voice."

"It's in his dreams," she assured me. "Did he say anything that might help?"

"Maybe," I said. "Look, I know you aren't going to
like this, but I have to talk to your father. I'll tell him I'm
working on my own in this case, repaying a debt to Thomas. But I have to talk to him, okay?"

She was silent for a moment. "Do you want me to set
it up?" she asked, her voice tight with tension.

"No, then he'll know you have something to do with it.
Leave it to me. I'll get in somehow. You sleeping okay?"

"Sort of," she answered. "It gets easier every day. I
almost hate that the big hole in my soul seems to be filling
in. I feel like Thomas is really leaving me now, that one
day soon I'll wake up and have completely forgotten him.
It makes me sad." She sighed. "It just takes so much energy, is all."

"I understand," I told her. And I did. I had clung to
grief for years after losing my parents, holding on to it
because, as a little girl, I felt it was the only way left to
honor their memory. Only the patient example of my grandfather had showed me that life goes on whether you get
with the program or not, so you might as well make the
most of it while you're here.

"I'll keep you posted," I said. "And take care of yourself."

"I will. I better go. I'm hosting a luncheon for some kids
who are trying to read two hundred books each by the end

of this summer. That's pretty amazing, wouldn't you say?''

I agreed and hung up. It was almost as amazing as wea-seling your way in to see the most powerful CEO in the state. Which I intended to do right after lunch.

I knew Randolph Talbot was in the office for the day because an ultra-well-trained secretary told me so when I called pretending to be a secretary for the governor. I didn't tell her who I really was because I doubted very much she'd be as big a pushover as the preteen working the tenth-floor reception desk.

Naturally, his office was on the top floor of the T&T building. Had I not intended to sneak in via the fire stairs, he would no doubt have been on the ground floor. As it was, I huffed and puffed my way up fifteen flights feeling very sorry that I had spent the night before fooling around instead of getting my nine hours of beauty sleep.

Once close to the inner sanctum, I slipped into the hall-way and checked the corridor. Only the holiest of the holy had offices near Randolph Talbot and the place was as quiet as an Irish bar on Easter morning. Every single door was shut. I imagined a score of high-ranking executives barri-caded in their suites, surrounded by mahogany and leather, guarded against the common public by karate-trained sec-retaries.

I wasn't far wrong. Shielded by a large potted palm, I peeked in one of the narrow windows that flanked the firmly shut doors to the chairman's suite and spotted an alertly erect secretary manning a front wrap-around desk. She was middle-aged, trim, tanned the color of pumpkin pie and wore her dark hair in a resolute helmet that looked stiff enough to play handball against. There was no way I was willing to tangle with her. She'd staple my ass to the floor as soon as sneeze. Plus, she probably had a security button embedded in that shiny desk of hers and I was not anxious to argue with a phalanx of rent-a-cops out to prove they deserved their hefty paychecks.

Instead, I took the cowardly prudent approach. I slipped into a hallway closet and waited until all that iced tea that I hoped she had gulped for lunch took effect. Sure enough, within twenty minutes, she headed for a discreet ladies' room at the end of the hall. The suite doors had pneumatic hinges and I caught them before they shut.

There was only one inner door and I wasted no time. Within ten seconds I was standing in front of Randolph Talbot's desk. Within three more seconds, I was looking down the barrel of a .44 Magnum. Good Christ. I prayed he wasn't about to ask me to make his day.

"Who are you and what do you want?" he demanded, his aim and voice steady. I couldn't help but notice that his custom-tailored suit matched his gun. *GQ* would be proud.

Fashion aside, I was in trouble. Randolph Talbot was even shorter than in his photographs—and his face was as flat and pugnacious as a hungry bulldog's.

"I'm Casey Jones, a private investigator," I said quickly, trying my best to sound calm. "I'm looking into the death of Thomas Nash on behalf of his family. All I need is five minutes of your time."

"Who the hell is Thomas Nash?" he demanded.

"Oh, come on," I said. "You know damn well who he is."

He glared at me.

"Five minutes," I assured him. "Five minutes and then I'm out of your hair." Speaking of his hair, I think it definitely was a toupee. But a good one. It was carefully arranged above a tanned face that I suspected had seen a facelift or two. Doesn't anyone grow old gracefully these days? More to the point, was he going to give me a chance to grow old at all?

"How did you get in here?" Talbot demanded, his eyes narrowing to slits.

"Your secretary isn't at her desk," I explained hurriedly. "I think she must be in the ladies room." I resisted the urge to hold my arms in the air. "Would you mind terribly not pointing that fucking gun at me?"

The secretary chose that moment to return, proving that she was even quicker on the draw than her boss. She popped her head into his office to ask a question, but her words slid into a gasp when she spotted me.

"How did you get in here?" she squeaked.

Talbot turned his gun on her like he was going to shoot her dead on the spot for daring to take a pee. Her knees shook and she dropped her steno pad.

"It's all right," Talbot finally told her after several scary seconds of intense contemplation. "I'll take care of her. If Fletcher calls, tell him I'll call back in ten minutes." She hurried away and I remained standing, staring at the gun.

"Sit down," he urged me, waving the pistol at a plush leather chair near his enormous desk. He slid open the top desk drawer and stored the gun back inside. "Can't be too careful in my position," he added. "Kidnapping is always a possibility. Look what they did to that Exxon fellow up in New Jersey."

I pitied the poor kidnappers who winded up with Randolph Talbot. No amount of ransom money would be worth the trouble, I suspected.

I sat in a chair and regained my composure. Truth to tell, when I had seen that gun swing up at me, I near about wet my beloved Ann Taylor pants—which were lined and had been obtained for a mere five bucks at the PTA Thrift Shop in Chapel Hill.

"Thanks for seeing me," I said, wondering if it was worth it to try to warm him up. Somehow, I didn't think so.

"Do I have a choice?" he said gruffly. "You don't look like the type who'd take no for an answer." He closed a file and moved it far away from my prying eyes. His desk was as bare as a landing strip. What was the point of having a huge desk if you didn't use it?

"Thank you," I said. "I think."

"Take it as a compliment. If you have to." He stared at me, calculating my black pants, white lycra stretch top and black leather boots. "Jesus, you're built like a linebacker."

"Now that I will take as a compliment," I said, smiling.

He didn't smile back. "Hurry up. You have five minutes. Start by showing me some identification."

I pulled out my fake ID, and slid it across the desk toward him. I wasn't worried. It was a good fake. In fact, it looks better than the real PI licenses North Carolina hands out and no one has been able to spot the difference yet.

Talbot examined the card without comment and slid it back toward me. "How the hell can I help? I barely knew Nash."

I remained calm, even though he was talking to me like I was a junkyard dog who had wandered in to chew on his carpet. At least I wasn't married to the jerk. What did I care if he was an asshole whose self-esteem depended on how many people he could terrify in any given day?

"I understand you knew the deceased," I said pleasantly. "That you had several conversations with him in the weeks prior to his death?"

Randolph Talbot was glaring at me, having switched from trying to intimidate me with his voice to trying to intimidate me with his burning eyes. He was good at it. He made Charles Manson look like Mr. Magoo. But I just smiled with even more pleasant determination and waited until he gave up.

"Where did you hear that?" he finally barked.

"Does it matter? Did you speak to him?"

"You're not the police," he said.

"No, I'm not." I paused. "Maybe they would be interested in knowing about it. I haven't told them yet."

It took about three seconds for him to weigh the implications of my remark. "I spoke to him several times," he admitted. "About matters that had nothing to do with his death, I'm sure."

"What did you speak about?" I inquired politely.

He hesitated again, using each silence as a symbol of his disapproval—and as a way to let me know that he didn't have to answer my questions, that he was merely humoring me because I wasn't worth the bother of confronting. "We talked about a number of things," he hedged.

"Like the recent harassment against him?" I suggested.

"As a matter of fact, yes." He glanced at his watch impatiently. "In fact, I called him after I heard through the grapevine that he was having trouble. I assured him that, under no circumstances, was T&T behind it. He believed me."

"Lucky for you," I observed.

"We were not behind it," Talbot snapped. "The day

we're reduced to pulling stupid stunts like that is the day I get out of this business. In fact, after my conversation with Nash, I sent out a confidential memo to our security people and all high-ranking executives outlining the situation and making it very clear that I personally abhorred it and wanted to be immediately informed if anyone heard anything indicating who might be behind the harassment of Nash.''

''Just in case one of your henchmen was being over-zealous?'' I asked.

He stared at my boobs, another ploy men use to intimidate the shit out of women. But I was wearing the equivalent of female armor: my underwire, reinforced spandex Warner bra and, believe me, it could withstand a lot more than dirty looks from dirty old men. I sat quietly, smiling back.

''Exactly,'' he finally said. ''I'm not going to screw around with this. If I say T&T had nothing to do with the harassment of Thomas Nash, you better believe that's the truth. No one runs this company but me.''

''When did this confidential memo go out?''

''About a month ago. Don't look to us for the trouble.''

I wasn't planning to. A month ago was two weeks before Nash's death. That was plenty enough time for his underlings to get the word. Yet the attacks on Nash had continued. He was probably telling the truth.

''I guess the Durham cops have talked to you?'' I said.

He eyed me carefully. ''They have not. I had my lawyer contact the police, to inform them of what I just told you and to offer to be of any assistance. They have yet to request further information from either me or T&T.''

''I guess they're more trusting than I am,'' I offered.

''Or smarter,'' he said.

I shrugged, perfectly happy to accept his implied insult. This annoyed him.

''You a dyke?'' he asked suddenly. ''You're built like one.''

''No,'' I answered in my deepest voice. ''Just a red-blooded, man-loving American girl blessed with big bones and a fondness for hand weights.'' I did not add that only a moron would think dykes came solely in extra large. Lord, had America learned nothing from the endless hype surrounding "Ellen"?

He grunted and looked at his watch. "One more minute," he warned me.

"About your daughter," I began.

His head whipped up and he glared at me.

"I assume you know she was involved with Thomas Nash," I said. My pulse beat faster in spite of my efforts to remain cool. His eyes burned bright when he was mad and I hoped I had not underestimated him. The .44 was, after all, only a drawer away.

"How much do you know about that?" he demanded.

"I know they were engaged. Did you?"

He stared at me for a moment before replying. "Of course I did. Do you think a daughter of mine could go out in public with someone and I not know? I have people everywhere who report back to me on what my children do. I don't like surprises. But this thing with Nash was just more of Lydia's nonsense, like trying to save the children of Guatemala. She was only doing it to spite me."

"You don't think they were in love?" I asked.

"Oh, *he* was in love," Talbot said with a pitying laugh. "Like a dozen men before him. Very in love."

Suddenly, I understood. "I see," I said quietly. "Nash called you to let you know that his intentions toward your daughter were honorable and you managed to let him know, without ever coming out and saying it, that the price of your daughter's hand was for him to drop his lawsuit against your company. Or perhaps I should say, lawsuits."

Talbot stared at me, his expression a cross between anger and admiration. "Not bad," he said. "That's close. You want a job?"

"Working for you? No," I assured him. "You had a number of good reasons for wanting Nash dead. Surely the police realize that."

"What the police realize, young lady, is that Thomas Nash had dropped his suit asking for more Clean Smoke royalties. And he'd withdrawn the harassment charges before that."

"What about the Hargett case?" I demanded. "The one involving marketing to underage smokers? Nash was going to testify against you on that one. He told me so himself."

His smile was reptilian. "He changed his mind. The Hargett case was settled the day Nash died. As was the Clean Smoke suit. His testimony was moot."

"I don't believe you."

"See for yourself." He pulled out two signed contracts from a file drawer and showed them to me. The first was an agreement signed by Thomas Nash dated the day he had died. It said that Nash was dropping his request for more Clean Smoke royalties in exchange for the princely sum of one hundred dollars.

The second agreement had been signed by Horace Hargett and his son days before Nash's death, though Randolph Talbot's signature was dated the day Tom died. I thought I knew to the hour when Talbot had signed it. I had followed Nash to the T&T building his last afternoon and seen him go inside. Nash must have visited Talbot right after Donald Teasdale, in his stupidity, had turned down his offer to settle the Clean Smoke suit.

Randolph Talbot was smarter than Teasdale. He had killed two lawsuits with one stone, agreeing to give the Hargetts money but only if Nash dropped the Clean Smoke suit first.

I scanned the Hargett agreement. In it, the Hargetts agreed to drop the lawsuit pending against T&T in exchange for a two-million-dollar settlement, to be paid directly to the family within three days. The lawyer's cut would be paid separately on top of the two million. That much money was peanuts to someone like Talbot, but it was a fortune to a poor mountain family faced with astronomical medical bills. Nash knew that, and that was why he had accepted Talbot's terms.

"You are a piece of work," I told him. "Not only did you use your own daughter as a hostage, you used those poor cancer-ridden hillbillies as bargaining chips to force a decent man into silence. What did you do? Offer to settle with the Hargetts only if Nash dropped the Clean Smoke suit?"

Talbot smiled and raised his eyebrows, hands folded smugly. "Once you know a man's weakness, you're half-way to beating him at his game. Thomas Nash had a serious weakness for justice. All I did was use it to my advantage."

I thought I knew Randolph Talbot's one weakness and I had a urge to use it right then and there. "Pretty bad planning on your part, wasn't it?" I said.

"What do you mean?" he asked.

"If you'd only waited one more day, Nash would have been dead anyway. He couldn't have testified. You paid the Hargetts two million for nothing."

His smile faded. I had hit him the only place it hurt—his wallet. "At least it proves my innocence," he said.

"Sure. But you could have gotten a damn good lawyer for two million dollars."

His eyes narrowed. Two little tusks and he'd have made a good warthog. "Are we done here?" he demanded.

"Almost," I promised. "I just need to know if you opposed Nash marrying your daughter."

"Opposed it?" His smile returned, twice as smug as before. "I applauded it. It solved a lot of my problems. Once he was in the family, it would just be a matter of time before I brought his company back into the fold."

"You were going to let him develop his new curing process and then buy him out?" I guessed.

Talbot shrugged. "Best way to get innovation—go out and buy it. He would have sold out to me, I have no doubt about it. Him and that partner of his."

"Franklin Cosgrove," I offered.

Talbot nodded. "Cosgrove's a whore. Always was. The best way to his heart is though his bank account. Just in case you're interested." He smirked and stared at my chest some more. Why did I have the feeling that there weren't a whole hell of a lot of female executives running around T&T?

"I'm not interested in *anything* about Cosgrove," I assured him. "Except whether or not he killed Thomas Nash."

Talbot shook his head. "Cosgrove had ten million reasons for wanting Nash to stay alive. I hear everything Nash was working on went up in smoke. All his files, all his research, everything.''

So Talbot's information was even better than mine. It didn't surprise me. "It's a shame about his work being wiped out," I remarked.

"More than a shame," Talbot pointed out. "No one else is even remotely approaching his methods. This industry needs a future."

"Did your daughter know you approved of her engagement?" I asked, wondering if Lydia had been lying to me.

Talbot laughed. "Hell, no. She'd have lost interest immediately. I know my daughter. Little Miss Rebel. I had to rant and rave against her even seeing him and hide that I knew they were engaged. I told Nash not to tell her that I even knew, for the time being at least, while I pretended to think it over. Otherwise, she'd have lost interest in him. Lydia's rather predictable, once you get to know her. Like most people."

I wondered if he had been able to predict that Lydia would ask me to prove whether or not he was responsible for her fiancé's murder.

"I have to disagree," I said politely. "In my experience, people are inherently unpredictable. That's what keeps me in business. I find it hard to believe that you know your daughter as well as you think you do."

The corners of his mouth twitched as he thought something over and I wondered what he was up to. "Why don't you meet her and find out for yourself?" he suggested. "I'm giving a dinner party tonight. You must come. It will give you a chance to meet Lydia and ask her all the questions you like about Nash. And you might meet some other people who could help in your investigation. When it comes to tobacco, Durham is a small town. Most of the people who really count in the industry end up eating around my table."

Gathering at the trough, no doubt. But I knew he had other motives for inviting me into his home. Randolph Talbot was like a human X-ray machine. The whole time I had been sitting in his office, trying my best to look unfazed and competent, his shark's brain had been sniffing out my weakness. And he had found it. Maybe it was the slight Florida cracker accent that gave me away, or my discomfort with his expensive chair, my worn boots, maybe even just the way I wore my clothes. Who knows?

But he had definitely ferreted out that I had been born and raised poor—and that the prospect of sitting down at a dinner table with people who had money might scare the shit out of me.

I hated him because he was right. He had found a way to intimidate me.

I was determined not to let him win.

"I'd love to come," I lied.

SIX

When you're raised within spitting distance of a swamp by an old man who has never even left the rural center of Florida, table manners are the last thing on the list of skills to learn. My grandpa taught me how to shoot, how to skin a squirrel and six different ways to get the catfish biting in the dead of summer. But he damn sure never taught me the difference between a salad and dessert fork. I was in over my head and I knew it.

If I couldn't act the part, I could at least look it. After all, that's the American way. It was only half past three. I had plenty of time to prepare.

I headed to a new thrift shop on University Drive and found a light blue raw silk pants suit for twenty bucks and a pair of almost matching heels that would do nicely. Then I hit the cosmetic aisle at Eckerd's and bought myself some new hair dye and makeup that was a little more subtle than my usual in-your-face shades. Finally, I spent a few minutes at a book store thumbing through Emily Post. I felt a little better by the time I left. I'd start from the outside of the silverware and work my way in. Unless they served snails, I'd be okay. No way I was swallowing the first cousin to a slug.

When I got home, I phoned my friend Marcus Dupree at the Durham Police Department. It was time to call in an expert.

"It's an emergency," I told him. "You have to come over *now*."

"What is this about?" he asked breathlessly. Marcus is six and a half feet tall, but his voice sounds like he's about to start serenading JFK at any instant. "I have to lie low at the department," he added in a whisper. "They're still trying to figure out who helped you last time."

"Relax," I told him. "This has nothing to do with work. I need your help getting dressed for a fancy-ass dinner party tonight."

"I get off in ten minutes and I'll be there in fifteen," he said and hung up.

What a pal.

Reassured, I sat down and began reading the hair dye instructions. I knew Marcus would arrive as promised. He is one of the most dependable people I know. As the oldest in a huge family, he has shepherded nine younger siblings through to adulthood so far, without losing even one to crack cocaine or alcohol—no small feat for a poor family in Durham, where the modernization of neighborhoods too often means bringing in the latest designer drugs from New York City. Marcus had helped at least six younger sisters prepare for high school proms. He ought to be able to help me with one dinner party.

Three hours later, I was behind schedule but my transformation was complete. Marcus had declared my intentional black roots to be "too crude" a statement for the soirée in question and had bleached my mop of uncooperative hair a lovely shade of yellow. At least that had been his intention. Unfortunately, he'd decided to first strip it of its previous bottled color and chemical overload set in. By the time we were done, I was sporting hair the color of a new copper penny.

The weird thing was, I liked it.

"It's you," Marcus declared. "It gives you an 'X-Files' sort of sensual authority. When you turn around and glare, it will give the men shivers."

"That happens already," I told him. I adjusted the blouse beneath my silk suit. "The tag itches. It's driving me crazy."

"Take off the blouse," Marcus ordered. "Go without. Let me lend you my pearls." He dug a strand of ivory pearls from his duffel bag while I ditched the shirt. After he fastened the necklace around my neck, he experimented with several hair styles. We finally settled on piling my hair in a big wad on top of my head—Marcus had some idiotic French name for it—and letting a few strands escape. It wasn't Ann-Margret, but it would do.

"I'm trying for a 'just rolled out of bed with a millionaire' look," he confided, loosening more strands of newly red hair and arranging them along my neck.

I admired the pearls against the rather spectacular cleavage of my silk suit minus a shirt. "Good call. This is elegantly sleazy in a very deliberate way."

"Exactly," Marcus agreed with satisfaction. "Which is just the statement you want to make tonight." He steadied me by my shoulders and looked into my eyes. "There is no point in hiding who you are, Miss Casey. I'm afraid that your light is just too bright to hide under a bushel."

"Meaning what, Marcus?" I asked. "That I should shoot and skin the family cat at dinner?"

"Meaning," he said sternly. "That you should just be yourself."

"Just be myself?"

"Just be yourself," he repeated.

"This from a man who dresses up as a different movie star every night?"

He waved his hands, dismissing my skepticism. "Some of us happen to be chameleons. But there is only one you."

"You sound like Confucius," I said.

"Honey, that's because Confucius was more southern than both of us put together," Marcus explained. "Think of it. He was always telling people what to do and no one ever knew what the hell he really meant."

He had a point. "Okay, Marcus," I agreed. "I will be myself tonight. But thanks for making me a little bit. . . . more me. I'd hate to give that Randolph Talbot bastard what he wants."

"You're most welcome, Miss Casey," Marcus answered graciously. His brow furrowed in serious thought. "You might want to snag a rich man tonight," he counseled. "Life has got to be easier when you have money." Seeing as how he had paid for every one of his siblings to attend college, Marcus knew what he was talking about.

"I don't like any of the rich men I've met so far," I told him.

"Send them my way," he suggested brightly. "I'm easy to get along with. If I can handle two hundred policemen a day, I can handle anyone."

"Which reminds me," I said, remembering why I was going to such lengths for the evening.

"Oh, no," Marcus answered, backing away as he correctly read my tone of voice. "You promised me this had nothing to do with work."

"I just want to know if the cops have any leads on who killed Thomas Nash," I said quickly. "I heard Cole and Roberts caught the case. You don't have to give me anything confidential."

"There's nothing to give," he assured me. "They have zippo. Big nada. No one knows who did it. Or why. It's a cold trail."

"You're telling me the truth?" I asked sternly.

"Girl Scout's honor," he promised, holding up three fingers.

"That's the Boy Scout oath," I said. "I think you're confused."

"Aren't we all?" he replied.

The Talbots' wrought-iron gate had been unshackled for the party. It swept open in a grand arc as I pulled up to the estate. A tuxedo-clad guard stepped from the shadows to check my name against a clipboard. He waved me in and I steered my decrepit Porsche along a winding asphalt driveway for a good half mile before I encountered civilization. Any doubt I had about which of the Talbot homes would be the site of the party disappeared when I came upon the first of the matching three-story mansions. It was blazing with more lights than an Italian Christmas display.

I wasn't the only one running late. Groups of people scurried down a stone walkway toward the front door. Some of the women wore fur wraps, a real stretch given that it was at least ninety degrees without a smidgen of breeze to rearrange the humidity.

As it turns out, those women wearing furs had obviously been to a Talbot party before. A penguin would have felt at home inside the mansion. Anyone who could afford central air conditioning for that sprawling house was rolling in the bucks big time, I thought. And maybe that was the real message behind freezing the zookies of the assembled guests.

I was ushered by a poker-faced butler into a series of linked rooms decorated with well-dressed people in various stages of drunkenness. Take it from me, rich people who are drunk and obnoxious aren't any more interesting than your average street bum drooling into his bottle of Thunderbird.

I side-stepped half a dozen old geezers flanked by bored wives who looked young enough to be their granddaughters. Then I encountered what was surely a pack of embittered ex-wives in one room, since they fell silent as I approached and stared at me until I drifted out of their orbit. Excuse me for being under fifty and swimming with estrogen, I thought as I escaped their malevolent glares.

Several of the rooms opened onto side rooms. It was like wandering through a museum. I kept expecting to find a mummy case parked in an alcove. Clearly, the furnishings belonged on display: exquisitely painted vases, turn-of-the-century marble statues and an endless array of oil paintings featuring Talbot ancestors whose sole shared characteristic looked to be, from their dour expressions, a genetic predisposition toward gas.

I was surprised to spot Franklin Cosgrove in one of the side rooms, sitting on the arm of a love seat and leering at a ripe blonde poured into a turquoise cocktail dress. Both of them held classic martini glasses and I kept expecting Nick and Nora Charles to refresh their drinks at any moment, though my true hope was for Asta to appear and bite Cosgrove on the ankle. He didn't see me and I kept going, wondering what in the hell he was doing at the house of a competitor who, that very afternoon, had called him a "whore."

I thought I'd discovered a sanctuary when I wandered into a small empty room with curved walls and a marble fireplace, but T&T's marketing head Donald Teasdale traipsed through with a woman hanging onto his arm. She was even tinier than he was. I wanted to ask them if they were looking for Gulliver, but I didn't have the chance. Teasdale glared at me with distaste and hurried away. Okay, so mingling was proving a challenge. I'd find a kindred spirit soon. Or, even better, a waiter with a tray full of drinks.

Just as I figured there was no end to the number of rooms—or the number of unpleasant dinner guests—I was rescued by an ancient but elegant-looking old woman who was lounging on a mustard-colored divan in one of the side rooms. She wore a long-sleeved black evening gown with a scoop top that showed off a sapphire necklace around her crepey neck. The blue of the stones set off the silver of her upswept hair nicely. For someone who was in her seventies, she was quite the dish.

"Come sit here, darling," she ordered me in a throaty voice, patting the other half of the small sofa she occupied. "You look bored and contemptuous, which tells me you must be a woman of good breeding and taste."

"I'm neither," I confessed. "But I'd still love to sit down."

"Then do so immediately," she ordered, and I obeyed. There was an authority to her smoky voice, a hint of steel lurking beneath the genteel drawl. Up close, she was like a rose that had dried past its prime, her beauty faded and brittle, her skin coated with an almost invisible dusting of decaying gray.

"Bring us champagne," she ordered a passing waiter and, before I had time to smack my lips, I was holding a well-filled glass of bubbly.

"No wonder everyone is drunk," I said. "With bar service like that."

She laughed unexpectedly, a booming, contagious sound that filled the room. "The service is good because I pay their salaries," she assured me. "I am Marie Talbot and this is my home. That's why I'm hiding out in this obscure room. No one can dare tell me otherwise.''

Holy Mary, Mother of God. Or close to it. ''You're kidding,'' I said.

She looked at me over the rim of her glass. ''Why would anyone pretend to be me if they weren't, my dear?' she asked. ''I'm as old as the hills and twice as weather-beaten. All my friends have died off from cirrhosis of the liver. My gardenias have been eaten by weevils. And my son Randolph is an ungrateful little bastard who married a psycho for his second wife. Together they're ruining the character of my grandchildren and withering my family tree on the vine. My only hope is my granddaughter Lydia. She reminds me of myself—a pearl emerging from the swine.''

I opened my mouth to comment, but she wasn't done by a long shot. Her monologue would have turned Randolph Talbot's toupee gray.

''I'm one of the Savannah Balls, you know,'' she said. ''In fact I was the belle of the Balls. Every distant cousin you could name pursued me, and plenty of other men, too. But I was determined to marry that incorrigible coot, Frederick Talbot, just to make my daddy unhappy. So I did. And when I did, I entered the seventh circle of hell.'' She glanced around. ''I expect Dante to start sketching me at any moment. That's why I'm posed like this. Also, I'm too drunk to move.''

I stared at her, so fascinated that I forgot to guzzle my champagne. ''You don't pull any punches.''

''Well, dear, you're a private investigator,'' she said. ''I assumed you would want to know something private. I could tell you about my latest female operation, if you prefer. I've had hundreds. I'm as plastic as a Barbie doll from the waist down.''

''How did you know who I was?'' I asked. ''I'm practically in disguise.''

''I know who everyone is,'' she said. ''And everything they do. I insist on having a last-minute list of every person who sets foot in my house and, if I don't get it, there is no party. I like to know who's sneaking up on me, my dear. Not to mention who might have stolen the heirloom silverware." She smiled, revealing yellowing teeth. "I'm not talking about you, precious. I'm sure you're completely trustworthy, since your honor is all you have. Who knows? I may even hire you myself. I do believe Randolph's second wife is having an affair. I'm a little curious to know who the lucky fellow may be."

"I'm a little busy right now," I said, not wanting to explain that I was already booked to air her family's dirty linen—by her granddaughter.

"I imagine you are busy," she said, raising her arched eyebrows. "Especially with a neckline like that."

She held her champagne glass out behind her, over the back of the sofa, and I swear that a waiter appeared from the shadows and dutifully refilled it. She took a sip. "Who really hired you to look into Thomas Nash's death?" she asked. "Was it Lydia? I hope so. That man made her very happy. Oh, yes—I knew all about their 'secret' engagement. And I am furious that someone has taken him from her."

"What makes you think Lydia hired me?" I asked, gulping down my champagne. Unfortunately, no waiter rushed forward to refill *my* glass.

"I didn't get where I am by being stupid," she said. "Randolph's father Frederick was idiotic, you know. A complete moron. He would have ruined Teer & Talbot had I not come along. It's a good thing Frederick died before I had him declared senile."

"How old was he when he died?" I asked faintly.

She waved a languid hand. "Oh, forty. Maybe forty-five. I forget." She took a jeweled cigarette holder from an exquisitely beaded handbag and affixed a slender cigar to it. The procedure was as precise and graceful as a Japanese tea ceremony. I watched, transfixed, as she lit the cigar and blew smoke quite deliberately in the face of a beefy man who was lurking rather obviously nearby.

"Herbert is eavesdropping again," she confided. "That should do the trick."

The man coughed and moved a few paces back, glaring at me.

"Why's he giving *me* the evil eye?" I complained.

"You're the one who blew the smoke in his face."

"Because he can't afford to glare at me." The old woman blew more smoke his way. "I pay his bills. He's the Talbot family lawyer. You should talk to him. If you can bear it. He's even more stupid than my late husband was."

I laughed. I couldn't help it. This woman was completely free to tell it like it was. And that's exactly what she was doing.

"Aren't you afraid your son will get angry that you're talking to me?" I asked.

"My son is a cruel and indifferent man," she confided, then paused for a gulp of champagne and a drag on her cigar. "He invited you here to frighten you with his money. I can't stand bullies. What about you?"

"I don't like them either," I said, staring at my empty glass.

She waved her cigarette holder and it was magically replenished. Maybe it wouldn't be such an awful night after all. I'd just stick close to Lucrezia Borgia.

"No, I mean, 'What about *you*?' " she said. "Tell me your story so I don't have to talk to these people. You have no idea how many parties I've been to with the same old faces. They bored me the first time I met them and, for most of them, that was at least thirty years ago. They whine endlessly about the same old troubles, only now they're having them with different people—their second wife, their new husband, their spoiled child who has grown into a surly teenager, their latest banker, another dishonest servant. Talk to me please, and do not whine. I'd be eternally grateful."

A pert brunette tanned the color of pecans and packed into a short white dress darted into the room, then scurried by as if afraid the old woman might bite her.

"See that one?" Marie Talbot asked, nodding toward the rapidly disappearing woman. "Look quick now, darling, before she dies of skin cancer. She is married to a man three times her age, but right now she's heading to the library to meet my grandson for a quickie. She has the morals of an alley cat."

"What about your grandson?"

"He has no morals at all." She dragged on her cigar and sighed. "Don't avoid the subject. Tell me your story."

There was no way I was walking away from the lady, not when she was overflowing with Talbot family secrets. If nothing else, I was greatly entertained and happy to pay the price of admission. I told her about my upbringing, about my parents being killed when I was seven, my grandfather stepping in, the lack of money—hell, the lack of running water—the hot cotton and beet fields, the barren soil, the nearby swamps, the ragged clothes. I told her about growing up bigger than the other kids and how I'd learned to use my physical strength early.

"And in case you're wondering," I added. "Red isn't my real hair color."

"Believe me, dear, I wasn't wondering. But what about men?" she demanded. "Why are you living here instead of in Florida? Tell me. Some stupid man is behind it, I'm quite sure."

"More like a stupid woman," I told her. "As in me. My life was such a mess down there that I knew I'd never untangle it. I came here to start over." I could not confess to her why I was really in North Carolina—that I was fleeing a drug conviction and the memory of a year and a half in a Jacksonville prison. Instead, I just told her about my ex and his many unpleasant personal habits.

She sighed when I was done. "I envy you your independence. I was born at the wrong time," she confided. "If only I had been born five years later, I could have run off and joined World War Two. Maybe married a Frenchman. Someone with courage and honor—or at the very least, a charming accent." She paused and considered another scenario. "Or if I had been born twenty years later, I'd have marched with Gloria Steinem to the White House and helped women take over the world."

"I don't think Gloria was actually into marching," I said dubiously as a waiter refilled my glass yet again. "She was too busy shaving her legs."

"Then with Betty Friedan," the old woman said. "Surely, she marched. She was positively weather-beaten."

"No," I said carefully. "I think Betty spent a lot of time indoors, writing."

Marie Talbot was thinking hard, her cigar balanced between two ruby lips. "I know," she finally said, triumphantly. "Bella. Tell me Bella Abzug didn't march. I dare you."

"Okay," I conceded. "Bella probably did march. At least once."

"You see," she cried. "And I could have been with her." She shook a fist playfully and diamond tennis bracelets slid up and down her bony arm. I'd seen one of them for sale during a gawking expedition to *Jewelsmith*; it had won a design prize and been priced at over twenty-four thousand dollars.

"But no," Marie Talbot moaned theatrically, "I get stuck in the middle, raising a dreadful child in the dreadful fifties, surrounded by lazy, stupid men. And my crowning achievement is giving birth to a man who has facelifts, for godsakes, and would rather count his money than pay attention to his own sons."

She stopped abruptly and stared at me with dark, aware eyes. "So who really hired you?" she demanded again.

Before I could reply, I was saved by the devil himself. Randolph Talbot hurried up to us, no doubt appalled by my proximity to his mother.

"Miss Jones," he said hastily, grabbing my elbow and dragging me away from the grand old dame. "We mustn't let Mother monopolize you. She always traps the most interesting guests."

I was touched by his concern. Behind me I could hear Marie Talbot's derisive snort and I waved a hasty goodbye.

"Remember the Alamo!" she called gaily after me.

"What were you talking about?" Talbot demanded as he hustled me back through the sitting rooms.

"Oh, Texas," I murmured, hiding a smile.

"Mother drinks," Talbot said tersely. "Don't believe a word she says."

I believed every syllable that had poured from that old lady's mouth. And if Randolph Talbot didn't want me to meet her, he should have thought twice about inviting me to his damn dinner party.

"May I have my elbow back?" I asked.

"What?" He stared down at my arm. The flesh had turned red from his grip. "Sorry." He released me and anxiously rubbed his jaw. "Have you met my daughter Lydia yet? I think she's in the blue room. Come with me."

He marched me into a room painted the color of a robin's egg, then stopped and looked around for his daughter. His glance lingered on me and he blinked.

"You look different from this afternoon," he said. "What is it?"

"I've lost weight," I confided. Maybe if I'd dyed my hair purple, he would have noticed.

He blinked again, then spotted Lydia in the far corner. "There she is. Come this way." He manhandled me over to Lydia and made formal introductions. I mumbled something and avoided her eyes.

"I want you to tell her everything you know," he instructed Lydia. "Nash's family has hired her to look into his death and I want one hundred percent cooperation from the Talbots." He nodded to me. "Excuse me. There's someone I must speak to."

Having accomplished his goal of separating me from his mother, Talbot dumped me with his daughter and set off in search of richer company.

"Thank you for not telling him," Lydia said in a low voice. She looked like a knockout in a white pantsuit. And she was also wearing no blouse beneath it. Together, we looked like a pair of flight attendants for Air Force One.

"No problem," I assured her. "So far, it's been very interesting. I met your grandmother."

"Oh, lord." Her eyes got wide. "Mimmi's an experience."

"She certainly is. She seemed to know about you and Nash. Did you tell her?"

Lydia shook her head. "She found out on her own. She has more spies in this town than Daddy. I'm not surprised she knew. But she never said a word to me."

"She thinks a lot of you," I said. "As opposed to the rest of your family."

Lydia smiled, but it took effort. "I'm not sure it's a good thing to have Mimmi thinking of me at all."

"Are you enjoying the party?" I asked. She seemed depressed.

Lydia shrugged. "I feel like I'm a robot walking around and going through the motions. No one knew I was engaged to Tom, so they don't understand."

"Well, besides your grandmother and father, Franklin Cosgrove had guessed something was going on," I reminded her.

Her face scrunched up in disgust. "Frank has a strange way of expressing his condolences. He keeps trying to pick me up."

"I think he's gone on to a horse of a different color," I told her, thinking of the woman in the short turquoise dress. "Or something close."

"I'm trying to figure out why he's here at all," she said. "Daddy's up to something."

"I was wondering that myself," I said as I spotted Cosgrove heading our way. "Here comes the man himself. I think I'll make tracks."

"I can handle him," Lydia assured me. "Good luck. Happy hunting." She managed a smile that transformed her face and I reminded myself that it was dangerous to like a client too much. Many of them were guilty as sin. Liking clients was a luxury I could not afford.

I left Lydia to cope with Franklin Cosgrove and thought about wandering back to where the old lady sat. But my private investigator instinct kicked in instead. Marie Talbot had declared that a passing brunette was on her way to meet one of Lydia's brothers for a little one-on-one. I wanted to know if what the old lady had predicted was true. After all, following cheating spouses was my specialty. A little practice wouldn't hurt. And I wanted to meet the brothers.

I asked a waiter for directions to the library, then casually wandered down the halls, smiling aimlessly at everyone I passed. How old was this grandson anyway, that he was boffing someone on his grandmother's couch? Lydia had said she had two brothers, one in college and one who was twelve. What would I do if it was the underage brother? Rescue him? Take a number and wait in line? Listen—I didn't put anything past this spoiled, well-watered crowd.

The library was at the far end of the house. I passed back through the room where I'd met Marie Talbot, but she had decamped for wetter pastures. Two rooms later, I was confronted with an enormous oak door that had to lead to the library since it was a dead-end. I was hesitant to simply barge in—after all, this was the first closed door I had encountered in the Talbot mansion. On the other hand, I could hear distinct sounds issuing from behind the heavy oak, especially if I crouched really low and cocked an ear at the base of the door where it met the marble floor. Either someone was reading the diaries of Anaïs Nin aloud, or someone was not reading at all.

The doors were locked. Do you think that stopped me? I took my maxed-out Visa card from my evening bag and slid it between the two sides of the door. I suspected it would be a simple spring mechanism, given that it was an interior door. The lock was easily pressed back and I stepped inside the darkened room, quickly surveying the empty fireplace and massive bookshelves that lined the walls. Moans were coming from behind a couch positioned in front of a far wall. There was a white dress puddled at one end of the sofa and a pair of dress pants draped over the opposite arm. One hairy, well-muscled leg protruded from behind the sofa and I was pretty sure it didn't belong to the brunette. For a moment I was lost in thought, trying to figure out where the hell the matching leg was and what page of the Kama Sutra they'd worked up to. But it was apparent from the well-toned calf muscles that whoever was engaging in hanky panky was old enough to know better and that I'd best find a more suitable time to meet Lydia's brother. I slipped from the room and left the doors unlocked, in hopes that the brunette's elderly husband might discover his wife and add some excitement to the dinner party for us all. Hey, obviously they got off on doing it in public. I was only trying to add to their ambiance. Besides, they were being *very* tacky.

My appetite is always dulled by public displays of sex but, even so, it seemed like the dinner hour would never arrive. I decided to wait it out with the riff raff in the sitting rooms, but I was only one room away from the library when a young boy dressed in a blue blazer and khaki pants rounded the corner at full speed, head down and out of breath. He careened into me and we both bounced off the same armchair and into a wall.

"Whoa," I said. "I'm pretty sure there's a thirty-five-mile-an-hour speed limit in town unless otherwise marked."

He hung his head. "Sorry, I was looking for my brother."

"You must be Lydia's little brother," I said. "I'm a friend of hers. I mean, we just met. But she seems very nice."

He looked up and I was treated to a roundish face sprinkled with freckles and a mop of reddish-brown hair that would have curled had the owner not so fiercely plastered it down for the night's festivities. Two large strands had escaped on either side of his forehead and curled upward like miniature devil's horns. It gave him an impish air at odds with his sad face. It was far too serious a face for a twelve-year-old boy.

"What's your name? Mine's Casey," I said.

"Haydon," he mumbled, looking uncomfortable.

"You're really hating this party, aren't you?" I said.

"Yes," he replied fiercely. "And when I find Jake, I'm going to rip his arms from their sockets and nail his legs to the floor."

"Ouch," I said. "What brought that on?"

"He stole my money. Again. I had fifty dollars saved up for a new Seiko and he took it. I know it was him. He takes everything of mine."

"How old is your brother?" I asked, a bit taken aback at the thought of multi-millionaires, however young, pilfering from one another.

"Twenty-two," he said sullenly. "Every time he comes to the big house, my money is missing. I know it's him."

"Well," I lied, moving to block his view of the library

door. "He's not at this end of the house. Tell you what—I'm a private investigator." I pulled a business card from my evening bag and gave it to him. "Call me anytime you need help proving it, okay?"

He looked impressed and immediately forgot about his brother—thank God. At twelve, he was about thirty years too young to witness the floor show taking place behind us.

"Cool." He turned the card around, then back again. "Do you have a lot of spy stuff you use?"

God bless Bobby D. Who'd have guessed that his adolescent preoccupation with James Bond–like devices would pay off so quickly? I walked Haydon Talbot back toward the other end of the house, regaling him with descriptions of Bobby D.'s ridiculous electronic excesses. Fortunately, he seemed more interested in night vision goggles than in tracking down his brother.

We had time for a good chat about the snobby kids who attended his private school before a waiter came and fetched him away, leaving me on my own. Drat. I was stuck with the boring adults again.

I made the mistake of making eye contact with the first person I saw and ended up being trapped by some beer-bellied yuppie who was losing his hair and insanely insistent that he had seen me play field hockey at Choate. I told him to lay off the Miller Lite and escaped, only to collide with Donald Teasdale.

"What are you doing here?" he hissed.

"I was invited. How about you?"

He glared and walked away into the crowd where, despite his balding head, a drunken woman spotted him from behind and mistook him for Lydia's little brother. I thought she'd faint when she called out Haydon's name and Teasdale's bulldog face whipped around, scowling indignantly.

Laughing, I retreated to a bar I spotted in one of the rooms. There, I pretty much drank myself into a stupor until dinner was announced. Silly me, spending all that time worrying about the silverware when all that these people really cared about were the drinking glasses.

There was a genteel stampede toward the dining room

when dinner was announced, and much inebriated lurching and confusion. I found myself elbow-to-elbow with the woman in the turquoise cocktail dress who had been flirting with Franklin Cosgrove earlier. I could see Cosgrove waiting in line at the other end of the room, searching the crowd for her.

"So you know good old Frankie?" I asked her in a woman-to-woman voice. I bent over her to shield her from Cosgrove's line of vision.

She looked at me uneasily. "Frankie? You mean Franklin?"

"Franklin, Schmanklin. They call him Frankie the Felcher down at Hotcakes, that topless truck stop outside Garner," I confided. "Miriam's cousin Harold told me. Frankie stops by at least once a week." There was a Hotcakes near Garner, but no Miriam or Harold. The thing is, in the South, if you sprinkle your statements with the names of enough relatives, it adds greatly to your story's veracity.

Her perfectly made-up face went through an amazing series of gyrations, finally settling on slow-burning rage. "What else do you know about him?" she asked, eyes narrowing.

"Well," I said cheerfully. "He gave Miriam's sister Candace the clap, which was poetic justice since it was Candace's roommate who first gave it to Franklin. But then Candace passed it on to the pastor of her church and pretty soon the whole choir was infected. I hear Franklin can't even show his face in Salisbury anymore, much less the First Baptist Church. They'd run him out of town."

"Thanks," she hissed, her eyes narrowing even more. She peeled away from me and headed for a far door, putting as much distance as she could between herself and Cosgrove.

One small step for woman, one giant step for womankind. Cosgrove deserved much worse, but it was a start.

The dining room was immense, with an entire wall comprised of windows that looked out on a lit garden. Round tables had been set up all around the room to give diners a view of the flowers and koi pools outside. A long head table was set up along the far wall. The Talbots and their closest hangers-on were already seated there by the time the herd arrived, leaving us to scramble for spots close to the hallowed hosts. I watched, amused, as Franklin Cosgrove found his date, only to see that both seats on either side of her were taken and that she was no longer speaking to him. Good news traveled fast in this crowd: he was rebuffed at several more tables before he ended up sandwiched between two old ladies whose pendulous bustlines wedged him in place tighter than a muskrat trapped in mud. He would no doubt spend his entire dinner accidentally elbowing their enormous breasts and having to apologize.

I found a spot—not by accident—near the beefy man who had been identified by Marie Talbot as her family's lawyer. Our table was in the middle of the room and surrounded by so many other identical tables that I felt like we were attending a charity banquet. I prayed rubber chicken was not on the menu, then turned to my companion to make small talk. Emily Post would have been proud.

"I understand you're the Talbot's family lawyer?" I said pleasantly to him.

"What's it to you?" the beefy man growled, running a finger under his tight shirt collar as he gulped down a glass of what smelled like straight bourbon. His face was glowing the color of a medium rare steak, which was appropriate since that's what probably had gotten him into pulmonary trouble in the first place.

I explained who I was and what I was doing and emphasized that Randolph Talbot had promised me "one hundred percent" cooperation, in hopes that the name of his employer might penetrate his bourbon-soaked brain.

It did. He warmed slightly and boldly offered that his name was Herbert Norsworthy. Then he moved his chair a few inches closer to mine—which wasn't what I'd had in mind—and offered to answer any questions that did not violate client-lawyer privilege.

In order to keep a lid on what I was asking, I was forced to bend close to him and nearly whisper, which gave the rest of my table the impression that I was being picked up by the old coot. Not that their opinions mattered. A more motley crew I'd seldom seen before. My table of twelve held an assortment of bored, aging men, insipid younger women and a few suspicious old ladies. They were more interested in where the hell the salad was than in sex.

"What do you know about the harassment lawsuit Nash was bringing against T&T?" I asked the lawyer before he suffered a heart attack before my eyes.

"Not much," he said, his bourbon breath wafting past my ear. "T&T's corporate lawyers responded to that one. But he also initially filed a harassment suit against Randolph Talbot personally and I was involved with that one."

"Against Talbot personally?" I asked. "Doesn't that imply that he had evidence Talbot himself was directly involved?"

The lawyer shrugged. "You'd have to ask Nash's lawyer about that. The suit was dropped before we got to the evidentiary stage."

"Did Nash's lawyer try and settle it?"

The man's laugh was like a bear growl. "You bet. And we would have settled, too. Randolph's a big believer in cutting your losses and moving on. But the Nash fellow said he had changed his mind completely. He didn't want money. He didn't want anything."

A waiter arrived and set a wild green salad dressed with a balsamic vinaigrette down in front of us. Herbert Norsworthy stared at his with disdain. I guess it didn't have enough cheese, chopped eggs and Thousand Island dressing glopped on it for him. He pushed it away, but I dove into mine, aware that a handful of leaves wasn't going to do much good when it came to soaking up the bottle and a half of champagne I'd had so far.

"How far did Nash go before he dropped the suit?" I asked, curious as to how much evidence may have been gathered.

"Far enough that it was unusual Nash dropped it," the lawyer explained as he crammed bread into his mouth. "Court date had been set for next month."

"What did Nash's lawyer say when he called you with the news?"

"He didn't call. Nash did himself."

That surprised me. "Really? What did he say?"

The lawyer waved his highball glass in the air for a refill. "He said he was dropping the harassment suit. He apologized for taking up my time. He sounded like the nicest litigatee I'd ever run into." He shrugged. "Go figure."

"Why do you think he dropped the lawsuit?" I asked.

The lawyer shrugged again. "I figure either his evidence didn't pan out, they'd filed prematurely or Talbot paid him off under the table. Not that I'd ever advise a client to do that. I wouldn't even suggest it, except to make sure you understand that Randolph Talbot had no motive to kill Nash."

"Why would Nash settle under the table?" I asked. "I didn't think court judgments like that were taxable."

"They're not, little lady. That's not the issue." He smiled at me with well-bonded teeth. "The issue is Nash's lawyer. He would have gotten at least a third of any settlement or judgment. I figure maybe Nash cut out the middle man and took something from Talbot under the table. But I didn't ask. I know when to keep my mouth shut."

Yeah. Except when he'd been drinking bourbon.

I was doubtful that was what had happened. It was possible, but I thought Talbot's explanation more likely: Tom Nash had dropped the suit out of loyalty to Lydia and to force a Hargett case settlement. Still, it wouldn't hurt to run a check on Nash's finances.

"Do you know anything about the other lawsuits against T&T?" I asked.

The lawyer patted his well-rounded belly. "Nope. And I don't want to. Show me a tobacco company lawyer today and I'll show you a man with an ulcer." His smile grew broader as a pair of waiters arrived with red meat all around.

There aren't many people in Durham with the bucks and the balls to serve filet mignon with béarnaise sauce in this day and age. But Randolph Talbot was one of them. Thank God. I turned my attention to the dinner in front of me and the all-important decision of whether to switch to red wine or stick with champagne. A glass of merlot set in front of me decided it. Time to mix and match.

Soon after dinner, a squadron of waiters removed the

empty crème brûlée dessert plates. The hubbub of the room abruptly ceased as Randolph Talbot rose from his place at the head of the main table and clinked his knife against the rim of his wine glass for silence.

"I have an announcement to make," he said.

The room grew still, but the mood was broken when a woman sitting to the right of Talbot quite distinctly hiccoughed. She giggled and put a hand to her mouth, eyes wide. Talbot glared at her briefly, then looked back up at the crowd.

If that was Lydia's stepmother, Randolph Talbot hadn't done too badly in terms of looks when it came to choosing a second wife: she was very pretty, with silky black hair and a finely carved face. But her sense of elegance left a little to be desired. She was listing to one side, like a disabled sailboat. Throughout the subsequent announcement by her husband, I could hear her alternating between hiccoughs and giggles, as if she were adding the punctuation marks.

"As you know, T&T Tobacco has grown steadily over the past two decades to dominate a number of key market niches here and overseas," Randolph Talbot intoned. My eyelids drooped, but flew open at his next surprise statement.

"We are determined to continue this growth into the new century and so I am happy to announce tonight the acquisition of King Buffalo Tobacco by Teer & Talbot." He waited out the buzz that greeted this announcement with a benign despot smile, then held up his hands for silence. "Of course, King Buffalo recently suffered the tragic loss of one of its guiding partners. However, the company was fortunate enough to have two superior minds at her helm and it is the surviving partner, Franklin Cosgrove, who I believe will prove instrumental in guiding both King Buffalo and T&T to new success in the future. Franklin?"

Cosgrove rose from his seat between the two old gargoyles and nodded majestically, as if he were simply too pleased to put it all into words.

A whore, eh? If so, he was an expensive one. Cosgrove had said his investment bankers were working on selling the company, but come on—Nash had barely been dead two and a half weeks. Could he really have pulled it all together in that short of a time? I needed to find out fast if that was possible.

"Franklin will be heading up a new division of T&T devoted to natural products such as King Buffalo's premium blend," Talbot continued. "And he will also take over as head of marketing for all of T&T's brands."

I heard a choking noise at the table behind me. I turned around to discover Donald Teasdale staring at Randolph Talbot, his tiny mouth open in outrage.

What a bastard. Randolph Talbot had brought someone in over Teasdale without telling him, then broken the news in front of a room full of strangers. God, but I was glad I worked for myself.

"With Franklin Cosgrove's help," Talbot continued, "I am confident that we will be able to complete the circle of innovation T&T needs to lead the tobacco industry into the twenty-first century!"

This stirring statement was met by predictable applause and, judging by the enthusiasm of the crowd, almost everyone had enjoyed the filet mignon and béarnaise sauce as much as I had.

"In conclusion," Talbot ended, "this evening is a celebration. Drink up," he ordered the crowd. "I positively command you to eat, drink and be merry!"

As the crowd laughed obediently, I searched for Lydia among the many faces. I found her at one end of the family table and our eyes locked across the room.

God almighty, how cold-hearted could the girl's father possibly be?

Randolph Talbot had barely waited two weeks to capitalize on Nash's death. It didn't say much for his sensitivity, not to mention his innocence.

Lydia's glance dropped and she suddenly looked very small, hunched over the long white tablecloth with her eyes fixed on her wine glass. She was sitting between her youngest brother and a man I immediately pegged as her other brother, Jake.

He was in his early twenties and had the same high

cheekbones and slender mouth as Lydia. But his most prominent feature was one of those skinny, long noses you only find on rich people: it seemed to start in the middle of his forehead and not stop until it had fallen off his chin. Roman nobility run amok. He had black hair that was slicked straight back with gel and gleamed in the reflected glare of the chandelier above. Even from a distance, I could tell his eyes were very dark—and fixed on Lydia.

What I couldn't figure out was why he had a satisfied smirk plastered on his face. All he lacked was a mouse tail twitching from one corner of his too-pretty mouth. Maybe banging someone else's wife behind his grandmother's sofa was his idea of the ultimate thrill, but I suspected that his gratification was fueled by an even darker motive. I think Jake Talbot was enjoying his sister's discomfort—which meant that yet another person had known of Lydia's secret engagement to Thomas Nash.

With family like this, who needed enemies?

Suddenly, I just wanted to be back home in my own cheap apartment between my own threadbare sheets. I was sick of all the Talbot's money. I was sick of their selfishness. I hated the doting crowd and I hated all the glitter. None of it was worth a single second's worth of the pain I saw on Lydia's face.

There she sat, surrounded by her entire family and dozens of fawning strangers. Yet she was—except for me—completely alone in the world.

SEVEN

I woke the next morning with a rancid champagne hangover that symbolized my disgust at ever having been awed by the Talbots' money. If I hadn't been so intent on sucking up all the expensive bubbly I could hold, I'd be feeling like myself instead of a coroner's leftovers. And for all I knew, I'd been swilling Andre and not Krug. It wasn't like I could tell the difference. When you grow up drinking moonshine, it's all uphill from there.

I arrived at the office to find Bobby D. munching on breakfast burritos—the foulest invention in gastronomic history and, in the hands of someone like Bobby, a public safety issue.

"Hey, babe," he greeted me cheerfully, as black beans dribbled down his chin. "You look like you lost a fight with a pole cat."

"Hung over," I explained. "And sick to death of people who have money."

"Then you're in the right place," he said, sliding open his desk drawer. "Seeing as how we are poor." He rummaged around and produced a small orange vial of pills. "Take two of these. They'll help."

"What is this?" I asked, examining the label.

"Tylenol-3. Prescription only. Works like a charm."

"What are you doing with them?" I asked.

"Doc gave 'em to me the last time he lanced a batch of my boils." He bit off half a burrito and chewed with a contented sigh.

"I had to ask," I muttered, shaking out three of the pills for good measure.

"Have a Pepsi," Bobby offered sympathetically, sliding a cold one my way. I washed down the pills, savoring the sugar water that flooded my veins.

"Hair looks good," he offered. "I got a soft spot for redheads."

"Keep it soft," I advised him.

"You gonna dye your cuff to match the collar?" he asked.

"Soon as my racing stripe grows in," I confided.

He greeted this lie with an enthusiastic wiggling of his eyebrows.

"How was the gay bar?" I asked as my blood sugar began to climb, bringing sweet relief. "Gonna switch teams?"

He shrugged with a full mouth. "My client's husband never showed, but the bartender says he's a regular. I'll catch him there sooner or later."

"Did you enjoy the show?" I asked, knowing it had been amateur drag night.

Bobby nodded. "Some of the guys were prettier than a lot of my dates."

I kept my mouth firmly shut.

"They could sing, too. Sounded just like Whitney Houston and whats-her-name, that French-Canadienne dame."

"Celine Dion?" I offered.

"Yeah, just like her. This guy came out in a sailing cap and evening gown, then did this whole *Titanic* thing. Made you want to cry. And you couldn't hear the difference between him and the real thing."

"He was lip-synching, Bobby," I explained patiently.

"Oh," he said, unfazed.

"Anyone hit on you?" I asked nosily.

He shook his head. "Naw, I think it's pretty clear I'm a straight shooter. But I did pick up a new client."

"You're kidding."

Bobby shrugged. "What do I care what two people do to each other in the privacy of their bedroom?"

"True," I agreed, "so long as they eventually cheat on each other and hire us to prove it."

He slid a business card across the table toward me. "I met this guy. He thinks his boyfriend is cheating on him with a health club instructor. He hired me."

"You're going undercover at a health club?" I asked skeptically. Bobby D. couldn't go undercover with a circus tent.

"Naw," he said, slurping down his Big Slam. "I'm gonna nail him the old-fashioned way. I'm gonna hang out at the gay bar and nab them together."

"Good for you," I told him. "It's time you got back to work." I examined the business card. "Hey, this guy is an investment banker."

"Sure," Bobby answered with newfound liberalism. "A lot of those guys look perfectly normal. More respectable than you or me, even."

That wouldn't be too hard. "Think you could call him up and ask him a few questions for me?" I asked. "There's some business dealings I don't quite understand that might help me with the T&T case."

"Sure," Bobby said expansively. "We shared a couple of brews. Nice fellow. Older than his boyfriend. He's being taken advantage of, sounds to me. I feel kind of bad for him. How come I never feel bad for the husbands whose wives are cheating on them, but this guy gets to me?" He looked to me for an answer.

"Maybe he reminds you of the son you never had," I said with a straight face. Then I outlined what I needed to know from his newest client.

When I was done, Bobby stared at me thoughtfully. "What is it, babe?" he asked. "You seem more bothered than usual about this case." Despite his disgusting personal habits, Bobby is not without his insightful moments.

"I'm having trouble putting my finger on a motive," I said. "I feel like I'm being fed false information, but I can't figure out what."

"Money," Bobby said firmly. "How many times I got to tell you to follow the money? Forget the rest of the crap and look for the bucks."

"That's the trouble," I said. "The money motives are screwed up. Randolph Talbot was no longer being sued by Nash, and the Hargett case was no longer an issue. So there goes that motive. And if and when Talbot ever makes money off Nash's death, it's going to be a long time down the road, which doesn't make sense for someone who already has as much money as Talbot. And while there's no one I'd love to put in a Central Prison cell with a horny convict for a roommate more than Nash's partner, Franklin Cosgrove, he lost big bucks because of Tom's death. I just don't think he did it."

"So who inherits Nash's half of the business?" Bobby D. asked. "Because now they'll get half of the purchase price Talbot pays for King Buffalo, right?"

I looked up, surprised. "Of course. Pretty stupid of me." Bobby has an admirably sneaky mind and I sometimes forget to take full advantage of it.

"Trust me," he said. "Look into his family to see who inherits his half of the business, or any other money he might have had, for that matter. Not to mention insurance. Trust your gut on Randolph Talbot if you don't think he did it and look somewhere else."

"I can't afford to do that completely," I told him. "My assignment is to find out positively, once and for all, if Talbot had anything to do with Nash's death. But the only way I can do that is to find out who did cause his death."

Bobby nodded slowly. "Check out the whole Talbot family finances," he advised. "You say Nash was marrying into the family. Maybe that threatened someone's inheritance."

"How?" I asked, not following.

"Maybe Nash would have gotten a piece of the pie automatically, as Lydia's husband," Bobby suggested. "Or, sometimes, people skip generations when they bequeath. For tax purposes. And if there is no third generation, they leave it in trust for when one comes along. After a period of time, the money reverts to the second generation if no grandchildren are born."

"Meaning what?" I asked. "That rich people are better at evading taxes?"

"Meaning that knocking off Nash guarantees he ain't ever gonna have children with Lydia Talbot. So maybe someone else gets a lot of money."

Comprehension dawned. "Duh," I said.

"I know someone down in Wake County probate," Bobby offered. "Let me look into it for you. She'll know someone in Durham County she can call. Who died recently in the Talbot family?"

"How recently?"

"Last twenty years?" he suggested. "Greed's got no statute of limitations."

"No one," I said, thinking hard. I looked up. "Maybe the mother. Lydia's mother died eleven or twelve years ago. She had money of her own."

"That's good," Bobby said, taking notes on his ancient legal pad. "I'll look into Nash's will and finances while I'm at it. It's probably been filed pretty recently. Anything else?" He waited, pen ready, my obedient servant.

I stared at him in surprise.

"Come on, babe," he said, irritated at my expression. "You said you wanted me to get back in the saddle. You gonna take me for a ride, or what?"

"Thanks," I said. "I appreciate it."

"It feels good to be back in charge," Bobby replied. "Maybe work will revive my appetite."

Oh, well—there's a downside to everything.

Thanks to extra, extra-strength Tylenol, my pounding headache soon dulled to a minor throbbing. I forced myself to drink two cups of coffee, which banished the problem entirely, then set about deciding what the hell I should do while Bobby did my work for me. I remembered my conversation with the Talbot family lawyer the night before and decided I needed to speak to Nash's civil attorney as soon as possible for more information on the defunct harassment lawsuits. If anyone knew the details of the harassment, it would be him.

I checked my notes, then tracked down a lawyer named Harrison Ingram III, who had an office in Brightleaf Square. When a secretary answered, I decided that a con-

fident approach was called for. I introduced myself as a
private detective investigating the death of Thomas Nash
and asked to be put through.

"Wasn't that awful? Tom was the nicest man," the sec-
retary said, confirming that Ingram had, indeed, been
Nash's lawyer. "I felt just terrible about it. So does Harry.
We both went to the funeral and cried like babies, espe-
cially when his parents and brother came down the aisle.
And the brother—well, he was so upset. It was just tragic."

Too bad I'd missed it. You can learn a lot at funerals, if
you can keep your eyes open. Oppressive heat seems to be
a requirement for services in the South.

"Then I guess Mr. Ingram will be ready, willing and
able to assist me?" I suggested, hoping to move things
along.

"I'm sure he will," she chirped back, "but he's not here
right now. He had a case over in Hillsborough this morning
and then he has to drive out to Alamance County to see
some new clients. I don't even think he's going to be in all
day."

"Will you let him know that it's urgent we speak?" I
asked.

She promised, took down my information and hung up
with a chirpy farewell. She was clearly a member of the
Stepford Secretaries Club.

I heard an impatient cough. Bobby had contacted his new
client who was an investment banker and now stood in my
doorway, his portable phone in hand.

"The guy says the sale of King Buffalo was quick but
not impossible. Want the inside dirt?" He handed me the
phone.

"Hello?" I said grumpily, since I hate it when other
people decide I should get on the phone and then stick one
in my face.

"Bobby said you wanted the details on the King Buffalo
sale?" a pleasant voice asked.

"*Sure.*" Cancel that last complaint about phones in my
face.

"We're not handling it," Bobby's client said. "My
firm's too small. But I heard the scuttlebutt. It's a small

investment banking community around here." The guy had
a nice voice, full and rich. He was probably gorgeous, too.
Not that it mattered. I lacked the equipment to play one-
on-one with him.

"So what was the story?" I asked. "Isn't two weeks
quick for a sale?"

"Sure," he admitted. "But in this case, the company was
privately owned and there were only two owners, so there's
not as much paperwork. Besides, when a key man dies in
a small company like that, it often folds up shop. With Nash
being the entire R&D department, there was no question
about King Buffalo hitting the block. Cosgrove sent out
feelers the day after Nash died, saying King Buffalo was
up for sale. We heard about it by late afternoon. One of
our clients was interested in a bid, but it was too late. Talbot
had jumped on it. I suspect Cosgrove knew Randolph Talbot was waiting for the chance to buy him out."

"You mean Cosgrove and Talbot may have had talks
about selling out even before Nash died?" Maybe that was
the motive. Cosgrove told me he'd heard about Nash's
death the next afternoon, when he called in from the road.
That meant he had phoned his investment banker immediately after hearing the news. Talk about not wasting time.

Bobby's client was quiet, thinking over the question.
"It's possible they had talked about it in the past, but if
what you're getting at is a reason to kill Nash," he said.
"I don't think this is it."

"Why not?" I asked.

"Nash *was* King Buffalo's future. And he was on to
something big. He would have made Cosgrove a multi-
millionaire many times over within three years if he had
lived. The man was a genius and, more than that, he knew
what the market wanted. If they had waited another year,
even, and then gone public—they could have cashed out
big. There's no way Cosgrove killed Nash for the money.
In fact, if I were the guy who'd killed Nash, I'd be worrying about Cosgrove coming after me. He must be furious
his money ticket got punched."

If that was the case, Cosgrove was a good actor. "What

about the possibility that Talbot killed Nash so he could buy the company cheap?'' I asked.

''Killing Nash destroyed the value of just about everything that company had,'' the banker explained. ''The only thing left to buy after Nash died was the King Buffalo brand name and market niche. It's not even worth what Talbot is now paying for the whole company. He's getting no bargain.''

''So why is he doing it?'' I asked.

''To get Cosgrove, I suspect. The guy is a marketing genius.''

''It's nice to know shallow, image-obsessed, incredibly selfish people have strong career options these days,'' I remarked.

''I see you've met Cosgrove,'' the banker answered with a laugh. ''Life is not fair. If life were fair, Cosgrove would be cleaning out toilets and my boyfriend would be in love with me.''

''If it's any consolation, your boyfriend is obviously nuts,'' I told him.

''Thank you. Anything else you need to know?''

''No. Just good luck and thanks again.'' I hung up, reluctantly moving Cosgrove and Talbot back down my mental list of suspects. That left me a very short list. I handed the phone back to a smiling Bobby D. He loved it when his connections paid off.

''Do a good job for this guy,'' I ordered him. ''You're right. He deserves better.'' It isn't often Bobby and I get a cheating-spouse client we both like.

Bobby rumbled off and I sat glumly at my desk. There wasn't much I could do until I talked to Nash's civil lawyer, and Bobby's earlier advice still rang in my ears. Maybe I ought to widen my net. I could talk to Sanford Hale, the farmer who'd been dropped from Nash's pilot tobacco-growing program. And I ought to meet Nash's family as well. They were probably still grieving, but I couldn't afford to wait any longer.

The Internet is a stalker's paradise. Within minutes, I not only had addresses for Sanford Hale and Tom Nash's parents, I had printed out maps that gave directions to their houses down to the block level. Hale lived in Norlina, a small town near Lake Gaston. The Nashes lived in Vance County just outside Kittrell. Both towns were within an hour's drive north of Raleigh. I could do it.

Suddenly, the idea of tooling around the Carolina countryside in my old Porsche seemed mighty appealing. I could cleanse my lungs of the rarefied air of the wealthy and replace it with some old-fashioned, down-home oxygen.

I grabbed my keys to hit the road. Bobby D. was busy on the phone when I walked by. He was sweet-talking women in court offices around the state as he tracked down my information, God bless him. He crooked a finger to stop me at the door.

"I need that cigarette pack mini-cam before you go," he whispered. "For tonight."

"Going back to the gay bar?" I asked, wiggling my eyebrows at him.

"A job's a job," he answered primly.

It felt good to leave the big city behind. I am, at heart, a country girl. My arteries feel clogged when I'm surrounded by too much concrete and auto exhaust. It was still fairly early, so I headed out to Norlina first, determined to track down the disqualified farmer. It was a great day to be on the road.

Late July can be a blessing or a curse in North Carolina. Some days, it's so humid that your shirt sticks to your back before you've even buttoned it up in the morning. On days like that, crops can look listless and parched beneath the burning sun. But every now and then, a wind sweeps in from the mountains, bringing rain to cool down the Piedmont foothills, making the farmland seem as green as a jungle bursting with lush growth. Thank God for my hangover that it was one of the cool days, with the thermometer in the low seventies.

Speeding cut a good ten minutes off my drive time to Norlina. I bypassed the tiny downtown area and stopped at a crossroads gas station and country store about a mile east of the city limits. My map had failed me. I needed directions.

From the outside, the building looked like it might last another ten days before it crumbled to the ground. From the inside, it was doing a thriving business as a meeting place for locals. Shelves were stacked with the assorted necessities of rural life, ranging from canned goods and dog food to engine oil and coils of nylon rope. Though an old-fashioned wall clock ticked steadily away behind the counter, time was clearly a low priority. The whole world seemed to slow the second I stepped over the threshold. The lighting was dim, the counters covered with a thin film of dust and the only air stirring was being pushed around by a huge ceiling fan located above the meager video rental section. Straightback chairs lined one of the walls, and were currently occupied with half a dozen men wearing dirty overalls and T-shirts, who were taking a midday break to enjoy a chaw and a cold Pepsi.

Some of the men were old and well-tanned from decades under the sun. They nodded and yupped, instead of conversing, and managed to give the impression that they seldom, if ever, moved from their seats. Others were younger, well-built with buzzed haircuts and big jaws. What they all had in common was a suspicious nature. They fell silent as I approached the register and eavesdropped when I quietly tried to get directions to where I was going.

"Do you know where Sanford Hale's farm is?" I asked the ancient geezer behind the counter. He had tobacco juice dribbling down his chin and a straight line across his forehead from where his hat had shielded the sun for umpteen years, creating a permanent boundary between tanned skin and pale skull.

"Sure . . . don't," he muttered.

This drives me crazy. People in the South start every denial with a "sure," which only gets your hopes up before they're dashed. Plus, I knew he was lying. The men behind me were being too quiet for the old man to be telling the truth.

"That's too bad," I lied back, selecting a handful of Slim Jim beef jerky sticks and a grape soda from the old-fashioned Coca-Cola cooler by the front door. "He might be coming into some money. I work for a lawyer out of Raleigh.''

"Sanford hates lawyers,'' one of the good old boys against the wall piped up. ''He won't let you in the door.''

Maybe not, but Einstein had just told me that Hale did indeed live near by.

"Oh, yeah?'' I said. "Why's that?''

"His boy got hit by a semi about five years ago,'' another man explained in an unhurried drawl. ''Still in the hospital. He's what you call a vegetable.'' A couple of his cronies nodded in silent sympathy. ''Big lawyer promised he'd get millions from the truck driver's company, but Sanford ain't seen a dime.''

"That's true,'' the old counter man piped up, unconcerned that his lie had been revealed. ''Best not to tell him that you work for a lawyer. He's likely to get out his shotgun and shoot first, then ask questions later.'' He hee-heed behind his crooked teeth and several of the other men shared in his merriment.

"Thanks for the tip,'' I told them, opening my knapsack and finding a twenty-dollar bill. ''Here. Keep the change. Now, where might I find him?'' I stared the old man down and he reluctantly took my cash.

"Keep your durn money,'' he said gruffly, sliding my change across the counter. ''Sanford's down the road there about two miles,'' he said, pointing out the screen door to the main road. ''Take a right at the first stop light. Go another half a mile and you'll see a gravel road to the left. It runs into his farm. You best be bringing him good news or you best not stop here again.''

"I am,'' I assured him, scooping up my purchases and heading for the door. ''Thanks.'' I wiggled my butt a little more than usual on my way out, because I figured the old guy didn't get much chance to ogle in these parts and I believe in being kind to my elders.

As I left the cool darkness of the old store behind me, their voices floated through an open window.

"You see the muscles on that gal?'' one of the men asked his friends.

"Yup,'' someone else answered. ''Reckon she could

wrestle my bull to the ground and still have enough left to whip me and my boy with one hand tied behind her back.''

"You'd like that, now wouldn't you?" another man retorted.

The men laughed at the thought. I shook my head and smiled. Never, ever, under any circumstances, assume that just because a man wears overalls and hides his eyes under a hat that he is in any way dumb or unobservant.

If you do, those country boys will get you every time.

The gravel road turned ugly a few yards down the lane. Potholes as big as a kiddie swimming pool threatened to swallow my Porsche every quarter mile or so. It looked like Sanford Hale wasn't big on welcoming company. Overgrown honeysuckle vines climbed the broken down sections of fence lining the road, and the surrounding fields were a mess of kudzu, fallen trees, goldenrod and Queen Anne's lace. But there was something peaceful and beautiful about the wildness. I stopped the car to negotiate a particularly nasty rut and heard the sounds of a Carolina summer day: bees buzzing, crows cawing and the trickle of a creek somewhere close by.

Heavenly—in more ways than one. Either I was hearing voices or there was a gospel choir nearby.

I inched forward, windows rolled down, as I strained to hear. Voices blended in the distance, punctuated by clapping and the kind of heartfelt "amens" and "hallelujahs" you only find in places like the Mount Zion Baptist Church. I was flooded with a childhood memory: people standing on pews, eyes rolled to the heavens, an old woman swooning to the floor. Where had that come from?

When I rounded the bend, I was in for another surprise. An immaculate farm was spread before me. Acres of tobacco stretched toward the horizon in tidy rows, the lower leaves already neatly harvested and the flowers carefully nipped from the tops, leaving sturdy palmlike plants with elephant-ear shaped fronds turning yellow beneath the Carolina sun. The lawn was a perfectly mowed expanse of green that surrounded a sparkling manmade pond, a white farmhouse—and a side yard filled with at least two dozen clapping, singing souls dressed in an assortment of jeans and casual wear. They were so caught up in the music that no one even looked my way as I pulled up behind a parking lot full of compact cars and the occasional old landboat.

The chorus was finishing up "One Of These Days" as I climbed the wooden steps to the porch and knocked firmly on the front door. I saw a few curious faces glance at me before a stout black woman in a purple dress clapped her hands for attention and started them off on a rousing version of "Put Your Hand In The Hand." I got so lost in the music that I never even noticed when the door opened and an elderly black man joined me on the porch.

"My wife's choir," he explained in a deep voice. He ignored my startled jump. "Got a big competition this weekend so they're rehearsing every day."

"They're really good," I told him. "I hope they win."

He nodded politely then waited for me to explain who I was and what I was doing on his front porch. He seemed in no hurry, so I took my time groping for the right approach, deciding, finally, that the truth might be the best bet. A man with an entire gospel choir on his side would not appreciate deception.

"I'm a private investigator looking into the murder of Thomas Nash," I said.

The old man's reaction surprised me. He'd been wearing a tan fishing cap and he quickly removed it. He held it over his heart, bowed his head and murmured, "God rest his soul." Then he began to mutter words I could not quite make out. Even a born-again pagan like me could figure out he was praying, so I waited until he was done before I started to grill him.

"Did you know Nash was dead?" I asked curiously.

The old man shook his head. "I been waiting for him to come and take soil samples," he explained. "I was wondering why he never showed up."

"Soil samples?" I asked. "Then you must be Sanford Hale."

"That's right." He opened the screen door. "Won't you come in and sit down? My wife has fresh pound cake and lemonade."

No one ever treats me cordially. I was dumbfounded and grateful. I followed him inside a small parlor crammed with a piano, overstuffed furniture, small round tables and photos of an extended family so large they made the Osmonds seem positively barren. I remembered what the men at the store had said about his son being a vegetable, but there was no hint of a hospital bed or other medical apparatus anywhere.

I sat on a flowered sofa covered by white doilies. The old man disappeared through a doorway and returned a few minutes later with a tray that held a huge slab of cake and two glasses of lemonade. It had been thirty years since I'd had fresh-squeezed lemonade. As I took a sip, I remembered suddenly and vividly that my mother made fresh lemonade for me one summer night almost thirty years ago, after I'd heard a man on the radio rhapsodize about it during an episode of "Lights Out." The memory was startlingly real, down to the tart first sip, the smell of the swamp, the odor of my mother's orange blossom perfume and the chirp of crickets out by the well. Then, in an instant, the feeling disappeared. Funny how a little thing like lemonade can stick with you for so many years.

But there was something else about Sanford Hale's tiny house crammed with memories that brought thoughts of my own family to mind. What? I shook off the old ghosts and took a sip from my glass. The lemonade made my mouth pucker, the way I liked it, and the pound cake was unbelievable.

"This cake is incredible," I admitted.

"Roses," he explained. "My wife Livinia makes it with rose petals. Secret recipe." I didn't care if it contained fertilizer. I scarfed up every crumb and accepted another slice when he offered it.

Sanford Hale waited politely while I ate. Here was a man in no hurry, who didn't care that the rest of the world had accelerated to a hundred-mile-an-hour pace. He was a farmer, time for him was measured in seasons, not minutes. It was rejuvenating just to be in his company.

"What exactly happened to Mr. Nash?" he asked when I was done with my second piece of cake. He settled back in a tattered brown Lazy Boy recliner that looked as if it had been his favorite chair for decades.

When I told him about the fire, the old man seemed genuinely shocked.

"Terrible way to go," he said. "A nice man like that."

"Nice man?" I repeated. "I thought he'd kicked you off his project?"

"That?" the old man said. "It was a misunderstanding, is all. It would have been corrected in time."

"What happened?" I asked.

"Mr. Nash got an anonymous call about me," Sanford Hale explained. "From a man who didn't leave his name."

"What did the man say?"

"He told Mr. Hale that there had been illegal dumping on my land, that I had let some chemical company drop their toxic waste here for a lot of money. He warned him that the toxins would leach into my soil and ruin Mr. Nash's crop."

"Was it true?"

The farmer's eyes flashed. "No one touches my land but me. It's been in my family ever since August of 1865, and you better believe I take as good care of it as my father and my grandfather and my great-grandfather before him. We don't hardly use pesticides on our crops, that's one reason why Mr. Nash chose me for the project in the first place. I was following his rules easily. No chemicals. No additives. Hand-picked off the tobacco budworms. Sprayed with organic compound every week, no questions asked. No sir, there was nothing in my soil the good Lord hadn't intended. The whole phone call was a lie."

"Why would someone do that to you?" I asked.

Sanford Hale shrugged, his massive shoulders rolling beneath his short-sleeved red-checked shirt. "Couldn't tell you. Jealousy, maybe. My tobacco wins blue ribbons at the state fair in Raleigh each year. Maybe someone just wanted to make trouble for me. That's all I can figure."

Or maybe someone didn't like a black farmer being so successful, I thought, though experience had taught me that when a man gets along with his neighbors for generations, race trouble is pretty rare.

"You must have been upset," I said, "to be accused like that."

He removed his hat and scratched at his scalp absently, his mind only half on my question. "I learned a long time ago not to get upset about lies. I just told Mr. Nash it wasn't true and he promised to come out and take soil samples. He'd get it straightened out, he told me that. In the meantime, I was what you call suspended from the pilot project. Mr. Nash said he couldn't afford for any rumors to get out and I understood that and respected it."

"Then why did I hear that you were upset?" I asked. "His partner says you were ranting and raving."

The old man thought for a moment, then his face broke into a bemused smile. "Sanford Jr. made that phone call. He was mighty upset that someone had called his daddy a liar. That was how he saw it. You know these young boys, they're a little hot-headed. Sanford Jr. more than some."

Outside, the gospel choir lifted their voices in a tune I had never heard. No wonder Sanford Hale kept his cool when faced with lies about his integrity. It would be impossible to live an angry life surrounded by such sounds.

"Is Sanford Jr. the son who was in that terrible accident?" I asked. "I mean no disrespect by asking."

The old man stared at me for a moment, his eyes clouding over. "That son can't talk on the phone. He's in what you call a perpetual care facility near Southern Pines. Sanford Jr. is my other son, the eldest of all my children."

"Would it be possible to talk to Sanford Jr.?" I asked. "Where does he live?"

"In the middle of the Atlantic Ocean," the old man replied, laughing at my perplexed expression. It was a sly, wheezing sound, one that let me know he was starting to enjoy our little chat. My continual confusion amused him.

"Pardon me?"

"Sanford Jr.'s in the navy. A career man. Spends most of his time on a carrier. He's a mechanic. Fixes jet plane navigational systems."

"How did he know about the pilot tobacco program?"

"He was on leave, loading up on his mom's home cooking, when Mr. Nash called with the bad news. He reported for duty again five, maybe six weeks ago.''

That ruled him out. Unless he was a very good swimmer. I sighed, and I guess my frustration showed.

"Sorry I couldn't help you out more," the old farmer apologized. "I don't like to hear of any man leaving the world that way. Least of all a nice man like Mr. Nash. He was out to the farm once and I could tell he loved the land, the way he sifted the soil through his fingers. I'm sorry he died that way."

So was I.

I thanked him for his time and gave him my card. He promised to call if he could think of anything else that might help. When that didn't perk me up, he disappeared into the kitchen and returned with half a pound cake wrapped in plastic. I'm never too proud to accept pound cake.

"Take this," he insisted. "Livinia's made enough to feed an army. Or at least a gospel choir." He laughed again and the sound followed me all the way out to the porch, where the choir had turned up the heat. They were rocking back and forth beneath the July sun, clapping their hands, throwing their heads back, swaying their bodies perfectly in synch with the music, like they were all part of the same joyous being. Which, I suppose, they were.

I stood on the porch beside Sanford Hale for a moment, listening to the choir sing. I became aware that Mr. Hale was intently watching his wife, as if seeing her for the first time. I followed his gaze. Her strong dark face glistened with sweat and little droplets danced from her tightly curled hair as she moved, the sun reflecting off the beads of moisture as if she was surrounded by a halo of diamonds. She was oblivious to anything but the music. Nothing mattered to her at that moment except for the sound she was sending up to the heavens. Her big arms cut through the air in eloquent curves, beckoning the choir to keep pace. I know that Sanford Hale thought her as beautiful as I did, and probably more so.

"She's really something," he said out loud. I didn't have to ask who he meant.

"They really are good," I told Mr. Hale as I shook his hand good-bye, anxious to remove myself from what had suddenly become a very private moment. "Good luck at the competition." I glanced toward the cars in his side yard. "And good luck to everyone who has to make it back down that road of yours."

He looked at me and laughed. "That's just some old abandoned back road you took in," he explained. "No one ever uses it. We leave it that way to discourage salesmen. Take the front way out." He gestured toward a neatly packed dirt lane that led between his tobacco fields. "It takes you right to Highway 55."

Like I said, those country boys will get you every time.

I drove away slowly, savoring the fading sounds of the gospel choir. My hangover was long gone, banished by the fresh air and sheer joy of hearing my own private summer concert beneath a clear blue Carolina sky.

Half an hour later, I was knocking on the door of a small ranch house located off a deserted two-lane highway near Kittrell. There was a pale yellow Chevrolet sitting in the concrete driveway. There was nothing remarkable about the house or the acre plot surrounding it. It seemed an unlikely place for a genius like Tom Nash to have grown up. When no one answered, I knocked again and double-checked the address to confirm that Nash's parents did indeed live there. Still no one answered. That would teach me to show up on doorsteps without calling first. I wondered what to do next.

A nap in the backseat seemed like a real possibility, but I decided it was better to work off my lingering hangover. I hopped back into my Porsche and hightailed it toward Youngsville, where Tom Nash's brother, and only sibling, lived. I'd planned to visit him tomorrow, but there was no time like the present. Maybe Bobby could look up his address for me.

I stopped at a 7-Eleven on the outskirts of town to call in for my messages. At home, a guy who wanted to sell me a health club membership and a woman pushing discount nutritional supplements had both left their office numbers. Maybe I could get the two of them together. When I called work for my other messages, Bobby intercepted the call to give me some unexpected news.

"This is a little weird, Casey," he warned me. "Are you ready?"

"What?" I asked, visions of Lydia offing Nash flashing through my mind.

"You wanted me to look into the will of the Talbot girl's mother, right?" he asked. "To see if there was any money there that might be a motive?"

"Right, right." I said impatiently. "Is there?"

"Not exactly," Bobby said. "When she died, her personal estate was evenly divided between her three children, which meant the will was pretty up-to-date since the youngest kid was only about one or so. So maybe she knew she was dying, is my point. Anyway, each kid got plenty. Her husband got nothing, but there was a paragraph in the will stating that this was because he was plenty loaded already and was entitled to half of their marital assets. It wasn't because she didn't love him."

"Hard to think of anyone loving Randolph Talbot," I said. "So what's weird about the will? She left it all to her kids and didn't play favorites."

"What's weird is that it turns out your client's mother died exactly ten years before Thomas Nash was offed. To the day," Bobby D. told me. "And you know what I think about coincidences."

"Yeah," I said. "They don't exist."

"Exactly."

"So what does it mean?"

"Beats me," Bobby D. said cheerfully. "Thinking is your department."

"Thanks for reminding me," I said. "Any news yet on the Nash estate?"

"That's interesting, too," Bobby said. "And it's just now being filed, so you didn't hear it from me."

"I hear no evil and speak no evil," I assured him. Two out of three ain't bad.

"This is the scoop on your dead man. First, I checked his bank accounts and credit history. No big deposits for the last three years, no big purchases, nothing unusual at all. So forget the under-the-table payment theory. So far as his will goes, he left everything to his brother, including his patents and future royalties, cash and half the stock in King Buffalo. It's a nice haul for the brother.''

"Nothing to his parents?"

"Nada," Bobby confirmed. "Maybe they're already loaded?"

I thought of the small ranch house. "They're not," I told him.

"Okay, maybe he hated them," Bobby conceded. "But there's something a little bit odd about the bequest to his brother."

"More weirdness?" I said.

"Not that weird. He left it in trust. In an airtight arrangement with a bank. The principal can't be touched by anyone and the interest goes to the brother."

"Why wouldn't he leave it to his brother outright?" I wondered.

"I figure he must be a dope fiend or something," Bobby said. "Or maybe he's prone to being sued or not paying his taxes. I don't know. But the way the trust is structured, no one but the brother can get money out of it. Not his creditors, not any future wives or ex-wives. The only exception is medical care for Nash's parents. The trustees may decide, at their discretion, to release money to the parents for healthcare purposes."

"So he didn't hate them," I said. "He just wanted to make sure his brother was taken care of more."

"It might be a Medicaid planning thing," Bobby offered. "Who knows?"

"Were you able to find out anything about the brother?" I asked.

"Not much. One of my gals thinks he throws pots for a living."

"Throws pots?" I repeated. "He has an anger problem?"

"No, he's a ceramics person. Squishes clay into shapes. Makes bowls and vases and shit."

"Here in America, we call that a potter," I told him.

"Whatever. You need his address?"

"You bet." I wrote the address down. "So the brother

is a potter who is either irresponsible, stupid or hooked on something other than phonics?"

"Sounds like it. Maybe you oughta go talk to him."

"Actually, I'm on my way to see him now," I told him. "Don't wait up."

"I'm always up," he said.

"Bobby," I explained patiently, "I am now going to call back for my phone messages. So don't pick up the phone, understand?" Bobby had a great deal of trouble understanding how answering machines worked and I had once been forced to call six times in a row before he grasped the concept of remote electronic retrieval.

This time I hit pay dirt on my first retry. There was a message from the redheaded guy I'd picked up at the bar a couple of nights before, which confirmed we'd been on different wavelengths all along. I didn't plan to return the call. And there was a message from Harry Ingram, the lawyer who had represented Nash before his death. He sounded overworked and in a hurry.

"Sorry I haven't been able to get together with you," he said in a voice so professionally sincere that I wondered if maybe they didn't teach it in third year law school. "I've been snowed under, but I just filed a huge suit today and have a couple of hours breather. I'd be happy to see you tomorrow if you can make it to my office in the morning. I'll be in after ten. No need for an appointment. You'll have my absolute attention. I'm making you my priority."

I felt like a Fed Ex package. I was a priority and could show up around ten-thirty. But, hey, I'd take the invite at face value and be there with balls on.

EIGHT

For decades, Youngsville had hummed along as a sleepy hamlet about twenty miles north of Raleigh. But several years ago, the lure of cheap Victorian houses within commuting distance to Raleigh had proved too much and an influx of doctors, professionals and families had changed the face of the town. Now it was another discovered haven soon-to-be homogenized. A Starbucks and Blockbuster Video couldn't be far behind.

I discovered Magnolia Drive behind an abandoned feed factory and followed the dirt road along an ugly hurricane fence bordering some cheap brick houses. Just as I was about to give up and turn around, I spotted a hand-painted sign promising that SUNFLOWER POTTERY was ahead. I kept going.

The lane took a wide turn into a patch of overgrown forest that led me deep into a shaded, still wild patch of land. Sunlight filtered through the limbs forming a canopy over the road, and birds flitted from branch to branch as my Porsche crawled past. After several minutes of bumpy travel, I began to suspect that my shocks would never recover from two lousy dirt roads in one day. The lane wasn't as bad as Sanford Hale's, but it was close—and a lot narrower.

I finally reached a dead-end blocked by a metal gate with an automatic locking device, video camera and speaker for live communications. An awful lot of security for a small town like Youngsville, I thought. I pressed a black button below a mounted speaker and waited.

"Who is it?" someone asked after a minute. He had a pleasant voice with a deep Southern accent.

I flashed my PI license at the video screen and explained who I was and what I wanted. He buzzed me in, no questions asked.

Sunflower Pottery consisted of a maze of abandoned wooden hen houses surrounding three sides of a small one-story home. The yard was a round patch of red clay with only a few bedraggled hydrangeas for color. A pond glistened in the distance behind some trees and an old blue tick hound snoozed under a far apple tree. It didn't even twitch when I climbed out of my car, so maybe the state-of-the-art security system was a good idea after all. There was a late model, blue Ford van parked close to the small house. Nice wheels. Expensive, too. And useful for hauling around pots and vases and shit, as Bobby D. would say.

Another hand-lettered placard was nailed to the front door of the small house and I knocked firmly in the center of the sign.

"Come on in," the same pleasant voice instructed me.

I entered an interior that smelled of wet earth and well water. The air was at least ten degrees cooler than outside, and the lighting so dim it took a minute for my eyes to adjust to what I was seeing: hundreds and hundreds of clay vessels in various stages of readiness. Large round bowls lined a shelf in the small entrance area, and vases crowded a wooden table. Plates were stacked from floor to waist height along the walls, while smaller butter dishes, cups and saucers, platters and pitchers toppled here and there in untidy rows. A long table stretched the length of the far wall and its surface was cluttered with even more pottery as well as jars of glaze paints, brushes, sponges, orange sticks, splotched rags and other supplies.

A man sat behind the table among a forest of tall vases, steadying one of the vessels on the countertop as he carved what looked like a cross-hatched pattern into the soft clay. He was too absorbed in his work to notice me.

"Don't bother to get up on my account," I said wryly.

He ignored me and continued to carve.

Okay, I could play along. I removed a stack of dishes from a small rattan chair and sat, waiting patiently until he was done.

After a minute of silence, he looked up and flashed me a smile that made up for the wait. "Sorry, I was in the middle of something. Didn't mean to be rude."

I started to say something smart ass, but the words died on my lips. He had the darkest eyes I had ever seen. We stared at each other from across the room and something profound stirred in my gut. My nerve endings started to hum, the air seemed to shimmy and my stomach did a flip-flop that rated an eight on the Richter Scale. It had been decades since a man had provoked such an immediate response in me.

I stared at the stranger. He looked like a sinister version of his brother Tom Nash, and sinister is my specialty. He had black hair cut very short around a lean, angular face. His dark eyes burned brightly against pale skin. He wasn't an outdoor man. His nose was narrow and straight above a long, thin mouth. It looked like he hadn't shaved in a couple of days, which made him all the more attractive in my book. Have him stripped and brought to my tent, please. Washing is optional.

"Hello," I said inanely, unable to take my eyes off of his.

He smiled at me and I swear the air in the room grew hotter by at least ten degrees. He wore a black T-shirt and I could tell, even from across the room, that he had amazing shoulders, narrow but well-muscled.

"And you're who?" he asked politely, his voice trailing off as he surveyed my outfit and blatantly checked out my legs. He did not have his brother's shyness.

"Sorry," I said. "I was staring."

"Hey, I'm used to it." He shrugged, which struck me as somewhat conceited. Reluctantly, I posted my first mark against him in my mental little black book.

"I'm Casey Jones," I explained. "I'm a private investigator and I've been hired to look into your brother's death."

"Who hired you?" he asked. I got the feeling he wasn't the kind of guy who went in for small talk. He didn't wait for my answer, but picked up another vase and began carving thin lines into its base.

"My client is confidential," I explained lamely.

He raised a dark eyebrow, letting me know he thought my reply had been full of shit. God, was it just me or was Beauregard Temple Nash even more attractive than his brother had been? Where Tom Nash had been unaware of his appeal, this man seemed dangerous around the edges, like he'd be happy to use his good looks to hurt you. I'm ashamed to say, the thought sort of thrilled me.

"Sorry," I apologized. "It's confidential for a good reason."

"Tom liked his secrets," the man said with a shrug.

"You *are* his brother?" I confirmed. "Beauregard Temple Nash?"

"Ouch," he said. "Just call me Burly and leave it at that."

Burly? He was so chiseled, he made the Red Hot Chili Peppers look dumpy. My eyes wandered to a framed photo jammed between two ceramic jugs on a table. It showed a bigger version of the man before me, taken when he had long flowing black hair and a narrow, nanny-goat beard. He was dressed in six feet of motorcycle regalia, with denim jacket, black boots, chains galore and a Harley hog parked behind him.

"That's you?" I asked, nodding toward the photo.

"In another lifetime," he replied, smiling at me over a mountain of pottery.

I remained seated across the room from him, afraid to navigate the tidy path that ran through the hundreds of fired and unfired pieces. Just looking at it all made me dizzy. Yet, despite our distance, I felt as if we were talking face to face. He had an oddly direct quality about him. I caught him staring at my legs again and my hormones kicked into overdrive.

"Could you answer some questions for me anyway?" I asked in my sweetest southern belle voice. "There's no obligation to, of course."

He gave me a long look that started at my high-top tennis shoes and traveled slowly up my calves to my thighs and black mini-skirt. What a stare. It was almost tangible. I felt like someone had just dribbled hot chocolate sauce up my bare legs. He took in my knit bodysuit and its metallic zipper like he was getting ready to unpeel me with his lips, then scrutinized my face with solemn concentration. I seldom get embarrassed, but the intensity of his gaze made me blush. It was getting hotter and hotter in that little farmhouse. Maybe even hot enough to remove a few items of clothing. I'd let him choose which ones came off first.

"That red's a nice color," he finally said.

"If you'd stop staring," I protested, "I wouldn't be so red."

"I meant your hair color," he explained. "It's not your real color, is it?"

"No," I admitted.

"What is your real color?" he asked.

"Hell if I know," I said, and we both laughed.

I wanted to get an equally thorough full-body look at him, but he was obscured from the chest down by mounds of dishes and a forest of vases. I had to be content with a nice upper body view. What I wouldn't give to see him without a shirt on. Mmm-mmm. That man could chop my wood any old time.

"So, will you answer a couple of questions?" I asked, forcing myself to concentrate on my work. After all, old what's-his-name had been killed and I had to find out who had done it to make my client, whoever she was, happy.

"Sure," he said. "Why not? I owe it to my brother. Besides, I don't get many women my age around here. Mostly, it's old ladies who wonder in to sniff around my 'art,' as they call it, before they buy a two-dollar bud vase and high-tail it home to their maids. I think I scare them. If I answer some of your questions, do you promise to sit there and let me look at you all I want?"

I'd prostituted myself for far worse. "Sure," I agreed. "I'll even cross my legs." I primly adjusted my mini-skirt, aware that his eyes were following every move I made.

"It's a deal, then." He put down the vase and crossed

his arms, staring at me as he waited patiently for me to begin. His face, when composed, fell into place with a perfect symmetry underscored by his pale skin and dark features.

Wow. What was it I wanted to ask him anyway? My gaskets had been completely blown and I found it hard to think. I was unprepared for the thousand basic instincts flooding my body, some of them more basic than others.

"A question?" he prompted me.

"When was the last time you saw your brother?" I asked, trying not to stutter.

"About a week before he died," Burly Nash answered. "We met for dinner."

"How did he seem?"

He paused, as if to compose himself. His eyes filled with tears, but he blinked them away quickly. A silence descended on the room while I waited for him to speak. I could hear the clock on the wall ticking loudly, then a dog barking in the woods in back of his house. Finally, he coughed and began again.

"He seemed the same as usual," he said in a softer voice than before. "He was preoccupied, but that's no surprise. My brother was obsessed with his work."

"I noticed that about him," I admitted.

"You knew him?" Comprehension dawned. "You're the woman he hired to guard him," he said. "I thought you had blond hair with black roots. Deborah Harry–like, that's what Tom said."

"I did at the time," I admitted, surprised Tom Nash had even noticed my hair color, much less bothered to provide his brother with so much detail. "So you talked to him right before he died?"

"Sure. He called me that night from his laboratory to say good-night."

Touching, but a little strange. Since when do fortysomething brothers call to tuck their little brothers into bed? Did Burly Nash have a mental illness or something? He seemed fine to me. Mighty fine, in fact.

"So you knew about the harassment?' I asked.

"I was the first person he told," Burly said, his gaze

lingering on my knees. "I was against his dropping the lawsuit against that jerk Talbot, but you know what they say. Love is blind."

"You knew he was in the middle of a relationship?" I asked evasively.

"I knew he was going to marry Lydia Talbot," he said. "I was going to be his best man."

"For a secret relationship, a lot of people knew about it," I pointed out.

"I think she was the one who wanted to keep it quiet," he said. "And out of the newspapers, unlike her last couple of attempts. Tom told me, but my parents didn't know. Still don't. Which isn't all that surprising. They didn't keep in contact with Tom very much, not since college."

"Did your brother get along with your parents?" I asked, thinking of the will that had omitted them.

Burly shrugged. "Barely. My parents are extremely religious, fundamentalist, actually. Tom made it clear every chance he got that he was agnostic, and that really drove them nuts. Plus, my father wanted Tom to take over the family farm and that was the last thing that was going to happen. Dad ended up selling out to an uncle when he retired. It didn't make him very happy. My mother follows my father's lead in everything, so both of them kept their distance from Tom after that, as punishment."

"For decades?" I asked. "That's a long time for such a small reason."

"Believe me, my father hated it whenever we disobeyed him. He was not used to being challenged and could be a cold son-of-a-bitch when we bucked him. Tom stood up to him and Dad found that unforgivable."

"Why didn't *you* take over the family farm?" I asked, wondering what his own background was. He was an articulate man, well educated and well spoken. What had been his goal in leaving the biker life behind?

Burly's dark eyes flickered at me, and I was once again unsettled by the unspoken questions that seemed to lurk in his gaze. "I guess I'm just not the farming type," he finally said. "Pottery is more my speed."

"Did you know your brother is leaving everything to you?" I said.

He shrugged. "I figured. He always said I'd never have to worry, that he'd take good care of me."

What *was* this? Maybe Burly Nash had schizophrenia or some other sort of illness that only showed itself intermittently. How could I ask him about it without being offensive? And since when had I worried about being offensive?

"Your brother sure seemed concerned about you," I said.

"He was." Burly stared at me oddly, but I ignored his gaze.

"Did he tell you much about his work?" I asked.

"Everything. Tom shared his whole life with me, just about every night."

This was getting stranger and stranger. "Even the Hargett case?"

"Especially the Hargett case." He nodded toward one of the windows. "I drove Tom up to the mountains about a week before he died, to visit the Hargetts." His voice faltered. "You've never seen anything like it. A crummy tarpaper house falling off the side of a rocky mountain. The father and son, both in bed, draped in oxygen tents and sounding like they were sucking down every problem the world had to offer. The mother with her dress hanging off her because she couldn't stop to eat. Grandchildren crying for food they couldn't afford. Mangy dogs running around under foot everywhere. Crops rotting in the fields." He took a deep breath. "It was no way to live in the first place, and it was damn sure no way to die. Tom gave the Hargetts all the money he had on him, and on the way home he talked for an hour about how he had to do something. Which he did."

"You mean settling all his other lawsuits against T&T if Talbot would throw the Hargetts some money?"

Burly nodded. "That was all Tom cared about. He wanted the old man and son not to feel any pain, and he wanted those kids to eat."

God, but there is enough suffering in this world to go around and then give us all second helpings.

"Any idea where your parents might be?" I asked. "I want to talk to them, but when I went by their house today, they weren't there."

"Mom is pretty broken up," Burly told me. "Last time she talked to Tom, they got in a fight over the phone and she never got a chance to apologize. They might be at my Aunt Margaret's in Alamance County, or . . ." His voice trailed off as he thought better of what he was about to say.

"What?" I demanded. "Tell me."

He shrugged. "I thought I heard some talk about a lawyer. Maybe they're seeing one."

"Oh, no," I groaned. "More lawsuits. What good will that do them?"

He picked up a vase and made a few tiny scratches in it while he thought his answer over. "Maybe they feel guilty?" he suggested. "About giving Tom such a hard time when he was alive. Maybe they want to fix things now that he's dead."

"You don't sound like you agree," I told him.

"Life is for the living," he said abruptly. He slammed the vase back on the table so hard that the soft clay bottom crumpled up in accordion folds.

"Your vase," I protested, staring at the mess.

"Do you want to go out with me?" he asked suddenly, the words sounding like a dare. "Maybe for dinner? Tonight?"

I was shocked at the anger in his voice. The silence after his announcement was abrupt. He stared and waited for my answer. I felt like his dark eyes could see right through my skin and clear down to the muscle that made my heart beat. I sat there mute, not knowing how to respond to his sudden change in mood.

He stared back at me, waiting. I didn't know what to say. I'd told myself time and again that it was a bad idea to go out with anyone involved in a case, but I had broken my own rule before and probably would again. This guy was different. He scared me a little bit, and thrilled me at the same time. I wanted to say yes, but his sudden anger put me off.

"I knew it," he said, pushing himself back from the table

before I could answer. "Don't bother answering, I get the message." His voice was a cold challenge. "If you won't go out with me, then at least have a beer with me. Think you could handle that? I'll get you a cold one."

He started toward me.

I stared, mouth open.

"Well, fuck *me*," I blurted out in astonishment. "You're in a wheelchair."

"I am," he said. "And believe me, I would fuck you if I could."

He wheeled past smoothly, his powerful arms maneuvering him easily through the cleared path.

"I didn't know," I said quickly. "I was just hesitating because I don't usually go out with anyone involved in a case."

"Sure," he said abruptly. He wheeled through an open door that led to a small kitchen and reached a half-refrigerator against one wall. He opened it, revealing a bottom shelf full of food and beer and a top shelf that held a single can of Budweiser, surrounded by a ring of dead flowers.

I followed him and stared over his shoulder. "What's that?" I asked. "It looks like a shrine."

"It is a shrine," he said, slamming the door and wheeling around in a circle. He nearly ran over my foot, on purpose I expect. He tossed me a can of Coors and I caught it in mid-air.

"It's the last can from the six-pack I drank right before I crashed my bike into a tree and managed to paralyze myself from the T-eleven vertebrae on down."

"What's that mean?" I asked.

"It means another half inch and I'd have been able to take you up on your generous offer." He popped open the can and held it up in salute. "Here's to my dead dick."

I was silent. What the fuck was I supposed to answer to that?

"What?" he asked defensively. "You think it's sick to keep the can of beer?"

"It is sort of an unusual memento."

"Well, some things should be remembered. Like a moment of stupidity that changes a life forever.''

"I'm sorry," I said.

"Yeah, yeah, yeah. Everyone's sorry." He threw back a few quick gulps. "Everyone's always sorry. I must be the most apologized-to man in the Western Hemisphere. People see the wheelchair and the 'I'm sorry's' just seem to spill out of their mouths like slobber from Zee Zee's jaws.''

"Zee Zee?" I asked. "Is that the hound dog outside?"

"Hound dog, girlfriend, best friend, faithful companion." His tone was sarcastic. He fiddled his fingers nervously against the side of the aluminum can. "Like I said, we don't get a lot of company."

I felt lower than the teats on a mama possum but, clearly, the last thing that would help would be for me to continue apologizing.

"I would never have said the things I said if I'd known you couldn't walk," I explained, remembering my opening shot about him not bothering to get up on my account.

"Forget it," he said. "I should have known when you started responding to me that you'd missed the wheelchair thing. What counts is that you don't want to go out with me now that you've figured it out." He was close to belligerent.

That made me mad. Real mad. "I guess you took a course in mind reading at the hospital after your wreck," I said.

"No. Mostly I concentrated on catheter insertion and two thousand ways to get off using your eyelids only."

"You can use your arms," I pointed out inanely.

"Great!" he said. "Want to arm wrestle?"

I let his sarcasm settle. "Okay," I conceded. "I don't know what to say and every time I start to say something, 'I'm sorry' does seem to come out. So I'd shut up, except that shutting up really isn't my style. Couldn't we just start over? I think you knew I didn't see your wheelchair. I think you were deliberately trying to trick me into saying 'yes,' so that you could make it even harder for me to say no later on because then I'd feel sorry for you."

He surprised me by laughing. "You lost me on that one, but, okay, maybe you're right. Sure, we can start over."

He adopted a formal tone of voice. "You wanted to ask me questions about my brother?"

"You're being a jerk," I said. "I meant, could *we* start over."

"Because I'm no longer a suspect?" he asked. "Given those twenty or thirty steps down to his basement lab?"

"Partly," I admitted. "But you could easily have hired someone to kill him." I only wanted to see his reaction. Maynard Pope had said it was an amateur and I believed him.

"I guess I could have hired someone," he said. "But I didn't. My brother was my link to the outside world and I loved him. I'd kill myself first."

"What do you mean?" I asked.

"I get around okay. I have a special van outfitted, thanks to Tom. I have the same friends I had before my accident. Most of them, anyway. I go places sometimes, especially when I'm drunk enough not to mind the staring or the constant talking over my head. Though, to be honest, my favorite is when people shout at me, like I was deaf or didn't speak English. I spend my days with my pottery and I'm good at it. Sometimes I even manage to convince a pretty woman to look me in the eye. But Tom, he was out there for me. He was getting out there and building something real, meeting people, fighting the good fight and calling me every night to tell me about it. Because he knew that all the crap I was filling my days with was just that, filler. So, yeah, I could have killed my brother, but believe me when I say that I would much rather have killed myself first."

He drank down the rest of his beer and crumpled the can into a ball, then gracefully arched it toward a far waste can. It clanked inside easily. "Two points," he said as I jumped at the sound. "Relax, I won't ask you out again."

"What am I supposed to say to that?" I said. "I come in here. I meet you and I like you. Okay, I admit it—I even think you're really good-looking and maybe the thought of us getting together is crossing my mind a little. But then you jump all over my shit and make me feel like a piece of insensitive scum." Now I had him. His nervousness was gone. He was starting to get pissed and I was glad.

"So is that your big technique with women?" I asked. "Trick them or insult them? Make them feel sorry for you or make them hate you?" I really wanted to get this guy back. He'd stirred up my feelings and then hurt them. "Stupid me," I continued. "I thought you really did like the way I look or, God forbid, like me. But I was just the first woman under the age of sixty to come inside your house and sit still long enough to be propositioned. It didn't matter who I was, did it?"

He whistled in admiration. "You're a real hot head, aren't you? I like that in a woman."

We stared at each other and a softer challenge came into his eyes, his anger giving way to a plea. I felt confused and slightly pissed at myself because the more we fought, the more my body reacted to his intense gaze as if he had all his parts in working order.

I think he could read my mind. "See that?" he said, nodding toward a shelf that held a large television and stacks of videotapes.

"Yeah. So you watch T.V.," I said. "I didn't think you were blind, too."

"Take a look at my video collection." He crossed his arms and smiled as he waited for me to obey.

I approached the T.V. cautiously, wondering what he was up to. There were three stacks of videos on top of the television set, each containing five tapes. I read the titles in amazement.

"You have *fifteen* copies of *Coming Home*?" I asked, perplexed. "That's a little weird, don't you think?"

He laughed. "Don't look at me. Every time my birthday or Christmas rolls around, some friend gives me a copy. I mean, have you seen it? It's depressing as shit. But they think it's going to be inspirational or something. Look around you. Do you see Jane Fonda anywhere?"

My eyes locked on his. "The point being what?" I asked slowly.

"Well," he said, his voice trailing off as he grinned. "Five of those copies are the director's version with special scenes cut from the original."

"Special scenes?" I asked.

"*Very* special scenes."

I started to smile in spite of myself. "I suppose you've watched those scenes over and over," I said.

"Not just over and over," he promised. "Forwards and backwards, too." He wiggled his eyebrows at me.

"You're bad," I admonished him, bursting into laughter. "No wonder no one will go out with you. You scare women away."

"Maybe, but why do I think that you don't scare so easily?" He was almost cheerful, sensing the tide of battle was turning.

He started to wheel toward me and I did something I rarely do: I panicked.

"Here's my card," I said quickly, thrusting it into his hand. "Call me if you think of anything else."

His glance dropped to my business card. "It has your home phone number on it," he remarked.

"Preprinted," I quickly pointed out, inane comments having suddenly become my specialty.

"Don't worry, Casey Jones, Private Investigator," he promised, reading from the card. He looked up. "I think you'll find it's pretty easy to run away from my advances if you don't want to be near me."

"I gotta go," was all I could think of to say.

"There's a completely modern bathroom through that door," he said, pointing. "Grip bars and all."

"No, I mean I have to go. As in *go*."

He started to say something, but stopped himself. Instead, he simply gestured toward the outside door. "Forgive me if I don't walk you to the door."

"Stop making jokes like that," I told him. I gathered my knapsack and calculated whether to touch him or not. In the end, I patted him on the shoulder like some horse's ass elderly uncle then backed out of the door, trying to smile. His shoulder had been hot under my hand, alive and hard and electric.

"Thanks for your help," I said, ignoring his stare.

"See you around," he answered in a tone I could not read.

"It was nice meeting you," I added. "Really." What in

the world was coming over me? If I stayed another minute, I'd rip off my clothes and throw myself into his lap.

I fled to my car and started the engine, anxious to put some space between us so I could think. As I was pulling out of the dirt yard, I heard someone calling my name. The sleepy hound dog named Zee Zee raised his head and stared lazily at the front door. Burly Nash was sitting in his wheelchair in the doorway, shouting after me.

I rolled down the window. "What did you say?" I asked, torn by an intense desire to flee and a need to look at him just a moment longer.

"I said, 'You can run, Casey Jones,'" he repeated. "'But you cannot hide.'"

He was still laughing at me as I headed down the bumpy dirt road, my mind in a tumble and my other body parts just as confused.

NINE

"Geeze, babe," Bobby D. greeted me back at the office. "What's that weird look on your face? You look like you overdosed on Krispy Kreme doughnuts."

"Nothing," I mumbled. "What's up?"

"No other money floating around this case of yours," he said cheerfully. "The Talbots all have clean credit records. None of them are hurting for cash."

He reverently unwrapped a virulently pink Hostess Snowball as he spoke. Bobby eats those things like a cat eats a mouse. First, he lovingly licks the coconut until it lies flat in the same direction. Then he takes the outer marshmallow skin in his teeth and peels it back so he can nibble at the cake underneath. After a few seconds of anticipation, he worms his tongue into the center and sucks out the cream filling before gobbling the rest as fast as he can.

I sat there, staring, as he plowed through two packages of Snowballs in a row.

"Want one?" he offered, pulling a fresh pack from his desk drawer. He'd been shopping the junk food aisles at Sam's Club again.

Oh, what the hell—why not? I unwrapped one and bit into it. It was sticky, sweet and vaguely comforting.

"You in love or something?" Bobby D. asked suspiciously.

I was astonished. "Why would you say that?"

"You got a faraway look in your eyes and you keep smiling at your shoes."

"That's ridiculous."

"I don't think so, babe. You want to know what I think?"

"No."

He plowed right on. "I think there's something in the air," he confided. "I see people all around me falling in love right and left. You think maybe some of those Research Triangle Park scientists are spraying Viagra into the air?"

"Bobby," I pointed out sensibly. "If they were spraying Viagra into the air, all hell would be breaking out in the local rest homes, now wouldn't it?"

This reply plunged him into several moments of deep thought, buying me enough time eat my Snowball in peace and think about Burly Nash.

"You got about a zillion messages," Bobby announced as an afterthought, following several moments of synchronized munching.

I sighed in exasperation. "Bobby, why don't you ever tell me things like that *first?*" I complained. "A zillion messages is significant, don't you think?"

He shrugged. "I figure it's more important to keep your blood sugar up."

Up? One bite and my blood sugar had hit the stratosphere. I shook my head, annoyed, and clomped back to my office in a show of privacy. Bobby didn't care that I was pissed. He was too happy I'd left him a bonus Snowball.

There were not a zillion messages, but there were five. Every single one of them from Lydia Talbot. She sounded increasingly hysterical with each call. I phoned her back immediately and was put through by Winslow, her butler.

"He's after me," she wailed into the receiver.

"Take a deep breath," I ordered her. "And tell me what's happened."

"Whoever killed Tom is after me now," she explained, words tumbling over other words in her fright. "I've been getting phone calls all day, from some guy using a creepy muffled voice. He uses different names of my friends to get past Winslow—and that means he knows who I hang out with. Winslow says he sounds normal at first, but when I get on the line he says terrible things in this scary, hollow voice."

"Like what?" I demanded.

"He'll kill my little brother if I don't leave Durham immediately. Or he'll come into my bedroom at night and put a knife in my heart. He says I have to leave town tonight or I'm going to die. He says I should give up and move to Savannah, where it's safer."

"Savannah?" I asked.

"It's where my mother is buried," Lydia explained. "I was there the day that Thomas died. I go every year on the anniversary of her death and put yellow roses on her grave. The caller knew it." There was silence and I could feel her tension through the phone line. "I think someone's outside my window," she whispered, close to panic.

"Stop it," I ordered her. "You'll make yourself crazy. You're surrounded by a ten-foot fence and armed guards at the gate. No one is outside your window." Too bad I didn't believe my own words.

Her silence lengthened. She remained unconvinced. "I guess not," she finally said. "I don't hear anything more. It must have been the gardener."

"Listen," I told her calmly. "I'm going to spҽ ꞁ the front gate guards. No one will get in or out unless the guards know them personally."

"But what if the caller *is* someone I know?" she wailed. She had me there.

"It's going to be okay," I promised. "Can you go out of town? It might not be a bad idea."

"I could, except for tomorrow night," she answered. "I can't just up and leave. There's this big charity ball at Memorial Auditorium in Raleigh. I'm chairing it, so I can't possibly skip it. It's to fund prep school scholarships for underprivileged kids. I *have* to be there. It's what I've been working toward all year. We may raise almost a million dollars."

"Okay," I said, thinking fast. "Tell me more about the

event." How was I going to protect her in the crowd?

"It's like a debutante ball, only it's for women who've already made their debut. It's going to be just like the night they first made their debuts, only now they'll be thirty or forty or fifty years old. Some of the families have three generations of women bowing at once. The idea has caught on like wildfire. People are paying a thousand dollars each just to attend and another five thousand to take a bow. We have nearly five hundred people coming. I absolutely have to be there."

Oh my God. Hundreds of aging debutantes in the same ballroom. A mosh pit for matrons-in-training.

"I *have* to be there," she repeated into my silence.

"What about before that?" I asked. "Can you stay home until it begins?"

"I need to make a million phone calls and have my hair done and . . ."

"Do it all from home," I ordered her. "And I'll be with you tomorrow night." My God, the sacrifices I make. It was the last place on earth I would feel comfortable, but Lydia was hyperventilating on me and I had to do something.

"Would you?" she pleaded. "I would feel so much better with a bodyguard."

She was right, but why did it have to be me? Nothing strokes the old ego like being surrounded by five hundred people who have more money and education than you, not to mention better breeding and better teeth. I was going to feel like an old nag on the way to the glue factory taking her last look at the thoroughbred pasture.

I made a stab at weaseling out of it. "I didn't do Tom a lot of good as a bodyguard. Maybe we should get you a guy who could act as your escort."

"I have an escort. Besides, I trust you," Lydia insisted. "You're the *only* person I trust, Casey. I don't even trust my own family right now."

"What do I wear?" I asked, at a loss. How the hell would I fit in?

"I don't know. I can't think. Just wear a dress. No, wait.

Come over here tomorrow. We'll alter one of mine. My
maid can do it.''

"We'll have to alter at least *two* of yours if it's going to
fit me," I warned.

"We can do it," she said. "Mariela can do anything with
a needle and thread. Just don't let me be killed by this
maniac, Casey. Haydon doesn't have a person in the world
who cares about him except me and my grandmother.''

I noticed she wasn't as concerned about her other
brother. Of course, judging from his performance in the
library the other night, he wasn't alone in the world.

"You're going to be okay," I assured her. "But after
the ball, leave town until we figure this out, promise? Only
not to Savannah. To someplace that no one else knows
about. And you'll stay away until I say it's okay? Agreed?''

"Yes," she said. "This is terrible. This is the most terrible thing that's ever happened to me. First, someone kills
Tom. And now, someone is after me and I don't even know
what I did wrong.''

"We'll take things one step at a time," I said. "Starting
with tomorrow night. We'll talk in the morning.''

"Wait. Don't go yet," she blurted. "You need an escort.''

"What did you say?" I asked.

"You need an escort. Everyone there will be part of a
couple. It's tradition. All the women have escorts, even the
youngest ones. You'll stick out too much if you don't. And
he has to wear a tuxedo.''

"I know how to alligator wrestle," I explained. "I can
shoot the eyes out of a snake at one hundred paces. And
the last guy that crossed me ended up with his balls full of
buckshot. But I really don't know anyone with a tux who'd
be willing to go with me to something like this, especially
on twenty-four-hours notice.''

"You *have* to find someone," she insisted, her panic
rising again. "I don't want anyone to know I'm being
guarded. Do you know what the newspapers would do with
that information? It's been hard enough keeping my relationship with Thomas a secret from the press so that I can
mourn in private. But reporters are starting to hear rumors.

It's just a matter of time. I have no privacy to begin with, being the daughter of—''

''Okay, okay,'' I assured her, cutting off her hysteria. ''I'll find someone.''

I mentally rearranged my schedule so that I could be with Lydia. But I couldn't afford to put off seeing Harry Ingram, Nash's former attorney, not when it had taken so long to get in to see him.

''Don't go out in the morning,'' I ordered her. ''Not even for coffee at Foster's. And wait for me in the afternoon. I have to question Tom's lawyer before I come to your house. He might know something about the harassment.''

''Okay,'' she agreed. ''I promise.''

''Good. Now put me through to the front gate guards.''

I hated to hang up when she was still in shock, but I figured she was safe for the time being. She was surrounded by a squadron of servants, a wrought-iron gate, and acres of open land. And, unfortunately for her, her family.

After a long conversation with the gate guard, I felt better. They promised to patrol the grounds and have two guards monitoring the video surveillance cameras twenty-four hours a day. For now, at least, Lydia Talbot would be safe.

An hour and many other phone calls later, I reached the reluctant conclusion that I badly needed to upgrade my stable of men. I couldn't find a damn person to escort me to the over-the-hill debutante ball. Jack pleaded poverty; he had to work. He suggested his red-headed friend, but I'd never be that desperate. Once a person has been designated as a one-night stand, it's too tough to recast them for an encore.

Attempted calls to other male friends were met with either a no answer or an outgoing message saying they were on vacation until the end of August. What the hell, did they think this was Paris?

I finally reached a gay doctor I knew, but not even begging could convince him to hobnob with the society crowd at Lydia's ball. He was a plastic surgeon and said he'd run into too many of his patients there.

As a last resort, I called Doodle, my fireman ex with the

cracker-hating mama. He thought I was crazy to even suggest it.

"What in the flapdoodle have you been smoking, girl?" he asked. "You want an escort so you'll fit in, so you're going to show up with a six-foot-four black man at an all-white event? People would be asking me to refresh their drinks and shit all night long. You must be desperate."

Great. Now I'd humiliated myself in front of an ex-boyfriend by making it plain I could not find a date even if I pleaded for one.

Burly Nash popped into my mind, as he had been every ten minutes or so since I'd met him earlier that afternoon. No contest that he'd look great in a tuxedo with that dark hair of his. But his wheelchair posed a small problem, investigational ethics aside. If I needed help or backup, he'd be neither.

In the end, I decided to borrow an escort from Bobby D., preferably someone with bodyguarding experience. I knew two other private detectives in Raleigh and was unwilling to be seen in public with either. Maybe Bobby would have a colleague who could pass for civilized.

I spent the rest of my Friday night reading *Car & Driver*, then called him at home just past midnight, when I knew he'd be back from his gay bar surveillance gig. He answered the phone, huffing and puffing like the little engine that could.

"One of those transsexuals give you a ride for your money?" I asked.

"Har-har," he answered back good-naturedly. "More like I was giving my king-sized waterbed a workout with an understanding little lady. Just affirming my heterosexuality after my walk on the wild side. Know what I mean?"

Yeah, I knew what he meant. My memory wasn't that bad.

I heard feminine giggling and Elvis crooning in the background. But I wasn't anxious for the logistical details. I'd gotten a peek at Bobby's bedroom once and had wondered ever since how the waterbed supported his weight and withstood all that sweaty action. It had to be like the tropics inside that bed. There was probably an entire eco-system thriving in his mattress, sea monkeys and all.

"Can you dredge up an escort for me?" I begged. "This is an emergency." I explained why it was imperative that Mr. Dream Date have a tuxedo.

"No problem-o, babe," he said at once. "I'll escort you myself. I've been wanting to get a peek at one of them debutante balls for years."

"Forget it," I said. "I don't want anyone thinking we're an item, not even strangers."

"Fine," he said cheerfully. "I'm sure you'll come up with someone. Now, if you'll excuse me, I have a little project I'd like to finish."

"Oh, all right," I agreed crossly. "You're on. But you better wear a tuxedo."

"No problem-o," he promised. "I've got that James Bond thing going, you know. My tux is always at the ready."

James Bond? Hardly. The closest he came was to look like Odd Job with a bad toupee. "For godsakes," I added. "Do something with that toupee of yours. It looks like a raccoon died on your head."

"I'll forgive you that slur on my manhood," he answered in a dignified voice. "But for your information, you are speaking of *my* hair, not a toupee."

"It's only *your* hair because you bought it," I retorted.

"If you're going to be a world-class bitch about this," he said calmly. "You can go rent a male escort for the evening."

"Okay, okay," I said grumpily, wondering myself where all my antagonism was coming from. Annoyance was bubbling from me like lava from an incipient volcano. "It's a deal."

"You mean, 'It's a date,' " he pointed out with a greasy chuckle.

"Whatever," I grumbled and hung up.

To tell you the truth, I felt like pulling the draperies from my windows, kicking a dog, pinching a small child or smashing a few plates for fun. And it had nothing to do with Bobby D. What the hell *was* my problem? I sat at my kitchen table, staring out at my tiny backyard. Fireflies flitted in the shadows, their pinpoints of light dotting the darkness. I used to like spending Friday nights alone. It beat fighting the date-night crowds. But tonight had sucked.

The problem, I realized, was that there was no one in my life willing to escort me, at least no one I wanted to go with. Because the person I really wanted to go with was still a stranger, scared the hell out of me—and could not even walk.

The next morning, I worked off my hormonal frustration by lifting weights until my muscles burned. Then I showered and dressed like a candidate for Mormon momhood before I headed out to Brightleaf Square and the offices of Harry Ingram, attorney-at-law. It always helps to look respectable when you're trying to convince a person to act unethically. I learned that by watching lobbyists in Washington on CNN.

I arrived at his office closer to eleven o'clock than ten, and realized I'd have to hurry to get to Lydia by early afternoon. Despite the fact that it was Saturday, one of those leathery, alarmingly tanned and, I always imagine, gin-swilling women of an indeterminate age was holding down the reception desk. She gave me a professional smile, but I could see the cash register toting up behind her alert eyes. She'd pegged me as a potential client. I wasn't obviously limping or in pain, but maybe, God willing, I was rotting inside and they'd be able to sue the bejesus out of someone.

"I'm a private investigator here to see Harry Ingram," I explained, dashing her hopes. "About Thomas Nash. My name is Casey Jones."

"Casey Jones?" she asked, her carefully plucked eyebrows scrunching up quizzically. "That name sounds familiar." She stared at me. "Wasn't your daddy famous or something?"

"He was a railroad engineer," I said solemnly—and she believed me.

A few swift punches of the intercom buttons later and I was sitting in a comfortable leather chair across the desk from Harry Ingram, Esquire.

He was the jolliest lawyer I had ever encountered, all round and quivering and cordial. I expected him to burst into a chorus of "I Love To Laugh" at any moment and float toward the ceiling. He was pudgy, with rapidly thinning hair that had been combed together into one dashing swirl at the center of his forehead. It made him look like Mr. Tastee Freeze in a suit. He wore a beautifully cut dark suit over a professionally laundered white shirt. This meticulous outfit was set off by several heavy gold rings and a thick necklace. There aren't a lot of guys running around wearing gold chains in the South, except for the Italian imports. But for Harry Ingram, it worked. He looked like a prosperous pasha who had decided to dabble in the law just for something to do while he rested in between bouts with his harem.

"How can I help you?" he asked expansively, gallantly leading me to a chair.

"Thanks for seeing me. I understand you were Tom Nash's lawyer?"

"I served as his lawyer in a specific civil matter," he explained gravely. "Regarding libel and harrassment matters. I understand he had other lawsuits pending that involved patent royalties, but that sort of thing requires a specialist. I am strictly a personal-injury–related lawyer." In other words, he was a high-class ambulance chaser.

"That's okay," I assured him. "I really only need your help with details on who may have been harassing Nash before he died. There seems to be a general consensus that the same person may be responsible for his death. And that this person may have been Randolph Talbot."

He eyes widened. "Indeed? That is interesting news, indeed." He drummed his carefully manicured hands on the desktop. They were soft and pudgy. "There are limits to what I can reveal," he said somewhat apologetically.

"Your client is dead. Surely attorney-client privilege can be waived."

He stared at me for a moment, thinking. "Who did you say hired you?"

It was my turn to apologize. "I didn't."

He nodded thoughtfully. "His brother, I expect."

I shrugged. "Can you help?"

He pursed his lips and stared off into the distance, weighing the moral implications of what I had requested. "I don't break attorney-client privilege," he said. "It's problematic."

"Look, it's an old case. The client is dead."

"That's not entirely true," he countered.

"Tom Nash isn't dead?" I asked incredulously.

He laughed quietly, as if I amused him too much for words. "It's not entirely true that it's an old case."

"What *can* you say?" I asked. If he wanted to split hairs, fine. Maybe it wasn't an old case. But it sure as hell was a defunct one.

"It's unusual circumstances. Perhaps I could make an exception," he mused, his voice trailing off. He reached a decision. "All right. I'll tell you what I know. In general terms only, however. I must be careful, you understand."

"Sure," I agreed. "Generalize away." I hadn't expected him to agree and I was grateful to have finally found someone who could contribute hard facts.

"Thomas was being maliciously pursued by someone out to destroy his professional reputation," the lawyer explained. "It started in late spring, with leaks to the media and false press releases stating that his research was compromised, his results tainted, even that he was taking money from big tobacco companies to falsify his conclusions."

"Who issued the releases and instigated the fake leaks?" I asked.

"There is strong evidence that they came from inside T&T Tobacco."

"What kind of evidence?"

He hesitated. "This didn't come from me, Miss Jones, you understand? But there were fax number imprints on some of the media communiques matching internal machines at T&T. And mailed notices that used paper matching T&T's second sheet letterhead. That sort of thing."

"What else?" I asked. Matching fax numbers? A little obvious, I thought. Would anyone be that stupid?

"After word leaked that Tom was going to testify for the Hargett family in their lung cancer lawsuit, the harassment escalated to a personal level." He sighed. "Frankly, I thought Tom treated the threats far too lightly. Unfortunately, as it turned out, I was right."

His tiny hands would have been delicate even for a woman. He folded them and sighed. "It's only the good who die young."

Thank you, Billy Joel. "What sort of things concerned you?" I asked. "Tom told me about the dead rabbit in his mailbox and the threatening letters and phone calls. Was there anything else?"

"What do you mean?" he asked.

"Was there anything else that concerned you in particular?" I repeated.

The lawyer looked startled. "Are you telling me that Thomas hired you *before* his death? I thought someone hired you afterwards?"

"Yes, I'm telling you that," I explained. "As a bodyguard. Though, as it turns out, I was barely able to put in twelve hours on his behalf before he was killed."

The lawyer looked bewildered. "If Tom still considered the harrassment bad enough to warrant a bodyguard, why wouldn't he continue with the lawsuit?"

"I don't know." I wasn't about to give away my theories.

The lawyer shook his head. "I don't get it. But then, I never understood why he withdrew the lawsuit in the first place when the evidence against T&T was so compelling."

"Do you really think so? I don't find the fax number or matching letterhead evidence all that compelling," I confessed. "That's an easy setup."

He leaned forward and whispered. "Miss Jones, I'm going to take a chance that you can keep your mouth shut and tell you something that it borders on the unethical to divulge."

"Hear no evil, speak no evil," I whispered back.

"Exactly." He nodded. "We had hard evidence that Randolph Talbot himself was *personally* involved, with the threats on Tom's life."

"What?" I could see Talbot hiring goons to do his dirty

work. I couldn't see him duct-taping rabbits, not in his hand-tailored suits.

"Yes. And I absolutely can't say more." He sat back in his chair. "But, trust me, there was direct evidence linking Talbot to the crimes. It would have prevailed in a court of law, take my word for it."

I thought back to all Thomas Nash had told me and factored in the new evidence. Had he really loved Lydia Talbot so much that he would ignore her father's attempts on his life? "I don't get it," I said.

"You're telling me." Harry Ingram looked troubled. "When Tom told me he was dropping the lawsuit against Randolph Talbot, I begged him to reconsider. I told him that he was making a big mistake to let Talbot get away with it, that the attempts would continue."

"What did he say to that?" I asked.

The lawyer shrugged. "He assured me that Randolph Talbot would no longer be a problem. He said he had taken care of it in his own way."

Oh, God. Please don't tell me that Thomas Nash was marrying Lydia just to get her old man off his back and on his side? For the first time, that possibility raised its ugly head and I didn't like it one bit.

"Did he explain what he meant by that?" I asked the lawyer.

Ingram shook his head. "I pressed for details and he wouldn't give them."

I thought of what Lydia had said about reporters snooping around lately. The news of her relationship with Nash would be public knowledge soon enough. And I had to be sure about a couple of things. It was worth giving the information away to know.

"Would it surprise you to learn that Tom Nash was engaged to Randolph Talbot's daughter?" I asked.

He stared at me, cupid mouth open.

"That's right," I said.

His face grew thoughtful as he thought back to their conversations. "It would explain . . . a lot of things," he said in a halting voice.

"It would indeed."

"I can't believe it," Ingram was saying, shaking his head. "Nash and Lydia Talbot?" He stared at me. "No offense, Miss Jones, but my client was a bit of an absent-minded professor. And Lydia Talbot is one of the most beautiful women in Durham. I've met her at a few parties and such. We move in the same circles."

I checked out his gold rings more thoroughly. None of them were wedding bands. Another son-in-law wanna-be.

"Look," I said. "If I get any closer to finding out Talbot did it, I'll need your evidence. It may be the only way to convince the police to take me seriously."

He looked pained. "I'll have to think about that. I have my reputation to protect. People have to be able to trust me, even from the grave."

"Okay. Fair enough. Think hard." I rose to shake his hand. It was soft and round and warm, like a hot cross bun in my hand. "Thanks for your help today."

"I'm only sorry I couldn't be of more help." He started to walk me to the door but I stopped short, remembering something.

"Wait," I said, "there is a way you can be of further help."

He glanced at the clock anxiously. "If I can . . ."

"Did you ever consider anyone else a suspect?" I asked. "It's easy to get so focused on one person that you lose perspective. Maybe someone was just setting Randolph Talbot up to take the blame, killing two birds with one stone."

The lawyer looked pained again. "We did look into the farmers Thomas had contracted with for his pilot program."

"Exactly," I said. "I had the same thought, but the fire destroyed his records, so I don't know who they are. I don't suppose?"

He beamed. "As a matter of fact, I do."

He marched over to a file cabinet, delighted to be of help, and opened the center drawer, extracting the correct piece of paper within seconds. He was a meticulously organized man. "Keep this," he said, handing me the paper. "I still have several copies left. It's a complete list of the participants in his program. I talked to each of them on the phone.

I don't think any of them are a threat, but you never know. Maybe you can find out more. I just didn't have the time to visit personally. Maybe if I had . . .'' He looked sorrowful again, as if he could hardly bear one more tragedy. For a personal injury lawyer, he was a mighty sensitive soul, although it probably helped him in front of the jury box.

I scanned the list. At least twenty names, and I'd only tracked down one of them so far. ''A lot of farmers for one little program,'' I said.

''Science,'' the lawyer explained with a shrug. ''Go figure.'' He extracted a card from his wallet. ''In case you ever get injured, Miss Jones,'' he murmured, trying to disguise the hopefulness in his voice.

I took the card without comment, then found my own way back toward the reception area. I was just in time to hear the receptionist greeting an elderly couple. From her chirpy enthusiasm, it was clear that, unlike me, the two old people were clients.

''Good morning to you both,'' she was saying brightly. ''Please have a seat. Mr. Ingram will be with you shortly. Can I get you some doughnuts? Would you like a magazine? Is the temperature in here comfortable enough for you?'' From the way the receptionist was fawning over them, it was obvious they represented a hefty legal fee— and that she shared in a bonus pool. I wondered what she'd be offering the old dude if his wife hadn't come along.

The old couple shook their heads while murmuring endless protestations back. She was not to trouble herself one iota on their account.

I sidestepped the politeness orgy and fled. Who had time for such niceties? Or the temperament.

Brightleaf Square was only a few blocks from my apartment and the morning was perfect for a leisurely walk. The clear sky was a cross between Duke and Carolina blue, and a cool breeze stirred the hot summer air. I walked slowly, thinking about the possibility that Nash had only been using Lydia Talbot to get her father to back off. It just didn't seem in character for him. But I'd been a worse judge of people before, God knows, just ask my divorce lawyer.

The charred ruin of Nash's house still sagged in the

morning light, though a bulldozer was now at work leveling out the surrounding destruction. Another week and only an empty lot would mark the spot. It would be as if Tom—and his historical home—had never existed.

When I passed the T&T building, I popped in to pick up a Diet Peach Snapple and give Dudley a hard time. He was sitting on his stool behind the counter, doing his Stevie Wonder routine.

"The Great Dudley," I said. "He knows all and *sees* all."

"Now Miss Jones," Dudley complained. "Why do you always want to give me a hard time? I'm just trying to earn a living like anyone else."

"Yeah," I said. "Illegally."

"That red hair sure looks good on you," he said, changing strategy, but only after looking around to see that no one could hear.

I didn't answer. I was too busy staring at the newspaper rack before me, which featured the *Durham Herald-Sun* and a front page headline that read FAMILY OF SLAIN SCIENTIST FILES WRONGFUL DEATH SUIT.

I thought of Burly Nash and got a sick feeling in my stomach. I grabbed the newspaper and walked away while reading it.

"Hey!" Dudley shouted after me. "That's thirty-five cents. You want to cheat an old blind man?"

"Fleece it off the next customer," I mumbled as I frantically scanned the article. Had Burly been lying to me?

I sat on a bus stop bench and examined the paper from end to end.

Burly was in the clear. But his parents had filed a multi-million-dollar civil lawsuit against T&T Tobacco as well as a separate civil suit against Randolph Talbot personally, charging that both had directly contributed to the premature death of their son, Thomas Nash, and the loss of millions in potential future earnings and royalties.

The article was short on facts and long on filler about the Talbot family finances. But one fact stood out above all others—and it was a whopper: the combined bid for damages was in the neighborhood of $150 million and change.

I got to Lydia's within half an hour, but it was too late. She'd learned about the lawsuit a few hours earlier over her morning coffee and newspaper.

"My father didn't even have the guts to tell me face-to-face," she said. "I'm sure he heard about it yesterday."

"You'll get dragged into it," I warned her. "I don't see any way around it. Once the trial starts, your name will come up. They'll use you against your father. It's going to be a media circus. I think you need your own lawyer."

"Oh, God." She was looking out her sitting room window, watching a gardener prune the boxwoods along the driveway. "What if everything they say is true? What if Daddy did have something to do with his death?"

"That's what you hired me to find out," I told her. "And I will find it out. Before the lawsuit begins, believe me. You'll know soon enough."

"I almost asked my father to escort me tonight," she said softly. "As a peace offering. But my stepmother Susan wanted to go. God knows it's her only chance to get near a debut. I knew she'd throw a fit if he'd been unable to escort her. So I asked my little brother instead."

"Jake?" I asked, thinking of her brother with the too-pretty face.

"No. A friend of his already asked him to escort her. Haydon's going to be my escort. He's very excited. It's the first time he's ever worn a tuxedo."

Well, hell, if I'd known twelve-year-olds qualified as escorts, I could have gone down to the video arcade last night and saved myself a lot of trouble.

"I don't want to upset you further," I said. "But don't you think it's kind of weird that Tom was killed on the anniversary of your mother's death?" Hey, she was already in a hopeless mood. May as well drag her down further.

She thought about it. "No. But wait until the press gets hold of that." She looked out the window again. "Father is doing his best to keep my involvement with Thomas out of the papers. I guess it's selfish of me, trying to keep it a secret. But I'm just afraid that if it gets turned into a story, it won't seem real anymore. And this empty feeling is all I have left of him, know what I mean?"

I nodded. I did understand. "So you're talking to your father still?" I asked.

She nodded. "I phoned him when I saw the newspaper. He swears he had nothing to do with Tom's death." A look of horror crossed her face. "Oh, God. My father will know I've hired you, if you show up tonight."

"Don't worry about it," I told her. "I don't think it matters anymore, anyway. There's nothing he can do to stop me if you're worried that he might intimidate me into dropping the investigation. Besides, I'll only be one of a whole stampede of people on his ass, now that the lawsuit's been filed."

"He said something funny about you this morning," she said. "Something like, maybe it was time to give you a call."

"Give me a call?" I repeated, an ominous feeling nibbling at the edges of my brain. Boasts aside, I didn't have the power to go head-to-head with Randolph Talbot.

Lydia nodded. "That's what he said."

"Have you had any more threatening phone calls?" I asked her.

"No. But I told Winslow that I wasn't taking any calls. I can't bear anything else this morning." She shook her head resolutely, as if trying to clear it. "I better start making my own phone calls right now or someone will fail to show up tonight. I always confirm with the caterers, wait staff, florist and musicians. You never know who'll give you trouble."

A lot like her grandmother, I thought.

I left Lydia to her business and went in search of another telephone. God knows there were enough rooms to meander through. Lydia was supposedly living in one of the estate's "cottages," but her cottage was three times as big as any house I'd ever lived in. I couldn't imagine spending my life surrounded by such luxury. But an afternoon of it would be just fine.

The phone in the sunroom was free. I sat back in a chaise lounge and pretended that I owned the place. Winslow, the butler, brought me a Pimm's cup in a tall glass, without even being asked first.

"I see you read minds," I told him, a remark that elicited a quick smile from him. He bowed as if to go, but I stopped him with a question. "Winslow, did you ever meet Thomas Nash?" I asked.

"Certainly, ma'am," he replied politely. "A perfect gentleman."

"Were they in love?" I asked him. "I mean, really in love? In your opinion?"

He looked taken aback, as if his opinion was entirely beside the point. "Why do you ask?" he said carefully.

I wondered how much to tell him. "I am trying to figure out how Mr. Nash's feelings for Lydia may have affected his business dealings with Mr. Talbot."

He grasped my meaning at once. "I would say that Mr. Nash genuinely loved Miss Talbot," he explained. "And that he would have given up any amount of money or material goals to have made her happy. I have seen many people together who do not love one another, but must pretend that they do." He paused, struggling to remain discreet. "Mr. Nash and Miss Talbot were truly in love. Which makes this house all the more sad today. This has not always been such an unhappy family, Miss Jones. Death has made it that way." Having said more than enough, he bowed again and was gone.

I sat there, sipping my drink and thinking that over. All that money and all that unhappiness. It didn't make me feel any richer.

I have deeper relationships with my answering machines than any human being I know. I decided to check in. When I called my office machine, there was a message waiting for me from Randolph Talbot. He'd left his private number at home. I called him back and was put through immediately by a woman with a professionally polite voice. Was I moving up in the world or what? Butlers. Pimm's cups.

And now little old me was on the "A" list for one of North Carolina's business titans.

"Miss Jones," he growled, in what I think was an attempt at politeness.

"Yes," I said, injecting as much boredom into the syllable as possible.

"I'd like to hire you," he barked.

"What?" I almost dropped my drink.

"I said I'd like to hire you. Can you come see me this afternoon?"

Shit. What was I supposed to do now? "No," I said. "I'm booked up. I'm on surveillance and I can't leave the job." I didn't add that I was slurping down liquor on his dime with my feet up on his furniture.

"But I need you," he said, and his voice had an oddly human quality to it. I was very nearly touched. Until I remembered that I was talking about Randolph Talbot. Human had nothing to do with it.

"My help in what?" I asked suspiciously.

"Proving that I'm innocent of these charges," he thundered, returning to his old style. "Have you read the newspapers this morning? I'm accused of murder on the front page!"

"I have read them," I admitted.

"It's nonsense," he sputtered. "Absolute nonsense. There's no evidence. Someone is out to get me. I could give you a dozen men who might be behind this. I want you to prove my innocence and find out who is setting me up. I want you to do it quickly, before my name is dragged through the mud."

His voice softened. "I have my daughter to consider," he said. "It's unthinkable that she be subjected to worrying about whether I had her fiancé killed or not. Can you imagine what her life will be like once it's public knowledge they were engaged? We'll be the laughing stock of the state. We'll end up in *Vanity Fair* as one of their high society crime features."

When the sheer horror of this last potential disaster brought him to a sputtering halt, I butted in. "Speaking of your daughter," I said nervously. "I think it might be better if you hired someone else."

"Why's that?" he demanded. "What the hell is that supposed to mean?"

Had this man ever, in his entire life, uttered the phrase, "Have a nice day?" I think not.

There was no other way to put it, other than being blunt right back. "Because I'm already working for her," I said. "And finding out whether you did or did not kill Thomas Nash is at the top of my list of duties, so far as I'm concerned.

"Hello?" I said into the silence that followed.

I heard heavy breathing, and then the line went dead.

Well, too damn bad. At best, he was guilty of callous cruelty toward his own daughter. At worst, he was a murderer. It was about time he worried about what Lydia thought of him.

Wait a minute. Even if Randolph Talbot had been the one to kill Nash, what in the world could he possibly gain by making threatening phone calls to his own daughter? Maybe the old guy was being set up.

I sat there, thinking it through while I finished my Pimm's cup. I could hear Lydia murmuring on the phone in the adjoining room. My fitting wouldn't be for another half hour, so I searched my mind for something to do. Call for a box of bon-bons? Have a manicure and pedicure? Demand a private session with the cabana boy?

I settled for calling in for my messages at home.

Burly Nash had phoned. A wave of heat washed over me when I heard his voice, a combination of dread and delight flooding my nervous system simultaneously. The flush traveled from my head down to my feet as I listened, turning my legs limp. It was just like the time my brakes locked on my old Chevy Impala and I steered around nine different cars in a single intersection, receiving the applause of people driving by as I sat, parked on the shoulder, numb and unable to breathe, once it was all over.

"Casey," Burly was saying in a halting voice. "I know you don't care, but—I didn't know about the lawsuits. I'd have told you if I had known. I'm trying to reach my par-

ents now. If I find out what's going on, I'll call you back."
He was silent for a moment. "Call me if you get a minute,
okay?" He left his number. "I really need to talk to you."

I replayed the message a couple of times just to hear his
voice, then realized how ridiculous I was being. Next I'd
be etching his initials into my notebook. Besides, I had a
fitting to attend.

Lydia's maid Mariela may have been able to work mir-
acles with a needle and thread, but subtlety was not her
strong suit.

"Big butt! Big butt!" she exclaimed over and over in a
thick Mexican accent as she shook her head and measured
me for a dress. "No can we use Miss Lydia's dresses. No
way. Big butt. Big butt. Flat like floor but wide like chair.
Big butt."

"Okay," I told her. "We get the message." I jumped
down off the love seat. No sense being on display, what
with my big butt and all. "What now?"

Lydia was sitting in a chair next to a table that held an
untouched plate of fresh fruit. She'd eaten maybe half a
grape. No wonder her clothes wouldn't fit me. "What?"
she asked, distracted.

"Big butt!" the maid insisted again, pointing at me.

"Will you knock it off?" I snapped at her. "You've got
a rather grande coo-coo yourself." My knowledge of Span-
ish, while small and on the vulgar side, is nonetheless useful at times.

"Order something from Dillard's," Lydia suggested
wearily. "Call them and tell them what size. I have an
account there and they'll deliver."

I was left to cope with the problem on my own. Dis-
cussing my fashion needs with the geriatric sales lady on
the other end of the line turned out to be like trying to
negotiate a peace settlement in a language I didn't understand.

"Formal? Semi-formal? Black tie?" she asked.

"I don't know. Try fancy ass to the max."

"You want a . . ." she hesitated, "a fancy ass on the
dress?"

I sighed. "Just send me something that disguises a big butt, okay?" I glared meaningfully at Mariela, but she just beamed from her spot at my elbow, pleased to have had some input, however indirect.

"I have a wonderful dress that might be perfect," the old lady croaked. "It was ordered for a formal wedding but the bridesmaid gained too much weight. We had to put her in something a little more expansive. The underlines are clean and classic, but it has a flair that updates it for the nineties. Very fun and chic."

I had no idea what the hell she was talking about so I agreed to take the dress. At least she wasn't fixated on my big butt.

What I ended up with was a strapless evening gown colored a deep jade that was made out of some sort of fabric that gave you plenty of shine but no wrinkle. The thing cut straight to the floor, making me look taller than I was. And, of course, strong like a bull. Unfortunately, it had been "updated for the nineties" via two big bunches of fabric atop each hip. This was fun and chic? It looked like giant cabbages were sprouting from my hips.

"No way," I announced firmly after a quick peek in the mirror. I grabbed the maid's scissors and pulled one of the offending fabric goiters out as far as it would go. It was anchored at the base with heavy-duty thread but I hacked away until it detached. I repeated the process on the other side while Mariela watched, eyes wide. When I was done, I had a dress instead of an agricultural exhibit.

"Look good now," Mariela told me, as she made a few adjustments in the waist. "Dress very good for—"

"I know," I interrupted. "Very good for big butt."

Damn. I did look good. Too bad it would be wasted on Bobby D.

My triumph was short-lived. I looked nowhere near as good as Lydia Talbot. She was born to formalwear, and I was but an impostor cloaked in borrowed finery. It showed.

Lydia wore a dove-gray evening dress with a vaguely Chinese air about it, the top fitted tightly to her slender figure and the bottom hugging her curves to the floor. Her hair had been swept up and anchored with gardenias, one of the passing fads of the moment. She looked effortlessly elegant and totally unaware of it.

Actually, unaware was an understatement. I think it's more accurate to say that Lydia didn't give a rat's ass how she looked. She was too busy worrying. She alternated between staring at the window, distracted, and lunging for the phone to dial someone else and bark new orders.

"You look great," I told her.

She stared at me with a dazed look, like a baby bird that has just fallen out of its nest.

"Are you okay?" I asked.

"We may as well go," she said, "and get it over with."

TEN

The limousine sagged to the left when Bobby D. clambered on board, sending Lydia's little brother Haydon sliding across the slick seat to crash into the side window. The kid stared at Bobby, open-mouthed. I guess he didn't realize they'd not only freed Willy, they'd given him a tuxedo, too.

I had to give Bobby credit. He looked great. His tux fit perfectly. He was sans toupee and what remained of his hair was gelled back off his forehead, giving his scalp a healthy pink shine beneath the dome light.

"Dodd," he told Lydia formally, offering his hand. "Bob Dodd."

Oh, God. He really *did* think he was James Bond.

"I'm not calling you 'Bob,' " I warned him. "People named 'Bob' are normal. No way you're a 'Bob.' "

"You can call me anything you like," he said cheerfully. "Just so long as you call me for supper."

Lydia's little brother thought this hilarious. I, who had heard it eight thousand times, did not.

Bobby squeezed his way onto the seat and, by some anatomical fluke, managed to wiggle his right hip violently until I was squished against the window and had given up my share of the seat. Yet not a muscle on his left hip had so much as twitched. Lydia sat on the other side of Bobby as cool and undisturbed as a nymph reflected in a pool of water.

"What's that sticking out of your pocket?" Lydia's little

brother demanded, staring at a tiny wire that snaked out of Bobby's right-hand pocket and led under the jacket into his pants.

"Yeah, what is that?" I chimed in. "Don't tell me your tux has air conditioning?"

"It's a recording device," Bobby explained with dignity. "In case I overhear anything interesting."

This immediately left me wondering if Bobby was dabbling in blackmail, but Haydon Talbot was clearly impressed. He and Bobby embarked on a long discussion of spying devices while Lydia and I sat, wedged beside them, each of us glum and lost in her own thoughts. I slipped a hand inside my borrowed evening bag and checked on my Colt .25. It was one of the smallest automatics ever made and very hard to find, especially on the black market. I'd paid out the nose for it. But it fit into almost any tight space, including my waistband, and was perfect for undercover work—even if you did have to be standing on top of someone to gain any stopping power. I checked to make sure the safety was on. I did not want it to go off inadvertently and plug some old deb in the butt during her moment of relived glory. On the other hand, I did want it at the ready in case trouble reared its ugly head. I checked the clip. Still loaded. Look out bad guys, here I come.

We arrived at Memorial Auditorium in one piece and what a motley crew we made. The uniformed valet who opened the door for us must have thought he was welcoming a busload of clowns from the circus. First, little Haydon climbed out looking alarmingly like Chuckie the Doll in a good suit, thanks to his overflushed cheeks and slicked-back hair. Then Lydia stumbled out in a near-coma, followed by a huffing and puffing Bobby D. who, with his tux and pocket watch, looked exactly like a giant version of the Monopoly man. By the time I got my chance to escape, the attendant was peering anxiously over my shoulder wondering who the hell else the limo might hold. I don't think Elvis himself would have surprised the guy.

"Thank you, my good man," Bobby told the attendant before I could drag him away. "Always wanted to say that," he confided in a whisper as we approached the blazing lights of the entrance hall.

Lydia swayed at the front doors and I steadied her with a hand on her spine. "Easy does it," I told her. "You can do it. Think of all those underprivileged kids dying to wear Tommy Hilfiger."

She wasn't really hearing my words, but she did read my reassuring tone. "I'm afraid of my father," she whispered suddenly. "He's going to be here."

"I don't think your father has anything to do with this," I assured her and, in doing so, realized that somewhere during the long day I had made the decision that Randolph Talbot was every bit as much a victim in this mess as Lydia. Whoever was framing Talbot made a mistake in threatening Lydia. And that meant the killer was getting desperate. My job was to find out why.

Bobby D. stopped in the doorway, backing up traffic, while he hitched up his pants like Jethro getting a grip on his britches. When he was done, the waistband hung about an inch below his nipples, making him look like Tweedle Dee and Tweedle Dum.

"Nice move," I hissed. "Too bad you're not wearing white socks." I tugged his pants back down to the vicinity of his waist, which had technically disappeared several decades before.

"The microphone cord is too short," he whispered to me. "It was pulling the microrecorder out of my pocket."

"I'm going to store that microrecorder up your ass," I threatened him as we plastered smiles on our faces and followed Lydia and her brother inside. "There is no reason to be walking around recording people tonight. It's sheer prurient interest on your part."

"What's prurient interest?" Bobby D. asked, sidetracked.

"Prurient interest is more proof that you don't need Viagra," I told him as a distraction so I could confiscate the recorder and store it in my bag.

"Holy shit," Bobby said with a low whistle. "We're not in Kansas anymore."

I looked around. He was right. The impressive lobby had

a ceiling about ten stories high and was heavy on gleaming marble, fresh flowers and two-ton chandeliers. Urns and pillars littered the place. Lydia's decorations had catapulted Memorial Auditorium way past Greek Revival and into Greek Resucitation. But there were too many people to make it safe for Lydia to mingle. I frantically scanned the crowd for sudden movements, all the while talking to Bobby out of the corner of my mouth.

"Can you believe this?" I mumbled, looking at the well-heeled crowd around us. The smell of money—and *Giorgio*—was overpowering.

"Wee doggies," Bobby exclaimed. "There's some tasty female pickin's here." He looked like he'd stumbled into the outlet store for Willie Wonka's Chocolate Factory. His tongue hung out and droplets of drool glistened on its tip. "I love gussied-up women and everyone here looks like they're wearing a prom dress."

"Yeah, with yard-wide inserts," I said.

It was true. For every young, well-toned former deb lounging around in her slinky Prada gown looking sophisticated and starved, I counted at least five plump battleaxes clad in poufy white dresses junked up with all sorts of bustles, sashes and bows. I kept expecting Aunt Pittypat to scurry past, murmuring about Scarlett's lack of decorum.

Damn. I'd lost Lydia. I abandoned Bobby to the hordes as I tracked the bobbing flower in her hair across the lobby and into the main ballroom. She was immediately swamped by a crowd of already tipsy partygoers. Unlike the real deb-utante ball, alcohol at this particular charity function seemed to be the beverage-of-choice. I checked out the crowd surrounding her and, while they were well lubri-cated, they also seemed friendly. I relaxed against one wall and kept a close eye on Lydia, occasionally searching for would-be assassins and, I admit it, some source of liquid comfort.

So much for having an escort. Bobby D. was already lost in the crush. After a couple of minutes, Haydon joined me against the wall, which I appreciated. Such gallantry in a young lad, I thought to myself, until I caught him staring at my chest. Mariela had gone overboard tightening the bodice. My breasts spilled out of the gown like two pink puppies trying to escape. Haydon was obviously in the big boobs stage of adolescence and fascinated by them.

"So what do you think?" I asked him—about the ball, not my boobs.

"It seems kind of crowded," he said. "I wonder if it's always like this?"

"I doubt it," I assured him. "This is like fifty debutante balls squished into one." And, indeed, it was. Excess seemed the theme of the night. There was enough white satin bunting to decorate a Confederate hospital camp and massive vases full of flowers perfumed the air. It made my nose itch. I prefer to smell like soap or, better yet, not smell at all.

"Oh, no." Haydon's voice grew small. He pressed against the side of my dress until he almost disappeared behind me.

"What is it?" I asked.

"There's my brother Jake. I don't want him to see me."

Too late. Jake Talbot was heading our way with a beautiful and very young debutante-type on his arm. He was flawless physically, with clear, tanned skin, a lean body and a head of glossy black hair. He was undeniably good-looking and only a couple of years younger than a lot of my ex-boyfriends. Yet I hated him on sight. Maybe it was the memory of the smirk plastered on his face as he'd watched his sister's pain at the dinner party where I'd first seen him.

"There's the squirt," Jake Talbot called out in an overly playful voice that did not disguise the hostility lurking in it. "Look at the little big man tonight."

He grabbed his brother by the arm and dragged him out from behind me. Haydon shrank back, but his brother jerked him to a halt in front of the young girl. "What do you think, Alicia? Who's better looking? Me or my brother?"

Haydon turned pink and Alicia looked confused. Not being a pedophile, she was slow on the uptake.

"Come on," Jake demanded. "Who do you think is going to carry on the Talbot good looks? Me or him?" He grabbed his little brother's chin and bent over, pressing their cheeks together, demanding an answer. That was when I decided Jake Talbot was a jerk. The event had officially started half an hour before and already the little shit was plowed.

"Need some more input?" he asked his date when she stood in befuddled silence. He grabbed the waistband of Haydon's pants and pulled it out, peering downward before nodding toward the girl. "Come on. Take a look and then you can decide."

"That's enough," I said. It was time to put a stop to it.

Jake Talbot actually jumped. I don't think he even realized I was there. I guess I was just too old and haggard for his eyes. He froze, his hands on his brother's pants, looking confused.

"I said that's enough," I repeated.

When he didn't move fast enough, I pried his fingers from the fabric, doing my best to break a couple of them in the process.

The jerk took a jab at my breast bone, using the palm of one hand to shove me backwards.

I plastered a big smile on my face for the benefit of onlookers, stepped quickly behind him, pinned one arm to his side and twisted the other at a painful angle behind his back.

"Keep your nasty little hands to yourself, you piece of shit," I warned him between clenched teeth. "And if you even look cross-eyed at your little brother while I'm around, I'll shove those capped teeth of yours down your throat. Understand?"

He started to struggle and I tightened my grip. Sure, he was twenty-two years old and fairly strong. He probably played a lot of tennis, maybe some soccer or pickup basketball. But he was basically a lazy spoiled brat whose strength would fade as he continued to pack away the sauce and eventually packed on the pounds. His slimy little high-society ass was no match for mine. I lifted weights four times a week and lived for moments like this. I twisted his elbow backwards another quarter turn for good measure.

"Ouch," he said involuntarily, as Haydon and the girl watched in silence.

"Apologize to your brother," I ordered him. People were starting to glance our way and I laughed gaily, hoping it would look like we were just horsing around. Instead, the laughter made me sound positively maniacal. Which, apparently, was just the touch I needed.

"I'm sorry," Jake hissed at his brother.

I released him and shoved him against the wall. "Good. Now go ask the bartenders to break out the coffee early."

"Who the fuck are you?" he challenged me, rubbing his sore elbow.

"Don't use language like that in front of your little brother again," I warned him. "Or I may be forced to kick your sorry ass from here to Tallahassee."

I glared and he backed down immediately, stumbling off with his still-confused date while casting backward glances at us.

"Thanks," Haydon said when we were alone again. "Where'd you learn to do that?" He stared at my shoulders in awe. God bless twelve-year-old boys. My muscles had instantly eclipsed my boobs in his hero-worshipping little brain. I was a goddess. Xena, Princess Warrior, had nothing on *moi*.

"Oh, I picked up a few moves here and there," I said. "What do you say we have some fun? Feel like dancing?" I grabbed his arm and led him toward the dance floor. Lydia sat at a table on the edge of the madness, greeting one person after the other with automatic grace, a parody of Grace Kelly in action.

"I don't know how to dance," Haydon protested. He balked at going further and dug his heels into the ground. "No way."

"Okay," I agreed. "Then we'll hang out here."

We hovered on the edge of the dancing crowd, listening to the Peter Duchin Orchestra playing their version of funky tunes while we tried to stay awake.

"You don't like my brother much, do you?" Haydon asked after a moment.

"Nope," I confessed. "How ever could you tell?"

*   *   *

The night wore on and the crowd grew more raucous. Fortunately, Lydia did her best to stay in one place, obeying my strict orders. Her table was along one side of the enormous dance area and she sat at it for most of the evening, graciously greeting a steady stream of well-wishers. Meanwhile, her stepmother was frantically downing a steady stream of gin and tonics. The poor woman was in over her head and she knew it. Though impeccably dressed, her eyes were wide with fear and her mouth had settled into a drunken smirk. Randolph Talbot was nowhere to be seen. He was either too ashamed to confront Lydia or too embarrassed to be seen with his inebriated second wife.

I suspected he was holding court in the lobby, where a large group of men had gathered to smoke cigars and talk business. The way they chewed and licked and sucked on those cigars was telling. There's a reason gay men rarely smoke them.

I was two seconds from abandoning my job in order to track down a stiff drink, when I felt a tap at my elbow. Harry Ingram, Esq., stood politely at my side, arm extended, the perfect picture of a successful personal injury lawyer all spiffed up for a night on the town. Uh, oh. I knew what was coming next.

"Might I have this dance?" he asked.

I looked around nervously. Haydon had disappeared. "What are you doing here? I imagine you and Talbot aren't exactly friends."

"Business is business," he assured me. "And I can't afford to be afraid of Randolph Talbot in my business. Please, I am escorting my mother and she is far too old to dance. May I?"

What choice did I have? He was determined. We waded into a sea of gyrating bodies. I knew, with sudden clarity, that I was at the epicenter of white America.

The dearth of grown men inside the auditorium had led to a curious phenomenon on the dance floor. Scores of grandmotherly types were boogying down with their grandsons, giving the whole scene a surreal air. I suspect the young men were hearing cash registers in their ears, not the flaccid music, but the women were having a good time. They looked a little ridiculous in their ruffled dresses bobbing to such rousing tunes as "Copacabana," but they were having fun and more power to them. At any rate, Lydia was safe. Unless one of the old debs pulled out a hatpin and went for her jugular, she was likely to survive the party.

Turns out I was the one in trouble. The band launched into a stuttering Isley Brothers medley and my dance partner leapt into action with alarming enthusiasm. I watched, open-mouthed, as Harry Ingram popped into the air, clicked his heels together and swept both arms over his head as if he were a tree being buffeted about by the wind. It was as if his secret ambitions to be a jazz dancer exploded in one terrifying moment on the dance floor. The crowd cleared away as Ingram bowed, twirled, bent and pirouetted his way into our collective memories. I was astonished that such a plump, soft man could sustain the pace—and somewhat dismayed at having to stand there, lamely bouncing my knees and trying to look cool, as my lawyer companion performed an interpretive dance that belonged in a Jules Feiffer cartoon, not on a dance floor in Raleigh, North Carolina.

I was so busy pretending not to be with him and scheming about how I could slink away that I did not notice at first when an argument broke out near Lydia. A lull in the music gave way to angry voices and I immediately dumped my dancing partner and high-tailed it to her table in case my services were needed.

Two old ladies—we're talking in their eighties—were arguing furiously across the table from Lydia. One wore a white feather concoction on the side of her head like a 1920's babe. It bobbed up and down angrily as she spoke.

"I should be in the middle, Lydia. My debut was right here in North Carolina." The look she gave her opponent made it clear that the second woman was from further south where, as everyone knew, white trash trickled like water from a leaky hose.

"Piddle," the other old lady retorted. "I made my debut in Atlanta and that's a much larger ball. I should be at the center."

"Please, Mrs. Worthy, Mrs. Tate," Lydia pleaded. "I'm sure we can work something out."

"I'm not standing rear-end to rear-end with *her,* if that's what you're getting at," the first old lady—Mrs. Worthy—announced. "Only one person should be in the middle of the spoke. And that should be me."

I was vaguely aware of the source of their argument. They were jostling for top dog honors in the famous debutante wheel that was yet to form. For some unfathomable reason, every year at the debutante ball, one girl stands in the middle of the presentation area while the others circle around her. Everyone is connected with ribbons and flowers, like a giant wagon wheel.

In my opinion, this reduces the center deb to nothing more than a human Maypole, but people are mighty keen for the honor. These two old ladies, having anchored the center decades before, now wanted another shot at glory.

At first, their argument had the genteel overtones of well-bred southern ladies. I was not fooled in the least—and neither was anyone else in earshot.

"It's quite a taxing responsibility," Mrs. Worthy announced sweetly. "I believe it should go to someone capable of fulfilling its physical requirements with style and grace. If I'm not mistaken, May has back trouble, poor dear."

Translation: "Mrs. Tate has grown fat and clumsy, while I have starved myself for decades in preparation for some unknown emergency just such as this. I ought to get *something* for all those pieces of peach pie I sacrificed."

Mrs. Tate countered with her own reasoning. "The spoke of the wheel is a symbol of all we hold important to southern womanhood. I believe it should go to someone whose social background and breeding are unimpeachable."

Translation: "My husband makes more money than yours and I happen to know that your younger sister had a baby out of wedlock in 1959. You better let me stand in the center or I'm going to announce it for all to hear."

Mrs. Worthy retaliated with a few innuendoes of her own. "The true measure of a woman's worth is in how well she passes southern values on to the next generation," she murmured modestly. "I have three lovely daughters, all of whom made their debut right here in this auditorium."

Translation: "I'm still pissed that Mrs. Tate squeezed out a bunch of sons to carry on her husband's name while all I popped out was a batch of spoiled daughters. Besides, I shelled out a fortune for those girls of mine when they made their debuts and now it's payback time."

"Now, now, Constance," Mrs. Tate tittered playfully in reply. "This isn't one of those dreadful gender issues at all."

Translation: "You bitch. I'll take you to the mat if I have to."

Mrs. Worthy lost it. "I paid over five thousand dollars for the chance to—" she began.

I cut her off before she could finish. Even I knew it was tacky to bring up money at a benefit for underprivileged kids. They'd be talking about her *faux pas* for generations to come if I didn't intervene and save her.

"I have a suggestion," I said sweetly, putting a hand on Lydia's shoulder so no one would question my authority. "Why don't we let the *oldest* of you be in the center? Age before beauty, so to speak."

There was a profound silence around the table. Neither woman wanted to admit that she was older than the other.

"Come on," I prodded them. "Let's have it. Which one of you is older?"

"Oh, she can do it," Mrs. Worthy conceded crossly, her chin held high. "I'm quite sure she's several years older."

Mrs. Tate looked as if another war might break out at this, but Lydia intervened. "How lovely of you, Constance. I'll have the florist deliver one of the large centerpieces in the lobby to your home for your graciousness. And I think that *you* should lead the procession onto the presentation floor."

Mrs. Worthy looked mollified and the two old ladies scurried away to begin their preparations for the wheel.

"Thanks," Lydia said as the rest of the crowd dispersed to resume celebrating. "I didn't know what we were going to do."

"At your service," I told her. I confessed how badly I

needed a drink. "I'd kill for one," I admitted. "But I can't find a waiter."

"Get one from the bar," she insisted. "Please. I'll be fine right here."

She was probably right. Her stepmother was the only one within striking distance and she was far too drunk to attack anyone. In fact, I feared she might puke at any moment. I gathered a handful of white linen napkins from the empty seats around the table and hoarded them nearby, just in case. Hey, I'm a full-service detective.

"Back in a sec," I promised.

I made my way through the crowd, aware that an excited murmuring was spreading through the auditorium. The presentation of former debs would begin soon and couples were starting to drift into place.

Great. That meant more elbow room at the bar.

I ordered a Tanqueray and tonic, reminding myself that not drinking on duty was not nearly so important as preserving my sanity. The bartender scurried to make my drink and I checked out the long tables of food and punch arrayed against one wall while I waited. As a concession to the younger members of the crowd, a large punch bowl filled with red liquid dominated one end of the table. Oranges floated around a huge chunk of lime sherbet that poked from the middle of the bowl like a lush deserted island surrounded by a sea of blood. This was not as strange as it sounds. The South takes its punch very seriously and if you don't have at least three lurid colors competing for attention in your cup, then you've failed miserably as a creative hostess.

The rest of the refreshment tables were filled with platters of tiny sandwiches, ham biscuits, fruit kabobs and all sorts of regrettably healthy goodies. I planned to cut a swath through the food as soon as I had a drink.

Uh oh. I was too late. Bobby D. had planted himself behind the food table. I'd have to hurry to get in my licks.

But wait. He wasn't eating. I stared in astonishment. He was laughing heartily with a fat woman dressed in a lilac evening gown. She had a mop of unruly gray curls topped by a funny little hat with a feather that jiggled whenever she laughed. She laughed a lot. In fact, she seemed to find Bobby hilarious. I could hear her booming merriment all the way across the room.

I claimed my drink, checked on Lydia, then spied on Bobby for a few moments. The two of them were having the time of their lives. The fat lady kept plucking tidbits of food from her plate and hand-feeding Bobby, who, I swear, would approach each piece of food like a giraffe: his lips would nibble slowly closer until they closed over the morsel, then he'd give her fingertips a gentle lick before retreating. Each time he did this, she giggled and the feather on her hat bobbed. Then they switched places and Bobby began to hand feed her.

The woman in lilac lacked Bobby's eating finesse. In fact, she practically engulfed his hand each time she lurched in for a bite. But the two of them seemed mighty entertained by this pastime, so who was I to complain?

I wondered what was up. She was a little older than most of Bobby's many conquests and had to be pushing sixty. She was also as fat as he was. The lilac satin did nothing to disguise her barrel shape. But she had a sweet face, with round cheeks and twinkly eyes and a rosebud mouth somewhat at odds with her boa constrictor style of eating.

As I watched, Bobby leaned over and whispered something in her ear. She blushed and the feather jiggled again. Then she put a hand on his arm and whispered something back that caused Bobby to erupt in bellowing laughter. He was acting positively giddy.

Good God. Maybe those Research Triangle scientists *were* spraying Viagra in the air. Was everyone in the world but me finding a mate this week? I was starting to feel like all those solo animals left behind when Noah's Ark pulled out from the dock.

As I turned to get back to work, my eye caught a flash of movement at the punch bowl. Lydia's college-age brother, Jake, was bending over it, yet he held no cup in his hand. He straightened up and slid his right hand into a pants pocket. Had he been spiking the punch? Most of the people at the ball were of drinking age and obviously preferred the bar. Spiking the punch seemed redundant. He hurried away before I could question him. I watched as he wormed his way through the crowd, seeking his date.

I shrugged it off and went in search of Lydia. I found her behind a bank of heavy red velvet curtains, inspecting an enormous set of movable white stairs and directing the initial procession. She had decided to forego her own chance at making a second debut so that she could oversee the event. She was pairing women with their escorts and handing out bouquets of long-stemmed roses.

Some of the women were staring anxiously at the backside of the movable stairs. I didn't blame them. In order to reach the top of the artificial stairway—where the crowd gathering in the ballroom area would see them—the women first had to ascend a far steeper set of steps backstage. For some of the older lovelies, particularly the tipsy ones, this was likely to be a real challenge. The escorts could be in for more than they had bargained for. Why is it that you can never find a Sherpa when you need one?

Gradually, husbands and wives lined up between younger girls and their dates, and everyone got busy squirming and primping their way into perfection. Lydia marched down the emerging line, straightening bow ties, loosening necklines, adjusting bows and rearranging roses in the crooks of elbows.

"Everyone looks magnificent," she announced.

I had to admit, I was impressed. There must have been a hundred women in line, and every one of them had been magically infused with a ramrod posture that would have made a marine sergeant proud.

"Let's go out front," Lydia whispered to me and we quickly claimed seats at her table. She sat next to Haydon and I had the honor of keeping her stepmother from falling over into her paté.

The lights in the auditorium dimmed and the orchestra began playing some classical tune I'd heard before but could not pinpoint. My one drink had been strong enough to fell a Kentucky Derby winner and I was a bit light-headed. Between the music, two-story stage set and the roar of the crowd, I felt as if I were watching the beginnings of a Vegas revue. I would not have been surprised had six

topless showgirls popped into view, carrying Siegfried and
Roy on their shoulders. In fact, I would have preferred it.

Instead, the music swelled and the lights rose dramati-
cally on a resplendent Mrs. Worthy, posed at the top of the
majestic sweep of stairs. Her shoulders were held back, her
cloche hat perfectly still, as she basked in her moment of
glory.

"Presenting Mrs. Constance Ann Broadhurst Worthy,"
a deep voice slowly intoned over a public address system.

Applause broke out and she stepped gracefully down the
wide staircase, roses balanced in one arm, her other hand
lightly looped around her husband's steadying arm. Mr.
Worthy was something of a fox, especially considering his
age. He had silver hair and a jaunty handlebar mustache
that curled upward at each end. Mrs. Worthy held her chin
high and her expression was one of solemn dignity. Mr.
Worthy was less formal. He beamed out at the crowd as he
proudly escorted his wife down the stairs.

Mrs. Worthy was followed in succession by every one
of her three daughters, each of them well into middle-age
by now and, yet, oddly beautiful when seen one after the
other, as they were.

It could have been ridiculous, so many women of varying
sizes and wearing unflattering dresses, taking turns parading
down the staircase like Norma Desmond seeking her
closeup from Mr. DeMille. But it was oddly moving, instead. Lydia had decreed that every mother be followed by
each of her daughters and the effect was inspiring, at least
to this motherless daughter.

I sat in the darkness next to Lydia, surprised at my own
reaction. Most of the women were well over thirty and few
embodied the ideal of a fresh unspoiled deb. Yet each
looked special, standing in her moment in the spotlight as
her name was announced, a gentleman on her arm guiding
her down the stairs as if she were the most precious of
cargo. The oldest women, in particular, took on a beauty
that transcended the physical, especially when followed by
their daughters. It was something in their bearing, I decided,
a certain set in their shoulders, that told everyone of how
very proud they were of the lovely young—and not-so-

young—ladies that followed them. It was as if they finally
had the chance to say to the world, "Yes, I have spent my
life in what some may consider a frivolous way, but look
at what I have created. This is my family."

It would have been so easy to make fun of them. They
had the advantages I'd never had: money, great teeth, expensive clothes, years of hairdresser appointments and the
luxury of believing that appearances could be everything.
Yet I had no stomach for ridicule watching them.

Lost in thought, I watched the endless procession move
down the stairs. At the base, the men silently disappeared
into the shadows and the women began taking their place
in the famous wheel. I had one surprise when I realized
that Franklin Cosgrove was at the benefit, acting as escort
to a plain-faced, middle-aged brunette. Why would Nash's
business partner be here? Then I remembered Lydia's theory that he was shopping for a new, rich wife. If so, what
better place for browsing than here, amidst a sea of mon-
eyed candidates?

Old Mrs. Tate would be out last, I suspected, her traditional first place in line having been given to Mrs. Worthy
in the name of politics. As the supporting cast of women
took their positions on the main floor of the ballroom, I
heard a sound like a Weed-Eater sweeping through grass.
Lydia's stepmother was sobbing behind me, emitting a
keening that sounded like a cross between a snivel and a
steady whine.

What a mess that woman was. She was slumped over a
highball glass, sniffling into her cups. Good God. Was she
mourning a never-realized dream of being a debutante,
which was *really* pathetic, or had something terrible happened to her recently? I watched for a moment, trying to
get a reading, and finally decided that she was crying because every cell in her body was saturated with alcohol and
she was in dire need of some serious rehab. I ignored her,
as everyone else at the table was doing, and returned to
watching the spectacle.

"How do you think it's going?" Lydia whispered to me
in the darkness.

"Perfectly," I said. "Are you starting to relax?"

"A little," she whispered back.

I wished I could say the same. It wasn't until Mrs. Tate
had made her grand entrance at the rear of the procession,
then taken her place at the center of the wheel, that I could
take a deep breath. It couldn't last much longer now. A few
chosen escorts had been moving discreetly through the formation, linking each deb to her neighbors and inward to
the next concentric circle of the wheel with ribbons that
stretched from bouquet to bouquet.

Finally, as Mrs. Tate took her place in the very center
of the formation, the other former debs began to revolve
around her slowly. Her silvery-gray dress made her look
like a tugboat in the middle of a harbor celebration, but her
joy was unmistakable. As the crowd burst into loud applause, her extra pounds and years seemed to melt away.
The music swelled, signaling a special moment and the
crowd fell silent.

I watched, astonished, as Mrs. Tate slowly but steadily
began to curtsy to the crowd.

"My God," a woman across the table from me gasped.
"She's doing a Texas bow!"

A murmur spread through the crowd as Mrs. Tate curt-
sied even more deeply, her stout body bending all the way
to the floor until she touched her forehead to her knee and
rose again. All without the benefit of an escort. I don't
know how she did it, maybe she'd secretly been taking
yoga lessons for the past six months, but, damn—I had to
join in the standing ovation that followed. The old dame
had done it with style.

A general sort of hysterical relief swept through the
crowd once the grand presentation had been completed. The
bartenders were kept busy as former debutantes stormed the
bar for their rewards. Lydia was swarmed with people offering their congratulations and both Mrs. Worthy and Mrs.
Tate were basking in their well-deserved glory. Bobby D.
was lost in the crowd, no doubt cooing with his oversized
turtle dove. I noticed she had not attempted the stairs or a
bow. Probably too busy feeding Bobby.

At one point, Randolph Talbot finally materialized out

of the pack to grasp Lydia's hands. He had abandoned his alcoholic second wife but was ready to reclaim his victorious daughter.

"A magnificent job. I am so very proud to have you as my daughter," he told Lydia, his eyes shining with what seemed to be genuine pride. I suspected he really wanted to say more, like please forgive me for being the kind of father who would even be suspected of murder, but now was not the time or place. He gripped her hand so tightly, I feared he might damage it. But Lydia did not flinch. She stood, locked in a smile of triumph with her father.

"You are the most beautiful woman here tonight," Talbot told his daughter. "And you're a genius for coming up with this idea."

I heard an unladylike snort behind me. Susan Johnson Talbot had lurched to life. She knocked over one of her many highball glasses. A clear liquid seeped across the tablecloth like blood from a vein. She thrust a braceleted arm toward Randolph Talbot, nearly taking my nose off in the process.

"That's right," Susan Talbot slurred in a drunken drawl that was equal parts nastiness and desperation. "She's your little princess, isn't she? A perfect darling. Except she was screwing the one man who was going to—"

"That's enough," Talbot ordered her sharply. Heads turned. Lydia's face crumpled. I did my duty.

"Bathroom break," I announced loudly. "And you know how we women like to go in pairs." I smiled at the onlookers and grabbed Lydia's stepmother by one arm, hoisting her aloft.

"Let's go, cupcake," I ordered her grimly in a low whisper. "Bedtime for Bonzo."

Before she could protest, I hustled her out through the crowd, eyes searching for a bathroom. I wanted to stick her head in the toilet and flush repeatedly, but knew I'd have to settle for sponging her sorry ass off with a damp paper towel. Maybe I could lock her in a stall until she sobered up.

As we staggered past the lobby, I noticed Harry Ingram caught in a similar situation. He was supporting a very

old—and very drunk—lady with both arms as he dragged
her toward the front doors. His dancing days were over, at
least for now. It was obviously time to put good old Mom
to bed. How depressing. Mother's Day must be a barrel of
fun around the Ingram household.

But I had bigger problems ahead. What the hell? I
rounded a corner and there was a long line of young women
waiting to get into the bathroom, most of them looking
mightily distressed and in imminent danger of peeing in
their deb pants.

"Emergency," I muttered grimly, shouldering past the
line. If I couldn't get a stall, I'd settle for a sink. Susan
Johnson Talbot was turning green.

I dragged my drunken burden into the marbled bathroom
and propped her up against the counter. She slumped over
the basin like she was getting ready to blow lunch. I
grabbed the back of her dress and held her aloft, hoping
I could butt my way into an empty stall.

We were in luck. The handicapped stall was empty. I
knew why: one of the biggest controversies among southern
women is whether or not a perfectly able person is supposed to use the handicapped stall when it is not in use.
Now, there wasn't a handicapped person within ten miles
of Memorial Auditorium at that moment, but most of these
women were so loathe to do the wrong thing that they
would not use the special facilities, no matter how desperate
their situation.

I was of a different opinion. It's not a parking space, for
godsakes, and most of us aren't going to be in there for
more than a minute. Use it and cruise it, was my motto. I
dragged Susan Talbot inside and held her head as she up-
chucked a couple fraternity parties' worth of liquor. For
this I get $100 an hour?

Normally, the sounds coming from our stall would have
inspired a few murmurs. When no one seemed to care, I
realized that some greater force was at work in the ladies
bathroom. For starters, the smell of sulfur was everywhere
and I could hear the scratch of matches being lit up and
down the line of stalls.

This was not as bizarre as it sounds. Every well-bred

southern woman is taught from junior high school on to carry a pack of matches in case she pollutes the bathroom while others are waiting to use it. A flick of the non-Bick and the odor was gone, meaning you didn't have to lurk in the stall for fifteen minutes pretending to adjust your pantyhose when you were actually attempting to wait out either the smell or the other people in line, whichever disappeared first. Wearing a skintight evening gown with no pockets was no excuse to shirk this important responsibility. Which was why these women were lighting up matches faster than the crowd at the end of a Lynyrd Skynyrd concert.

My question was—why? I dragged Susan Talbot out of the handicapped stall and a desperate deb trampled me in her haste to claim it. From her contorted face, it was clear she was well beyond convention and in dire need of relief.

I stood, bathing Susan Talbot's face with cool water, as debs took turns upchucking in the sink or racing to the toilets.

Oh, my God. What if the chicken salad was bad? Lydia would die from the embarrassment.

Then it struck me. With few exceptions, all of the sufferers were young. And it had been the older women, those less concerned with their figures, who had hit the food tables the hardest. So why were mostly young women suffering?

I let go of Susan Talbot as my brain formulated the answer. She slumped to her knees and caught the counter with her elbows, laying a cheek against the cool porcelain as she half-dangled to the floor. I ignored her and continued to puzzle it out. Young meant . . . no liquor. No liquor meant the punchbowl.

The punchbowl meant Jake Talbot.

The little shit had put something in the punch that had wreaked havoc with the delicate gastronomical systems of these flowers of southern womanhood.

When I found him, I was going to rip his head off and serve it up on a platter for the dogs.

I left Lydia's stepmother in a heap on the floor and raced from the bathroom, scanning the crowd for Jake Talbot's smug profile. Ten minutes later, I was still searching. No

way was I giving up. I was madder than a wet hen. I finally
spotted him heading out the front door. I slipped behind a
marble statue and waited a moment, then quickly walked
out into the hot summer night, ignoring the gaze of Randolph Talbot and his cigar-smoking cronies as I hurried
past.

Jake was turning the corner of the auditorium, heading
toward the darkness of one of the parking lots. I followed
him, using shadows and shrubs to hide my presence. My
stupid dress fit me like skin and made it tough to crouch
down. I was tempted to hike it up to my waist but settled
for ripping the side seam up to my thigh. It gave me more
maneuvering room and wouldn't look all that out of place
once I dragged his sorry ass back inside for a public flog-
ging.

The parking lot was deserted. Long rows of luxury vehicles and assorted sports cars gleamed beneath the safety
lights. I ducked behind a black Lexus for cover and
watched as Jake Talbot stood, waiting, near the end of a
row. After a moment, a thin black man dressed in red baggy
trousers and a dark-striped poker-dealer shirt stepped from
the shadows. He wore a floppy Dr. Seuss top hat that he
held onto with one hand as he quickly walked over to
Lydia's brother.

What followed was a soundless ballet enacted on street
corners and park benches everywhere: the stranger passed
a plastic package over to Jake. Jake put it in his pocket and
handed the stranger a fistful of dollars. The two nodded
good-bye, then strode away in separate directions.

Okay. Add drugs to Jake Talbot's resume as a slimeball.

I followed Lydia's brother back toward Memorial Auditorium, wondering just how I would break it to his sister—and if it had any bearing on the death of her fiancé.
Maybe I'd have a little private chat with Jake on my own,
instead.

Randolph Talbot was waiting for me near the edge of
the front lawn, a good twenty feet from the well-lit entrance
doors. "Miss Jones," he said loudly as I tried to slip past.
I had no choice except to stop.

"Mr. Talbot," I replied, stepping toward the light. I had a sudden urge to flee.

"Taking a break?" he asked, clipping the end off a fresh cigar and holding it up to his nose.

"You might say that. It's been quite a successful evening, hasn't it? You must be very proud of your daughter." I left before he could answer me.

Too late. Jake had been lost in the crowd and I couldn't find Lydia, either. The ball was breaking up and chaos reigned. I tried to battle my way back inside, but was constantly pushed back by the departing crowd. By the time I reached Lydia's table, it was empty and being cleared by a pair of weary-looking waiters.

It was stupid of me to have ever left her side. Figuring that everyone had to eventually pass through the exit, I returned to the lobby and took up a spot outside the main bank of doors. I was just in time to see Jake Talbot climbing into the passenger seat of a late-model Porsche—with Franklin Cosgrove at the wheel. The two men pulled away from the curb and I watched the car make its way to Person Street, where it turned left and headed toward downtown. My, my, I thought. Very interesting, indeed. What could Franklin Cosgrove be up to with Lydia's little brother?

I waited outside in the evening air, watching the other revelers depart and wondering about the connection between Jake and Cosgrove. Half an hour later, my thoughts were interrupted by Lydia herself.

"There you are," she said, grabbing my arm. "My father can't find my stepmother. Got any ideas where she might be?"

"Floor of the bathroom?" I suggested.

Lydia rolled her eyes. "Leave her there," she decided. She gave the parking valet a ticket and turned back to me. "What's your friend doing with Fanny Whitehurst?" she asked, nodding toward Bobby. He was framed in the exit doors and rapidly heading our way.

"Hell if I know," I confessed. "Maybe he thought she looked like his type?"

"Then your friend has good eyesight," Lydia explained.

"Fanny just won half of her husband's assets in a big divorce battle. She's worth forty million dollars."

"Holy shit," I said. Yes, it was totally low-class of me. But wait until Bobby heard. I couldn't wait to tell him.

"Casey, babe!" Bobby bellowed happily as he charged across the sidewalk, towing the fat woman behind him. "You've got to meet my new main squeeze. I'm telling you, it's love at first sight. This is Miss Fanny Whitehurst, a former Miss Asheville and currently the toast of Raleigh."

The woman collapsed in giggles at Bobby's excessive pronouncement. Her big bosom vibrated like someone had dropped a quarter in her slot. "He's being silly," she protested in a fluttery voice. "You are a big tease, Bob. Now you just stop that." She was holding a lilac fan that matched her dress and she playfully bopped Bobby over the head with it.

Bobby grabbed her and pulled her close, squishing her up against his bulk. "Fanny's husband just left her for a woman thirty years younger," he announced, shaking his head in disbelief. "Can you believe that some man would let her go? Why, this is the most good-natured woman I've ever met. And I've known plenty." He wiggled his eyebrows and I resisted the urge to slap the silly grin off his face. Traitor. He'd found someone.

"He left me for some skinny, snippy thing with no appetite," Fanny added. "She used to be my personal trainer. Now she's training him. Good riddance to bad rubbish. They deserve each other. As for me, I'm out to have some fun!"

She pulled her floor-length dress up a few inches and did a sprightly jig, inspiring Bobby to join her. The two of them capered away on the sidewalk, oblivious to the curious stares they were attracting. I decided they had spent the entire evening hanging mighty close to the bar.

Lydia and I stood shoulder-to-shoulder, watching the spectacle, too tired to comment. It had been a long night.

"Where have you been?" a young voice asked, interrupting our reverie. Haydon Talbot raced up and grabbed his sister's arm. "I'm tired and I want to go home. Where's the limo?"

"Coming," Lydia promised.

"He's vibrating," Haydon said to me.

"What?"

"That fat man you're with is vibrating."

The kid was right. Bobby's left-hand pocket was jumping and jiving like he had a couple of jitterbugging ferrets stored inside it.

"Hey, Bobby," I yelled across the sidewalk. "Is that a snake in your pocket or are you just happy to see me?"

He stopped jigging and glanced down. His face lit up. "Cool," he said as Fanny stepped closer. "My new forwarding device works." He pulled yet another ridiculous electronic device from his pocket and began to unfold it. "If someone calls the office and tries to leave a message," he explained. "I can program it to automatically forward it to my cell phone instead."

"Bob Dodd," he barked into the receiver, hoping to impress Fanny. He listened intently and his face changed expression. "Sure, she's right here." He held the phone out to me.

I looked at him suspiciously. "Bobby," I warned him.

"Some guy named Burly for you," he answered with a shrug.

I grabbed the phone. Burly was breathing heavily on the other end.

"Burly?" I said tentatively. "You okay?"

He cut me off. "Look, Casey, I'm probably overreacting and you're gonna think I'm just coming up with an excuse to call you, but I've been getting weird hang-up calls for the last couple of hours and the electricity just went out in my house and I was thinking that maybe you could stop by and help me look a—"

His words were cut off by a tremendous blast that echoed into the phone. I heard a crash followed by a series of smaller crashes, more heavy breathing and then he was back on the line. "Someone just shot out one of my side windows," he whispered into the phone. "I've got to hang up and call the—"

The line went dead.

"Shit," I shouted, pounding it with the heel of my palm.

Bobby looked at me, perplexed, and I thrust the phone at him.

"Make it work!" I ordered.

He grabbed it, pressed a few buttons and listened to it. "The phone works fine," he said. "It ought to. It cost me over—"

"I need a car," I yelled at the small crowd that had assembled. "Anyone. Give me your car keys. A man's life is in danger. I have to borrow a car."

Lydia was staring at me, shocked into stillness.

"That was Tom's brother," I said. "I have to have a car."

"Jake's keys," Haydon piped up, tugging on his sister's elbow.

Lydia's eyes widened. "That's right," she said. She opened her evening bag and dug among its contents, retrieving a small silver key chain. "It's a red Lamborghini in the far parking lot. He was too drunk to drive it home, so I made him give me his keys. Be careful of the—"

I didn't wait to hear more. I grabbed the keys from her hand, hitched up my skirt and started running.

ELEVEN

Under any other circumstances, driving a Lamborghini race car retooled for road use would have thrilled me. In my present state, I was terrified. The car flew down New Bern Avenue, hitting seventy miles an hour within seconds. But the suspension was iffy and the steering was loose. Keeping her steady was like wrestling jello. It was either slow down and call for help or speed up and save Burly solo.

I eased off the gas and fumbled for Bobby's cellular phone. There was way too much shit coming down on my shoulders for me to do this on my own. I stared at the LCD panel, wondering how the hell you got a call to go through. I hate phones when they're connected to a wall and I really hate them when they're not. Consequently, I am cell-phone challenged—and I was sorry for it now. Finally, after several false starts, I managed to press enough buttons to bring up a code that indicated all was ready. I dialed Anne Morrow's phone number at the Raleigh Police Department. I was a little skinny on friends around the RPD and Detective Morrow was my only hope.

Nothing happened. I had failed to satisfy the great cellular gods and my call would not go through. Disgusted, I threw the phone on the seat next to me and veered to the right, where I zoomed up the exit ramp for the Beltline. I punched down the accelerator until I was cruising at a hundred miles an hour. I reached the cutoff for U.S. 1 North within two minutes and squealed around the exit curve to the main drag, where I blew past a procession of cars crawling along at the legal speed limit toward a stop light. A blare of horns sounded behind me as I ran a red light and hit a stretch of empty highway.

Youngsville is about ten miles north of Raleigh, just beyond a stretch of U.S. 1 that was once rural farmland and was now wall-to-wall shopping centers. It wasn't even midnight, and it was a weekend night, so the road was crowded with people in various states of sobriety. I wove through traffic, honking my horn, jumping the curb, clipping the sides of construction cones and generally creating havoc in my wake. It would only be a matter of minutes before someone with a little more technological sense than I had ratted me out to the cops via car phone. Good. I needed all the help I could get. If that meant pulling into sleepy downtown Youngsville with a screaming squadron of Wake and Franklin County deputies on my ass, so be it.

I reached open country and knew I was close. I slammed the gas pedal to the floor and the speedometer crept over a hundred. The car actually steadied at a higher speed, the engine in its element. I prayed that no one heading toward me would attempt to pass the car in front of them on the narrow two-lane highway. Cars swept by on the opposite side almost as fast as I spotted their headlights.

My heart was hammering in my chest as I fought to keep calm and wondered how to best approach Burly's house.

With help, I thought, with help. What was I thinking? I could not do it alone.

I reached the exit for Youngsville and screeched to a halt at a deserted stoplight on the edge of town. Two horses stood in the moonlight behind an electric fence, staring at my Lamborghini with impassive eyes. I grabbed the cellular phone and examined every inch of it, finally noticing a set of upper buttons below the LCD display. After a couple of tries, I figured out that you had to press the "Send" button after dialing the number in order to complete the call.

God was in a good mood that night. Detective Anne Morrow was working the late shift and answered her phone with a businesslike, "Yes?"

My story tumbled out in a confused mishmash of details that left her thoroughly confused.

"What?" she said. "Slow down, Casey. Where are you?"

"In Youngsville," I told her, pulling out onto deserted Main Street and heading toward Burly's house. I gave her as much of the truth as I could. "One of my clients is pinned up in his rural home with an unknown assailant taking potshots at him. I think it's the same person who killed Tom Nash and burned down his house a couple of weeks ago in Durham. You familiar with the case?"

"Sure," Anne said. "Friend of mine in Durham is working it."

"My client is Nash's brother," I lied. "I think he's in real trouble. I'm on my way now, but . . ." I stopped, the enormity of Burly's predicament hitting me.

"But what?" Anne demanded.

"He's paralyzed from the waist down," I explained as I neared the dirt turnoff for Burly's property. "He's going to have trouble getting away quickly."

"Oh, shit," Anne said. "Hang up and get there. Do what you can, but don't tell anyone I said so. I'll call the Franklin County sheriff for you. Tell me where the house is."

I gave her directions and hung up just as I reached the right turn down the rutted lane and nosed the Lamborghini into the thick grove of trees.

"This is insane," I thought as the sports car bounced and squeaked its way from pothole to pothole. Where was an armored car when you needed one? I was a perfect target for anyone lying in wait.

I was thick into the woods and was forced to slow to a crawl along the dirt lane. The moon hovered behind a cloud and the shadowed branches of the heavy overhanging trees reached down like hands in the dark to stroke the roof of the car as I crawled through the thick growth.

I stopped for a moment, planning to roll down the window so I could listen to the night silence outside, hoping to pinpoint where any disturbance—or stalker—might be coming from. The window refused to budge. I tried every button without success and could find no manual override. They were stuck shut. I cursed Jake Talbot's choice in ostentatious cars as I remembered the litany of problems outlined in the *Car & Driver* magazine I'd been reading the night before: windows that stick, leaky roofs, poor handling and, worst of all, bat-wing doors that often won't open. Oh God, it was all I needed, to be stuck in a $320,000 sardine can while Burly lay fifty feet away, just beyond my help.

Unfortunately, I didn't hear sirens in the distance. Trapped or not, I was the only help he had nearby and I had to get to him—if he was still alive.

I cut the engine about thirty yards from his front yard clearing. The darkness of the woods was comforting, until I realized I'd have to crash through the metal security gates since I needed more room to open the car's ridiculous bat-wing doors.

I revved the engine, checked my seatbelt and stomped the gas pedal to the floor. The car leapt forward and crashed though the aluminum gate with the lingering screech of metal ripping metal. The Lamborghini bounced to a stop in Burly's front yard and I cut the engine. The silence was profound. I crouched just below the dashboard, waiting for my eyes to adjust to the darkness. Finally, I slid the sunroof open and listened as the high chirping of the night peepers resumed after the racket I had made. If there was someone out there in the woods, he had been there for a long time. The night animals were unconcerned.

My pupils dilated gradually and I began to make out objects where rough shapes had been: the darkened house, the surrounding hen huts, Burly's van parked beneath the pecan tree, a mound of broken pottery.

There was a lump to one side of the front door and I realized with a pang that it was Zee Zee. From the way his body twisted to one side, head flopped over his stomach, I knew the old hound dog had to be dead. That frosted me big time. I was pretty sure Burly loved that dog more than he cared for most people. Hell, the poor old pooch probably had no teeth left and was too old to be any real danger, unless the killer accidentally tripped over him in the dark. Why go and kill him? Just meanness, I figured, pure meanness. I could feel the rage rising in my gut, overwhelming caution.

Funny how anger can make you both foolish and brave. I ripped the skintight dress I was wearing even further up the side, extending the slit all the way up to my waist until I felt less like a sausage trapped in its casing. I stuck the cellular phone into the back of my industrial strength control-top thigh-cuts and slipped my Colt .25 under the tight elastic waistband near the slit, where I could get to it easily. I tucked an extra clip of ammunition between my pantyhose and underwear, then pressed the button to open the bat-wing doors so I could shoot me a dog killer.

The doors wouldn't budge.

Frustrated, I beat the dashboard with the heel of my hand. Only a jerk like Jake Talbot would drive a piece of shit like this. What was I going to do? I examined the sun roof. I might be able to wiggle out of it but, while I was, I'd be perched on top of the damn car like a mechanical duck in a shooting gallery. Not that I had a choice. I stuck my head out like a prairie dog peeking out of its hole and looked around. All quiet on the western front. I wiggled my shoulders through and prayed my big butt would not choose this time to be a problem. It was like working the cork out of a bottle of wine, but I did manage to claw my way onto the roof without getting a hideful of buckshot. I slid down the front windshield to the hood and dropped to safety between the car and the house.

Ducking low, I crab-walked toward the front stoop and stopped to check on Zee Zee. I ran my hand over his body to be sure he was gone. He had fur like velveteen, cold velveteen. Poor Zee Zee was dead all right and had been for a while. He'd done his best to protect his master, sounding the alarm and standing guard on the front stoop. But he'd died in the line of duty. Sounder would have been proud.

I tensed. It was suddenly quiet. Way, way too quiet. No crickets. No tree frogs. No owls. Nothing but the sound of my heart hammering in my ears.

"Now!" I thought to myself as I threw my body against the front door, hitting it with my shoulder. The air around me exploded as a shot boomed in the clearing and I was showered with shards from the door's stained glass window above. Someone had opened fire from the edge of the woods. I hit the door again with my shoulder and this time the lock tore away from the frame. I rolled forward as the thin wood cracked beneath my weight and I landed hard in the tiled front hallway of the house.

"It's me! It's me!" I said quickly. "It's Casey. Don't shoot."

The sound of a gun hammer cocking in the darkness was not reassuring.

"I'm over here," Burly called out. "On the floor. My wheelchair is between us, so be careful. I had to hit the ground when the first round of gunshot broke out the west windows. I think he was out front and then went around back. I can't figure out what he's doing, why he's walking around the house."

The night wind shifted, sending a gust through one of the broken windows. I sniffed the air. "I know what he's doing," I said grimly as the tang of kerosene filled my nostrils. "We have to get out of here *now*."

Count on me to state the obvious. But how exactly could we get out of there? I wasn't about to sling Burly over my shoulder and make an end run for the car. No way I could shimmy up the hood and dunk him through the sunroof without both of us getting killed.

"Can you drive right now?" I asked. "Do you have the keys?" I knew his van had hand controls and wasn't sure I'd be able to figure them out quickly enough. Burly would have to drive.

"Sure," he promised. "If you can get me to my van, I can get us out of here."

A new gun blast boomed through the house. Wood splintered on the wall behind me. It was followed by another explosion, and a stack of clay pots to my right shattered in a noisy burst.

"Shotgun," I said.

"He has a handgun, too," Burly reported. "I think he's trying to smoke us out with the shotgun and then he's going to pick us off with the pistol."

Good Christ, who were we up against? Buffalo Bill Cody?

"I don't think we can make it to the van," I told Burly. "Not with this idiotic dress I'm wearing." I slid the Colt out of my waistband and took aim at a window, just to feel like I was doing something. Burly lay on the floor beside me, his upper body pressed against mine as we huddled together for courage.

"Cops are on their way now," I whispered. "We're going to have to wait it out. Keep him from torching us until help comes." That meant keeping the killer busy.

I took a pot shot out the window closest to the latest blast just to let the fucker know he wasn't getting a free ride. When a huge boom answered me, shattering the hallway mirror, I quickly reconsidered my strategy. I crawled on my hands and knees toward the center of the room and dragged back as many chairs, pots and end tables as I could grab, piling them in front of Burly like a barricade.

"Got your gun?" I asked.

"You betcha." A click in the darkness told me he was ready to use it. "I've been saving ammo until I can see him. Until now, he's been all over the place."

"Listen," I said, putting my hand on Burly's arm as the faint sound of sirens filtered through the heavily forested acreage. Beneath the thin flannel of Burly's shirt, I could feel his coiled muscles, hard and smooth. They twitched beneath my touch, but I could tell that he was calm. Probably calmer than me.

"It's going to take them awhile to get down that lane," Burly muttered. "If they can even make it. What are they driving?"

"It's deputies," I explained. "As in sedans—and more firepower."

The words were barely out of my mouth when a blast shook the front hallway. The killer was blowing a hole in the front door and all I could think was *"Why?"* Was he planning to come in, guns blazing?

"Stay down," I ordered Burly, as if he had a choice. I scrambled to the foyer and kicked over a long table that held a row of pots, then used it to barricade the door. I shoved it in place, then braced it with a stack of chairs.

"He's moving around to the side," Burly warned me. "I can hear him breathing through the walls. He's pretty winded."

"One person or two?" I asked, sidling along the wall, picking my way through the broken pots, trying to stay quiet but hoping to get a shot off before the killer got a shot in.

"One," Burly whispered. "Just one. Someone big, though, from the sounds of it. Big and out of breath. Zee Zee's not barking. I think something is wrong."

I didn't have the heart to tell him. I was too busy worrying about being blown away through the walls. We were trapped in a flimsy old farmhouse, meant for mild Carolina winters and hot summers. The exterior walls were no more than a single board thick and I could hear the faint crackle of someone in heavy shoes creeping around the corner of the house, only a few feet from where I crouched on the other side. I held my breath, terrified that the unseen killer might start blasting through the wooden planks.

"Look out," Burly yelled. "In the window above you!"

I dove over a mound of pots, hitting my shoulder hard on the wooden floor. I rolled to safety behind the corner of an interior wall that led to the kitchen, but there was no sound of gunshot. It was something far worse. The remaining glass in the window was knocked in by something heavy, like a brick, and the smell of burning kerosene filled the small house.

"Shit, shit, shit, shit," Burly muttered as he crawled on his elbows through the broken pottery toward me. "I think he's getting ready to throw a torch in."

Burly's useless legs whipped back and forth behind him as he clawed his way to the kitchen. He grabbed my arm and we froze, staring at the living room window together. An old glass Pepsi bottle filled with kerosene and stuffed with rags spiraled through the air, almost graceful in its flight, spinning across the shattered debris of what had once been Burly's home, painting the interior with an illuminated arc of light. The flaming rag left a smoky trail that signaled death, yet I found it both terrifying and oddly beautiful.

The bottle exploded against an interior wall, showering the main room floor with droplets of fire that quickly spread in pools and ran in trickles across the floor, igniting lamp shades, throw pillows, magazines and books.

Burly gripped my arm and dragged me deep into the kitchen, as far from the flames as we could get. I stood up for a better look.

"Behind you!" Burly screamed, his gun cocked and ready as he took aim toward the lone kitchen window behind me. I spun around and hit the floor on my stomach, propping myself up on my elbows to take aim. A piece of buckshot whizzed past my head so closely I could hear the whine in my ear. We fired at the same time, our pistols exploding in unison as we blew out the kitchen window and sent someone scurrying for cover in the bushes outside of it.

"Did we get him?" Burly asked.

"Hell if I know. Think I'll make sure." The sounds of the sirens grew louder as I scrambled to a position on the other side of the refrigerator, then jumped up on the kitchen table and poked my hand out the broken window, firing into the bushes.

"This is for the dog, you fucker!" I yelled out into the darkness as I emptied my gun. When all you're waving is a .25, you have to aim for the head and squeeze off as many rounds as you can.

"Jesus, Casey, you're gonna need those bullets," Burly yelled. "Get down or you're gonna get hit."

"No, I'm not," I declared, loading my spare clip into the chamber. I was hoppin' mad now. I leaned out the window, seeking my prey, emboldened by the screeching of the sirens. I was starting to spot the flashing reflections of approaching cars. Red and blue beams swept over the tops of the hardwood and pine trees in an eerily festive dance of color. It looked like half the sheriff cars in Franklin County were tearing down Burly's lane.

I took another shot at the nearest clump of bushes. "Anyone who kills an old dog is a goddamned coward," I yelled out the window. "I'm gonna put a bullet through your yellow hide one day. You understand?" I shot twice more.

The table was pulled out from under me and I nearly cut my arm on a piece of glass as I toppled backward and fell to the floor. Burly gripped my upper arm with incredible strength and dragged me to the floor beside him.

"Get the fuck down, you lunatic," he hissed. "Don't get up until I tell you."

"He killed Zee Zee," I told him between clenched teeth. "And he's damn sure trying to kill us."

"God, you're a hothead," he said in a tone halfway between exasperation and admiration. "I'm sorry about old Zee Zee, but you getting shot right before my eyes isn't going to make it any better."

He pulled me to him and I stopped struggling, aware that my mouth was only inches from his. Behind us, in the living room, the fire had reached the couch and flames were starting to build. Heavy black smoke billowed toward the shattered windows and the smells of melting plastic and burning fabric filled the air. We huddled face-to-face in the flickering darkness as the sound of screaming sirens grew louder. The shadows of flames danced across the angular planes of Burly's face and his eyes burned as dark and bright as the fire behind us. I could feel my heart beating against my dress, just inches from the beating of his heart.

"Is that your pulse?" I asked, placing my palm against his breast bone, feeling his heart hammering beneath my touch.

"Yup. Contrary to popular belief, I have a heart," he whispered back. His hands slid down the long length of my dress and he pulled the fabric upward, trailing his fingers along the muscles in my thighs. He paused. "What the hell is this?" He pulled the cellular phone out from where I had tucked it into the back of my panties and held it up. "You are weird, Casey," he said, shaking his head. "Really weird."

The moment had passed. "Much as I like this position," I told him, "we're gonna die if we don't move soon." Obviously, the cop cars had reached the clearing. I could hear the crash of metal meeting metal, and the sirens sounded like they were going off inside my head.

"Wait for the cops to actually set foot in this damn house," Burly ordered me. "We've gotten this far. Let's keep it together. Stay low and you'll be able to breathe."

The crackle of police radio static mingled with the pop of the flames that were rapidly building in the living room. Someone coughed outside the front door. "Anyone in there?" a deep male voice called out.

"In here!" I yelled. "To the right of the front door." I heard thumpings and crashes as the deputies tried to break through the makeshift barricade. There was no time to wait. I rolled Burly over on his stomach and tried to remember how Doodle used to sling me over his shoulder and march around my bedroom.

"Hold on," I said to Burly, grunting as I lifted his dead weight. God, please help me, I prayed, and while I'm at it, thank you for the thunder thighs. I slung him over one shoulder, staggering into the wall as I veered and bounced my way through the smoke to the front door. The smoke was inescapable and it clogged my throat in a thick, choking ball. I'd only gotten a few yards when bodies crashed through the barricade and hands reached out to help me, taking Burly from my arms and supporting me as I stumbled from the house. The cool air outside hit me like a spray of water and I gulped in the fresh oxygen.

"He's paralyzed," I croaked inaudibly to two deputies who were trying to stand Burly on his feet and getting nowhere. He kept crumpling to the ground and being hoisted aloft again. Burly wasn't helping any, either. He was starting to laugh hysterically and I was beginning to wonder if he had lost it.

"I'm cured!" Burly yelled, arms outstretched, as one of the deputies propped him against a tree only to gawk as Burly slid to his butt in a hydrangea bush.

I coughed up smoke and spit out a wad of gunk. "He can't walk!" I screamed to the deputy. "His wheelchair's inside!"

Slow on the uptake or not, the deputy was brave. He headed right back into the fire, returning a minute later with Burly's wheelchair still in one piece. Part of the backing was scorched, and a bullet hole had pierced the leather right where Burly's heart would have been had he still been sitting in the chair when the shot was fired.

"Thank God," Burly said. "It's my lucky day."

Was he out of his mind? I stared at him and he grinned, his white teeth a Cheshire cat semicircle in the dark-sooted mask of his face.

"It took months for the factory to custom-build my chair," he explained cheerfully as he was helped into it and we were hustled far from the flames of the house. The fire was spreading rapidly now, devouring eaves, licking at the hen houses, blowing out what was left of the glass windows, exploding unseen bottles with a rapid series of pops.

"Oh, God." I stared back at the flames. "All your pottery."

Burly was wheeling himself to the edge of the clearing. "Forget it all," he said, without even looking back. "Tomorrow is another day."

Burly had been right about the dirt road. The fire trucks couldn't get down it. There was nothing to do but watch the wooden structure and surrounding hen houses burn to the ground while the deputies and arriving volunteers dug a fire trench around the property and formed an old-fashioned bucket brigade that stretched from the pond on the far side of the smoldering hen houses into Burly's front yard. Old Zee Zee was gone, his body removed by some official who either had a practical streak or a soft heart.

I sat next to Burly on a stump that was pitted with deep slashes from where it had once been used for splitting logs. I was exhausted. It was all I could do to keep the strapless bodice of my tattered dress from falling around my waist. Anything else was beyond me.

"We need some marshmallows," Burly decided. He sat content in his wheelchair, watching the flames as they climbed into the night sky. He felt it, too, that hypnotic effect that the fire seemed to hold for us all.

"You seem mighty cheerful for someone who's seeing his whole life go up in smoke," I said. We were holding hands, like seventh-graders at a weenie roast.

"I've had worse things happen to me," Burly explained.

"And now's as good a time as any to start over." He smiled at me. "You saved my life."

"Any time," I told him, then paused. "Except never again, okay?"

"Okay."

We stared at the flames for a few moments without speaking. I was the one who broke the silence.

"Where are you staying tonight?" I asked him.

"With you," he said happily.

"Good," I said. "I need a ride. That Lamborghini is a piece of shit. And no wonder. It belongs to Lydia's brother."

Burly looked over at it. "I don't think he's going to be too happy about its present condition."

"What do you mean?"

"It looks like three deputy cars ran right up its ass."

He was right. The Lamborghini had been rear-ended by at least three of the sedans barreling into the clearing. The first crash had apparently caused the bat-wing doors to finally open, and they had lifted skyward just in time to be clipped off by more arriving cars.

What was left of the chassis gleamed richly in the reflected glare of the fire. The sleek red body was crumpled but still obviously expensive, its ostentatious glory dwarfed by the practical lines of the surrounding police cars, like some rich cocaine kingpin flanked by a phalanx of weary flatfoots.

"Who did this to us?" I wondered out loud, staring at the fire. "And what the hell is going on?"

"I'm being purified," Burly answered. "That's what's going on." He stretched his arms out wide, as if the heat of the night were not enough and he needed the warmth of the fire. "Ashes to ashes and dust to dust."

"If the killer can't get you, then I guess I must," I added, poking his ribs.

"Come and get me anytime," he agreed with a grin.

"Someone want to tell me what the hell is going on?" a voice boomed out behind us. "And if the two of you are okay."

I'd never met the Franklin County sheriff before and,

under other circumstances, might have considered him a fine specimen of Homo sapiens, preferably erectus. He was middle-aged, with thick dark hair going gray at the temples and a very nice body beneath a clean-pressed uniform. But that night, I wouldn't have cared if he had looked like Gregory Peck and Antonio Banderas all rolled into one. I was grateful, however, that he was treating us as victims instead of suspects. It may have had something to do with the upcoming election and the fact that Burly did live, vote and pay taxes in his county.

It took half an hour to go through our story and the sheriff listened carefully without interrupting. I got to hear Burly's version of events, from start to finish: he'd been sitting quietly, reading with Zee Zee at his feet, when the hang-up calls began. Then, the old dog had grown restless. Burly let him outdoors for a quick break, but the hound refused to come back inside. He kept standing at attention near the front door, occasionally letting out a soft growl. This was enough unlike Zee Zee to make Burly start to get nervous. He'd watched out a window for a while, noticing only that more birds than usual were taking off from their roosts among the trees and that the usual forest sounds had given way to disturbed rustlings and warning cries. At first he'd thought it might be a black bear passing through; they were not unheard of it in the Piedmont area of North Carolina. They sometimes wandered in from the east, despite all the real estate development of recent years. He doubted it was a bear, however, since he couldn't smell one and since Zee Zee was not exactly the type to hang around when one was headed his way. Then Burly began to hear the crackle of twigs being stepped on in the woods and grew alarmed, thinking poachers might be on his land—or worse. When the electricity went off, he decided to call me. He was too embarrassed to phone the cops right away, he explained. He thought maybe he was overreacting.

I thought maybe he was looking for an excuse to call me.

But then a shotgun blast shattered the first window and the phone line was cut in the middle of our conversation. That was when he'd known he was in real trouble. He'd hit the ground, gotten his gun and extra ammo out of the wheelchair's storage box and held on until I arrived.

The sheriff looked at me like he couldn't understand why anyone in his right mind would call me for help. That was when I remembered I was wearing a strapless jade dress torn to the waist and covered with soot and grime. I looked like a cross-dressing chimney sweep.

"I don't usually dress like this," I explained. "I was at a debutante ball."

This only made the sheriff stare even harder. I had the urge to whip out my Colt and nail a few trees just to prove my self-worth, but wisely contained myself. He'd already examined my fake P.I. license a little longer than was comfortable given my paranoid state. I wasn't anxious to belabor the topic of my occupation and credentials.

"Where can I reach you in case I have more questions?" he asked. I gave him my home and office numbers, then he turned to Burly. "What about you?"

We looked at each other and Burly shrugged.

"Just call me," I told the sheriff. "I'll find him."

"I just bet you will," the sheriff said, smiling enigmatically. He closed up his notebook and stared at the fire, then pushed his hat back and scratched his forehead. "You two both look pretty bad off. Want a lift to Wake Med?"

We assured him that, under no circumstances, were we headed that way. Neither one of us relished a night spent watching drunks and drug addicts stagger off the streets and into our view. Nor were we in the mood to answer more questions.

"He can go home with me. I'll take good care of him," I volunteered, wheeling Burly toward his van.

"I just bet you will," the sheriff answered with the same maddening smile.

"What is with that guy?" I complained as I climbed in the passenger seat and waited for Burly to maneuver his way on board. I knew better than to help him.

"He's got your number," Burly said cheerfully. "Like I said, Casey, you can run, but you cannot hide."

A prickle of annoyance rippled through me, but at the very same time, I felt like throwing back my head and laughing. Something about Burly got under my skin but when it did, it burrowed straight for all the right parts.

It took a while to inch the van through the crowded yard and out the narrow lane, but Burly was content to take his time. He was whistling, seemingly oblivious to the fact that his house was now a burning pile of rubble behind us.

"Jesus," I complained. "You're about the most cheerful person I've ever seen in the face of disaster."

"Disaster?" he said, smiling at me. "This is the best thing that has happened to me in years. Did you see how we blew out that kitchen window together? Man, we were incredible. I could tell what you were thinking the second you thought it. We make a great team."

We said little after that. I didn't even ask why he stopped the van at Wake Med after all, then disappeared inside for half an hour and returned with a large plastic bag full of strangely shaped objects that my nosy inner child longed to snoop through. No such luck.

"Mind your own business," he said when he caught me looking. He stored the bag under his seat. "Take it from me, you don't want to know."

"Who cleaned you up?" I asked, noticing that his face had been wiped free of soot and grime, his cuts cleaned and his hair washed.

"Debbie," he said, lifting his eyebrows and wiggling them. "Night nurse in the ER. I know her from my check-up visits here."

I stared at him for a moment without speaking, taking in his satisfied smile. "They just love you, don't they?" I finally said, disgusted. "All those nurses. They wait on you hand and foot, swab you down with wet washcloths and eat you up with a spoon. I am sitting next to the poster boy for paraplegics."

He shrugged. "I can't help it if the nurses love me. You gotta admit it, I'm kind of cute when you get right down to it." He was teasing me, but I was too irritated by the thought of some overripe blonde in a tight white dress lathering up his torso to be a good sport about it.

"What is it with nurses?" I complained irritably. "Stick

a white dress on a woman and the men go gaga, never mind if she has a face like a baboon's butt and a build like Jabba the Hut.''

"Debbie has neither," he said smugly.

"Shut up about Debbie," I ordered him. "Take me home and swab me down. I'm the one who did all the work back there."

"That's cute," he said, pulling out onto New Bern Avenue. "You're jealous. I didn't know you cared."

"Actually, I'm too tired to care," I said, leaning my head back against the seat and yawning as a wave of weariness overtook me. "And I am *so* damn tired of wearing this dress."

"Can't say I've ever seen anything like it," he agreed. "That is one mangled, ugly dress." He paused for the punch line. "But it looks good on you."

"Fuck off." For an all-purpose expression, it was hard to beat.

"You can take it off right now, if you want," he offered. "Or the second we get to your apartment. I think a hot bath is in order, don't you?"

I glanced at him, wondering what he was up to. "Burly . . ." my voice trailed off. "Don't go getting any ideas, now. I'm too tired to move."

He sighed contentedly. "I'm not planning to climb in the tub with you, Casey. All I'm asking from you is to borrow your bathroom for fifteen minutes, all by my little old self, along with a washcloth, towel and a sinkful of warm water. Followed by the loan of half your bed tonight. I wouldn't dream of asking for more."

That was annoying. Wasn't he even going to *try*?

"Then why are you so cheerful?" I asked.

"Because," he explained, "it has taken me only forty-eight hours to not only get into your bed, but also get inside your head." He looked over at me and grinned. "Considering what a hard head you have, I consider that quite an accomplishment."

TWELVE

I woke late the next morning and lay contentedly in bed beside Burly, my head resting on his chest. His face looked different when it was still; it seemed softer and lacked the hard lines that his leanness lent him when he was awake. His eyelashes fluttered and his eyes twitched beneath the lids. I wondered if he was dreaming of running—or maybe of what it had been like when he was still able to make love.

I thought about that for a moment until my curiosity got the best of me. Moving slowly so as not to waken him, I lifted the sheet and peered beneath it at his legs, wondering what it was like to feel no life in them. He was wearing a pair of plaid boxer shorts I'd lent him and he had wrapped a hand towel around his colostomy bag, which was fine with me. Even *my* curiosity has its limits. His legs didn't look all that shriveled, like I thought they might, though they were on the skinny side and nowhere near as developed as his torso and arms.

He caught me peeking. "Casey, honey," he drawled sleepily. "The South is going to rise again before that thing does."

I dropped the covers, embarrassed. "Sorry, I was just being nosy."

"No problem, but I'm going to have to claim my right to look in return." He lifted the sheets and peered down at my legs. I was wearing nothing but an oversized T-shirt—

hey, I gotta air it out sometime—and it had bunched around my waist in the middle of the night.

"My God," he said in a soft voice. "But that is a beautiful sight."

The lower part of my body melted in a puddle, but my head took flight. "It's late," I said, rolling for the safety of the bedroom floor. I stood up and stretched, which was stupid, since it only provided Burly with another peek.

"Quit looking at me," I complained.

His laughter made the whole bed shake. "I feel pretty good right now, Casey. I'm going to sit here and watch you get dressed. You don't mind, do you?"

"Look away," I agreed. "But in return, I want a shoulder massage. It's killing me. I busted down about three doors and hit the ground twice last night. It's a wonder I didn't dislocate it."

"Sit here," he ordered, patting the bed beside him.

I crawled up on the bed and sat Indian-style beside Burly while he massaged the muscles in my back. I let out a groan of contentment. "You have incredible hands," I admitted, then froze as an unbidden and graphic image unfolded in my mind, a pornographic preview of exactly what those hands could do. A wave of heat washed over me.

"You okay?" Burly asked gently. "Did I hit a nerve?"

"No, no," I managed to murmur. "I'm okay." I was floating on a wave of contentment, wondering what had brought the two of us together.

"I'm so sorry about your brother," I said suddenly, my words a surprise to us both. "But I'm glad we met each other."

His hands encircled my body as he pulled me close and held me there. "That's one reason I like you so much, Casey. You never really knew my brother, but you sure have taken his death personally. Everyone else says how sorry they are and blah, blah, bah. But you're not going to quit until you find out who did it, are you?"

"Nope," I promised. "I'm not."

"He was a good guy," Burly said, his voice breaking. "I can't think of anyone who would want him to die."

"Maybe they didn't want to get your brother," I told

him. "Maybe they really wanted to get Randolph Talbot. To ruin his reputation."

He was still, thinking about it and, when he spoke, I heard the anger in his voice. "My brother better have died for a more important reason than that. Find out for me, Casey. Please? I need you to do that for me."

"I will," I promised, overcome with a sudden urge to make him smile. I wiggled out of his embrace, got too close to the edge of the bed and tumbled to the floor. "Want some coffee?" I asked from my spot on the carpet.

"Sure," he agreed, laughing. "But better make it ice water if you plan to flash me like that again."

I struggled to my feet and primly tugged on my night shirt. "Milk or sugar?"

"Both. I guess that means I get to sit here and let you wait on me hand and foot. Got a white dress and stethoscope you can squeeze into?"

I ignored him. He leaned against the headboard, watching, as I raced around my tiny apartment doing things that would keep me away from the bed. For a man who couldn't walk, he always seemed to be one step ahead of me. The fact that he was calm only made me more nervous. I had this awful feeling that I was in a fight being fought with weapons I had never seen before. He was winning, and I was still trying to figure out the best way to approach the battle.

"You have a million phone messages," he pointed out helpfully when I brought him a cup of Carolina latte (that's when you shake the milk carton really, really hard before you pour the froth on top of strong coffee).

I stared at the blinking light, then reluctantly turned up the volume on the answering machine and played the messages back. Time to get back to real life. Bobby D. had checked in to make sure I was okay and Lydia had called three times, first wanting to know if Burly was safe, then demanding to know what the hell was going on and finally asking if I could meet with her and her father at noon. We had been summoned.

I had less than an hour to dress and shake the fog from my brain. I called Lydia and arranged to meet her at her father's office a few minutes before noon, then chugged a cup of coffee. Thank God I had showered the night before, savoring the water against my skin, the washing away of soot and grime.

"Wonder why Talbot wants a meeting?" I said as I sat in a chair and tugged on a pair of black stretch jeans that had fit perfectly three trips to Biscuitville ago.

"Something to do with money?" Burly guessed.

"Now what would make you say a thing like that?" Of course it had to do with money. Randolph Talbot didn't think about anything else.

"Do you really think someone is setting him up?" Burly asked.

"I do," I admitted. "Too neat for me. Life is messy."

"Then I'm going to tell my parents to drop the case against him," Burly said suddenly. "Besides, suing Talbot won't bring Tom back. My parents have been talked into it by some lawyer. I don't think their hearts are in it. Once they find out Tom was engaged to Lydia, they'll drop the suit against her father. That's the kind of people they are. You'd understand if you'd ever met them. Want to?"

"Don't go there," I warned him. But then I thought over what he had said. "You're sure they would drop the lawsuit?"

He nodded. "If Tom loved Lydia Talbot and she loved him, they're not going to cause her any more pain than what she's already gone through."

I thought about it. The attacks against both Lydia and Burly had escalated after the new lawsuit was announced. Maybe they were connected. "Where are your parents now?" I asked.

"I don't know. I talked to them yesterday at my aunt's, but they were leaving there early this morning." Burly watched me slide a knit top over my sports bra. "You are built like a brick shithouse," he said appreciatively.

"That's very romantic," I conceded. "Next you'll be telling me that I don't sweat much for a fat girl."

He grinned. "Stick around and I'll show you my idea of sweet nothings. Hey, it's Sunday morning. Let's stay in bed and eat doughnuts and read the newspaper together."

I threw a pillow at him. "Get up. Or whatever it is that you do. And get dressed. I rinsed your shirt and jeans out and hung them over the shower rod to dry. You're welcome, by the way, but that's the extent of my domestication. I have an appointment with Randolph Talbot at noon. Do you have anywhere to stay? Someplace to go? A nurse to wow, perhaps?"

"I'm going to head out to my parents' house and call around for them from there, see if I can track them down and talk to them about the lawsuit. Then I think I'll start looking for an apartment, while I decide what to do next."

"Look near Durham," I told him, pulling on my boots. "It's cheaper to me."

"Nearer to you, too," he offered, unwilling to let even the slightest of Freudian slips slide by. He positioned his wheelchair beside the bed, checking inside the storage compartment for his gun before he sidled onto the seat.

"Burly," I said. "I can't believe you're carrying your gun around like that. It's dangerous. Any crackhead could take it from you."

"I have a permit," he said. "What's the big deal? It helped save your ass last night. Besides, you think people here are too nice to rob a cripple? Think again. I'm easy pickins. At least I am without old Jesse by my side." He admired his Colt .45 and checked the chamber to make sure it was loaded, then stowed it back inside the storage box.

"You could stop a buffalo with that thing," I said, somewhat jealous.

He smiled. "Get out your Colt. I'll show you mine if you'll show me yours."

I ignored the invitation. "Don't go blaming me when you shoot your foot off."

"At least it won't hurt if I do," he countered.

I guess he had to make jokes like that before someone else did. But I didn't think they were funny. "Aren't you worried about your parents?" I asked, changing the subject. "Hasn't it been a couple of days since they've been home?"

He shrugged. "They're just hiding out from the press.

They hate attention. I'm going to call their lawyer today. He'll know where they are."

"Who's their lawyer?" I asked curiously.

"Same guy that was representing Tom before," Burly said. "Which makes sense. He already has the evidence and everything."

"Harry Ingram?" I asked, gulping down my second cup of coffee. No wonder he was so fucking jolly. "Since when?"

Burly shrugged. "I don't know. Mom told me yesterday."

"Who hired who?" I asked.

Burly shrugged. "I'm pretty sure he contacted my parents first. Or maybe he was at Tom's funeral, I can't remember. But looking up a lawyer is not something my parents would do on their own. They live their lives scared of making waves. They'd be too frightened of what Talbot might do in retaliation to think of suing him on their own. I suspect they were talked into it."

That explained why Ingram had leaked information to me. He wanted me to strengthen his case for him without having to pay me for it. What a guy.

"In that case, I think I saw your parents in Ingram's office," I said, checking the clip on my .25 before making sure my mascara wasn't running down my face. If you're forced to kick ass, why not look good doing it? "I interviewed him yesterday and saw two older people in the lobby. They had white hair, clothes from Sears, sensible glasses, no signs of overeating, matching Hush Puppies."

"That sounds like them," Burly said, interested. "Did they look like they had never even committed so much as a misdemeanor in their lives? That they sat in the front row of church every Sunday, tight-lipped and pissed that the world around them was full of sinners?"

"Yup. That was them."

"They're good people," he said after a moment of shared silence. "They're just a little inflexible."

"Don't apologize to me," I said. "They seemed like good country people. My kind of people. I wasn't making fun of them."

Burly was quiet, probably lost in thought about all the ways he had disappointed his well-meaning but perpetually disapproving parents over the years.

I brought him his clothes and made myself scarce in the kitchen while he dressed, then wheeled him out to his van. I was glad I lived on the ground floor so we could avoid an argument about helping him up or down the stairs.

"Nice car," he said, admiring my Porsche. "A classic. You ever work on it yourself?"

"Sometimes," I said. "Little things. Mostly I take it into my friend Jimbo down at Faircloth's."

I stood beside the van as Burly activated the mini-lift and pulled himself behind the wheel. I was willing to settle for a handshake, even, but he just shut the door in my face. "Thanks for the save, Casey," he said, cheerful once again.

"That's it?" I complained. "I ruin my best evening dress saving your ass and that's it? Not even a high five?"

"That wasn't your dress," he pointed out. "Not your style. And I've been thinking about us. I decided that if you want anything else from me, you'll have to come right out and ask for it. Sorry. But I know you better than you think, and whether or not to get involved with me is one hurdle you're going to have to get over on your own."

"What's that mean?" I asked, outraged. He was out-flanking me again.

"It means I'm not in the business of convincing people to care for me. You know who and what I am. Take it or leave it. Let me know when you decide."

I wanted to get mad at him, but Burly followed this pronouncement with a smile that made my stomach flip-flop and then took off down the road.

I had a feeling that I had just been played as smoothly as a trout being brought to shore by a master fisherman. I hopped in my Porsche and zipped past Burly at a light—just to let him know that he could eat my dust—and cut him off at the next turn. He didn't react exactly as I hoped. He started honking his horn and waving an arm out his window, then chased me down at the next light.

"What?" I asked him. "Change your mind?"

"Something's the matter with your alignment," he said.

"You've got a shimmy in the front and something shiny flew out into the street when you accelerated at that last turn. You better take a look."

"Yeah, right," I said skeptically.

"Casey." He shook his head, exasperated. "Someone tried to kill us last night. And now I think your car is driving funny. If you don't think there might be a connection, then you're not as smart as I give you credit for. For all you know, there's a bomb under the chassis. Use your head and quit acting so macho."

He roared off without a backward glance, leaving me to deal with it on my own. I wanted to deck him, but I couldn't exactly figure out why.

The fact of the matter was that I *was* as smart as he gave me credit for. I got the hell out of the car and called my friend Jimbo, who arrived in ten minutes and examined the underside before assuring me that no bombs were present.

While he checked it again, I searched the road for the shiny object Burly had seen flying from underneath the car. It took a couple of minutes of dodging traffic, but I finally found a large bolt in the street about a block behind me and brought it back to show to Jimbo.

He was hooking my Porsche up to his tow truck so he could haul it back to his shop for a better look. I handed him the bolt. He turned it over in his hands.

"This here looks like a bolt from one of your CV joints," he told me.

"So?"

"So, that's what connects your transmission to the wheel, Casey. If your CV joints fail, your car's gonna fall apart and that's not something you'd want to have happen on the highway at a high speed, know what I mean?"

I knew what he meant. "Find out if that's what it is," I told him.

"Sure," he agreed. "Call me later on this afternoon."

With my car out of commission, I hoofed it over to T&T Tobacco, but not even a hike calmed me down. I was nervous about the meeting with Randolph Talbot. So was Lydia. I met her outside the elevators in the deserted lobby and we rode up together, exchanging no more than a few muttered words about the night before. I started to tell her what her brother, Jake, had done the night before, but she looked like she had enough problems, so I kept quiet about it. If the grapevine didn't pick up that half the debs had puked their guts out at the end of the ball, I wasn't going to spill the beans. Maybe people would chalk it up to an epidemic of bulimia, anyway. I did tell Lydia about the Lamborghini, however, and she took the news about her brother's car being destroyed calmly. She mostly seemed relieved that Burly was okay.

"I never got a chance to meet him," she said. "But Tom loved him a lot. He said that Burly was a really brave guy, his hero even. He admired the way he had turned his life around after the accident that paralyzed him."

This was a side of Burly I had never really considered, what with my being too busy fighting him and all. I guess she had a point.

"What do you think this meeting is about?" I asked as we approached the twelfth floor.

"Your guess is as good as mine." She was biting her lower lip nervously and her makeup was sloppy. I realized that she had a lot more to lose during this meeting than I did. I hoped to God her father wasn't about to confess.

There was no sneaking into the inner sanctum for me this time. Randolph Talbot's secretary practically carried me and Lydia across the threshold in her arms, then fussed around us, taking coffee and soda orders until I wanted to swat her. She finally departed with an obsequious nod. Old Talbot must have paid her pretty well to have her there on a Sunday, kissing ass so religiously.

"This is my lawyer, Robert Klein," Lydia's father explained, gesturing toward a thin man who was wearing a four-thousand-dollar suit, two-thousand-dollar shoes and a ten-cent smile. He was sitting in a deep, coffee-colored leather chair. His long legs were crossed and a thin cigarette dangled from one hand.

"I thought your lawyer had a fat red neck and was about two cheeseburgers away from a heart attack," I said.

Talbot did not smile. "I have retained special counsel in

the matter of the civil lawsuits filed against me and my company a few days ago,'' he explained evenly.

''So that's what this meeting is about,'' I said, resisting the urge to add ''Aha!''

Talbot's eyes narrowed. ''What else would this meeting be about?'' he asked.

I shrugged. ''You tell me.'' I had an inexplicable desire to make this as difficult on him as possible. Maybe it was some misguided attempt to protect Lydia, but I was desperately afraid that he was about to hurt his daughter very deeply.

''Why don't we make this quick?'' Talbot's lawyer suggested as he smoothly flicked open a gold cigarette case with one hand and extracted a fresh smoke without offering either me or Lydia one. ''We're both very busy men.''

I looked at Lydia and shrugged. ''Suits us. We're both very busy women.''

Lydia stared straight ahead without speaking.

''I have an announcement that I would like the two of you to hear before I release it publicly,'' Talbot said to me, avoiding his daughter's gaze. ''But before I go into details, I would like for you to answer some questions, Miss Jones, for the benefit of my daughter.''

I jumped when he said my name. I couldn't help it. He had a way of spitting it out that made you think he was one step away from hitting you with it.

''Fire away,'' I said, perhaps a poor choice of words.

''In the course of your investigation, have you uncovered a shred of evidence that would indicate that I was involved in the death of Thomas Nash in any way, either directly or indirectly?''

I pretended to think it over. It didn't make him sweat.

''No, I have not,'' I finally said. ''I have seen some evidence, but I believe it was manufactured.''

''Have you uncovered any evidence that would lead you to believe I attempted to influence his relationship with my daughter in any way?'' he then asked.

''Well,'' I began, wondering how to word it. ''It depends on how you—''

''What Mr. Talbot means,'' his lawyer interrupted, ''is

whether or not you have any reason to believe he discouraged Thomas Nash from seeing Lydia.''

"No, I have not," I said truthfully. "Nor have I uncovered any evidence that Thomas Nash was unfaithful to Lydia or anything but a deeply caring fiancé."

Lydia's eyes had glazed over and I wasn't sure how much she was hearing.

"Have you uncovered anything that would lead you to believe I ordered anyone else to harm Thomas Nash?" Randolph Talbot persisted.

I shook my head no. What was he getting at?

"Do you personally believe I had anything to do with it?" he asked me, showing me he had some guts after all.

"No, I do not," I admitted. "I think you were set up."

Talbot let out a long sigh, one of the first signs since I had met him that he was human after all. He seemed to grow smaller then, maybe a few years older, too, as if he had been somehow humbled by admitting that my answer mattered.

"Did you hear that, Lydia?" he asked.

"Yes," she said, the single syllable ringing through the room.

"Does it convince you at all that I am innocent of having had anything to do with the death of the man you loved?" Talbot asked her, and though he tried to sound authoritative and in control, his words trembled as he spoke.

Lydia stared at me for a long time, as if I were the suspect and not her father. Perhaps she was trying to decide if she could trust my judgment after all. Or, maybe, she had simply taken too much Valium that morning.

"Yes," she finally said. "That does convince me."

"Good." Talbot settled back in his chair. His lawyer emitted a nearly inaudible grunt and uncrossed his legs. Now the games could begin.

"I want there to be no misunderstanding about what I'm going to tell you next," Talbot said.

I knew what was coming an instant before the words left his lips.

"I am going to settle the two lawsuits with the family

of Thomas Nash,'' Talbot said. "For sixteen million. It will
be announced in the press tomorrow.''

"What?'' Lydia asked, looking from her father to his
lawyer. "You just said you were innocent.''

"Innocence, unfortunately, has nothing to do with the
law,'' Talbot's lawyer jumped in, using his most pompous
courtroom voice. Where was a paperweight when you
wanted one? The man needed a good beating about the
arms and face.

"It's a business decision,'' I interrupted, just to let them
know that I was no stranger to corporate-speak.

"Exactly.'' Talbot gave me a grudging glance. "The
Nashes have agreed to settle for less than one-tenth of the
original amount and my insurance company has advised me
to take the deal. They will cover the entire amount if I do,
both my personal and corporate liability. The risk of fighting the matter in front of a jury is simply unacceptable. As
your friend Miss Jones has said, I have been set up and the
evidence, while manufactured, may nonetheless be convincing.''

So now I was his daughter's friend, Miss Jones, eh? It
would be Casey and Randy next.

Lydia looked at me for guidance.

"It will keep your name out of the newspapers,'' I explained.

"Exactly.'' Talbot's lawyer beamed at me. I was such a
quick study. And I'd taken the bait with an open mouth,
too.

Fuck him and the horse he rode in on. "What do you
want from me?'' I demanded.

All three of them stared at me.

"What is it?'' I insisted. "You didn't summon me here
to be polite. What do you want from me?''

The lawyer's nose wrinkled in distaste at my approach,
but Talbot couldn't have cared less.

"I want you to drop the investigation,'' Lydia's father
said.

"Why?'' I asked, wondering how much he knew about
how very little I'd gathered in my so-called investigation.

"Because it is time to let this thing die,'' he said, not

even noticing that his choice of words made his daughter wince. "My family has been through enough. It's time we got back to normal. I will not tolerate a continuing cloud of suspicion over our heads." He appealed to his daughter. "Lydia, darling, I don't know who killed Tom or why, and there is nothing I can say or do that will bring him back to you. But sixteen million is a lot of money and his parents are donating the entire amount of their proceeds to a foundation to educate children against smoking. The money will go to a good cause. Someone *has* paid for his death. I have paid for his death. Please accept the situation as over. Our family has gone through enough."

Don't do it, Lydia, I willed her silently. *Grow a backbone, girl, grow a backbone.*

She was staring at her father. As an outsider, I could not even begin to fathom what unspoken message was passing between them. I would never know, I realized. I lived in a different world.

"All right," she said calmly, rising to go. "Come on, Casey. We can have a cup of coffee and settle up your fee."

"No need," the lawyer interrupted smoothly. He was a human snake with a rattle so faint you'd never notice it until he bit you. He passed me a white linen envelope. "I'm sure this will more than take care of her fees and expenses."

I should have crumpled it up in a ball and bounced it off his condescending forehead. But if I did that, I'd never know what price Talbot thought I could be bought for—and that was something I had to know. Clearly, he assumed I was a whore. Whether I was an expensive one or your garden variety street walker remained to be seen.

"A pleasure doing business with you," I said calmly, accepting the envelope and joining Lydia at the office door.

The two men watched us go without comment.

We rode down in the elevator in silence, then walked to Main Street, still without a word. "Okay," I finally said. "What gives?"

Lydia sighed. "My father is right. Nothing is going to bring Tom back. It's time to let it go."

"How can you say that?" I asked angrily. "Don't you want to know who killed him?"

"I thought I did," she said, then her voice slowed. "But now I'm not so sure." She looked at the envelope in my hand. "Does that cover it?" she asked.

I pulled open the flap and peeked inside. "Yup," I said. "That covers it. And then some."

"Cash the check," Lydia ordered me. "You earned it. Take my father's conscience money. If you don't want it, give it away. Or use it to forget you ever knew a Talbot. This family is nothing but bad luck."

She turned around and walked away, leaving me holding a check for $25,000 in my hand.

"How much?" Bobby D. asked me again, still incredulously, when I told him about the payoff on Monday morning. "That's a lot of money." He whistled as visions of expensive spy devices danced in his head.

"Yeah," I agreed. "So what did I find out that's making Randolph Talbot so nervous? Hell if I know what it is."

Bobby D. considered the problem. "Who have you been looking at?"

"No one," I admitted. "I've been too busy protecting Lydia from threats, wearing stupid-looking dresses and pulling people out of fires."

"Does Talbot know that?"

"I don't think so. I get the feeling Lydia's not telling him much."

Bobby chewed thoughtfully on a licorice stick. Bits of black candy studded his teeth like he'd been eating ants. "Have you said anything to Talbot that might have tipped your hand or given him an idea of what you were up to?" he asked.

I shook my head. "Nope. Yesterday, I said jack shit to him. When I saw him the night before, I kept it quick. Before that, I was my usual smart mouth, but I didn't give away any information."

"You saw him the night of the shindig?" Bobby asked.

"Yeah. While you were romancing your future ex-wife, I was on the job. I followed Jake Talbot to the parking lot and ran into his father on the way back in. He was standing on the sidewalk smoking a cigar and looking important.''

Bobby wagged the licorice stick at me. "Well, there you have it, Casey. He saw you following his son. *Capiche*?''

I capiched. "He thinks his son has something to do with it, and wants to stop me from looking at him further," I realized.

"You got it. So what are you going to do?" Bobby asked.

"Follow his son around," I said. "Of course."

"Of course," Bobby agreed.

One thing Bobby D. and I both believe is that money ought to mean nothing when it comes to the law. Randolph Talbot was hoping to buy his son's way out of trouble and that only made us more determined to nail the spoiled little brat. If he'd had anything to do with Nash's death, I would get Jake Talbot.

It would cause Lydia pain but, on the other hand, her little brother Haydon would probably rejoice.

"I don't have much on him," I admitted. "Only the fact that I can't stand his snotty rich ass, that he's downright cruel to his little brother and that he zoomed off with Franklin Cosgrove last night after meeting with some tall drug dealer in the parking lot.''

"You sure it was a drug dealer?" Bobby asked.

I nodded. "The guy handed over something to Jake in exchange for cash, and he was wearing a top hat with a striped shirt like a poker dealer in an old-time saloon. What self-respecting black guy in Raleigh, North Carolina would wear something like that unless he was a dealer?''

"I know that guy," Bobby D. sputtered, little bits of black licorice tumbling from his mouth as he spoke. "He's a fixture at the Pony Express. I ought to know. I spent two nights there secretly taping the joint.''

"You sure?" I asked skeptically. I'd forgotten that Bobby had spent Thursday and Friday nights playing tourist at a gay bar while I was out battling killers.

"I'm sure," Bobby insisted. "You never see him without that hat. Look, Casey, it makes sense. The Pony Express is only a block from Memorial Auditorium. The guy probably *is* a drug dealer who works out of the bar, and if he's Jake Talbot's connection . . .'' His voice trailed off and he looked at me, eyebrows raised.

"I don't think so," I said firmly. "I saw Jake boffing some babe behind a sofa with my own eyes, and if you're insinuating that Franklin Cosgrove is his boyfriend, forget it. I have lots of proof he's just a plain old heterosexual slimeball, though in my humble opinion he'd screw a poodle if it stayed still long enough."

"So what are the two of them doing together?" Bobby asked.

"Drugs," I told him. "That has to be it. They're drug buddies. Birds of a feather snorting coke together."

"So find the dealer and ask."

"Are you sure it's the same guy?" I said.

"See for yourself." Bobby hefted himself from his chair and trundled over to an empty desk against one wall. He slipped a micro video cassette tape into a standard cassette converter, then popped it onto a VCR that was connected to a television on top of the desk. Ever since the Rodney King incident, half the world walked around with video cameras on their shoulders. So Bobby spent a lot of his time with potential clients explaining that their footage of the little wifey gardening in a tube top and flirting with the next-door neighbor was not grounds for divorce in a North Carolina court.

"This is the tape from a couple of nights ago at the Pony Express." Bobby explained. "Watch. My client's boyfriend is that blond guy at the end of the bar. He came in alone and I was hoping to catch him with the health club instructor, but no one ever even came up to say 'boo' to him."

"Instead, you got tape of a bunch of closeted Raleighites trying to act like they weren't all nervous as hell to be hanging out at a gay bar?" I guessed.

"You got it, babe."

I watched, impressed, as Bobby's tape played. For a camera shaped like a fake cigarette pack, it did a damn good job.

"I propped my lighter up under it," Bobby explained.

"To get a better angle. Little things like that distinguish a great detective from a mediocre one."

Yeah, so did getting off your duff once in a while, but I didn't bring it up. I'd gotten off my duff plenty on this case and it had gotten me nowhere.

"Hey," I said. "That guy in the green golf shirt is on the city council, and that guy's on some sports show that runs on Channel Five."

"That's nothing," Bobby said. "Wait until you see the guy who lives with—"

"That's him," I interrupted. "It's the guy in the top hat. Play it back."

The image was grainy because of low lighting conditions, but there in the corner of the picture behind Bobby's mark was a row of bar stools arranged along a side wall near a cigarette machine. The drug dealer was leaning on the chair closest to the machine and every time someone came up for a pack of smokes, they'd try to feed in a couple of dollars without success, then appear to ask the guy for change and hand him a fistful of money.

"Cute," I said, knowing what was coming next. The customer would put in several dollar's worth of quarters, select a brand at random and then ask the dealer for a pack of matches. The guy in the bowler would reach into his knapsack and palm a bulging matchbook, then hand it to the customer. Everyone would look satisfied and smugly clever, as if they had just smuggled an ocean liner of drugs past the coast guard.

Business was booming, by the way. There were enough people in line at the cigarette machine to sell out a Garth Brooks concert.

"I can't believe the bartender doesn't know what's going on," I said.

"He probably does and just doesn't care," Bobby said. "I get the feeling the tips are pretty sweet around that place. He doesn't want to endanger anyone's good mood, know what I mean? He may even be getting a cut."

I mumbled an absent-minded "yeah" because I was too busy staring at the screen. I had just seen a star basketball player from N.C. State not only come up and conduct a transaction with the drug dealer, but also plant a big wet one on him before he sashayed off. "This is better than 'Hard Copy,' " I said.

"It's a great little camera," Bobby agreed. "Take it back and use it for a couple of days while you tail the kid. Give the video option a try. My client's called off the case, so I don't need it. They're reconciling. Until next week, that is."

"I'm gonna go talk to him," I told Bobby. "Tonight."

"The dealer?" Bobby looked skeptical. "You're gonna have trouble fitting in."

When I looked offended, he added, "I'm not saying you don't look like a dyke."

"Well, isn't that a relief." I rolled my eyes.

"The trouble is," Bobby explained. "I didn't see any dykes at all in there and I was at the bar two nights in a row."

"So?" I countered. "I'm a woman who looks like a man. I can certainly look like a man trying to look like a woman."

Bobby stared at me in admiration. I guess he'd never seen *Victor, Victoria*. "That's mighty sneaky of you, Casey. Want me to escort you? I got a date with Fanny, but I could cancel it."

I was touched. I knew he'd gone gaga over Fanny. It was a true sacrifice on his part. On the other hand, who wanted to hang out with a gawking Bobby at a gay bar all night?

"No thanks," I told him. "I'll get Marcus to take me. How are things with Fanny anyway?" I wiggled my eyebrows.

Bobby looked offended. "Please, Casey. When have I ever been the type to kiss and tell? Besides, Fanny Whitehurst is a real lady. I intend to treat her like one. She likes me the way I am."

"What are you talking about?" I said. "All your women like you the way you are, or they wouldn't be going out with you." I couldn't quite understand it myself, but it was the truth.

"No, they don't," Bobby said. "They like the things I do for them. The flowers, the dinners, the presents, the notes. All that stuff. I've got to work hard, you know, being the way I am and all.''

"What way is that?" I asked, mystified by this new Bobby before me.

"Fat," he said bluntly. "I'm fat."

I felt terrible—and terribly touched. "Oh, Bobby," I protested. "That's not true. No one cares if you're fat."

"*Fanny* doesn't care if I'm fat," he corrected me. "We've decided we're going to get even fatter together."

"Well, isn't that romantic?" I started to say, but the unexpected glimpse of Bobby's insecurities stopped me. Then, I nearly asked him if he knew that Fanny was loaded, but something stopped me there, too. Maybe it was the memory of Lydia's wistful voice as she talked about trying to find someone who loved her for who she was, not for what she had in her bank account.

"I hope it works out for the two of you, Bobby, I really do," I finally told him, instead. "She's not your usual type, but maybe that's a good thing."

"No, she's not my type," Bobby agreed. "I usually like 'em a little younger and a little slimmer, but you know— we have such a good time together and I don't have to worry about my waistline and when I hear her laugh, well . . ." He shrugged and tapped his heart with a fist. "Love. Go figure."

Go figure, indeed. The two of them having sex would look like those fake sumo wrestling contests the Durham Bulls staged between innings, but if Bobby and Fanny were having fun then who the hell was I to criticize? Other than a jealous, bitter, incredibly horny single person who spent far too many nights alone, of course.

I headed for my office and phoned Marcus with my plan for that night. He readily agreed to be my beard at the Pony Express so long as I paid for everything and helped him make an engineer from the Research Triangle Park jealous.

"He's really hot and I have to have him. So hang all over me, Casey," he instructed. "Tongue my ear. And remember to light my cigarettes for me."

"I'll be a perfect gentleman dressed as a perfect lady,"

I promised. ''That means no tongue, but it's a go on the cigarette lighter.''

I hung up and got back to work. I needed some wheels. I'd taken a TTA bus into the office, surrounded by northern implants eager to help the environment and disgruntled southerners embarrassed not to have a car. I wasn't anxious to repeat the experience. So I arranged for a rental car to be delivered to the office, then spent the rest of the afternoon trying to locate a good photo of Jake Talbot and Franklin Cosgrove online, occasionally taking a break from my Internet skimming to see if Burly had called and left a message for me at home. No luck.

I had better luck with the photos. I found Jake Talbot in a group shot taken at last year's debutante ball, downloaded it onto my system, then isolated the image of his face and printed it out at four times its actual size. Not bad. His overbred nose was unmistakable.

A photo of Franklin Cosgrove was even easier to find. His mug was plastered all over the place, usually attached to some aging socialite who'd needed an escort for the evening. Geeze, but he was one step short of a gigolo. The only difference was that he was holding out for one big payday, instead of mooching it in installments. It would be sweet to tie him into this mess somehow. I'd love to take him down.

At the end of the day, I drove my rented Escort back to Durham. They'd delivered a white car despite my request for a dark one, and I spent the rush hour drive time trying to figure out why all rental cars are white, when no one ever actually chooses one that color when they buy a car for themselves.

I stopped by Faircloth's to ask Jimbo how the work on my Porsche was going. As usual, a couple of his co-workers stood around, staring, while we spoke. I always had to fight an insane urge to rip open my blouse and flash them when I stopped by Faircloth's. Those guys definitely needed to get out more.

''That friend of yours who made you pull over saved your life,'' Jimbo told me as he wiped his hands on a greasy cloth far more filthy than his fingers.

"Why do you say that?"

"Someone loosened the bolts on all four of your CV joints," he said. "If they'd fallen off at high speed, your car would have stopped dead in its tracks. You would have, too, probably."

I thought about it. "It isn't a natural occurrence?"

He looked at me with pity. Alas, as a nonmechanic, I was one of the washed and unenlightened. "All of them bolts wouldn't go like that at one time without help," he explained in a slow drawl. "Plus, there's scratch marks up and down the shafts. Someone used a pair of pliers to loosen 'em. You got you a serious enemy, Casey. One who knows cars."

Well, I hadn't noticed Richard Petty trying to force me off the highway, so that left about eight million other North Carolinians as possible suspects. "Did you fix everything?" I asked.

Jimbo nodded. "I still got to clean things up. It's a little greasy down there. She might burn off a little smoke unless I wipe things down."

"Don't wipe her down," I said. "Leave her as she is for a couple of days, okay? And don't touch her again. I'll pay a storage charge or whatever I have to."

He looked at me, perplexed. "If that's what you want," he said.

"It is," I assured him. "And thanks, you cute thing, you." I pinched his oil-smudged cheek and left the reverse imprint of my thumb and forefinger on his skin. He ducked his head, embarrassed.

"You be careful now, Casey," he mumbled.

"I can take care of myself, Jimbo," I assured him. I took pity on him and didn't give him a kiss good-bye. His friends stood around, watching, as I left.

"How can I look more like a man?" I asked Marcus, peering into the mirror at a Casey that he had created using a crinoline Donna Reed dress, curling iron and pumps. My hair flipped up at the ends like I should be pointing at an early Frigidaire and chirping about the joys of housework.

The retro-drag look was very *in*, according to Marcus, and I had the hips and breasts for it.

"Just pump some iron before we go," he decided, "So your muscles look cut. And let me soften your makeup."

"That's it?" I asked.

Marcus looked apologetic. "You didn't have far to go, honey."

"Thanks," I said dryly. "That's what I get for just being myself."

Marcus had opted out of drag in favor of an incredible charcoal zoot suit that made him look seven feet tall and more dapper than Cab Calloway. I got a good look at him under the street light in the bar's parking lot and whistled in admiration. "You are so Chicago," I told him. "You are positively smokin'."

"I'm in love, Miss Casey," he explained as he opened the door of my car and helped me out into the Pony Express parking lot. The place was jammed.

"Not you, too," I complained. "Bobby's right. There's Viagra in the air."

"Not Viagra," he corrected me primly. "Love." He broke into a pretty good version of "Love is In the Air." There was no lip-synching for Marcus.

"I'm gonna become a nun," I mumbled. "It's the only acceptable justification left for being single."

Entering the front door of the Pony Express was like stepping into a monsoon. A roar of music and voices filled the air, sweaty bodies surrounded us and giant floor fans did their best to cope with the heat. I stepped in front of one and it blew my skirt straight up past my shoulders.

"There goes your secret," Marcus mumbled. "And don't think there weren't a whole bleacher full of boys standing around waiting for a peek at your package."

They wouldn't be looking at me anymore. I found Marcus a seat at one end of the crowded bar, dutifully lit his cigarette and ordered a round of daiquiris from the bartender. Hey, if I'm gonna look like Donna Reed, I have a right to drink my liquor through a straw.

I surveyed the packed room. Everyone looked alike: buff,

well-dressed and reeking of personal care products. The titillation factor faded quickly. Unless they're sleeping with me, I don't much care who people sleep with, and so I wasn't as surprised as Bobby D. to discover a large percentage of Raleigh's movers and shakers moving and shaking their booty with the boys.

"There he is," Marcus said, gripping my wrist with the strength of a boa constrictor.

"Who?" I asked, looking around for the dealer.

"My new husband. The engineer."

"Good God, Marcus." I complained. "That guy belongs on a Wheaties box."

I left Marcus to bat his eyelashes at some All-American buzz-cut collegiate type and kept an eye on the corner of the bar nearest the cigarette machine. Two daiquiris later, the dealer showed up wearing his top hat and carrying a black knapsack, which he placed at his feet as he took up a position near the machine.

He'd hardly had time to loosen his prairie collar when a line formed to his right. I gave Marcus a nod and took my place in it, behind a beefy man with very red ears and khakis that were several sizes too small.

Years of waiting outside ladies rooms has taught me patience. I was calm, cool and collected by the time it was my turn.

"This is the story," I said softly when the dealer turned expectantly to me, his hat pulled low over his forehead. "Take a good look at this." I opened my leather purse— which was light blue and matched the goofy dress—then pulled a fake gold badge out of the bottom of it. I flashed it at him, then quickly stowed it back inside. The dealer didn't even blink.

"What do you want?" he asked in an accent that was vaguely British.

"I want to talk to you outside for ten minutes."

"About what?" he asked, his eyes sliding to the line waiting behind me. I was costing him business. "You gonna bust me?"

"I don't care about you," I told him. "I care about two of your customers."

"I don't give up my customers," he said, his mouth tightening. I realized his accent was Jamaican. "It wouldn't be brotherly of me."

"It's not very *Jah* of you to be selling coke," I whispered tersely. "Whatever happened to 'peace, love and ganja?' "

"Profit margins," he hissed back with a terse smile.

"These are two rich white guy customers," I persisted. "Straight guys. And I'll give you two hundred and fifty dollars for talking to me for ten minutes."

That was one one-hundredth of what Randolph Talbot had tried to buy me off with. I thought it an appropriate sum.

"Now you are talking, mama," he said. "Why didn't you say so in the first place?" He took my elbow and slung his backpack over his shoulder. "Back soon," he told the next guy in line as he gently guided me toward the front door with exaggerated charm, as if we were heading for a dance floor to cha-cha.

We sat in the front seat of my car and I was impressed with his calm. "You don't seem too nervous," I told him.

"You're no cop," he said. "I know every cop in this town. And you're paying me good money. Besides, I know who you want to ask me about. They're bad news and getting sloppy. Too much of a good thing." He sniffed loudly. "Get rid of them for me. I don't care."

I pulled out the computerized photos of Jake Talbot and Franklin Cosgrove. "These guys?" I asked.

His mouth curled up in distaste and he clicked his tongue against his teeth in disapproval. "Those guys, they have too much money. But they always try to get me to go down on my price. And they have big mouths. Especially that one." He pointed to Jake Talbot. "What do you want to know?"

"What can you tell me about them?" I asked.

"I know that Daddy has lots of money," he said, placing a long finger on Jake Talbot's face. "Because he acts like he owns everything he sees." Then he touched Cosgrove's image. "And this one is sucking up to the other boy. He wants something from him. Maybe money, maybe a way to get to Daddy."

Or to his sister, I thought. "Sucking up?" I asked. "You think?"

"Sucking *up*, not off." The dealer smiled. "They come to the bar sometimes, but only for the drugs. They think they are slumming, you know what I mean? But those two would not be into men." He bumped his fists together. "There's not enough power in being with a man for them." He looked disdainful. "Those two, they like being on top. That's why they like the White Lady so much."

"Which white lady?" I asked.

He stared at me patiently and tapped his nose. "This white lady."

"Oh, yeah, right." I felt as unhip as someone's grandmother. Another reason why I hated the drug scene.

"She makes them feel bigger than they are," he added. "I think they go for meek women who are afraid of them. Maybe lonely ones."

"Or desperate ones," I offered.

"Lots of those," the dealer said with a sly smile. "Especially if you have some of what old Spencer here is selling to make the lady less desperate. But me, I like men." He looked me over. "Even when they dress like a woman. You look good, mama. You almost fooled me. I thought you were all woman at first."

"I *am* a woman," I explained.

He stared at my biceps. "Then you are not their type, I think. Maybe you are *my* type. I'm not a flyboy all the time, you know. Just when I work here."

"I'm not meek, not lonely, not desperate, not in the market and definitely not in the mood, so stay on your side of the car, Bubbah," I said, just to make sure we were clear on where things stood. The last thing I needed was to have to fend off an omni-sexual Jamaican coke dealer. "How often do they buy drugs from you?" I asked, to get him back to business.

"Only that one *buy* the drugs," he replied, touching Jake Talbot's photo. "The other one just *do* the drugs. He thinks if he doesn't pay for them, it means he doesn't have a problem."

"*Do* they have a problem with it?" I asked.

He shrugged. "The redhead who won't buy has a problem here." He tapped his nose. "The other one has a problem here." He tapped his head. His eyes narrowed as he noticed the pocketbook on my lap, probably figuring out, correctly, that there was plenty of room for a gun among all of the fake badges, Kleenex and lipstick holders I had jammed in there.

"Why are you asking me about these two men?" he said, staring at a bulge in my pocketbook. He'd realized that it was from a barrel, not a portable phone.

"They may have killed a man." I told him.

The dealer threw back his head and laughed—which scared me more than anything else he had done yet. "Not those two," he insisted, his shoulders shaking with silent merriment. "Like I say, they are chicken." He clucked a couple of times and laughed again. "They the kind who like their victims small. Besides, together, they don't have two balls between them."

I wished I could be as sure. "Where do you usually sell to them?" I asked. "Here?"

"In Durham," he explained. "I go see my customers there first on weekend nights, then I stop by Chapel Hill and I end up the evening here with the night owls. I have a route see, like a bread truck. Only I get to keep the bread." He smiled and a gold tooth winked at me in the glow of the street lamp. "Time management is my secret. I'm a good businessman."

"Where in Durham do you meet them?"

He named a noisy beer bar in the heart of downtown that was a haven for white Duke students and old white bums. "Seems to me you'd kind of stick out in a place like that," I said. "Not to be rude."

"That's true. But it's good business for me to stick out," he explained. "People know what I am. I am a walking billboard."

"Great when you're trying to be discreet," I said sarcastically.

His smile grew wider. "Like I say, I know all the cops."

"When did you last see these two guys?" I asked.

"Tonight, mama."

"But you just sold this one some stuff Saturday night," I said, waving Jake Talbot's photo. "I was watching."

He shrugged again. "He is a good customer. Maybe they have a party planned. Who knows?"

"Are they usually alone when they buy from you?" I asked.

"Sometimes girls are waiting back at the table. One night I see a fat man watching them and later I think he joined their party."

"What makes you say that?" I asked.

He shrugged again. "He was watching the two of them and I was watching him. When the two boys come to me, I think to myself, 'Is that fat man a cop?.' But then I say no, he's too soft-looking to be a cop. When I sell them the stuff, they leave. The fat man, he gets up and leaves right after them."

"What did he look like?" I asked curiously.

The dealer shrugged. "Fat and white. That's all I remember."

"That really narrows it down," I said. He'd just described half the men in the South.

He shrugged again, apologetically this time, and held out a hand. "You said two hundred and fifty dollars to answer your questions for ten minutes."

I gave him the money and he grinned happily at the bills. "You want a sample, maybe?" he asked me, gold tooth twinkling.

I shuddered. "No thanks. I've spent my whole life trying to learn to be happy where I am. I'm not about to take a drug that only makes me wish I was always some place else."

He nodded. "Smart lady. Lucky for me, not everyone thinks that way."

"Lucky for you," I agreed.

When we reentered the bar, I could practically hear the collective sigh of relief that filled the room once the packed partiers spotted their supplier again. God forbid people have a good time on their own. They might have to live with themselves for fifteen minutes that way.

I returned to the bar and explained to Marcus that I had

to go, but he hardly heard a word I said. He was deep in conversation with the engineer and I was only in the way.

"I'll give him a ride home," Mr. Blond Buzz-Cut promised, earning me a dazzling smile from Marcus in lieu of a good-bye.

I left Marcus to his future and headed back to Durham in hopes of tracking down a little bit of the recent past.

THIRTEEN

I now knew Jake Talbot and Franklin Cosgrove were drug buddies and so despicable that not even their dealer wanted their business. But I had nothing to connect either one of them to the murder of Thomas Nash. So why was I about to don my gay apparel and follow them around Durham? Because Randolph Talbot had wanted to discourage me from following his son so badly that he had parted with twenty-five G's—and I intended to find out the reason why. I don't know the going rate for hush money elsewhere, but in Durham, $25,000 can buy a lot more than one person's silence on a murder.

I stopped by my apartment to change into something that didn't make me look like Beaver Cleaver's mom and found a message waiting from Detective Anne Morrow. She was calling on behalf of her Durham cohorts and wanted to know what the hell was going on with Burly Nash and did it have anything to do with the death of his brother?

Good question. But I had no answer, so I didn't call her back. Instead, I wiggled into my black jeans and a black leotard top, which looked a little New York for downtown Durham on a Monday night, but I was intending to skulk around in the bushes and the right outfit in the South makes *all* the difference, no matter what the social situation may be. I left my Colt at home. Sidearms are not standard issue when you're trying to pass as a college student in Durham, at least not yet. I stuffed Bobby's fake cigarette pack camera into my back pocket and headed out to track down my two least favorite people.

Downtown was insanely busy. It turned out that the final summer school session had ended that day in preparation for exams and scores of liberated, academically indifferent Duke students—which is close to an oxymoron—had decided to celebrate. I checked in at the bar where Jake Talbot supposedly purchased his drugs, and though the bartender readily admitted Jake was a regular and had been in earlier, he could not say where he had gone next. I folded the computerized photo back into my jeans pocket and hit the strip.

Main Street around Brightleaf Square includes several blocks' worth of cavernous bars that cater to the student crowd, beer-drinking professionals and, in some sad cases, professional beer-drinkers. First stop was Down Under, which was jammed with sweaty softball players and inebriated dart enthusiasts who were taking turns drunkenly tossing razor-sharp points within inches of each other's eyes. And people think rock climbing is dangerous.

The bartender claimed he had no time to answer my questions, but a ten-dollar bill changed his mind. He pointed me in the direction of Satisfaction and I high-tailed it across the street to Brightleaf, where, over a pint of Foster's, a cooperative female bartender directed me a couple of blocks down the street to a new bar called the Loop.

"Tonight's opening night," she explained. "Everyone's headed that way."

I thanked her and followed the raucous sounds of a bar band cranked up several hundred decibels over the legal limit. People who live near colleges are either masochists or fools. I ought to know, I'm one of them.

The Loop was located on a dark side street off Main, next door to a funeral home—which probably cut down on the noise complaints considerably. The building had housed an old-fashioned department store decades before, then stood empty until the Loop moved in. I wasn't convinced another college bar was an improvement.

Picture windows lined the exterior of the building and I peered inside them, searching for a familiar face. It wasn't easy. The place was packed and new lighting made it difficult for my eyes to focus. Bright neon lights flashed in a constant circle in the center of each window, red chasing red in an electronic frenzy that beckoned drinkers inside.

I squeezed into the sweaty, dancing crowd. Signs behind the bar advertised twenty-five-cent beer, which explained the chaos. The floor was so sticky with beer that my boots stuck to the linoleum. I heard a giant sucking sound down south every time I lifted a foot. Ross Perot would have felt vindicated.

The band was screeching away on a low platform at the other end of the room. I returned to the front and stood in an elevated bay window that had once been a showcase area for mannequins. I stared over the top of the crowd, searching for Jake Talbot.

I spotted Franklin Cosgrove first. He was leaning against the far end of the long bar, talking to a petite brunette whose white tennis shorts barely covered her butt. The edge of her white cheeks winked at the world in twin crescent moons. Her father would have fainted had he seen her. She was attractive enough, but, if she was flirting with Cosgrove, chances were good she was no rocket scientist. He was getting a little long in the tooth for this crowd. She was proof that there was always some silly misguided co-ed willing to mistake his sleazy lust for sophistication.

As I watched, the brunette tossed her head back in a classic flirting gesture, flipping her long hair behind her into some poor slob's beer. Neither one of them noticed. She continued to shake droplets of beer from her damp hair like a poodle whenever Cosgrove made her laugh. God, was I that inane when I was picking someone up in a bar? I hoped not.

A dark corridor to the right of the band stretched toward the back of the building, leading to the rest rooms. Jake Talbot emerged from this hallway with a redhead clinging to his arm about three minutes after I set up station in the front window. The girl looked a little wobbly, as if she'd had about a keg too much to drink. Jake steadied her and leaned her against the wall, then handed her a fresh beer. Like she really needed one. One more sip and she'd be ready to book a room at Betty Ford for the month.

I moved closer, unconcerned about being spotted by either Talbot or Cosgrove. Both men were hot on the trail of college bootie and unlikely to notice me unless I lost forty pounds and fifteen years.

As my eyes adjusted to the dark interior of the club, I realized that the tavern had a door in the back that led out onto the sidewalk of the side street. Jake and his redhead claimed a small spot of floor near this door, where they were easily visible through the windows. I'd be better off tailing him from outside. I slipped out the front door and chose a dark doorway across the side street from the bar. An abandoned textile mill stretched the length of the opposite block. Its dark loading bays gave me plenty of cover.

I don't know what I expected the two men to do next. Clearly, they were deep in the eightball they'd bought from their dealer and planning to party the night away. But they were my only lead and so I waited. I took some footage of Jake and his redhead through the window to test Bobby's camera, then killed some time wondering if there could be a connection between Tom Nash and drugs. Who knows what he was using in his laboratory? Maybe Jake Talbot had gotten high one night and run out of fairy dust, prompting him to break into Tom's lab and eventually leading to disaster? No theory is too farfetched when drugs are involved. I've heard junkies boast about punching out their grandmothers for a fistful of change.

About fifteen minutes after I took up my spot across the street, Cosgrove and his brunette left the bar by the front door. They staggered down the sidewalk toward his Porsche in the kind of boozy embrace that people with a shred of dignity are embarrassed to discover they've indulged in once they sober up.

Now that the two drug buddies were splitting up, I was faced with a dilemma. I decided to stay put on Jake's tail for a very scientific reason: I hated him more. He was still standing near the rear door, shielding the redhead from the rest of the bar with his body. Her head was starting to droop now and the beer mug in her hand was dipping lower and lower toward the floor. If Jake didn't make his move soon,

he'd be better off nipping next door to the funeral home
for a more responsive partner.

He made his move. The back door of the Loop opened
and he steered the redhead outside by her elbow. She
promptly bounced off a street lamp into the gutter. Jake
caught her on the way down and hoisted her back aloft,
then guided her toward a red Miata parked at the curb. Its
top was down, revealing a leather interior. He probably had
hundreds of them lined up in his garage like Matchbox cars,
for those pesky times when his Lamborghini quit on him.

He poured the girl into the passenger seat, then leapt over
the driver's side door—proving he was a hell of a lot more
sober than she was—and roared away down Main Street. I
jogged after him, reached my rental car near Down Under
and hopped inside, still keeping an eye on his tail lights.
He was at least three blocks ahead, but I caught up with
him at the corner of Ninth Street and Main. I expected him
to turn left and head toward his family compound, but he
turned right on red and roared down Ninth Street like a jet
about to take off from a runway. A few blocks later he
turned left and I cut through the parking lot of George's
Garage restaurant just in time to see him zoom down the
entrance ramp for I-85. If I didn't know better, I'd say he
knew he was being followed.

With the top down on his Miata, he was easy to spot
among the more staid Buicks and Chevys clogging the
highway. I dropped in a few cars behind him as he slowed
for a construction lane, confident that he had no way of
knowing that I had exchanged my Porsche for an Escort.
He sped north past Durham, heading for Raleigh via Highway 70. I eased back a few cars and relied on the stop-and-
start traffic to keep him within easy spotting distance.

A few miles later, he turned right abruptly and wound
back into a patch of overdeveloped land that was clogged
with the ubiquitous brick apartment complexes popular
with students and the transient Triangle crowd.

When he turned into one of the smaller apartment complexes, I pulled my car over onto the shoulder of the main
entrance road and waited until he had parked and helped
the nearly incapacitated redhead from the car. If she lived

in the complex, I was surprised she'd been coherent enough to tell him.

I left my car where it was and crept into a row of red-wood bushes, keeping low to the ground and occasionally raising my head to check on their progress.

The redhead's legs buckled beneath her, and every time Jake got her to stand up, her knees wobbled then turned inward and she collapsed again. By the time he reached the concrete entrance stairwell, he had her by the shoulders and was practically dragging her up the steeply inclined brick walkway. I hid behind the Miata as he took a set of keys from his pocket, then unlocked the door of a first-floor apartment. He looped his arms under her shoulders and heaved her inside, her head lolling back and her body limp.

I didn't like the smell of it at all. None of it fit. She was too drunk to talk, so why had Jake taken her here? She was also too drunk to drive, so maybe it was her car and maybe those were her keys. But she had seemed nearly comatose from the time she'd laid her head back in the passenger seat and I had witnessed no talking or communication between them so far.

What the hell was he up to?

The apartment complex was quiet. It was past one and most of the residents were already in bed. I looked around, saw no one, and crept toward the building, scrambling up a crumbling red dirt hill to get there.

The apartment was built on the side of a steep hill that had been planted with Bermuda grass in a futile attempt to keep it from eroding. Though the entrance was level with the top of the hill, the rest of the apartment extended over the slope, so that the windows were higher than normal above the ground. I could tell lights were being turned on inside the apartment, but could not see above the window ledge into the rooms.

I stretched as high as I could and touched the rough surface of a concrete window ledge, then dug my fingers in and tried to pull myself up. I managed to claw my way up to eye level and found myself staring into a bedroom through a ten-inch gap in the curtains. The lights were on, but I did not see either Jake Talbot or his companion. I pulled myself up further and rested on my elbows, my legs dangling in the air, listening to water running in a nearby bathroom. Maybe he was trying to revive the redhead.

Unfortunately, I also heard car engines. A pair of vans turned into the entrance road of the complex. I couldn't afford to be caught dangling from a windowsill—how the hell would I explain that to the cops?—so I dropped to safety and landed in some prickly holly bushes. Ouch. Whatever happened to good old boxwoods? I crouched behind the stiff curtain of leaves, waiting as the two vehicles crawled past, speed bumps making them cautious. Neither turned into the parking lot nearest me and when they were gone, I sat in the darkness below the window, trying to come up with a plan. Above me, I could hear voices coming from the bedroom.

"Lemme go," a high voice mumbled before lapsing into gibberish.

Jake Talbot laughed and I heard a crash. Someone had fallen into furniture.

"Stop it!" the female voice said, this time more sharply. There was a slap and then silence, then laughter from Jake, followed by more crashing sounds.

Okay. I am into game playing as much as the next sex fiend, but I know consensual sex when I hear it—and this didn't sound like some friendly romp between friends. It sounded perilously close to rape.

I pulled the miniature video camera from my back pocket and clamped it between my teeth, then jumped up and gripped the windowsill with my fingertips, slowly pulling myself upward until I could get an elbow onto the concrete ledge. I balanced there long enough to take the camera from my mouth with my free hand and position it between the curtains. I pressed the record button and angled the lens into the room at a bed pushed against the wall opposite from the window. I scraped my elbow badly trying to sustain my weight, then once again fell to the ground, this time avoiding holly bushes in lieu of a patch of monkey grass and cedar chips. It was an improvement. I looked around for a tree to climb and saw nothing but a few ane-

mic crepe myrtles, no higher than my shoulders. Cheap
landscaping bastards.

Above me, I could hear Jake laughing. The sound made
the hair on my arms stand on end. It was a quiet giggle, so
steady it was almost a hum. The man sounded loopy—and
absolutely ecstatic. "There, that's perfect," he was saying
happily. "Ooops. That way, I think. Here, let me help
you."

There was a thud and I was sure the girl had fallen off
the bed. Jake burst into laughter but this was followed by
the sound of glass breaking. Jake swore and I heard another
slap. The girl gave a pathetic squeak, as if she had no energy left for a scream.

Okay. That was enough for me. It was maddening being
able to listen, but unable to see. Maybe they were best
buddies and did this every Monday night, but I didn't think
so. I wasn't sure what the penalty was for *coitus interruptus*
between two consenting parties but I knew what the penalty
was for a raped woman: a lifetime of wondering "What
did I do wrong?"

I tore up the hill toward the apartment entrance, rounded
the corner and gathered speed just before I hit the cheap
hollow core door with my right shoulder. The lock tore
away in a chunk of wood and I tumbled inside, banging
my head on the narrow hallway wall. I scrambled to my
feet and dashed toward the bedroom, wishing that I had my
gun with me.

I found Jake Talbot standing above the naked redhead,
a Polaroid camera pointing down at her motionless body.
He was so zoned out he had not even noticed the front door
being battered down. He was peeling off his underwear
with his free hand and he froze, half-naked, turned toward
the door when I entered the bedroom at full speed.

"Get the fuck off her," I said, grabbing his shoulders
and flinging him against one wall. The camera bounced off
the bedside table and its flash exploded. Jake slid to the
floor, his mouth open in surprise. He'd been hoovering up
so much white powder that tiny flakes wafted from his nose
like snow. I ignored him and checked the girl. She had a
pulse, but was unconscious. She was also completely naked

nd her vulnerability made her seem years younger than she probably was, though she could not have been more han nineteen or twenty.

"You miserable little prick," I told Talbot as I wrapped he girl in a sheet. "You fucking little coward. Can't handle a real woman, huh? You have to knock yours unconscious irst?"

He stared at me, his eyes glittering with an intense brightness that I knew was from way, way too much coke. People can get dangerous when they're tanked up like that and I searched the room for a weapon. A bedside lamp had been knocked to the floor earlier and the light bulb broken. I kicked the shade and broken glass away from the stand, then unplugged the cord from the wall and wrapped part of it around one of my fists, drawing the remainder of it taut. I'd be able to loop it around his neck or jab him with the jagged base of the broken bulb if he tried to come after me.

He wasn't coming after anyone. He leaned against the wall, mouth open, and stared at me. "I know you," he stammered. "Who are you?"

"I'm your worst enemy," I told him. "And I mean that sincerely. Your nightmare has just begun." Yes, I sounded like a character in a B movie but, frankly, it was like being trapped in one.

He stared at me, mute, as I lifted the girl from the bed and slung her over one shoulder. She didn't weigh more than a hundred pounds. After lifting Burly a couple nights before, the little redhead was nothing.

Talbot followed me to the front door in his underwear, perplexed and zoned-out. He gazed at the splintered wood sadly. "Where are you taking her?" he complained, as if I had just snatched his favorite toy from him.

I looked at him, standing there in his idiotic Calvin Klein briefs, eyes glistening, lips in a pout, his long nose quivering because he couldn't have his way. And I lost it. Completely.

Every grudge I'd ever harbored against people who had money when I had none, exploded in me. Every guy I'd ever met who acted like he was too good to be seen with me melded into one arrogant image: Jake Talbot. And every time I'd been pressured as a young, dumb kid into doing something I didn't want to do with a man unfolded in my mind and converged in a single rush of adrenaline that ignited into violence.

I wanted to destroy the pathetic bastard before me.

I lashed out a foot, kicking upward. The weight of the redhead slowed me down a little—which probably saved Jake Talbot's balls—but I hit him square on with all of my weight behind the kick. He screamed like I'd taken a chain saw to his leg, slammed back against the cheap hallway wall, then slumped to the floor, his hands clutched to his crotch as he began to howl.

A door across the hallway opened and a young black guy stuck his head out. "What the fuck's going on?" he asked, taking in Talbot curled up on the floor and me, standing with what looked like a mummy slung over my shoulder.

"Just taking my little sister home," I told him.

He shrugged and shut the door, happy to mind his own business. But his presence jolted me back to reality.

I wanted to kick the shit out of Jake Talbot. I wanted to kill him, in fact, and I had no doubt that I could—or that I would be doing the world a favor. Because I had a feeling the redhead wasn't the first woman who'd ended up wrestling with him in her underwear. But it wasn't up to me to be the judge and jury, at least not in this particular case.

And, to be perfectly truthful, while Randolph Talbot's $25,000 hadn't been enough to make me walk away from the murder of Thomas Nash, I guess it was enough to make me walk away from Jake Talbot before he was maimed for life.

After I reclaimed my camera from the windowsill, I drove the unconscious girl to Durham Regional Hospital. If she was overdosing on something, I didn't want her on my conscience.

I staggered through the doors of the emergency room like Frankenstein bearing the little girl who had befriended him. A muscular attendant rushed to my rescue and took the unconscious girl from my arms. He was Native American, probably a Cherokee, and wore an enormous bear claw necklace around his thick neck. His hair was tied in a long black braid and he had an infinitely kind face. I felt as if a thousand pounds lifted from my shoulders when I saw him.

He carried her back to the triage room and laid her on a stretcher, then stood guard as if to protect her from evil. At first, the nurse on duty barely disguised her distaste, assuming that the redhead was one more co-ed too stupid to know when to quit drinking. But after I explained the situation, her attitude changed abruptly. She exchanged a glance with the attendant. He strode from the room. I followed. He picked up a clipboard on the check-in desk and flipped to a sheet of paper near the bottom of the stack. He read through it, then pushed a red button on the wall and picked up the phone.

A doctor came rushing out of an inner hallway and I followed him back to the triage room. He meant business. He checked the pupils of the girl's eyes and monitored her pulse. Then he ordered a toxicology scan, IV drip and a private room, stat. The girl was whisked away before I could blink.

No one told me anything.

When I returned to the waiting room, the front desk attendant avoided my eyes. He turned away, leaving me to stare at his long black braid and broad shoulders. I knew something was up when he didn't even bother to ask me her name or request other data. When a hospital passes on insurance information, you know bigger forces are at work.

I waited under the harsh fluorescent lights, alone and feeling vaguely guilty, listening to the hum of the vending machines. The only other person in the waiting room was an old white bum sleeping upright in his chair, one hand wrapped around a bloody, badly bandaged thumb.

I was almost asleep myself when the cops arrived, anxious to talk to me. Not a couple of bored uniforms, either, but two serious-looking detectives in plainclothes, their badges and notebooks at the ready to convince me they meant business. I didn't know either one of them, which meant they weren't homicide.

"What's the big deal?" I asked as they examined my credentials, always a heart-stopping moment for me. "I thought this kind of thing happened all the time in a college town."

"Depends on what you think happened," the taller and thinner of the two men answered, handing me back my license without comment. "Why don't you tell us why you were following her in the first place?"

I gave them an abbreviated version of events, one heavy on evasion and light on truth. I said I'd been tailing a college kid because a client suspected him of having an affair with his wife and had stumbled onto his meeting with the redhead by accident.

They wanted to know Jake Talbot's name. I wasn't sure I wanted to give it.

"You're putting me on the spot," I said. "Client confidentiality and all." God, but I hated to sound like a lawyer.

The shorter, fatter detective didn't like that much. "You're interfering with an ongoing investigation by the Durham Police Department," he said gruffly. "I don't think you want to get into a pissing match over this."

I looked at them, surprised. "What are we talking about here?" I asked.

The two men exchanged glances and that was when it hit me.

"Shit," I said, disgusted. "The guy who's raping Duke co-eds."

The plump detective raised his eyebrows but said nothing.

"Look," I pleaded, "if I were that girl, I'd give you his name in a heartbeat. But how do I know she wants to press charges, or even have this incident known by anyone other than you and me? That's something I think she's entitled to decide for herself. You know as well as I do that if this gets out, her photo will be all over the papers." And *how*, I thought to myself, once the media found out that Jake Talbot was involved. Gag order or not, the national press would swoop on it and the poor girl would end up on "Hard Copy."

"Look," the tall detective said grimly, "you could be our first, only and, hopefully, last reliable witness if this guy is the one."

Good God, and I'd videotaped the entire episode.

"What do you mean?" I asked, feeling as guilty as if the video camera in my back pocket were a kilo of cocaine.

"This is part of the whole rape drug trend sweeping this great country of ours," the first detective said sarcastically. "The victims are doped at the bar where the perp first spots them and he's good at what he does. He doesn't move in on them until they're so far gone that they don't even remember meeting him the next day. We don't have a single clue, not even an artist's sketch based on some figment of a vic's imagination. The drug causes them to black out, even though they look like they're walking and maybe even talking. These girls are missing hours on either side of the rapes, and the friends they're leaving behind in the bars are usually drunk as hell. They can't tell us doodly-squat."

The fat one got impatient. "Yeah, lady," he interrupted. "So decide if you're going to protect a scumball or maybe side a little bit with your sisters."

"What makes you think she's a victim of the same guy?" I asked.

"She fits the profile exactly. That's why we were called. Every emergency room in the Triangle is on alert to let us know when a potential victim comes in. We saw one in Raleigh Saturday night, found wandering near NCSU, which means the guy is really starting to get around. We'll know for sure when the drug screen comes back, but I'm willing to bet my badge she's part of it."

When he finished, the tall detective stood calmly, waiting for what he had said to sink in.

I tried to think. If Jake Talbot was the campus rapist, my only regret was that I hadn't kicked his balls up and out his ears. I'd be happy to do what I could to put the guy behind bars where he could find out for himself what it was like to be on the receiving end of a rape.

But I had meant it when I said I thought it was the girl's right to decide whether or not to pursue charges. It wasn't a copout. I'd had more than one client in the past who had been raped and come to me for help tracking down her assailant. None of these women wanted the cops involved, none of them wanted to take the stand and testify. They just wanted help finding the bastard who had done it to them.

I'd done my job and located the guys. My clients had taken their vengeance from there, no questions asked by me. After a couple of times, I'd learned not to try and convince a raped woman to take her pain public. She either dealt with it privately or worked it out in court but, either way, it was her call, not mine. Besides, the one client who changed her mind and pressed charges ended up embroiled in a lawsuit for slander, teaching me how much the search for justice could cost a woman on top of what she had already paid.

Like it or not, it was the redhead's decision.

"I'm sorry," I said. "I can't make that call yet. Let me talk to the girl."

The fat detective threw his notebook to the floor in disgust. "Oh, that's just great," he said angrily. "While you're busy protecting her feelings, he's going to be right out there doing it some other woman. Have you thought about that?"

I had. "Just let me talk to her first," I asked. "Then I'll tell you what I can."

The fat cop started to protest, but his partner dragged him away to the other side of the waiting room. We sat in silence, in opposite camps, for the longest hour of my life. Not even the sympathetic glances of the desk attendant, who'd overheard our conversation, made me feel any better.

Finally the doctor appeared. "She's conscious," he said. He looked confused when all three of us hopped to attention. "Her name is Karen Wilson. We've notified her parents. They're on their way down from Richmond."

The doctor said nothing more until we were down the hall. "Keep it short," he ordered as he led us back to an elevator. We rode to the third floor in silence, the short detective glaring at me and the tall one staring at the ceiling.

We reached the girl's room and I stopped, blocking the

entrance. "Alone?" I asked in my nicest voice, knowing that only a few degrees separated skating on thin ice from being forced to try and walk on water.

The tall detective nodded and pulled his partner back. They retreated to the hallway as I crept inside. I had no doubt that they would eavesdrop once my back was turned, but I didn't plan to say much anyway.

The young girl looked tiny lying in the glaring white hospital bed, surrounded by pillows and machines. Her face was pale and mottled with vivid freckles that had been masked by makeup earlier. Her eyes were open and staring dully out the window, tears running down her cheeks. She had a black eye and a cut in one corner of her mouth that had swelled to an angry red. Her right cheek was bruised and purplish spots marred her arms. A long scratch led down her neck and across her chest, until it disappeared beneath the sheet.

She mumbled something and I leaned over her to hear better. "What did you say?" I asked softly.

"I want my mom," she repeated in a weak voice. Tears trickled down her cheeks and ran into a deep groove etched around her mouth. She had aged about ten years in the last four hours.

"They've called her," I said. "She'll be here soon."

"I don't want her to know what happened to me," the girl said suddenly, struggling to sit upright.

I gently pushed her back in the bed. "Nothing happened to you," I assured her. "Not like you think."

"It didn't?" she whispered.

"He didn't get a chance."

She lay back against the pillow, eyes closed. "I can't remember," she said. "I remember being at the bar and then I couldn't find my friends in the crowd and . . ." her voice trailed off. "Then I was here and my body really hurts down there and I thought, oh no, I thought . . ."

"I stopped him before he could," I assured her. "You don't remember meeting a guy at the bar?"

She shook her head. "I mean, I met a lot of guys, but I don't remember one in particular. Are you a police-woman?"

I explained who I was and that I had been following someone when I saw her leaving the bar. "I didn't see him do it, but the police think he dropped something in your drink. I wouldn't be surprised if he had. He's that kind of guy."

"Then you know who he is," she said. She frowned. "Did you tell the cops?"

I shook my head.

"Why not?"

"His father has a lot of money," I explained. "When the papers find out, the news will be everywhere. They'll learn who you are eventually, no matter how much the courts try to keep your name out of the media. His father will make sure of that to scare you off. Your photo will probably be printed. But no one will ever explain exactly what happened, so everyone else will always wonder what he did to you. People will talk about you and you'll know it. Do you go to school here?"

She nodded weakly. "At Duke," she whispered. "I'm going to be a sophomore. My parents let me come up a few weeks early to find a nice apartment."

"Off Highway 70?" I asked.

She shook her head. "On Anderson Drive. Why?"

"He took you to an apartment off Highway 70."

"Oh." Her voice grew smaller as she become lost in the thought of what had happened to her. "And you followed me there?" she asked.

I nodded. "I couldn't see exactly what was happening but I heard enough to make me break down the door."

"And if you hadn't . . ." her voice broke and she started to cry. I let her cry it out for a couple of moments, handing her tissues from the box by her bed. Finally, she took a deep breath and sat up straighter. "My head hurts," she said. "And I want to throw up."

"That's the drug he gave you," I explained, moving the plastic basin closer just in case. "The doctor gave you more drugs to counteract it. You're going to feel lousy for a couple of days."

"So this guy is rich and he's going to get away with it?" she asked suddenly, anger overcoming her fear.

"Not if you don't let him," I said. "That's what I wanted to ask you. If you give me your permission, I'll tell the police everything I know. They'll press charges. And they'll probably find enough evidence to tie him to other rapes as well. If you don't want me to tell them, I won't say a word." Which didn't mean I wouldn't find another way of dealing with Jake Talbot.

She thought about it. "What if I just want to forget the whole thing?" she asked, avoiding my eyes.

"He might do it to someone else," I said. "In fact, he probably will. And I doubt I'd be around to stop it."

"Meaning some other girl would get hurt even worse than me?" she asked.

"Much worse," I told her. "Take how you feel right now and multiply it by a million. That's how that girl would feel."

There was a silence.

"I don't know what to do," she said. "What if no one believes me? What if no one believes you?"

I took the camera from my back pocket and placed it on the bed in front of her. "I have this," I explained. "It's a camera."

"You have pictures?" she asked, horrified.

I nodded. "Videotape of him talking to you in the bar, then leading you outside. And what happened later, in the apartment. I filmed it through the window of the bedroom."

"I want to see it," she said, reaching for the camera.

I stopped her, thinking of how she had looked when I burst in the bedroom, her pale legs splayed and her limp body flopping all over the bed as Jake Talbot experimented with her, propping her up first here and then there, like she was an inflatable doll instead of a human being.

"It's a miniature tape. You can't see it without an adapter," I explained. "And I don't think it would help you to look at it, anyway."

"Will the police have to see it?"

I nodded.

"And the people in court?" Her voice faltered.

I considered it. "The judge will probably agree to let the jury view it privately, if they get to see it at all. It may not come to that. Once this boy's lawyer knows I have it on tape, he may convince him to take a plea. You may never have to testify.''

"That's good," she said hopefully.

"It's only a chance," I said.

There was a silence and I could hear the steady tick of the big industrial clock on the wall of the room. Thirty seconds passed like an hour.

"Okay," she finally said, "I want to press charges. Because of what you said about the next girl."

I patted her hand. "You're going to be fine," I told her. "I can tell you're strong. And now I know you're brave, too. You were definitely worth saving."

She smiled at me tentatively. "Where are the cops?" she asked.

"Outside. Want me to tell them to come in?"

She nodded. When I opened the door, I found both detectives standing on the other side, noses practically glued to the door, like impatient guests who've been kept waiting.

"She wants to press charges," I said as the men entered the room and stood on either side of her bed.

"His name?" the plump one demanded impatiently.

"Jake Talbot," I said. "His father is Randolph Talbot. Of T&T Tobacco."

The two men exchanged long glances, then stared at me. The short one looked disgusted.

"You wanted to know," I said with a shrug.

"You're absolutely sure?" the tall detective asked. "You have proof?"

I nodded and held up the video camera. "Film at eleven," I promised.

FOURTEEN

When it comes to memorable encounters, some people will always have Paris. But Marcus Dupree and I will always have the third-floor men's room of Durham Police Department headquarters.

Six hours after leaving the hospital with the two detectives, I was crouched in a stall waiting for Marcus to take his morning cigarette break. I was bruised and grumpy from lack of sleep. Three hours snoozing on a bench had done nothing for my temperament. But that wasn't what was bothering me.

What was bothering me was that I knew there had to be a connection between Jake Talbot and the murder of Thomas Nash. What was it?

I was perched on the lid of the toilet pondering this mystery when the main bathroom door opened and the clean scent of vanilla floated across the room, soon followed by the pungent aroma of Virginia Slims.

"Marcus!" I called out in a deep voice. I was rewarded with a squeak. I burst from the stall and found him frantically waving the air with long fingers, trying to diffuse the smoke.

"Smoking in a public building is a misdemeanor, even in North Carolina," I informed him. "I'm going to have to place you under house arrest."

"You scared the bejesus out of me," Marcus complained as he took a deep drag on his cigarette. "Plus you look terrible, I'm sorry to say."

"I feel terrible," I said. "I was up all night long."

"Happily, I can say the same thing," he said with a satisfied smile. "Fortunately for me, engineers are every bit as precise as rumor has it."

"Yeah?" I was interested. "Tell me more." I needed to try on a few new professions for size. Policemen and firemen were starting to bore me, and potters were proving to be a problem.

"Sorry. A lady never tells." His voice dropped to a whisper. "What are you doing *here*. What if someone sees you?"

"Relax. I'm on official business." I told him about Jake Talbot and my long session with the two detectives. I called them Frick and Frack. Marcus informed me they were actually Joyner and Jones.

"You're mixed up with that rape case?" His eyes opened wide in disapproval. "Lord, Casey. That's causing a shit storm in the department this morning. And you're telling me it's all your fault?"

"All *his* fault," I corrected him.

"Are they putting the *squeeze* on you?" he asked hopefully.

"Worse, they're demanding the truth."

Marcus shuddered. "Never tell them the truth, Miss Casey. They'll use it against you. I ought to know."

"I know," I agreed. "But I can't wiggle out of it."

His voice dropped to a whisper. "I hear they have *videotape.*"

"I'm the one who took it."

He looked genuinely shocked. "You really are in it up to your elbows."

"I need your help," I told him.

"Of course you do." He stubbed out his cigarette. "Why else would you be lurking in *here?*"

"Is it safe for you to pull up any files the department might already have on Jake Talbot?"

He considered the question. "Today may be the safest day of all to do it," he decided. "Since everyone and his brother is interested in the file. They probably won't even bother to track who's getting access. I'll use someone else's code, anyway. I don't like this homophobic new sergeant. Think I'll use his.''

"Good. I'm interested in any reports involving Talbot that *didn't* result in an arrest, incidents that never made it to the official stage.'' Maybe I could find a connection between Jake and Tom Nash that was off the record.

Marcus nodded. ''In that case, I'll need to search the paper files. It will take a little longer. I can't just go pawing through the cabinets without an excuse.'' He looked in the mirror and straightened a tightly coiled curl so that it dangled over his left eyebrow. ''What else?''

"Have they gone to arrest Talbot yet?'' I asked. ''Frick and Frack are being jerks. They pumped me for all the information they needed and now they won't tell me anything.''

Marcus eyed me speculatively. ''How unusual for you not to be the one doing the pumping.'' He managed to make it sound obscene. ''But it so happens they went to arrest the gentleman in question. About two hours ago.''

I nodded, satisfied, but slightly pissed I had snoozed through all the action. I'd endured the foreplay and been screwed out of the finale. Still, having Jake Talbot in custody would buy me time to figure out what the hell was going on.

"Listen!'' Marcus commanded, a finger to his lips. ''Someone is coming.'' Heavy footsteps echoed down the hallway, accompanied by off-tune whistling. ''Sounds like that new sergeant.''

I hustled into a stall with Marcus pressed close behind me. I climbed up on the toilet bowl and balanced there as Marcus turned around so that his feet were facing the right way. ''Don't even breathe,'' he ordered me in a whisper.

The main door swung open with a bang and heavy footsteps entered the room. Someone belched softly as the footsteps wandered over to the urinal. We waited, holding our breath, while the interloper took a piss that could have flooded the Ganges.

"Good Christ,'' I muttered, unable to help myself. ''You guys need to cut back on the coffee.''

Marcus made a tiny mewing sound of amusement that caught the visitor's attention.

"That you, Dupree?" a gruff voice called toward the stall. "I would have thought a sissy like you would be hanging out in the ladies room. Trying to sneak a peek at my pecker?"

The bastard laughed and I could feel Marcus cringe. He endured a lot from people in general, but most of his co-workers had learned to live and let live. This guy was the type that would never quit. I wanted to punch him.

"That's a pecker?" Marcus answered politely. "I thought maybe you had a pet worm and were just giving him something to drink."

The guy made a kind of growl and zipped up his pants. "People like you make me sick with your—" he started to say. I cut him off at the pass.

I took a deep breath and belched as loudly as I could, punching it up from deep in my diaphragm. The effect was astonishing, if I do say so myself. A deep rumbling filled the stall as the long burp built to a crescendo, culminating in a final series of rapid pops louder than a Mustang back-firing.

When I was done, a profound silence filled the bathroom. Marcus was crouched, convulsed in silent laughter. I smiled, pleased at my effort.

"You ought to get that checked, Dupree," the sergeant finally said. There was something akin to a mixture of awe and respect in his voice. "I think you blew a gasket."

"Just peppers in my breakfast omelet," Marcus managed to murmur.

"Yeah, well, Jesus, man." The sergeant was silent, re-considering his assessment of Marcus as a sissy. "Hey," he finally offered as a sign of friendship. "Did you hear about the Talbot arrest?"

I thumped Marcus on his back, willing him to say something.

"What about it, Sergeant?' Marcus asked with polite interest in his voice.

"He's gone. Took a powder. Hit the road. They went to that apartment where he was last night and, when he wasn't there, they served a warrant at his father's house. It was a hell of a place, Joyner said. But the kid was gone. Someone warned him. They're checking flights out of RDU right now."

"You're kidding?" Marcus answered, sounding suitably grateful to be treated like one of the guys.

"Nope." The sergeant's footsteps moved toward the exit door. "Just goes to show you that the poor get poorer and the rich get away."

The door slammed shut behind him and I thumped Marcus on his back. "Out of my way!" I hissed. "Move, move, move!"

"No need to be a ruffian about it," Marcus complained, squeezing against the wall as I dashed out the stall door. "Glad to be of help!" he called after me, but I hardly heard his words.

I wanted to get to Lydia quick.

The guard at the front gate to the Talbot compound wasn't letting anyone in, and that included me.

"Come on," I pleaded. "She might be in danger."

He was a beefy guy who liked his cushy job and wasn't about to do anything that might endanger it. "Sorry, Miss. I've got my orders. No one except family."

"Can I call her?" I asked, staring at the phone on the wall of the guardhouse.

His lips tightened.

"Look, you know me," I pleaded. "Just let me call her. I'm not from one of the newspapers or a television station, for godsakes."

He reluctantly moved his big butt out of my way, like he was doing me a huge favor. I found the code for Lydia's cottage on a list by the phone, and dialed it, pretending I didn't notice that the guard was breathing down my neck.

"Winslow?" I asked, when the butler answered. "This is Casey Jones. We met a few days ago?"

"I remember you, Miss Jones," the butler said, ominously stripping the words of any inflection whatsoever.

"Is Lydia there? I really need to talk to her."

"Miss Talbot is sleeping," he said politely, but then his

voice deepened. "The doctor was just here."

Oh shit. She'd gone off the deep end. Who wouldn't after losing a fiancé and finding out her brother was a rapist in the span of less than a month?

"Has anyone else been to see her?" I asked.

"Her father. And her little brother is staying with her in the cottage. Under the circumstances, I think it's for the best." His tone changed just enough to let me know he was telling me information he knew was inappropriate to divulge to outsiders, but that he felt I needed to know.

"And her grandmother?" I asked.

"Mrs. Talbot is up at the big house."

The big house? It even sounded like a prison.

"Where is Jake?"

The butler cleared his voice and said carefully, "I do not know Master Talbot's whereabouts, Miss Jones."

"I need to speak to Lydia," I told him. "I'm concerned she may be in danger. I believe she must leave town now." Until I knew the connection between Jake and Tom Nash's death, I wanted Lydia safely out of the way. For all I knew, her own brother might hurt her.

"I'll have her call you when she awakens," he promised. "It won't be for at least three or four hours, I would imagine."

"Winslow," I warned him. "It's very important. She must call me."

"Miss Jones," he said solemnly. "You have my word that she will."

It was the best offer I would get. "Tell her I'll be at my apartment," I said. I hung up wondering what I could do next. Go home and get some sleep. Or, go to the office and start from the beginning, looking for a missed connection.

I headed for Raleigh, rumpled clothes and all.

Bobby was AWOL. He'd left a note saying he was driving down to the coast with Fanny to eat their way through Calabash, a tiny town on the edge of the South Carolina border that consisted of a dozen restaurants specializing in lightly battered seafood. Even Bobby and Fanny would have difficulty eating their way through Calabash. I wouldn't expect them back for a couple of days.

I was happy to have the office all to myself. I put my feet on my desk, stared at the poster of Jeremy Northam in *Emma* that I kept on my wall, and thought about the chain of events that had occurred. Nash dead. Randolph Talbot sued. Jake Talbot in trouble with the law.

There had to be a connection between Jake and Tom Nash's lives somewhere. A place where six degrees of separation turned into one.

I pulled out from my file on Nash and reviewed all of the photographs and newspapers clippings carefully, in the hopes of finding a place or event where their lives had crossed, courtesy of one of my suspects. So far, only Lydia fit the bill and I could not believe that she'd had anything to do with her fiancé's death since all she had gained was a broken heart. There was always Franklin Cosgrove, of course. He was drug buddies with Jake Talbot and partners with Tom Nash. But he had lost tens of millions when Nash died. Although, I realized, he had lost millions only in the long run. Technically, he had gained a big fat salary and new job from Randolph Talbot almost overnight. It wasn't much of a motive, though. There was nothing to stop him from jumping ship when Nash was alive.

Or was there? I made a note to find out if there had been any agreements preventing the two partners from splitting. I wasn't sure who had handled business affairs for King Buffalo, but Harry Ingram might know who had.

In the meantime, I had to find a connection. Maybe Harry Ingram could help with that, too. I hadn't asked him any questions about Jake Talbot and he did move in their social circle. He might know of a friend in common that I'd missed.

Desperate, I pulled out the papers that Ingram had given me a few days ago and reviewed the list of the farmers participating in King Buffalo's pilot tobacco-growing program. I scanned it carefully, looking for a familiar name, but did not find a single one I recognized. No connection there.

I put the list aside and tried Ingram's office. His secretary told me he was in a meeting and said he would call me

back. I asked if the meeting was with Mr. and Mrs. Nash
and she said he would call me back. I then asked if they
were going to accept the settlement with Talbot and, you
guessed it, she said he would call me back. I gave up and
said good-bye, asking if by any chance he could call me
back.

God, but a good secretary is annoying.

I started going through the newspaper articles on the Talbots again, found nothing, then logged on the Internet and
searched the archives of local newspapers one more time,
paying special attention to social events that might have
brought Jake Talbot and Tom Nash into the same orbit. But
Nash hadn't been much of a social butterfly and about all
I gleaned for my efforts was that Jake Talbot and Franklin
Cosgrove had plenty of opportunity to snort coke together.
Maybe they thought wearing a tuxedo while you did it
made it okay.

I expanded my search to include all online North and
South Carolina newspapers, and ran a request for any articles including the name Talbot or Nash. The most interesting hit was a two-column article from the archives of
the Morehead City newspaper, the Carteret County Crier,
that detailed the death of Lydia's mother over ten years
before.

I printed it out and read it carefully, growing increasingly
ashamed of my hatred for Lydia's brother as I did so. Jake
had been twelve years old and driving the family's speed-
boat in Bogue Sound when he'd veered too close to a
bridge and hit a sandbar that had shifted during a recent
storm. His mother was thrown from the boat and smashed
her head on a piling, losing consciousness and never re-
covering until she died ten hours later at Carteret County
Hospital.

There was a photo of the family leaving the hospital.
Jake Talbot was a gangly twelve-year-old adolescent, huddled in on himself with arms crossed and wrapped tightly
toward his back. He was bent at the middle, as if his stomach ached, and his head was turned away from the photographer's flash. Lydia stood at his side, dressed in a striped

T-shirt and shorts, her face so puffy from crying that she looked much older than she did even now. She held a bewildered-looking toddler in her arms. It was her little brother Haydon. He was sucking on a chubby fist jammed in his mouth and staring at his sister with solemn, puzzled eyes. An unknown man with thinning hair and wearing an expensive suit was guiding Lydia down the hospital steps by her elbow. He held a briefcase in his free hand. I did not recognize him. Another lawyer, no doubt. The Talbot lives were filled with lawyers.

Randolph Talbot was nowhere to be seen.

Oh, man. Casey Jones, hard ass detective, suffers a crisis of conscience. My hatred for Jake Talbot had taken on a black, malevolent life of its own and I was suddenly ashamed of it. I knew what it was like to lose your mother in the space of a few cruel seconds, to have your world changed in a single unalterable instant, to feel as if the sun had darkened forever in a big part of your heart. And I'd had nothing to do with my mother's death, while Jake Talbot had caused his.

No wonder he ran around, hating the world, hurting as many people as he could. And no wonder Lydia tiptoed around life's edges, afraid to take a chance, able to love someone fully only after he was gone. Only little Haydon had been spared—and that was only thanks to Lydia's need to live for someone else instead of herself.

All their money hadn't been able to do a thing for them.

But pitying Jake Talbot was a dangerous mind game. I forced myself to think of the young woman huddled beneath a sheet in Durham Regional Hospital, fearing that her parents might found out what had happened and stop loving her for something that wasn't her fault. Jake Talbot had done that to who knows how many other girls, and he had to pay. I couldn't afford to feel sorry for him.

I surfed the Internet for a while, hoping to find a connection between Jake and Nash, but found nothing to help. There was something wrong nagging in a deep corner of my mind but it would not come out into the light. Maybe there was no connection after all. Maybe Lydia was right.

Maybe the Talbots were cursed, and that was all there was to it.

I finally switched off the computer and called it an afternoon. I phoned Harry Ingram again, but he was still in a conference. Dollars to doughnuts, he was sitting across from Burly's parents. I left my home number and headed back to Durham, feeling achingly tired and absolutely discouraged. Maybe a little sleep would help. I knew that forgetting the Talbots for a few hours would.

I dreamed of my mother. She was trapped beneath the murky waters of the Florida bayou, her face pressed up against the surface, staring at me in terror, as if she were trapped beneath glass and drowning. I was in a row boat, grappling hook in hand, fishing the waters for her but unable to control my arms. The hook flung wildly in the air but I could not let it go, it was grafted to my arm like a clawed hand. There was a gospel choir singing in the background, and I knew the singers were lining the shore but I could not move my body to see them.

I heard a deep voice in my ear, a voice I had heard before. It was resonant, full of love. "She's really something," the voice said.

I woke, confused, groggy from afternoon sleep, still on the edges of the Florida swamp with the sounds of peepers and distant air boats ringing in my ears. The ringing grew louder and I reached out, fumbling for the telephone.

"Hello," I croaked. My eyes were blurred from deep sleep. I squinted at the clock. It was nearly six o'clock.

"Casey?" Lydia said, her voice sounding far away. "I guess you heard about my brother?"

She didn't know I'd had anything to do with his arrest.

"Yes," was all I said.

"He's gone," Lydia whispered. "My father sent him out of the country."

"What?" I asked, suddenly awake.

"This afternoon," Lydia explained. "Jake drove up to D.C. early this morning. I thought he was seeing a lawyer. But when I woke up half an hour ago, Winslow told me the news he had heard from the big house—Jake flew to

Vienna late this afternoon. I don't think he's ever coming back."

She burst into tears. I didn't blame her. Maybe Jake had been a bastard, but he was her brother and she'd just lost him as surely as she'd lost Tom Nash.

"Who knew about him leaving the country?" I demanded, my mind racing as I contemplated who to call and what I would say when I did.

"I don't know," she said. "I think it was my grandmother's idea. My father would have tried to buy his way out of it. My grandmother is smart enough to know that Jake went too far this time. But I can't be sure who suggested it. They didn't tell me anything until it was over."

No, and they made damn sure you were sedated until the deed was done, I thought. "I have to talk to you," I told her. "I'm coming over."

I needed to tell her how I had been involved with Jake's arrest, before she heard it from someone else. It was important to me.

"No," she said, her voice growing stronger. "I can't stand to be here any longer. I have to get out of here. I have to get away from them. This place is like a prison. There are reporters at the gates."

"Where's Haydon?" I asked.

"Upstairs playing video games. He doesn't know anything, just that our father is in a bad mood."

"Take him to the airport," I ordered her. "Can you send him to relatives in Savannah?"

"Sure," she said. "Midway has a flight every night at eight o'clock."

"Explain what happened on the way to the airport," I said. "Make sure he knows everything and that he knows it isn't his fault. He won't be surprised, Lydia, believe me. I think he knows your brother better than anyone. And make sure he understands that you'll be joining him soon." I didn't want her to go to Savannah; the killer knew she had a connection to the town, but I had to get her out of Durham and it was a start. She could leave tomorrow, stay there for a couple of days and then we could take it from there.

"Okay," she said obediently. "I'll get Winslow to drive me."

"Good. I think you better do it without telling your grandmother or father." I wouldn't put it past the two of them to trot out poor Haydon for the cameras as a symbol of the family's respectability. The kid deserved better.

"What do I do after that?" she asked.

I thought about it. "You could stay over here," I finally offered. I looked at my bra hanging off a doorknob and the pile of dishes in the sink. "Though I don't exactly think it's your speed."

"I need a drink," she insisted suddenly. "Please, Casey. Meet me for a drink. I need to sit in a normal bar alongside of normal people, enjoying a drink like I have a normal life."

It was a good idea. If we met for drinks at MacLaine's, my friend Jack would take good care of us and, in the unlikely event reporters followed Lydia there, he'd probably take care of them, too. Plus, she could book a room at the nearby Europa Hotel and stay as long as she needed.

Lydia agreed to the plan. After we hung up, I phoned Detective Morrow and explained that I'd heard a rumor about Jake Talbot flying out of Dulles. Anne thanked me, asked no questions, promised to notify Durham and hung up. I'd never known her to waste her time asking useless questions.

I stripped and stood in the shower until my hot water ran out, hoping to rinse away the unhappiness that the Talbot family seemed steeped in. The cooler water lifted the fog from my brain that sleeping in the day brings and I began to think ahead, trying to figure out what Jake Talbot fleeing the country could mean. I knew I was overlooking something. That missing piece still nagged at my brain. It was maddening, but I could not work it out.

I rubbed myself dry carefully. The cuts and bruises from the fire were starting to heal and my bones had lost their deep ache. But I still hurt all over.

I had a sudden urge to bring order into my life and dressed in a cobalt blue silk sheath dress with matching slippers, pinned up my still-red hair, and decided to wear my rhinestone earrings in the shape of spirals. It seemed like a long time since I had looked good, even longer since I'd felt good.

Hell, I needed a drink worse than Lydia.

I arrived at MacLaine's early. Jack was working at one end of an empty bar.

"What night is it?" I asked, claiming a stool. "This place is dead."

"Are things that bad?" Jack asked, inspecting my outfit. "You don't even know what day it is?"

I plopped my elbows on the bar. "You have no idea," I told him. "No idea at all. This case is a killer."

He stared at a bad bruise on my forearm without comment. "For your information, it's Tuesday. And your first gin and tonic is on me."

"Make it a Jack," I told him. "Neat."

He stared. "It's really bad, isn't it?" he asked sympathetically, pouring a huge dollop of Jack Daniels into a highball glass and setting it in front of me. "You look like a million bucks in that dress, you know. And that hair, well, what can I say? Maybe you don't deserve someone better than me, after all."

He leered cheerfully and I smiled in spite of my mood.

"Thanks," I told him weakly. "I figure this color of blue matches my bruises."

"Okay," he ordered me, pulling a stool over from the drainage sink and taking a seat. "Tell me all about it. That's my job, you know. The doctor is in."

I let it all out. From the death of Nash all the way to Lydia and my getting too closely involved with her, ending up with following her brother and what I had discovered about their family's secrets. But I didn't stop there.

Never drink Jack Daniels on an empty stomach. The whiskey burned a line of fire right to my gut then took a U-turn and went straight to my head. Before I knew it, I was not only relating my tale of woe about the case, I was heaping on the self-pity as well.

"Every time I turn around, someone else has fallen in love and is getting all sloppy about it. I feel like a leper and I was perfectly happy being alone before.''

"I know what you mean," Jack said, snapping a towel. "That stuff can get pretty nauseating. Think of it as hormone-induced insanity. Pity the poor fools. They'll learn soon enough.''

"That's not the worst part," I explained, then I told him about meeting Burly. "The guy tried to trick me," I complained, hardly noticing when Jack refilled my glass without comment. "He knew I didn't know he was in a wheelchair and he didn't say anything about it until after I was attracted to him.''

"So, what's the problem, Case?" Jack asked. "The guy is in a wheelchair. Big deal. You always wanted a man you could push around.''

"Very funny." I was annoyed.

"No, really, look at it in a positive light," he urged me. "You've always said the thing you hate the most about men is that they think with their dicks. Well, this guy can't do that. So, he's either thinking with his heart, or with his head, and either way, it's an improvement.''

"Maybe," I said dubiously. "But speaking of dick . . .''

"Look at it this way," Jack interrupted, not wanting to hear more on that subject in case his own performance crept into the discussion. "Between him and me, you'll have the perfect man. You and I can do our thing, and you and him can, well, sit around and connect. Or whatever.''

"That's all very fine and good, but who's going to take me dancing? You won't and he can't." I wasn't being entirely serious.

"Take lessons at Arthur Murray," Jack suggested. "Or go hang out with the Mexican guys at the Hilton on salsa night.''

"I don't know," I confessed. "It just seems so . . . *something*. So politically correct. Know what I mean?''

Jack rolled his eyes. "Look on the bright side. Maybe he'll pull out a gun and shoot up a McDonald's. That ought to make him politically incorrect in a hurry.''

"Don't joke about that," I warned. "He does have a gun. He carries it in the storage compartment of his wheelchair.''

"Of course he has a gun," Jack said reasonably. "The guy is a sitting duck for muggers. Look, Casey," he added, his voice softening as he leaned over the bar toward me. His smile was patient. "I know you, babe. Pretty well. We've been, how should I put it, upfront with each other for what, three years now?"

"We've been taking our clothes off and going at it like weasels for three years," I agreed. "Yes, that's correct."

"So I know you pretty well. And, forgive me for saying so, but you are, hands down, the stubbornest woman I have ever known."

"What's that supposed to mean?" I asked.

"It means, get off your ass and stop blaming this guy for your feelings toward him. Call him. He isn't trying to own you. He isn't going to erase you. He just wants to be with you. Is that such a bad thing? I told you a week ago, you need to fall in love. Trust me. It will cure what ails you."

"Great," I mumbled, raising the glass for another hit. "Now even you've turned sappy on me."

"I'm going to lose my patience with you," he warned, but stopped abruptly. He stared behind me, his mouth open. I was forgotten.

I turned around and spotted Lydia standing in the doorway of the bar. She was wearing a pale blue sleeveless dress and a string of pink pearls. Her brown hair fell in gentle waves to her shoulders. Grief had made her even more beautiful. She seemed more delicate than she had before, if that was possible, as if she might shatter if someone spoke too loud.

"Over here," I said, waving.

"Who's that?" Jack whispered in an odd tone of voice.

"My client," I explained as Lydia sat gingerly on the stool next to me. She placed a tiny blue-beaded bag on the counter between us. She smelled like lemons. Up close, I could see that she had applied her makeup carefully to conceal signs of crying. She looked as exquisite—and as unapproachable—as a geisha girl.

"White wine," she asked politely. "The best you have that's dry."

At first she took no notice of Jack, she was staring at her
pocketbook. But then, when he set the wine glass down in
front of her, she noticed his hands—which, believe me,
look as capable as they are. Her gaze traveled upward, over
his well-toned arms and lingered on his dark Irish face.

That was when it happened. She looked at him. He
looked at her. The air around us grew charged and I could
practically feel the ions bumping against each other in a
frenzied dance. Within seconds, I was odd man out.

"Jack McNeill," my soon-to-be-former bedmate said,
extending a hand.

"Lydia Talbot," she answered in a funny voice, reaching
out to meet his hand. They touched and, when the touch
lingered, I picked up my drink with as much dignity as I
could muster and slipped away to a corner table where I
could lick my wounds in private. Another one bites the
dust.

I didn't begrudge her the attraction. God knows, she
could use a little distraction right now. Nor did I resent
Jack for being attracted to her. I had no claim on him,
didn't want one, and was not in the mood for one of his
rough-and-tumble sessions anyway. That wasn't what was
bothering me at all. Truly.

What was bothering me was that the whole frigging
world was pairing up around me. Bobby, Marcus, Doodle
and his new girlfriend, now Jack and God knows who else.
While I, who didn't even want someone and who had been
perfectly content until now, was feeling bad about being
left out.

For a moment there, I hated the whole world. But especially Burly Nash.

"If you want anything else from me," he'd said, "you're
going to have to come right out and ask for it."

He was probably sitting by the phone at his parents'
house waiting for me to call, just so he could smirk about
it.

Who was I kidding?

I downed the rest of my Jack Daniels and headed for the
pay phone before I lost my nerve.

I was carrying his number in my shoe, if that tells you something.

He was there.

"You win," I said. "I want to see you."

He didn't sound smug at all. In fact, he sounded relieved. "I didn't think you would call," he said.

"I'm calling." I couldn't think of anything else to say.

"When?" he asked.

I looked over at the bar. Jack was lighting a cigarette for Lydia and she was trying to smile. "Now," I said, before I lost my nerve. "My place?"

"Great. I'll bring dinner." He cut off my protests. "I mean it. You sound really tired. I'll make you dinner and then maybe I'll rub your feet and you can fall asleep on the couch."

Hearing it, there was suddenly nothing in the world that I wanted more.

"Sounds great," I agreed.

"It'll take me an hour to get there. I'm in Kittrell."

"No problem," I said, hanging up. I felt strangely exhilarated, yet still afraid. As if I had just safely taken a big step toward a cliff in the dark but knew I would have to take another one.

I wandered back to the bar to tell Jack that I was leaving. He was alone, happily rubbing down the counter in front of Lydia's stool.

"What did you do with my client?" I asked.

"She's in the ladies room." He nodded toward the back. "She's really nice, Casey." His voice grew troubled. "You're not pissed or anything?"

I laughed. With Burly coming over soon, I could afford to. "No, I am not pissed. Just don't do your usual thing, Jack," I warned him. "No hit-and-run with her, promise? She's been going through a rough time."

He held up his hands to stop me. "Say no more. I have no intention of hurting her."

"Be careful yourself," I added. "She's on the rebound."

"I don't care. I have to go for it. Did you feel what I felt?" His eyes grew wide and he gave a sideways smile, in that really annoying way that people about to fall in love get when they're in the gooey stage and want to talk about it to everyone. "It was like the air changed or something. There was this . . . this *thing* between us." He moved a hand back and forth, staring at it, and I resisted the urge to roll my eyes. Look, he was a friend. Why piss on his parade?

"I'm happy for you," I said, insincerely, but he didn't notice. He'd found a victim to unload his happiness on and wanted to get it all in before she returned.

"It's so corny, but it's true," he said in a wondering voice. "It was like angels singing, you know, a whole choir of them. I looked at her and everything seemed to slow down and then there was this sort of silent music and . . ." he stopped, at a loss for words. "She's really something."

Oh. My. God. That was when it hit me. I knew where I had heard those words before. And I understood why they had come back to me in my dream earlier that day. I had first heard them while lingering on the front porch of a farmhouse near Lake Gaston, standing beside an old to-bacco farmer as he watched his wife lead her church's gos-pel choir in song. Sanford Hale. The farmer who had been asked to leave Nash's pilot program.

His name wasn't on the list that Harry Ingram had given me a few days ago. That was the detail I had been groping for earlier in the day. He should have been on the list of farmers in the pilot program.

Why wasn't he?

"Casey?" Jack asked. "You sure you're okay with this?"

"Sure, I'm sure," I told him absently. "No problem. Listen, can I use the bar phone? I'm out of change. And do you have a phone book?"

"Absolutely," he said, happy to atone for what his Cath-olic upbringing probably saw as a betrayal. He slid it across the counter toward me and I looked up the number for Harry Ingram, wondering if he'd still be in. It was past nine.

He picked up the phone himself. "Ingram speaking."

"Casey Jones speaking," I replied, matching his busi-nesslike tone.

"Ah, Miss Jones," he answered in his good-humored voice. "You got my messages then?"

"What messages?" I asked.

"I left one each on your office and home answering machines. Dolores said you called?"

"Oh, that's right. Yeah." I thought back to earlier that afternoon. What had I wanted? "I was calling to ask you if there was any contact, to your knowledge, between Jake Talbot and Tom Nash."

"Jake Talbot?" he asked doubtfully.

"Randolph Talbot's oldest son. Don't tell me you don't know who he is." He would by the morning, that was for sure. Though I kept *why* to myself.

"Oh, I know who he is." Ingram gave a lawyerly laugh. "The heir to the throne. I was just a step ahead of you, trying to figure out why you had asked. I thought this whole thing was being brought to a close . . ." His voice trailed off regretfully, as if he did not want to say more.

"Oh, can it," I told him, suddenly annoyed at his circumspection. "I know you're representing Nash's parents and that Talbot has offered a settlement."

"Well, then," he said, sounding relieved. "I just didn't want to betray any client confi—"

"I know," I interrupted. "Don't say it. I'm sick of hearing that word."

"Well, forgive me for asking," he said more politely. "But since the criminal matter is in the hands of the police and the civil matter is close to being settled, why are you still looking into it?"

"I can't tell you," I said with satisfaction. "Client confidentiality and all that."

He was silent and I hoped he was enjoying having the tables turned on him for a change. "Touché," he finally said.

"I'm just looking into it for my own edification," I lied to make him feel better. "It's no big deal. I hate loose threads."

"In that case, I'm happy to answer your question," he said. "No, I don't know of a connection between the two men. Does that help at all?"

"A little." It didn't. "I have another question for you, though."

"I'm always glad to be of service."

"You gave me a list of the farmers participating in the King Buffalo pilot tobacco program, right?"

"That's correct. But it's a dead end to pursue them. I checked each of them out personally. Or, rather, my regular investigator did." He managed, without saying so, to make it sound as if his investigator was a lot more on the ball—because he had balls—than I was.

"But did he check out Sanford Hale?" I asked.

"Who?" Ingram sounded confused.

"There's a farmer near Lake Gaston named Sanford Hale who was asked to leave the pilot program because of suspicion that toxic waste had been dumped on his property."

"I don't know anything about that," Ingram said apologetically. "Where in the world did you hear about him?"

"From Franklin Cosgrove," I said. "Then I went out to his farm and talked to Mr. Hale personally."

There was a long silence while he thought my news over.

"I'm completely perplexed," he finally admitted. "What did this Mr. Hale say? Anything to help our case?"

"Not much." That was all I would throw him until he begged for more. "Where did you get the list in the first place?"

"From Nash's office," Ingram said. "I can't remember who sent it over to my office. Their secretary at the time, I would imagine. Is it important?"

"It could be," I said, though I didn't really know.

There was another long silence, as if he were thinking things over. "Look, is it really necessary for you to continue this inquiry?" he asked. "Since you know about my relationship with the parents, let me be frank. They are distraught about their son's death and they want the matter put to rest."

"They're accepting the settlement?" I asked.

"Yes," he said. "And donating their share of the proceeds to a foundation."

"Don't be so sure," I told him.

"Why do you say that?" he asked, his voice taking on an edge of uncertainty for the first time.

"I don't think Nash's surviving brother wants them to accept the settlement," I explained.

"But they could easily lose if it went to court," Ingram warned. "Talbot is a powerful man and juries are tricky. It's too risky."

"You don't understand," I explained. "His brother doesn't want them to take any money at all. He thinks Talbot was set up for the fall. And that he isn't responsible for either the harassment or his brother's murder."

"That's ridiculous," Ingram said. "I have a file cabinet full of proof."

"So you say," I pointed out. "But I haven't seen it, so what am I supposed to tell the brother?"

It worked. What I had wanted for a long time finally came. There was a long silence while he considered my words and then he took the bait. He was going to show me his before I showed him mine.

"Okay," he conceded. "I can show you the evidence if you come over tonight. It has to be strictly hush hush, though. This breaks all the rules."

"I can't tonight," I told him. "I have a—"

"Casey?" Lydia interrupted. She was standing at my elbow, her blue purse in hand. "I'm sorry to interrupt."

"Hold on," I told Ingram, placing a hand over the receiver. "No problem. I'm just taking to Tom's lawyer."

She didn't want to hear about the past. "I'm going to go home and change," she said timidly. "And then, when Jack gets off work, we're going to drive to Grandfather Mountain and wait for the sun to rise. It's crazy, I know, but I need to do something crazy right now. Know what I mean?"

"I know what you mean," I assured her. She was right. She deserved a break. Telling her about Jake would have to wait. "Go. Have fun. Call me the second you get back. We'll talk then. You're in good hands. Believe me." To my great credit, there was absolutely no double-entendre lurking in my recommendation.

She waved a good-bye and gave Jack a long look that

elicited a goofy smile in reply. I rolled my eyes and returned to the phone.

"What's going on?" Ingram asked impatiently. "I haven't got all night. I've been working late just so I wouldn't miss your call."

"Sorry," I apologized. "I'm out with Lydia Talbot." That ought to cool his heels. "She was just saying goodbye."

"Lydia Talbot." He sounded alarmed. "Does she know you were talking to me?"

"Yeah," I told him. "So what?"

"The settlement, Miss Jones," he explained patiently. "You can't let *anyone* know I'm showing you the evidence involved. I could lose my license over this. The bar would yank it in a heartbeat. And she, of all people, must not be told. It could endanger everything. I thought you said you were working alone on this?"

"I am," I assured him. "Cool your jets. Randolph Talbot is not going to be the one to change his mind about the settlement. If I were you, I'd worry more about the parents."

"This is highly irregular," he said. "Maybe it's not a good idea after all."

"Look," I soothed him. "I can't come tonight, but what about tomorrow?"

"No one must see you," he said. "Meet me there at eight in the morning."

"Okay," I promised. "I'll wear a cloak and carry a dagger." Sheese, but people could get paranoid when money was involved.

We hung up, but Harry Ingram's paranoia lingered. Maybe it was contagious. That was the trouble when so much money was involved. It was impossible not to care about it one way or the other.

FIFTEEN

When Burly arrived just after ten, my landlady had already locked the front door to the lobby, a security measure she follows sporadically depending on whether or not she'd been watching reruns of slasher films again. Since the bell hasn't worked since 1953, Burly had to bang on the reinforced wire mesh window until I came to his rescue. He was holding a sorry-looking bouquet of wildflowers in one hand and a take-out sack of food in the other.

As I wheeled him through the foyer, we attracted a small crowd of nosy neighbors anxious to see what the commotion was about. Talk about spoiling a romantic moment.

"I hope you remembered the condoms," I said loudly as I wheeled him inside my apartment and slammed the door shut with my foot.

"Are they always like that?" Burly asked as he handed me the flowers and the sack of food. Exotic smells wafted up from the bag. Indian. *All right.* One step closer to the Kama Sutra.

"Most of my boyfriends slip in under the cover of darkness," I explained.

"I'll try to remember that next time," he promised.

"Thanks for the flowers." I examined a wilting rose. "It was nice of you to spare me the trouble of killing them myself."

"I picked them from the front beds along my parents' walkway," he explained. "They were all I could reach. I think it's too hot for them there."

"I love them," I explained quickly, sticking the ragged bouquet in a juice glass. "They go with the apartment."

We smiled at each other and I was suddenly conscious that I was still wearing my blue dress.

"For a tough cookie, you sure wear a lot of dresses," he said. "Lucky for me."

"It's a long story," I admitted. "I was trying to cheer myself up."

"That bad?" he asked.

"That bad." I pulled out a chair and flopped into it, reaching for my beer and sliding a cold one across the table toward him. "There's something about this case. It makes me feel dumber than a goat with its head in a bucket."

"What do you mean?" he asked.

"Usually when I take on a case, it's simple. I go full speed ahead. If I hit a brick wall, I bounce off. Eventually, I either solve the case or I don't. But I never spend a lot of time worrying about if I'm doing the right thing or if I'll be able to solve it. This one has me wondering if I can do anything right at all."

He thought about it. I realized that not one in a hundred people would have really listened to what I had just said. Most people would have made automatic attempts to soothe my ego. This guy wanted to do more.

"You grew up poor, right?" he finally asked. "You've made a few cracks about it."

I shrugged. "You might say that. I consider the four food groups to be grits, possum, syrup, and bacon grease. Why, does it show?"

"No, but that's my point. Growing up poor doesn't show on the outside, but it's there on the inside. It's all the money floating around this case that makes you feel inadequate. That's why I hate money."

"You have plenty to hate now," I pointed out.

He shrugged. "I'd rather have my brother."

Oops. "Point well taken," I said.

"The thing is this, Casey," he told me, reaching for my hand. "The Talbots make everyone feel inferior. That's what they do. They've been bred to it and no one around them can ever open their mouths without thinking of how much more money they have than the rest of us. If you care about the money, it's paralyzing. Just look at me.'' He smiled. ''But even if you don't care about the money, their attitude will get you and you'll still feel like shit. It's being around them that's making you feel that way. You're still the same person. You're strong and smart and it looks to me like you still bounce off brick walls.'' He touched a bruise softly and it gave me goosebumps.

''You think so?'' I took a gulp of beer. ''I feel kind of like a bull in a china shop next to Lydia Talbot.''

''That's exactly what I mean.'' He made a face. ''Tom went for women like that, delicate and sort of helpless. I like more juice in mine.'' He smiled. ''Lydia's a nice woman, I'm sure. But she's not you, Casey, and for all her money she'll never be you. And I don't think you'd like being her.''

I thought about it. He was probably right. ''But I hate this feeling of doubting myself,'' I admitted. ''I want to go back to feeling like me.''

''How about if I feel you instead?'' he offered and I threw a wadded-up paper napkin at his head.

''Let's eat,'' I suggested. ''Maybe if I pig out, I'll feel more like myself.''

He began unpacking the food while I headed for the pathetic little cabinet that held my entire meager stock of domestic possessions.

''My parents are seriously thinking of dropping the lawsuit,'' Burly said. ''I talked to them again late this afternoon.''

''Were they at their lawyer's office?''

''Yeah. I finally found them there. He'd been moving them around to different hotels to keep the press at bay. How did you know?''

''I called there a couple of times and Ingram was always in a meeting. I figured it was with your parents. When will they make a final decision on whether to go ahead or not?''

''After they talk to you.''

''What?'' I almost dropped the paper plates and plastic forks I was carrying.

''They want to talk to you first,'' he explained. ''I told

them that you had known Tom, that you thought Randolph Talbot was being set up, that you knew a lot more than anyone else about the case. I also said that you had saved my life and I trusted you. All the basic stuff, except that you were going to be my new girlfriend. I thought I better ask you that first."

I ignored his last comment. "That explains it," I said.

"Explains what?"

"Why their lawyer is so willing to let me paw through his evidence drawer. Ingram knows I'm going to meet with your parents and he wants to convince me of Talbot's guilt before I do."

"Could be. Is that good or bad?" Burly stared at me, listening intently. I noticed that he was wearing a coarse black cotton shirt that set off his pale coloring and dark eyes. Oh, mama. He had a beautiful mouth. My mind began to wander. What if he actually had played the director's cut of *Coming Home* backward and forward? I mean, if he couldn't do the rumba, chances were good he had learned to play the congas pretty well.

"Casey?" he prompted.

I jumped, nearly spilling the basmahti rice. "What?"

"Is that good or bad that Ingram's letting you see the evidence?"

"It's great," I explained. "I have been desperately searching for a lead on this thing. Ingram may think his evidence proves Talbot is the killer, but I think it's more likely that the evidence will point me toward whoever is setting him up."

"How?" Burly asked.

"Either by the wording used or the method. Who knows? I'll comb through the files carefully. Just not for the reason Ingram thinks."

Burly nodded. He liked it. "My parents have asked their whole church to pray for them, to guide them toward the right decision. So, your advice is right up there with God's."

"You're kidding," I said. "I didn't know multi-million-dollar lawsuits qualified for God's personal attention. Aren't people supposed to pray for a cure for cancer or that their precious son walks again or something?"

He stared at me, silent, and I suddenly realized what I had just said.

"I'm sorry," I said quickly. "I forgot. That was a poor choice of—"

"Forget it," he said firmly. "Or try to forget it. And remember, we agreed, no more apologies."

"Okay," I said, for once in my life willing to acquiesce to anything, so long as my big mouth grew a more sensitive side so that Burly would stay right where he was, sitting across the table from me. The air around us seemed to vibrate and I knew it was only partly the Jack Daniels that was simmering in my stomach. I didn't want Burly to go, and I was finally ready to admit it. I wanted him to stay for a long, long time. Maybe even until morning. Or next October.

"When do they want to meet me?" I asked, conscious that Burly was watching me eat. I moderated my usual shovelful of food to a dainty bite, then decided what the hell and attacked the chicken kurma with gusto.

"Tomorrow," he said. "They want to meet you at the lawyer's office in early afternoon."

"Okay," I agreed. "I'll be there anyway. I'll have just enough time to go through the files, then run and get something respectable to wear before they show up."

"Just be yourself," Burly assured me. "That will be enough."

"Funny," I told him. "I have another friend who always tells me that."

"Smart friend," Burly said.

We ate in silence for a few minutes and I found it surprisingly restful, no desperate babbling to fill in the quiet, no inane questions, no discussions of astrological signs or favorite sports teams.

When we were done, Burly asked me if I had found out anything new about Tom's death. I explained what had happened with Jake Talbot, but confessed that I wasn't sure it was related. Burly didn't even know that a warrant had been issued for Jake's arrest.

"What happened?" he asked incredulously. "Tell me again."

I described what had happened the night before, all the way to breaking down the door to get at the girl.

"Shit, Casey," he said, reaching for me. "That Xena princess-warrior stuff kind of turns me on." He grabbed my wrist and pulled me into his lap, lifting my feet and draping them over one arm of his wheelchair. He looked around at the five pieces of furniture that filled my three rooms. "You know what else I like about you? Your place doesn't look much like a girl's place, but it's you."

"Moose shit, but good," I suggested.

He smiled. "Hey, I know that joke."

"Another sign we're compatible," I offered.

"Want another one?" he said.

The kiss lasted a good ninety seconds and took us beyond every chapter in the Kama Sutra and all the way into Tommy Lee and Pamela Anderson territory. By the time it was done, I knew, without a doubt, that there was no way this man was leaving my house before the night was done. I'd tie him to the bed if I had to—and maybe even if I didn't. But most of all, whatever it took, I was going to find a way to make him feel as good as he was making me feel.

"Wow," he said. "That was downright electric. I swear I'm regaining feeling in my lower lumbar."

"Shut up and do that again," I demanded.

When we came up for air, I started to laugh. "I haven't made out since junior high school," I confessed.

"That was the only good thing about junior high school, don't you think?"

We kissed again and his hands began exploring parts of my body that no one had bothered to touch in decades, including myself.

"Let's move on to high school," he murmured, his hands sliding to the back of my dress. "I was voted most likely to seduce a teacher."

"God, you had a progressive yearbook," I whispered.

"It was an unofficial vote," he explained, unzipping my dress and letting it fall to my waist.

"Who voted?" I asked, trying to stay focused. "The football team?"

"The faculty."

I started to laugh again, my whole body shaking.

"Be still," he warned me. "I can't get your bra." He fumbled at the clasp and it came undone in a cascade of white lace and satin.

Burly peered inside one of the cups, inspecting the fabric.

"What are you looking for?" I asked.

"A holster," he said.

"Sorry, you'll have to go lower for that."

When I began to laugh again, he grabbed me around the waist. "It's like trying to pet a wiggling puppy," he complained cheerfully. "I don't have a chance of hitting the right spot in this position. Why don't you wait for me in bed? I'll be there in a minute. I have to do something in the bathroom first."

I stood up and he slid my dress and underwear off, his hands lingering on my body. "You have beautiful muscle tone," he said. "You won't hurt me, will you?"

"You wish," I told him.

He frowned for a second, the momentary crease of his forehead making him look like a little boy. A serious thought had intruded. "Before we get in that bed together, I want you to promise me one thing," he warned.

"Name it," I offered. "So long as it doesn't involve livestock, we're in business."

"Don't get mad at me if I tell you to do something, like move over here or put your hand there. I'm not trying to boss you around. I'm asking you for a good reason and, if you don't get hot-headed about being told what to do, I think you'll find it's worth your while."

"Okay," I said agreeably. "You'll be the first man in my life I've ever let order me around." Now was not the time to bring up my ex-husband. "But it's a limited time only offer, understand?"

He groaned and shook his head as he wheeled toward the bathroom.

I snuggled under the sheets, anticipating the delight of entering an alternate dimension, where dead men and money didn't exist and where all of life was warm and liquid, with just a touch of mystery—like Jack Daniels in the belly or the smell of cardamom in the air.

Burly emerged from the bathroom after a few minutes and wheeled to the edge of the bed. "Turn your back for a second," he told me.

I rolled over and waited while he maneuvered himself into bed beside me. His weight caused half the bed to sink and I rolled against him. He caught me there, running his hands up and down my body, leaving trails of heat wherever his fingers touched my skin.

I forgot about everything in an instant—fire, murder, greed, money, even the necessity of having our dance so carefully choreographed.

"Turn around," he whispered. "So I can see you."

I rolled over and pressed against his body. Finally. Talk about coming home.

"Show me how to make you feel good," I asked him.

"I will," he promised. "Right after I show you exactly how I feel about you."

"Casey." The whisper grew louder. "Casey, wake up."

I was deep in dreamland, lying on a hot sandy beach kissing a man whose face was a fire-filled oval and whose hands moved over my body like hot liquid. I ignored the interruption and struggled to hold on to the image.

"Casey!" Burly's voice hissed into my ear as he shook me awake.

I mumbled and pushed his hand away.

"Wake up," he whispered, his voice urgent and low. He pinched me and I squeaked in protest.

"Ssshh," he warned. "Wake up. Someone's trying to get in your front door."

"What?" My eyes were open in an instant, the dream forgotten.

"Do you have a boyfriend who has your keys?" he whispered.

"No."

"An ex-boyfriend?" he asked softly.

"No. Are you sure someone's at my door?"

"Yes." His voice was little more than a warm breath in my ear. "Listen."

I froze, every muscle in my body stiff with adrenaline. It was quiet in the apartment. I could hear Burly breathing next to me, the bedside clock ticking—and the faint rattle of my front door knob being turned.

"Can they get in?" Burly asked.

"No. I have a deadbolt," I whispered back.

"Did you lock it?" he asked as the rattling stopped and a faint click, click wafted toward the bedroom.

"Sure, I always lock the—" I stopped, stunned. Yeah, I always locked the deadbolt and chain. Except when I was too busy pushing someone in a wheelchair over the threshold in front of a crowd and slamming the door shut with my foot. I'd left it unlocked. There was nothing but a half-inch wedge of brass between us and the intruder.

As Burly reached for my hand, we both heard the door open in the dark, the lock giving way with a soft series of clicks that sounded like a snicker.

I moved a hand slowly out from under the covers and slid open my bedside table. Holding my breath, I moved my fingers over the bamboo interior, searching for my gun. Oh, God, I thought, as my fingers closed around the tiny Colt .25, what I wouldn't give for a .44 instead.

A barely inaudible bump, followed by a faint dragging swish, told me that the unseen intruder had hit the side of my sofa but recovered and reached the linoleum-floored hallway in one piece. Whoever it was moved slowly, waiting for his or her eyes to adjust. I decided to let twenty seconds go by, and then turn on the lights, hoping to blind them while I got off a good shot to scare them into freezing. Then I'd move in for the kill.

I eased closer to the lamp and Burly grabbed my arm, trying to pull me back over to his side of the bed. Either he didn't want me to leave him alone in the bed, or he thought we should stick together. But both of us were afraid to say a word for fear of drawing fire.

I counted slowly under my breath and, as I approached twenty, I mentally prepared to make my move. My ears were roaring as loudly as a pounding surf. I could hear my heart beating, yet I could also hear the faraway honk of a car horn on a distant street—as well as every soft step of the approaching intruder. I inched closer to the edge of the bed.

Burly pulled hard on my leg and I kicked him away. I couldn't just lie there and do nothing.

Twenty. I rolled quickly, grabbing for the cord on the lamp. I pulled. Nothing happened. I pulled the chain again. Still darkness.

My electricity had been cut off.

"Stay right where you are," I screamed as loudly as I could, scrambling to my knees on the bed and aiming the pistol with both hands. "I have an automatic and I'll spray the entire apartment if I have to."

"Hah." It was a grunt, nothing more, but it was enough to tell me my assailant was male.

"Who are you?" I asked loudly. "I like to know who I'm killing before I kill them." My money was on Franklin Cosgrove or Donald Teasdale.

There was no answer except for the soft click of a safety. He was playing it smart, waiting for me to make myself an unmistakable target before he shot.

My mind raced through my options and I desperately tried to calculate my advantages and disadvantages. I knew the apartment better than anyone. I could make a run for the armchair and crouch behind it. And I could leap over the sofa in the dark and be out the door in ten seconds, if I had to. But I was probably outgunned and, worst of all, Burly was stuck in bed, unable to move quickly without help. I couldn't just leave him there to be shot.

"I'm getting out of my bed now," I called out, false bravado making my voice boom in the darkness. "I plan to shoot first and ask questions later." Why should I be the only one scared?

I eased my feet onto the thin carpet of the bedroom floor and clomped closer to the window, leading the intruder's attention away from Burly. If I could just open the curtains, the glow from the street lamp down the block might help my aim. The light was too far away to be of much use, but it was better than nothing.

The intruder fired. I heard only a faint pop, yet the bedroom window behind me shattered in thousands of glass shards. They rained down on the floor behind my bare feet, making it impossible for me to safely back up. The intruder was using a silencer and that scared the shit out of me. It meant he had come for one reason only—to kill me and to get away with it.

"I mean it," I warned into the darkness. "I have a gun."

There was another soft pop. The mirror on my closet door shattered, the sound followed by the crack of wood splintering. The bastard had some heavy-duty firepower, all right. It had penetrated an oak door.

"Missed," I said loudly, trying to keep my voice from shaking. I was afraid to move toward the closet, but had nowhere else to go. Did I have anything stored in the closet that could help me? Something heavy I could swing, maybe a shoe to lob and draw fire away from the bed?

Why hadn't I bought a bigger gun?

The bed springs started to squeak—what the hell was Burly trying to do? I coughed to cover the sound. The intruder fired in my direction and I flung myself to the floor, rolling close to the edge of the bed just as a bullet hit the poster of Benicio del Toro I kept above my bed, breaking the Plexiglas cover with a sharp crack. That made me mad. Posters of Benicio are hard to come by.

I rolled back up to a kneeling position and fired off a series of shots toward the doorway. My gun sounded more like bubble gum popping than a deadly weapon. That's what I got for trying to be fashionable.

But I hit him.

I heard a grunt, followed by cursing. Then all hell broke loose. He retaliated by squeezing off a round that peppered the wall above my head.

Simultaneously, Burly began screaming. "Get down, Casey! Get down! His clip is empty. Move now, while he reloads! Get under the bed. Move away from the window. Move toward me. Get away from the door. I need to know where you are." For a man who didn't want to tell me what to do, he sure as hell was taking charge.

I hit the deck pronto and rolled under the bed as fast as

I could. My hand knocked against the metal leg of the cheap frame, cutting the skin and sending my gun flying into the middle of the room. Shit.

A deafening boom exploded in the close confines of the bedroom, the retort ringing in my ears only to be drowned out by another explosion, and then another and another. The echoes rolled through the room like thunder at ground zero.

Jesus, the intruder had two guns. One with a silencer and one without. That meant both Burly and I were dead.

"Burly!" I screamed "Burly! Where are you?"

No one answered. My head throbbed with the after-effects of close fire. I could hear the pounding of my own ear drums as loudly as if an Apache war party were at my elbow.

"Talk to me!" I screamed. If Burly was dead, the killer would be moving toward me next.

An incredibly strong hand gripped my leg and tried to drag me out from under the bed. I screamed and began kicking furiously.

"Let go of me, you motherfucker!" I yelled, pulling away and gripping the nap of the carpet with all ten fingernails. I kicked the hand away and scrambled to safety on the far side of the bed.

My ears were still ringing from the gunshots, making me partially deaf, and the air was thick with the smell of cordite. All I knew was that someone was behind me, someone with a strong grip and loaded gun. I ran to the window, heedless of glass on the carpet, pulled the curtains from the rod with one big rip and began to scream through the shattered pane. "Help me! Help! Call the cops! Someone call the cops." I shut my eyes and yelled it over and over, the hell with dignity. If I died, that bastard was going down with me. I'd make sure someone saw him leaving my apartment, whoever he was. He wouldn't get away with it. I grabbed the safety bars and continued to yell for help, waiting for a final boom before the darkness.

I had screamed for a solid thirty seconds before it hit me. Someone was calling my name from across the room—and that someone was Burly.

"Casey! Shut the fuck up, Casey!" he was shouting.

"I'm here. He's dead. That was me grabbing your leg. I killed him. I'm all right."

"What?" I stopped, hands gripping the safety bars, relief flooding my bloodstream with such force that I sank to the ground. "Burly?"

"I'm on the other side of the bed," he called out in a muffled voice. "I'm jammed between the bed and the wall. I fell off as I was shooting. My wheelchair rolled against the wall, I think."

"You're alive?" I asked, still unsure.

"For godsakes, Casey, yes, I'm alive. I just blew away the bastard with my Colt .45. I'm as alive as I'll ever be in my life."

He let out a rebel yell that filled the bedroom. It was a savage, lingering whoop of triumph that could have single-handedly carried the day at Gettysburg. If that didn't get the neighbors dialing their phones, nothing would.

"I can't believe it," I said, pulling open the curtains and crawling across the carpet, feeling my way in the dark until my eyes adjusted to the dim lighting. I saw the outline of a slumped body in the doorway. I was heading toward it when Burly stopped me.

"Oh, shit," he called out. "I think I've been shot."

"What?" I stumbled to my feet. "Where?"

"In the leg. There's something wet running down it, I can feel it with my fingers." He started to laugh. The sound was as edgy as his rebel yell had been. "At last, an advantage to being paralyzed. I can't feel a goddamned thing."

"Stop joking about it," I ordered him. "It could be an artery."

As I crawled toward him in the darkness, I heard loud banging at my front door. "What's going on in there?" a voice demanded. Murmurs backed it up.

"Come in," I called out in a totally unsuitable, automatic hostess voice. I was too focused on finding out how badly Burly was injured to comprehend anything else.

Burly lay on his back next to the bed, the Colt .45 still in his hand. "Oh, God, Casey. It was great. I knew if I could just get to the box on my chair, I'd have him. I reached over and—"

"Don't talk," I ordered him. "Just lie still."

"What's going on in here?" my landlady demanded in an outraged voice from somewhere in the darkened living room. "The front door's been forced open and what have you done with the electricity? What's that funny smell?"

"Nothing," I replied calmly. "Gunpowder. It's okay, Mrs. Scoggins. Some guy just cut the power line before he tried to kill me."

Oh great, that ought to reassure her.

"This is a respectable building," she began to lecture me.

"Call the cops," I interrupted in my most authoritative voice. "Somebody just tried to kill me."

"It's okay," a calm male voice assured me. "I've already called them. Do you need a flashlight?"

"Yes," I said gratefully. "Watch your step in the doorway. There's a body there. Can you bring the flashlight over here? My friend's been shot."

"Coming," the same calm voice replied. "It's okay. I can take a look. I'm a third-year medical student at Duke."

For once I was grateful that Mrs. Scoggins had jacked the rent up so high that only us old-timers and new yuppies could afford it.

The round glow of a flashlight bobbed toward me, but the man stopped short in the doorway and bent over the body.

"This guy is still alive," he announced after a few seconds. "Someone call an ambulance."

Sirens sounded in the distance. "I think one is already on the way," a female voice offered timidly from the hallway. She was congratulated on her foresight by a round of other voices. Geeze, when this was over, I'd have to give a potluck dinner so we could all get to know each other. At least no one was videotaping it.

The flashlight wobbled over to me and I was abruptly pushed away from Burly's side.

"Sorry," the med student mumbled, "but I need room to take a look."

I crawled on the bed, hoping to get a better view without being in the way. If anything had happened to Burly, I would never forgive myself. If his artery was severed, what would that mean? God, what if he—

"He's all right," the med student announced in a loud voice. "He's not shot. The bullet just hit his colostomy bag."

"Get out of here," Burly ordered suddenly.

"Pardon me?" The med student sounded offended.

"Not you. Her."

"Come on, Burly," I pleaded. "I just want to make sure you're okay."

"Wait in the other room," he ordered me in a peculiar voice.

I didn't argue. He meant it. "Give me your flashlight," I said to the med student. "I'll bring it right back."

I stepped around the splintered glass as best I could and made my way to the doorway. A bulky figure lay face down on the carpet. He looked dead to me. I grabbed his shoulder and started to roll him over.

"Hey, what are you doing?" the med student demanded, lurking like a disapproving Mother Superior at my elbow. He pulled my hand away. "Don't touch him. Give me the flashlight back. He's seriously hurt."

"Good," I said. "He tried to blow my head off."

But with Burly no more than embarrassed, the med student had turned his attention to the wounded man in the doorway. He was in no mood to suffer my presence. "Stand back," he said. "And don't touch him."

"I want to know who it is," I demanded.

"Don't touch him," the med student repeated, as if he knew only one phrase in the world. He lifted one of the intruder's arms and placed his fingers on the pulse point.

I would have argued but at least six cops chose that moment to barge into the apartment with their flashlights drawn. They shouldered their way through the growing crowd and filled the living room with their stamping, panting presence. They sounded like a herd of buffalo at rest. I could practically smell the testosterone in the air.

"What's going on in here?" one of the cops demanded.

"I'm a private investigator. The man in the doorway is

an intruder. He emptied his gun at me. My friend shot
him.''

I hoped that said it all. Apparently, it did.

''Turn him over so we can I.D. him,'' one of the cops
ordered the med student. The kid started to protest but
changed his mind in the glare of six bright beams trained
on his face. He gently pushed on the man's shoulders, rolling him over onto his back and lowering him face-up to
the carpet.

There, spotlighted in the dancing beams of a half dozen
flashlights, lay Harry Ingram, his face bloody and still. He
didn't look at all jolly.

''Oh, my God,'' I said. ''I know him. He's a lawyer.''

As if on cue, every flashlight in the room turned from
Ingram to me. I was illuminated in a spectacular glare.

''I do know him,'' I protested, reading the silence as
disbelief. ''He has an office in Brightleaf Square.''

The room was utterly still. Until Burly began to laugh.

''What's so funny?'' I demanded.

''You don't have any clothes on,'' he told me, laughing
harder. ''You're naked as a jaybird, Casey darlin'.''

The paramedics arrived for Act II. Red lights circled the
room in jerky intervals, a gift from the ambulance parked
outside. I tried to follow one dancing beam and it gave me
an instant headache. Disco lights gone bad.

I closed my eyes, content to sit and wait on one corner
of the bed, dressed in a comfortable T-shirt and gym shorts,
until the cops got around to questioning us. Burly lay
stretched out next to me. My neighbors had been shooed
back to their own apartments, where they were no doubt
busily calling one another on the telephone to discuss,
among other things, the fact that I was not a natural redhead.

There was a woman paramedic inspecting Burly's legs
by flashlight for glass shards, while the rest of her crew
worked on Harry Ingram under the glare of a portable stand
of klieg lights. Burly ignored the medic.

''You okay?'' he asked, reaching for my hand.

"I'm okay. You saved my life," I answered quietly. "Thanks."

"Good. That makes us even. I like an equal partnership, don't you?"

"I don't know if I like the idea of a partnership at all," I confessed. Burly's face fell in the weird glow of the ambulance lights. "But I know I like you," I added. "And I don't want you to go anywhere any time soon." I leaned over and kissed him. He locked his hands behind my neck and pulled me to him. The kiss lasted long enough for the paramedic to clear her throat.

"He needs to watch his heart rate," she said apologetically. "Maybe the two of you should knock it off for a little while?"

"Sorry," I said, settling back against the headboard to watch the rest of the emergency squad work on Ingram's unresponsive body. He was alive, but barely. And far from conscious. The white uniforms of the ambulance crew were stained with blood and he already had an IV of fresh plasma trickling into him.

"Is he stable enough to move?" someone asked.

"Just about," a grim-faced medic replied. "Let's lift on my signal." Six men took their positions around the body, preparing to lift him onto a metal gurney that had been lowered to the floor at his side. "One, two, three . . . lift."

They raised him from the ground about a foot, and gently eased him onto the pallet. The gurney's legs unfolded until it was waist high.

"Uh-oh," one of the paramedics on the far side of Ingram suddenly said. "I feel an exit wound along the spine."

A small crowd gathered as someone focused the portable klieg light on the gurney. "Yup," the first medic announced after a moment of probing. "Somewhere between the T2 and T4. Jesus, it feels like he was shot with a cannon. Even if this guy survives, no way he's ever going to walk again."

Burly was inconsolable. We sat, surrounded by strangers, caught in our own private anguish. It was a pain I felt but did not understand.

"I can't believe I did that to someone," he said. "It's totally freaking me out. What the hell does it mean?" He put his head in his hands. "You've got to get away from me, Casey, before it happens to you."

"But he tried to kill us," I said.

"You don't get it," he answered through gritted teeth. "To do that to someone is terrible. He'd be better off dead, believe me."

"How can you say that?" I answered angrily. I shook him by the shoulders, but he wouldn't look at me. "Would *you* rather be dead?" I demanded.

He shoved my arms away, "When this happened to me," he explained softly, "I wasn't the only one who ended up in the hospital, okay? There was a girl. She was only sixteen and she was driving a car coming in the opposite direction. She tried to avoid me, but she swerved and hit a steel and concrete barricade. She went through the windshield and bounced off the hood. When she fell into the road, another car hit her. She lived, but she's even worse off than me. Her whole face was crushed and she's never going to walk or even to be able to talk ever again. And now I've done it to someone else."

"Stop it," I ordered him. "You didn't do anything to Ingram. He brought it on himself. With his greed. Just greed. Pure and simple."

"Is that right?" a rough voice interrupted us. "I'd like to hear more about that, Miss Jones."

A beefy man with a crew cut stood before us, notebook in hand. He'd been standing there listening to us, soaking up every word.

"Fuck you," I told him.

Burly, in spite of himself, smiled. Maybe it would all be okay.

"Fuck me?" the man repeated cheerfully. "Sure thing. But I suggest we introduce ourselves first." He stuck out a hand and I shook it glumly. "Detective Richard Cole, Durham Police Department."

"Casey Jones," I mumbled back. "What are you doing here? I thought you were working the Nash murder."

"Oh, I am," Detective Cole said, flipping open his notebook. "Something tells me that I am."

SIXTEEN

Bobby D.'s theory is that proving "The lawyer did it" is the modern-day equivalent of saying "The butler did it."

I have to disagree. I think that's an insult to people like Winslow and his hard-working cronies everywhere.

Harry Ingram did it for the money. The worst reason of all. Not out of love, not out of envy or hatred. For the money. I guess business really was just business to him, and he couldn't afford to be afraid of his conscience. He stood to make over five million dollars as his share if the wrongful death settlement between Randolph Talbot and Tom Nash's parents had been signed. And he was prepared to kill anyone who threatened the settlement, whether it was Lydia, Burly or me.

I thought I understood his frustration. Death had never been his intention. It was too messy for a fastidious man like Harry Ingram. He was always just after the money all along. Unfortunately, all of us pesky supporting characters refused to play along with his plan, and he was forced into violence.

What I think happened is this: Ingram laid a careful trap for Randolph Talbot, first targeting Talbot as the perfect mark. After all, Randolph Talbot was one of the better known settlers of lawsuits in the state, famous for his desire to stay out of court. Then Ingram had identified the perfect candidate to be injured by Talbot—Thomas Nash—before carefully creating evidence to make it look as if Talbot was behind the harassment. Even Nash had been fooled.

But Nash had pulled out of the lawsuit out of love for Lydia and refused to reinstate it, without explanation, even when the attacks against him seemed to escalate. Ingram had watched as a year's worth of planning evaporated, before taking the businesslike step of confronting Nash in his laboratory one hot July night, a meeting that ended with Tom Nash lying on the floor dead, three bullets in his back and one fatal shot to the head. Killing Nash, Ingram probably reasoned, would give him a chance to file an even larger lawsuit, one based on wrongful death. The fire had been set to cover his tracks, to destroy any evidence Nash may have kept of their conversations together.

At least, this was the part of the story that could be pieced together. Detectives Cole and Roberts visited Harry Ingram in the hospital and, as they told me later, being a lawyer, Ingram knew enough not to say a word. But by the time they wheeled him into the Central Prison infirmary for pretrial confinement—no bail was granted on a murder one charge—the evidence against Ingram was starting to mount.

Annie the accelerant dog was the first to weigh in with a forensic snootful, discovering traces of gasoline on the floorboard of Ingram's car and in his closet where he had hung his arson outfit before packing it up to the cleaners.

Then the handgun used to kill Nash was found, neatly cleaned, lying beside a shotgun in the library of his mother's house. Why don't people ever get rid of the gun? Maybe they really are phallic symbols after all.

Circumstantial evidence also pointed toward Harry Ingram. He turned out to be the big city lawyer who had failed to carry through on his promises to the old tobacco farmer named Sanford Hale, whose son had been injured by a truck several years ago. Hale provided his side of the story: when Ingram had been unable to force a quick settlement out of the trucking company's insurance firm, he had disappeared in search of easier cases.

Later, when Sanford Hale turned up on a list of farmers in Nash's pilot growing program, Ingram grew afraid that his name might somehow come up. At the time, he was in the middle of representing Nash in the original harassment lawsuits against Randolph Talbot and T&T. He couldn't afford for Nash to hear any negative opinions about his abilities as a lawyer. So he had manufactured toxic dumping charges against Hale to have him removed from the program, and had taken Hale's name off all official lists for good measure. But what seemed like a good idea at the time, like many good ideas at the time, later came back to haunt Ingram. His actions were another piece in the circumstantial puzzle that backed the meager hard evidence against him.

The gun and traces of accelerant weren't a whole lot to go on for murder one, but the DA believed me when I told him that Nash's murder had been premeditated. I explained how Tom's death had occurred on the one night when Ingram knew Lydia would be out of town, visiting her mother's grave. He had lied to me when he pretended not to know that Lydia and Nash were engaged. The date was planned on Ingram's part, I felt sure, to guarantee that Lydia would not be around. His timing proved something else to me as well, though I kept it to myself for later investigation.

My little chat with the DA had an impact. Not being enamored of either legal extortion or of murder, the DA decided to seek the death penalty against Ingram. Unfortunately, someone beat the state to the punch.

Two weeks before his trial was to start, Harry Ingram was stabbed to death with a sharpened spoon in the infirmary of Central Prison by a person or persons unknown. If he'd been able to run for help, perhaps he would have survived, but Ingram had been confined to a wheelchair since that night in my apartment, paralyzed from the upper chest down. The real trouble was that Ingram's mouth had not been paralyzed and that, I suspect, was why someone paid to have him killed. Randolph Talbot? Perhaps.

I visited Lydia soon after Harry Ingram's death. She was packing up her cottage, moving out on her own, and we spoke surrounded by stacks of brown cardboard boxes and an air of lingering regret.

"At least no one in your family had anything to do with it," I offered.

I was lying, of course.

I drove away from the Talbot mansion for the final time in my life, wondering just how much Jake Talbot—who was probably swilling champagne in Berlin—had to do with Tom Nash's death. You see, like lines linking dots in a puzzle, I had tracked down the connections between Harry Ingram and Tom Nash's life.

My friend Marcus Dupree came through with photocopies of handwritten incidence reports filed away and forgotten in the year before Jake Talbot's last escapade. Twice, he had been brought into the station, once for drunk and disorderly, once for unlawful fondling and, in both cases, the charges were dropped soon after one Harry Ingram, Esq., arrived for a chat with the supervising sergeant. I believe, but will never be able to prove, that Jake was Harry Ingram's inside man, the accomplice providing access to Randolph Talbot's inner sanctum and details on Lydia's schedule and life—all key components of the five-million-dollar plan.

I wanted to know if I was right. It isn't often I hate someone on first sight and it was important for me to determine if my instincts about Jake Talbot had been on the mark. I reread my case notes and came up with two places where Ingram and Jake Talbot may have crossed paths.

First, I checked the lease on Jake Talbot's cheap apartment, the one that now had a broken front door. It had been rented by a company that eventually traced back to Harry Ingram. A neat arrangement, very convenient for a rapist. And, I suspected, a nice little payback for inside services rendered.

But how had Ingram gotten Jake Talbot on the hook in the first place?

The answer was the Pony Express. I showed Harry Ingram's photo to the bartender and he identified him immediately as a regular. My costly friend, Spencer, the drug dealer, added his two cents worth for a lot more out-of-pocket than that—Harry was the fat white man who had followed Jake Talbot and Franklin Cosgrove one night.

What I figure is this: Harry Ingram saw Jake buying drugs from Spencer and recognized him as Randolph Talbot's son. Maybe he also thought the kid was gay, or maybe he just had the good sense to know that when a lot of money meets a lot of drugs, trouble is soon to follow. I think he gave the kid his card and told Jake to call if he was ever in trouble.

When Ingram got a call from Jake in the middle of the night a few months later—begging him to come to the police station and bail Jake out without his father ever knowing—that was when Harry Ingram probably got to thinking about how he could turn Randolph Talbot into his own personal cash cow. He waited until he got a little bit more on Jake—another near arrest, more drug use, maybe even Ingram followed him and witnessed a rape one night. However he got him on the hook, he had the kid trapped tight. Ingram could have blackmailed Jake, but he was after bigger fish. Jake Talbot had no choice but to help set his father up in return for silence about his own miserable recreational habits.

I probably don't have all the details right, but in the end, it doesn't really matter. Jake Talbot will never have to pay. He's sowing his wild oats on a grand continental scale, summering in Nice, springtime in Paris, the fashion season in Milan. I hear he's cutting quite a swath through the ranks of Eurotrash these days, and is rapidly spending down his inheritance. A guy who thinks it's funny to poison the punchbowl is definitely going to have to start buying friends sooner rather than later.

Jake Talbot knows, and I know, that he will never set foot in the U.S. again. If he does, Detectives Joyner and Jones—and yours truly—will be waiting.

Like Mariela—Lydia's seamstress and maid—I hate loose ends. Which is why I paid a visit to the new offices of Franklin Cosgrove, now head of T&T's Marketing Department, on one fabulously cool day in late October. It was almost exactly three months after Tom Nash's death.

The last secretary must have outlived her usefulness, because a new secretary sat at the front desk, too busy shaking a bottle of hot pink polish and doing her nails to bother glancing at me when I came through the front door.

"I suggest you start reading the want ads," I told her as I barged past, headed for Cosgrove's office. "You're going to need a new job soon."

Her mouth was still open when she joined me in Cosgrove's office.

"Get her out of here," I told him.

He read the tone in my voice and obeyed.

When we were alone, he gave his very best smile and stuck out a hand. "Casey Jones," he said. "Am I glad to see you. What a job you did. Caught the killer and brought justice to all."

I looked at his outstretched hand.

"I'm not shaking your hand," I told him. "And I'd prefer to make this quick."

He blinked, but regained his charm quickly. "Please, have a seat. What is it? How can I help you?"

"I'm not sitting down, either," I said. "I'm here to let you know that you have two weeks to resign your job and move elsewhere. I suggest the West Coast."

"What the hell are you talking about?" he demanded, taking a seat behind his huge desk. He needed the courage of at least looking more powerful than me.

"I know you recommended Harry Ingram to Tom," I said. "It's the only way it could have happened. Why else would Tom have hired Ingram instead of someone else when the harassment started? I think you did it for money. Knowing what a scumbag you are, Harry Ingram approached you with his plan and offered to give you a cut of his settlement from the harrassment suit if you introduced him to your partner. It was a way for you to shake down Randolph Talbot and earn big bucks while you waited for King Buffalo to pay off."

"You can't prove it," he said. "I lost millions when Tom died."

"Maybe not. And I don't think you were happy about his death. But it didn't take you long to get over it and to start thinking about how you may as well profit from it. You said nothing when you knew who the killer was and I can prove you were involved as an accomplice after Nash's death." I pulled a series of small black-and-white

photographs from my back pocket and showed him the first
one. "See this?" I asked.

No way he'd be able to come up with the self-confidence
to ignore the photo. He leaned over his huge desk and examined it.

"What the hell is it?" he asked.

"It's your fingerprints in grease on the drive shaft of my
Porsche, left there the day you tried to kill me."

He started to speak and I interrupted him.

"I don't really care if you were doing it because Harry
Ingram told you to, or because Jake Talbot made you do it
in exchange for more of his magic dust. And I don't care.
But if you don't leave town, I'm going to the police with
this evidence of attempted murder and these photos to
boot." I tossed a stack on the desktop. "You can keep
those, I have copies."

"What are these?" he asked, thumbing through them.
"I'm drinking at a bar. Big deal."

"You're drinking at a bar with Jake Talbot the night he
attacked and tried to rape a girl. And I bet your hair and
fingerprints are all over his little love nest. Leave Durham,
or I will go to the cops and tell them everything. How you
and Jake were such nice drug buddies that you stalked the
bars together."

"I didn't know he was the rapist," Cosgrove interrupted
angrily.

"I don't really care," I assured him. "There's a fine line
between you and Jake Talbot, you scumbag, and I'm not
sure I'm in the mood to make distinctions."

"These don't prove anything," he said, sliding the photos back toward me.

"They don't have to," I explained. "And it doesn't matter if the cops ever bring Jake Talbot to trial or not. I'm
here to tell you that, unless you leave town, your name will
be leaked in connection with Nash's death and Jake Talbot's arrest. Everywhere you go, people will whisper and
point out that you are somehow involved. You'll never be
able to get a date in this town again, much less land yourself another babe with big bucks."

He frowned at me and his eyes glistened, almost as if

his feelings were hurt. "Why are you doing this to me?" he said. "I didn't want Tom Nash to be killed. I was furious when Ingram killed him. Tom was going to make me millions."

He still only cared about the money. "I am doing this to you because you are the scum of the earth," I said. "And I don't want to breathe the same air that you exhale."

I left him sitting at his desk and I guess he thought it over, because he quit his job the next day and moved to L.A. I heard he took a job in marketing at a major movie studio, but that he wants to get into producing and directing. Perfect. With his selfishness, coke habit and hatred of women, he ought to fit right in.

Besides, Cosgrove now has bigger problems than being on my bad side. The plain Jane secretary I'd felt so sorry for the day I first met him, turned out not to be so pliable after all. She turned Cosgrove in to the IRS and they came sniffing around big time, even calling Burly to ask if he knew anything about King Buffalo's records. A lot went up in smoke during the fire, but King Buffalo's accountants had thoughtfully kept backups of Cosgrove's expense reports and checkwriting habits. He could well end up in a nice cushy cell at a federal detention center, practicing his moves on prison guards.

I hope Plain Jane takes her cut of the IRS proceeds and uses it to hire a maid, so she can retire from ironing shirts forever.

The death of Tom Nash and the flight of Jake Talbot changed the lives of Durham's richest family, of course. Lydia left the family compound and took her brother Haydon with her. They bought a house in the middle of nowhere, near a tiny North Carolina town called Silk Hope. It was appropriately named for her new life, I thought, if only she had the courage to start living it.

I went out to see Lydia and Haydon after the move. I wanted to make sure they were safe, that they felt protected against unknown enemies, against friends who only wanted their money and against memories of family betrayals.

Haydon had slimmed down. He was sunburned and

happy, a rich boy turned farm boy, who loved the local
school and the anonymity it gave him. He also loved the
miniature wristwatch walkie-talkie set I brought for him.

Winslow, the butler, had made the move to the new
house. I found him out back in the stables, trying to subdue
one of Lydia's thoroughbred horses—her new hobby. He
looked resplendent in his formal riding wear.

"To the hounds, Winslow?" I asked him.

"Miss Jones," he replied with a formal bow. Some habits are hard to break. "I am instructing Master Talbot in
the art of dressage these days. It is a little-known talent of
mine that has had the opportunity to flourish here."

"You look happy," I said. "Tell me it's true."

"It's true, Miss Jones," he admitted. "I am happy. Master Talbot is very happy. I venture to say that even Miss
Talbot may be happy again one day."

Just then, three shrieking brown-skinned children raced
past us, throwing bunches of hay at each other. I looked at
Winslow.

"Mariela's children," he explained, fighting hard to keep
his composure. "There are two more in addition to those
three. She works as the housekeeper now and her husband
looks after the stables."

"One big happy family?" I asked.

He nodded his acknowledgment. "The first Master Talbot has ever known, I venture to say."

It was good news about Haydon, his shining face told it
all, but I found that Lydia had not been so resilient. She
was in her new study, surrounded by books and artifacts
and very little that had to do with real life.

I kept my visit brief, our words were cordial, the thanks
to me quite sincere. But when I left, I still had the same
feeling about her—she had been hurt too much and no
longer trusted life enough to open herself up to living it.

And that was what made her so special. I had fallen in
love with Lydia Talbot a little bit, I think, during the course
of my investigation. Like so many people before me, and
probably like many more in the future, I wanted to protect
her, to shield her, to prove to her that not all of life is about
loss and sadness.

But in the end, none of us can live for anyone else nor can we find life by hiding from it. We just have to wade through it. Until she decides to do just that, I'm afraid Lydia Talbot is going to remain an unattainable heart locked in the body of a woman who hates, but cannot live without, a very great deal of money. No one, not me, not Jack, not any of her peers, will be able to break through her caution.

I suspect Lydia will continue to live in the middle of nowhere, spearheading her charity events, taking occasional forays into the society that knows her. But it's going to be a long, long time before she ever pokes her head out into the real world again and she may even, like her grandmother, simply build a smaller world composed of expensive walls, fawning friends and endless distractions as a barricade against the outside.

Especially if or when Lydia ever hears the news about her stepmother. God knows, I'm not going to be the one to tell her.

A month after Jake Talbot flew to Vienna and freedom, Susan Johnson Talbot did the very same thing. I know because Winslow told me. No one is really sure if her leaving to join her stepson proves that she had maternal instincts after all, or if it is evidence of a darker theory, one proposed to me by Marie Talbot, the grande dame of that all-too-rich family, one July night when she tried to hire me to investigate her daughter-in-law's fidelity. My money is on the darker theory.

Regardless, I found a sort of justice in the news. I often imagine Jake Talbot, jetting from one European capital to another, endlessly pursued by a drunken woman who persists in sitting beside him wherever he goes, her champagne glass constantly toppling over to spill across the first class cabin carpet as her slurred voice asks, "Where are we going next?" Bon voyage.

The events of that summer killed Marie Talbot. Or, at least, pushed her over the edge. She had been battling liver cancer, as it turns out, so perhaps she came by her bile honestly. She was a marvelous old lady, but a ruthless one as well. I'm surprised she didn't manage to cut a deal with Mr. Death before she left.

When she died, she left behind instructions stipulating that she be buried in a $75,000 bright red Viper sports car. It was an appropriate choice, I do believe, for one so filled with venom. But a sad day, indeed, for sports car enthusiasts. It's said that, at the funeral service, grown men burst into tears when the first clods of dirt hit the fiberglass roof, and that they were still sobbing about it three days later. No matter. Both Marie Talbot and her Viper had run out of gas.

She still had a surprise left in store for me, however. A week after her death, a messenger arrived at my office with an envelope from one of Raleigh's biggest law firms. Inside was a check for $5,000 and a hand-written note from the old lady, to be delivered to me after her death.

I once said to you that all you had was your honor. Congratulations on keeping it, despite my son's best efforts. I envy you. You have more than all of us combined. How I wish that we could trade places and I could have your youth and you, well, you could have all of this. It means nothing in the end.

Enclosed is a check for your fees and expenses. This is to give you a choice.

I hope you will forgive me for my role in the flight to Vienna. He is, after all, my grandson and family is all I have left to care about.

Sincerely,
Amelia Marie Ball Talbot

I was touched she had remembered me and I understood what she meant about a choice. Later, I made the right one.

As for Randolph Talbot, he now lives alone in one of the big houses on the top of the hill, surrounded by his wrought-iron fence. I can't decide if he's trying to keep memories in or bad news out. Sometimes I wonder what he thinks about, late at night, after the servants are gone, when his obedient executives are home with their families, when even his lawyers have taken their leave. Does he sit there in his huge library, dwarfed by acres of books and costly possessions, and realize that he is now completely alone? Does he wonder if the choices he has made are worth it? Does he even care?

Or, does he contemplate the fact that he inadvertently turned in his own son? Because I am convinced that Randolph Talbot had no idea that his son was guilty of rape. I think he only knew that Jake was behaving erratically and may have had something to do with Nash's death. And knowing that, he had chosen to protect his son instead of choosing to help his daughter find justice. As a result, he tried to buy me and failed. He succeeded only in putting me on his son's trail.

I wonder if he realizes this? I think so. I sent him a coded message soon after the case ended. I spoke eloquently in his language. I suspect he understood.

Turning over the Talbot rock was a lot like rolling a boulder over the side of a cliff into a lake. The splash the Talbots made that summer in Durham and the ripples that radiated outward for months affected the lives of almost everyone who had come in contact with them.

The young redhead I saved from Jake Talbot wrote me a thank-you note, being a proper young southern lady. She thanked me for rescuing her and told me she was switching her major to medicine. She'd fallen in love with hospital life while there. But that was not all. She'd also fallen in love with the hunky Cherokee emergency room attendant, and now they were dating. He'd given her a bear-claw necklace of her own for strength. Some people have all the luck.

About a month after they received their settlement from T&T, Horace Hargett and his son both died from lung cancer on the very same day. I imagine it was God's way of telling old Mrs. Hargett that she had done her part and it was time to lay down her burden.

Two million dollars isn't the most money in the world, but it was the start of a new one for the surviving Hargetts. Burly keeps up with them in memory of his brother. All those little Hargetts will get to go to college now, at least many years down the road and, in the meantime, they'll be able to enjoy running water and something besides grits for dinner. They won't have to grow up like I did. It was an unexpected legacy that the dying Hargetts were able to leave behind for their families. Thanks, in large part, to Tom Nash, who had given up what was his due in order for them to gain justice.

Donald Teasdale was reinstated as head of T&T's marketing department after Cosgrove decamped for L.A. But he got fired again after the disastrous debut of a new company ad campaign that cost T&T forty-two million dollars and ten percent of their total market share. They should have asked me. I could have told them that no one wanted to buy cigarettes from a dancing pink pussycat. They'd gotten their subliminal signals crossed, for godsakes.

Bobby's investment banker eventually lost his cheating boyfriend to an aerobics instructor, but found true love—all thanks to Bobby D. and me.

We were sitting in the office one boring afternoon when two of our cases collided. We'd finally been able to prove that a client's husband was two-timing her with a man, and we'd taken the pictures to prove it. It was going to be a costly divorce for the hubby, and he was not pleased. He burst in the front door, intending to demonstrate to Bobby that being gay didn't mean you couldn't pound the crap out of another human being. Fortunately for us all, kismet struck.

Bobby's investment banking client had stopped by a few minutes before with a check for services rendered, and the two men met coming and going. They looked at one another, birds burst out in song, a fight was averted, coffee was offered and, several months later, the two men moved in together. They make a nice couple. Even Bobby's female client was happy. She got her fat settlement without any trouble. What did her soon-to-be ex-husband care? He was living with an investment banker and they were loaded.

Maynard Pope, Durham's arson investigator, retired shortly after the resolution of the Nash case. His new hobby is making barbecue sauce. He experiments with secret recipes, and participates regularly in competitions around the state. How that man can stand there—after all he saw in his long career—chowing down one charred rib after another, will forever be beyond my comprehension.

Even Dudley, the supposedly blind newsstand smooth operator managed to be caught up in the Talbot tornado that fall. He slipped on a wet spot in the lobby while coming to work one day, pitched headlong in front of the coffee vendor's booth, caught his foot on the cord of an electric percolator and plunged headfirst into the waterfall pool. By the time they fished him out from his electrifying experience, all of his hair had fallen out, he couldn't speak, his right leg was numb and he'd broken his left arm in two places. He recovered his speech a week later, just in time to negotiate a tidy settlement from Randolph Talbot in lieu of bringing a personal injury case against T&T. Dudley went home $600,000 richer and, I am sure, now has more than one younger girlfriend to depend on.

People had paired up all around me during that long, hot summer. By winter, we had all met with varying degrees of success at our attempts at couplehood.

Doodle got married to his new girlfriend and they had a big wedding. I was not invited. I guess his mama thought I might clash with the color scheme. I feel sorry for Doodle's wife, however. No matter what color she is, she's going to have her hands full with that mama-in-law.

Marcus got married, too. This time I was a bridesmaid. Marcus took pity on me and let me pick out my own gown. It had shoulders this time, and no cabbage-patch hips and was a deep blue to highlight my once-again bottled blond hair. My only concession to fashion was a modest bustle on my butt, which I wore only because my gluteus maximus is so flat that I and I alone could pull it off.

Marcus and his engineer stood before us, resplendent in their matching tuxedos, as they pledged to love one another forever. The church was filled with sobs of joy from his sisters and hallelujahs from his devoted mother. I think she'd figured out that an engineer's salary can go a long way indeed when you're putting your new siblings-in-law through college.

Burly was my date. He looked hot, hot, hot. We danced the night away at the reception. Marcus had gone whole hog and sprung for one of the large banquet rooms at the Governor's Inn. We took over the center of the dance floor and Burly was smokin'. He wheeled his chair around and around in circles while the crowd urged him on and I did an impromptu hoochie-koochie dance beside him. The festivities were brought to a halt briefly when my bustle got caught in one of his wheels during a down-slither and ripped from the back of my dress, exposing my control-tops. But Marcus's mama pinned her hat over the hole and we continued the party until the wee hours of the morning.

I like to think I haven't lost a friend with Marcus getting married. I've just gained someone who can fix my toilet when it overflows.

Lydia broke Jack's heart in record time and I'm not even sure that they ever even slept together. If not, it was a first—and probably a last—for Mr. Jack McNeill. I wasn't surprised. She was looking for distraction, he was searching for true love. A recipe for disaster. Jack took the heartbreak in stride, since it gives him a good story to tell on those slow nights when not much is going on at the bar and he's in the mood to reminisce pathetically about lost love.

Bobby eventually found out that Fanny had more money than God. I'm sad to report it made a difference. Suddenly, all the wonderful, silly little things they loved to do together seemed cheap and childish to Bobby. He felt she deserved more. I tried to get it through his thick head that if Fanny didn't care about the difference in their incomes, why the hell should he? He was inconsolable—and insecure—for weeks until Fanny hit on a solution.

She moved to Florida. Smart woman. Now she flies Bobby D. down every month for a week and lavishes money on him while he is there. They wine, they dine, they play with his underwater, super-sonar pinging and singing devices to their hearts' content. Then, when he starts to get uptight about his self-respect, she puts him on a plane and sends him back to me.

They could last forever this way. Who knows? In the meantime, Bobby's racking up the frequent flier miles each time he goes to see her.

Burly and I are a different matter entirely. Burly has a lot of money now, but I wouldn't dream of complaining. He paid for restoring my old Porsche, then bought a farmhouse in Chatham County where I can go whenever I get homesick for fresh air or the smell of pond mud. I also head his way when I'm in the mood for a long night of endless foreplay and incredible, imaginative sex. When people get nosy about our sex life, I tell them to mind their own business. It all comes down to one word anyway: "accouterments." You ought to give them a try.

I love Burly, no doubt about that, but I still see Jack every now and then for a tumble. He's a hard habit to give up. Burly doesn't ask me about him and I never tell. Besides, it's a different animal entirely, so the question of choosing one over the other never quite comes up.

When I am with Burly, it matters. It matters all the way down to my toes and in every cell in my body. I am never more alive. And when I'm with Jack, it doesn't matter at all—and sometimes that's a good thing. I've found that I need both in my life.

So Burly and I are building a life together that I suspect will end up somewhere in between a lifelong truce and a lifelong love affair.

We had two big hurdles to get over first. I helped him with his and he helped me with mine.

First, we took Randolph Talbot's check for $25,000 and burned it in the kitchen sink. We sprinkled it with jubi-jubi powder that Marcus's Aunt Clarissa sent me from New Orleans, causing the fire to spark and dance. As I watched the official bank paper curl, scorch and finally burst into flame, I felt released.

Randolph Talbot had many things in this world, but he did not have me. When his check was never cashed, he would notice—and he would know.

Plus, while I had no money, I could honestly say that money had no hold over me. I'd burned away being the girl from the poor white trash background forever. From now on, I'd just be me.

It was a grand gesture, but one I could afford. After all, Marie Talbot had sent me a check for $5,000 to cover my fee and expenses. She had given me the choice.

Burly exorcised his demons in a more difficult way. We drove down together to the perpetual care facility near Southern Pines, one of the few in the state. While he went into the room of the young girl whose life he had changed forever, I visited the youngest son of Sanford Hale.

The boy had been there for over five years. He was lying in his bed, a ghost of a human being, his dark body wasting away beneath the starched hospital sheet, curled up like a leaf drying in autumn. I wondered if any part of him was still left, and if there was a point in keeping him alive. Then I thought of his mother singing beneath the hot sun, of the hope in her face and the faith in her heart. And I thought about how, for some of us, the hope alone is enough.

When I made my way back down the hall, Burly was waiting for me in the lobby. He'd met his demon face-to-face, and she'd turned out to be an eighty-pound blonde in a twenty-thousand-dollar state-of-the-art plastic body suit. She'd been unable to speak, but Burly felt sure she had listened. She'd given him a signal, he said, one he thought was a sign of forgiveness.

But he would not tell me what it was.

Burly is like that. He has his secrets. He has a lot of things he likes to keep private. He, like Lydia, needs his barriers in order to deal with life.

I'm trying to respect that. I'm trying not to keep crashing through those barriers. But it's hard for me. Burly knows that. He says he loves me just for trying, then adds that sometimes I am more trying than at others.

Sometimes at night, we sit alone on his back porch and talk about maybe getting a dog. It has to be a hound, of course, preferably one so lazy it urinates lying down so neither one of us has to mess with walking the damn thing. But we agree that a dog might make us a family, and that's something we both kind of crave. I don't have a family, of course, except for my grandfather. And I still haven't found the courage to go home and look him in the eye. And while Burly may have parents, he doesn't really have a family. They're still just as disapproving as ever, doing wrong in their desire to do good.

So it looks like it's going to be a dog for us, as we search for a way to build a family. Burly thinks family is the most important thing in the world, he says realizing that was the one thing he gained from his brother's death.

I told him that it was easy for him to say, since he's rolling in the bucks.

"So what?" he said. "You and I both know that money can't buy you happiness."

"Maybe not," I conceded. "But you have to admit that—for some people—it sure as hell buys enough."